Sunset at Catoctin Creek

Catoctin Creek: Book One

Natalie Keller Reinert

Natalie Keller Reinert Books

Paperback ISBN: 978-1-956575-08-8

Cover Photo: bjorn999/depositphotos
Book & Cover Design: Natalie Keller Reinert

Books by Natalie Keller Reinert

The Catoctin Creek Series

The Grabbing Mane Series

The Eventing Series

The Alex & Alexander Series

The Show Barn Blues Series

The Hidden Horses of New York: A Novel

To Mrs. Kelbaugh, my history teacher at
Walkersville High School.
I borrowed your name, and I hope someday I can be as cool as
you always were.

Chapter One

Rosemary

E veryone said Catoctin Creek was prettiest at sunset.

Maybe it was the way the sun poured through the notch between those two smooth curves in the mellow, tree-covered chain of the Catoctin Mountains, flooding the rolling foothills and farmer's fields below with a rich light like molten gold.

Or, maybe it was the way the burbling creeks and brooks around the little town of Catoctin Creek caught the last lingering flickers of the sunset's afterglow on their rippling surfaces, gleaming brightly even as the sky overhead slowly faded from yellow, to blue, to black.

It might even have been the way the white siding on the old buildings lining Main Street turned pink when leisurely clouds drifting across the rural Maryland valley reflected the sunset's most blushing hues.

Rosemary Brunner thought her hometown's gorgeous sunsets were due to all of those things, plus one simple fact: Catoctin Creek was the loveliest spot in the world, a perfect slice of heaven on earth, and nowhere else in Maryland, or the Appalachians, or indeed North America, was as perfect a piece of heaven.

What was more, Rosemary knew with certainty that in all of Catoctin Creek, there was no lovelier spot than her own little farm.

Notch Gap Farm, the Brunner family homestead, had sat in a tree-lined little cup of a hollow in the foothills below Notch Gap for generations. As farms go, it was postcard-perfect: an old brick farmhouse built with German stoicism and love, a two-story bank barn with a faded red upper level and a fieldstone-flanked lower section, a tiny farmyard of split-rail fence surrounding its front doors, and a green front lawn flanked with venerable oaks and maples of wide girth and hand-sized leaves.

The farmhouse's stacked front porches faced eastward, and when drivers emerged from the little thicket of forest separating the farm from the winding country road, the house was framed perfectly by the mountains behind it. The view was so striking, Rosemary often had to stop her truck and just breathe it all in for a moment, and she had lived here for her every single one of her twenty-seven years.

The front lawn was bordered by the rushing waters of Catoctin Creek, just after the chilly little mountain stream of Notch Gap Run joined it in a noisy confluence within a dark patch of forest between Rosemary's farm and the neighboring property. Catoctin Creek, emboldened after gobbling up Notch Gap Run, chattered through stone-lined banks right into the center of its namesake town, some two miles away. By the time it reached town, it was wide and almost sedate in certain sections, but Rosemary's creek was a wild, rushing, ice-cold cataract.

The creek was never silent; day and night, the waters burbled away through their business, cutting vigorously into the clay banks and providing a bubbly little lullaby which was better than any white noise machine. Rosemary loved cool nights when she could sleep with her window open, and summer days with the living room windows pulled high, the creek talking endlessly, a ready friend in her lonelier moments.

This was the farm of her ancestors. Rosemary Brunner's great-great-grandfather had walked back to Notch Gap Farm after Lee's surrender at Appomattox, still wearing rags of tattered blue, to find Rosemary's great-great-grandmother waiting on the front porch. A great-great-great-someone (Rosemary had lost track of how many *greats* back he was) had first built a cabin here shortly after the end of the Revolutionary War. All those great wars over the years had left notches in her family tree—and that of everyone in Catoctin Creek, because this was not a place people left, nor a place very many people moved to—yet the overwhelming feeling here was of peace, gentleness, and a love for the simple pattern of changing seasons.

Rosemary wasn't thinking about peace just now, though, nor of gentleness, nor of the simple pattern of the changing seasons. She was thinking rebelliously of the dying January light and longing for summer, for long evenings which let her dawdle over her chores and play with her animals. She was pushing all of her emotion into being angry about the short days of late winter, because if she stopped to think about the dark, lonely night awaiting her on the other side of evening chores, she'd have to brush away tears from her cheeks while she was watering the horses.

And it was simply too cold for that kind of nonsense tonight.

The old feed store thermometer on the lower barn's sliding door read thirty-one degrees. Rosemary slapped her hand underneath it as she passed, feeling the old wood shudder beneath her palm. The lower barn was the basement level of the farm's traditional bank barn, which had been built against the hillside so that the huge upper level, made for storing hay, grain, and farming implements, opened onto the graveled farm lane above. Down here, facing the burbling creek and the farmyard, the lower barn was built with flinty Maryland fieldstone and filled with four pairs of wooden box stalls facing each other over two narrow aisles. Just eight stalls —not many, but enough for the horses of Notch Gap Farm Sanctuary, and Rosemary's chosen life work.

Smoke, the barn cat, came curling around her legs, his rough purr rumbling against the leg of her heavy work jeans. Rosemary flicked on the lights, and the old light bulbs in their protective metal cages cast a yellowish glow over the stables. Donors in the past had offered to update the stable, to put in low-cost fluorescent lamps which would throw more even lighting and fewer shadows, troublesome pits of darkness which made stalls hard to clean in winter, but Rosemary always resisted. She had always known the barn in this sepia light. Her father had milked cows under this gentle light, and she had braided her childhood pony's mane under it, waiting out the mud and ice of a Maryland winter, dreaming of summer rides beneath green trees.

Now, eight horses looked at her expectantly from under the warm bulbs.

"Hello, friends," Rosemary called, smiling as they greeted her with a raucous chorus of whinnies, neighs, and snorts. "Is everyone ready for their dinners?"

The lower barn was cool in summer, but downright chilly in winter, and the horses were wearing blankets to ward off the chill. They came in all sizes, which made moments like this, with all eight horses staring at her in eager anticipation, pretty funny: Rochester stood seventeen hands high and his ears brushed the low roof; Mighty-mite was twenty-four inches at the withers and Rosemary had cut down his stall door so that he could see out at all.

"Big horse, little horse and every horse in-between," she sang to their attentive faces, feeling her heart fill up with love. Rosemary's horses were her whole life.

They'd been in their stalls for an hour already, eating hay. In winter they spent the short daylight hours in the north pasture, which stretched up the hillside behind the barn and into the young woods which had sprung up over the old dairy pastures. Because some of the horses had been malnourished in the past and now had sensitive digestive systems, Rosemary made sure they ate plenty of hay to cushion their stomachs against the grain they'd eat for dinner. She liked to give them a nice long break to work through their roughage.

They all thought this was torture. It was *dark,* so it was past time for *dinner,* and they wanted her to know, pawing and circling and neighing to share their concerns.

Rochester kicked his door with one huge hoof, making a sound like a bass drum.

"*Roch*ester!" Rosemary snapped, and the big horse stepped backwards, his expression almost, but not quite, ashamed. "I can't have you tearing down my barn, monster. You're too big to be kicking like that."

Rochester wasn't just the biggest horse in her barn, he was the biggest horse she'd ever *seen*. The lofty black Percheron gelding barely fit under the low rafters of the stable. He used this to his advantage; in midsummer, when Rosemary started buying hay for the winter and filled the echoing upper level of the barn with fragrant first-cutting bales, Rochester would lift his nose up the gaps between the boards and nibble at the blades of hay which found their way through the rafters. He had his own personal buffet as long as there was hay above his head.

Rochester's stall was always messiest in the months between January and April, when the hay supply was waning, and Rosemary was always thankful when the longer hours of springtime turn-out arrived, just to get a break from his constant mess. It had taken her almost an hour to clean his stall earlier in the day. She peered in now and sighed. "How can you be so messy when you have a nice hay-pile in the corner? Stop turning in circles looking for roof-hay, goofball."

He blinked down at her, then whinnied again. *Food, please!*

Rochester was a full-fledged giant, but the other horses she'd rescued over the past few years ran the full spectrum of available equine sizes. On the larger end was Bongo, a chestnut Belgian cross Rosemary had gotten from the same auction as Rochester; on the smaller end was little Mighty-mite, a black-and-white pinto miniature horse who had come from a foreclosed farm down in the Tuscarora valley, and who now served as Rosemary's rescue ambassador at community events. In between there were Rosita, Talon, Miracle, Dumplin, and Kiki—all average-sized Standardbreds or Thoroughbreds who had spent time racing, pulling Amish carts, or both, and then fallen on hard times. None of them had to work for a living at Notch Gap Farm—Rosemary promised them that when she pulled them from their miserable former living conditions. They didn't owe anyone anything, these horses. They'd done more than enough for humans, twice over.

Rosemary thought humans were over-rated, anyway.

"Okay, food is coming. Keep it quiet, boys and girls," she told the hungry horses lightly. She hurried down the short passage between the stalls and the sliding barn doors to an ancient wooden door set into the wall. She opened it up and stepped down four wooden stairs into the old, stone-walled dairy.

The wooden steps groaned beneath her feet, the whisper of mouse feet went pattering away at her approach—"Smoke, you're slacking, buddy,"—and, where fresh milk had once been stored in cool repose under the hillside, Rosemary lifted small plastic buckets from the deep shelves lining the wall and turned to the steel trash cans where she stored horse feed. The little dairy was her feed room and tack room now, although the damp was hard on leather, meaning her saddles and bridles needed constant attention with soap and oil. Above the feed cans, a bulletin board scattered with old newspaper clippings and photos remained from the dairy's previous incarnation, a relic of her father's days. She glanced over them absently as she opened the cans and began scooping out measures of grain.

Catoctin Creek Farmer Takes Top Prize at State Fair

In the photo: Rosemary's father, smiling and young and as-yet unmarried, black hair slicked back stiffly, standing next to a spotted sow of astonishing proportions.

Notch Gap Farm Spared in Flood "For The Ages"

In the photo: the twin creeks merged into a vast river and sprawling across the hollow, their waters drowning the farmyard, lapping at the front doors of the barn and licking at the porch steps of the farmhouse, all made more dramatic by the grainy black-and-white print. Her mother stood on the porch, posing with one hand on the railing and one hand planted defiantly on her hip, her knee-length floral dress one Rosemary remembered from long-ago church Sundays. She'd dressed up for the photographer, confident the Brunner farmhouse could withstand any flood.

Catoctin Creek Rescue Takes in First Horse

In the photo: Rosemary, four years younger than tonight, but not noticeably different, with her curly dark hair springing around her shoulders and her pale, thin face wearing the weakest of smiles, lurked half-hidden behind a small dark horse. Her first acquisition for the rescue had been Rosita, a Standardbred mare she'd brought home from a Pennsylvania auction, kicking the trailer walls all the way. Her friend Nikki had insisted on the press coverage, calling the local Union *Sun-Register* to tell them the little town's native daughter and recent orphan was turning historic Notch Gap Farm into a rescue for abused horses.

"No one is going to give you money if they don't know you're here," Nikki had told Rosemary, waving away her protests. "And you're going to need *all* of their money."

Some things never changed, Rosemary thought, shaking her head as she replaced the trash can lids. Even though her friend was busy all of the time these days—when her aunt retired, Nikki had taken over the woman's venerable old Blue Plate Diner up on Main Street, and her life now consisted of chasing around a revolving door of high school girls who waitressed for a few weeks before getting bored and quitting—Nikki still found time to come out to Notch Gap Farm once or twice a week, a wrapped dinner in hand, so she could boss Rosemary around for a little while.

"Telling me how to live my life is the highlight of your week," Rosemary had once told her, grinning, in a way shy Rosemary Brunner never grinned at anyone else.

"Yours too," Nikki had replied with an arch smile. "I'm the only human you ever talk to."

This was essentially true, but Nikki never wanted to hear the truth from her on this front: the fact that Rosemary didn't *want* to talk to people made no sense to extroverted, bossy Nikki. By the time she'd turned twenty-three and decided to devote herself to horses, the last people left who Rosemary had wanted to talk to, with the exception of Nikki and her next-door neighbors, were her parents.

And they were gone.

There were newspaper clippings from *that,* too, but they weren't on the bulletin board. Rosemary didn't even know where they'd gotten to; shoved into a closet somewhere in the house, no doubt. She didn't need reminders. She knew she was alone in the world.

That was why she had the horses.

"Here you are, Smoke," she told the gray cat, who had followed her into the feed room and was currently twirling around her legs with some urgency. She gave him a handful of Meow Mix from the bag she kept on a shelf too high for him to reach. Old-timers would tell you the key to a useful barn cat was to keep them just a little hungry, or they wouldn't be good ratters. Rosemary was too soft-hearted to short Smoke at meals, so Notch Gap Farm probably had more mice than any other farm in Maryland.

Still, he was such a nice, fluffy cat, with a purr like an outboard engine. Rosemary dropped a pat on his head as he dove into his food.

"You're worthless, you beautiful thing, you."

She stacked the horses' feed buckets carefully and went back up into the barn. Listening to the horses dig into their suppers always put Rosemary into a good mood. Despite the darkness outside her little stable, despite the empty house waiting for her just across the dry winter grass, Rosemary sighed with contentment once everyone was eating up.

All in all, lonely winter nights aside, Rosemary was mostly happy. She knew the rest of Catoctin Creek generally thought she was pretty strange, and getting stranger, living up here alone at the ripe old age of twenty-seven, taking in horses like some sort of overgrown crazy cat lady—and maybe they were right, she didn't know. The fact was, Rosemary had never struck anyone as particularly normal, and her school contemporaries would have described her as a total weirdo, given to pointless blushes and stammering sentences. So how could she make a solid judgement now?

Rosemary could never explain her anxiety around most of the human race, or why she found speaking to strangers unbearable and to acquaintances not much better. She just knew she'd never felt true peace anywhere but at this farm, amongst trees and crops and animals, and although life alone here was often lonely, sometimes painfully so, she could accept this to be her lot in life. Call it shy, call it introversion, call it a crippling fear of conversation: Rosemary didn't know if her anxiety had a name, but she knew it had a cure, and that cure was staying snug at home, on Notch Gap Farm.

If she had to live here alone forever, so be it.

Chapter Two

Stephen

"This town goes to bed too damn early," Stephen muttered, squinting into the night over his steering wheel. The street-lights on Main Street were widely scattered and wanly lit, orange globes which seemed to cast the tiny town into a more profound darkness than if he'd been seeing it by starlight alone. He liked the lights, though. Stephen had been living just outside of town for four weeks now, and he was still put off by the deep darkness on the roads between Catoctin Creek and his late father's house.

He was also put off by the lack of dining options. Stephen had pulled into the Blue Plate Diner's small parking lot at precisely eight-oh-five p.m., only to find the Closed sign hung lopsidedly on the door. His knock had gotten the attention of the curly-haired young woman who seemed to be both waitress and manager, based on his past visits, and the look she gave him over her cash register was an expression he associated more with Manhattan than Maryland.

A look which said: *knock one more time and see what I do to you.*

This was fine. Stephen could respect attitude from a business owner when he tried to get something he wasn't due. He'd lived in New York City for his entire life; attitude was not a problem for him. Sleepy-eyed villagers, who wouldn't put a little hustle in their step when he needed a coffee to go or an answer to his questions, *they* were the issue. The sooner he got out of this mountainous corner of Maryland, the better. These people were slowing him down.

And starving him, apparently. Stephen considered knocking a second time, knowing the only other option for dinner was whatever bounty the shelves of the small gas station at the other end of Main Street could offer him, but he decided to respect the curly-haired woman's glare out of the reasonable conclusion that hers was the only restaurant game in town, and if he pissed her off too much tonight, he might not be able to get dinner from her tomorrow.

Gas station gourmet, it would be.

So it came to pass that hungry Stephen Beckett turned his father's old brown sedan back towards his father's old brick rancher with a large styrofoam cup of Coke to keep him alert in the darkness and a box of Hamburger Helper rattling on the passenger seat.

He was feeling unenthusiastic about both. He would have liked a latte over a soda, or at the very least an Americano, but Catoctin Creek's gas station offered only a large metal box with the dubious word *capochino* stenciled in a looping script, and the nearby hot plate of "freshly-brewed coffee" had long since turned to an oil-slicked pool of heartburn fuel.

Stephen could appreciate a farming community would not require a lot of late-night caffeine, but surely a few long-distance truckers or second-shift factory workers must pass through the town in the wee hours from time to time? Or perhaps not—he had not seen anything approaching even the lightest of industry since he'd first departed the suburban outskirts of Frederick, the bustling county seat. He'd seen no tractor-trailers around Catoctin Creek, either, other than the early morning milk tankers.

He had never understood why his father had moved out here, choosing to retire amongst the moo-cows and the baa-sheep and the rocky fields of waving corn, especially when it meant leaving behind New York City, his only son, and every connection he'd ever had. The Becketts were not a vast family by any means, but there were cousins in Woodside and in Woodlawn (was it a coincidence, that the twin Irish enclaves in Queens and the Bronx were named so similarly?) and there were old friends from the force who all got together regularly at bars with names like Tierney's and Sullivan's, the sorts of places where you grabbed a beer in a styrofoam to-go cup on your way out.

Not unlike the giant cup of Coke currently sloshing in his cupholder, Stephen reflected.

The point was, there'd been no reason for his father to leave the city. There was plenty waiting for a guy once he retired from the police department, *plenty*. Friends meeting up at union fundraisers; get-togethers with the cousins who had the backyard and the nice barbecue. Watching ball games on hazy summer afternoons in Coney Island; long, slow evenings swapping stories with old buddies in dark bars.

So when Gilbert Beckett sold the old apartment in Sunnyside and moved to western Maryland to rusticate in an unappealing, unhistoric ranch house, everyone who knew him had been stunned. Stephen, most of all. This was his *father*. Sure, he didn't see the guy much, but it was good to know the old man was in the same town as he was, living in the same slightly ratty two-bedroom where he'd always lived, the rectangular brick apartment house with its three narrow living room windows overlooking the honking cars on Queens Boulevard. Stephen didn't even understand how his father had learned to sleep in the uncanny silence of Catoctin Creek. How did a man born of asphalt and gasoline fumes adjust to damp clay and cow manure?

Stephen certainly hadn't made the adjustment yet. He'd come here just before Christmas to nurse his sick father, and found himself planning a funeral almost immediately. He'd meant to pack up the house, put it up for sale, and go straight back to the city. Life had proven to have other plans.

The headlights of his father's car lit up a deer along the side of the road. The whitetail seemed as big as a moose and he cursed, slamming his foot down on the brake pedal. The box of Hamburger Helper went sailing onto the floor, the dry pasta within rattling like pebbles, and Stephen thought wistfully of past pleasures, of ordering in Thai food and settling down to watch HBO in his flannel pajamas.

Instead, he had another ten minutes of driving on dark country roads surrounded by killer deer which leapt from the forest like four-legged agents of mayhem, hoping against hope for the house's finicky furnace to have remained operational while he was out all day pursuing financial security and a ticket back to his Manhattan existence.

Amazing how a perfectly good life could go so wrong, so quickly, he thought grimly.

Well, he only needed this land deal to go through and he'd be set to go back to New York. Once he had the zoning adjustments pushed through and the artist's renderings drawn up, suburbanites looking for more room would pay Stephen richly for the privilege of living in Catoctin Creek. Sure, it was a long drive from D.C.'s sprawl, but once they saw that pretty mountain view from their future backyards, they'd be able to justify the extra time in their cars. All Stephen had to do was buy the property, push the county zoning boards to do his bidding, and get the ball rolling on clearing and construction.

Then he could go *home* and get his life figured out.

The thought was all that got him through the long, quiet days here.

Stephen had spent this day down in Frederick trying to iron out details with the bank. He was ready to make a final offer on the piece of land he'd been eyeballing for the past few weeks. The fields were overgrown and the outbuildings were beginning to crumble, but the property boasted an incredible view of the twin mountains the locals called Notch Gap, a lovely fieldstone farmhouse, and a broad, stream-fed pond. Really just a widening of the creek, he'd been told—apparently Maryland had no natural lakes, which was a bizarre stat if he'd ever heard one—but it was still pretty. It would make a lovely entryway for a subdivision. He could imagine a rock-faced bridge arching gently over the pond, the rumble of Land Rover tires on its old-fashioned paving stones as residents drove home each night, eyes dazzled by the sensational sunsets they got up here.

He had spent several similar days in Frederick and was growing used to the little city; it was a pretty enough place, if a little choked with traffic from the D.C. commuters. There were decent restaurants and the people he dealt with were generally soft-spoken and kind, which had been a nice change of pace from New York when he was forced to work through funeral arrangements, hospital bills, and estate matters. There was a green park in the middle of town with a stately bandshell, an impressive carillon tower, and a lake filled with geese. There was a brick-walled college, and streets lined with stately Federal-era houses. Stephen went into well-appointed offices brassy with antiques, and spoke with courteous professionals. Maryland felt northern but had dabbled with being southern, and it showed in the way everyone moved a bit more slowly, and spoke a bit more gently, than their cohorts in the northeast.

Catoctin Creek, on the other hand, was not like Frederick. It wasn't like anything Stephen had ever experienced. Barely two roads, hardly any businesses to speak of, with only the Blue Plate for dining out and a grocery store which was five short aisles and one bored cashier reading paperbacks. He didn't even really live in Catoctin Creek, but fifteen minutes outside of the village by way of lonely, winding roads. Catoctin Creek was simply the closest town to his father's house, and the ZIP Code where his mail was directed.

Stephen couldn't quite believe he was living out here, at the top of a steep driveway which was still pitch-black with the fresh asphalt his father had laid down in the fall. The emptiness of his acre of green lawn and his three bedrooms of brown-carpeted house still spooked him. He'd been uneasy enough visiting his father here over the past few years, but the past month had been a true trial, and not just because no one, doctors included, had expected Gilbert Beckett to get sick so suddenly, go into the hospital so suddenly, *die* so suddenly. And when it happened . . . well, Stephen wasn't callous enough to say out loud that his father's death couldn't have come at a more inconvenient time . . . but he wasn't strong enough not to *think* it.

Suddenly, there wasn't just one deer in his headlights, there were four of them, wandering across the road on their spindly legs, unconcerned by the passage of time. Stephen slammed his foot down again, said a few blue words, braced for impact, closed his eyes, hoped for the best. When he opened them a few seconds later, the car was stopped and the deer were watching him, their big eyes startled, as if no one could have expected a car to appear on this stretch of road.

Stephen supposed they were probably right. He sat for a minute watching the deer, who finally decided he was harmless and shuffled off through the brush along the roadside. A worrisome thought occurred to him: he'd been driving for a while . . . shouldn't he be home by now? Stephen picked up his phone and tapped the map app, but the little wheel began to spin and he had a feeling it was just going to keep on spinning. He'd stopped deep in a little valley, a glen between two steep-sided foothills.

Well. He knew the driveway turn was definitely somewhere nearby, simply judging by how long he'd been driving out of town, but he couldn't remember which little unmarked gravel lane belonged to his father. Belonged to *him,* now. If he could find it in the dark, he could keep it another night.

He tapped his phone a few more times. Nothing.

Apparently the mountains and forests weren't about to let modern technology tell him how to get home. What was he supposed to do now, consult the stars? Stephen looked up through the moonroof of his father's old Toyota. The Milky Way twinkled faintly through the tinted glass, and gave away no secrets.

"I'm lost in the woods with a box of Hamburger Helper," Stephen said aloud. "How long can I last on dried noodles?"

Eventually he got up the nerve to start driving again, but now it was more clear than ever: he was lost. These desolate country roads all looked alike, their curves dipping into hollows and running briefly along the shores of stoney creeks, cold water shining in his car's headlights. Sometimes there was a guardrail when water appeared, but occasionally the creek seemed to run right alongside the pavement, the cracked surface slowly succumbing to the rushing water. Stephen began to suspect this was the only way to tell if he'd left the actual road for some old farmer's right-of-way. He wondered how trigger-happy the locals were out here in the Catoctin Mountains. The place *seemed* pretty civilized, all plaid shirts and blue hair in the diner, old Volvos alongside the battered trucks in the gravel parking lots, but what did he, Stephen, actually know about life in western Maryland? Nothing.

Finally Stephen turned up a gravel lane which he thought seemed vaguely familiar. The driveway twisted a little like his father's, cut through trees a little like his father's, even went uphill a little like his father's, but instead of opening onto a broad bald hilltop where his father's ugly little house sat like a toad with a prince's view over the valley, the driveway dipped again and took him over a wide, rushing stream. The wooden bridge rattled alarmingly beneath his car's tires. Stephen held his breath until he was on the other side.

Ahead of him, Stephen saw a farmhouse. The white paint of a front porch glowed gently in the starlight, and a second-floor window formed a yellow rectangle of light. A middle-aged Ford truck was parked in front of an old garage nearby, and he could just see the hulking shadow of one of those big two-story barns built into the hillside beyond.

Stephen sighed and pulled his car up behind the truck. Turn around and fight another battle against the labyrinthine country roads, or ask for help? His decision was quickly made for him. He saw a shadow move to the window and move the curtains aside for the briefest of seconds. There was a moment's pause after the curtain closed again, then a new light flipped on, lighting a window at the center of the house. The hall light, he figured, watching the tableau unfold before him. Next came the downstairs hall light, and finally the porch light.

At last, once the icy yard was illuminated, the front door opened and a figure swathed in a heavy coat stepped onto the porch.

Stephen surveyed the figure. No gun, he decided. Unless it was a little one hidden in that coat—but he liked his chances better without a shotgun hoisted in the air. He opened the car door and slowly got out.

"Hello?" the person on the porch called. It was a woman's voice, Stephen noted, feeling even better about his chances of escaping unscathed by bullets. "Do I know you?"

"I'm Gilbert Beckett's son," Stephen called back, hoping the name meant something to her and he hadn't accidentally driven to the next town, or into Pennsylvania. "You knew him? Everyone knows everyone out here. Anyway, I'm Stephen."

"Oh," the woman said, sounding confused. "Why are you here?"

"I got lost," he admitted, walking towards the porch. "I'm not used to these twisty roads, and it's really dark out tonight. Am I *anywhere* close to my dad's house?"

The woman laughed. She had a pretty laugh, light-hearted and musical. The moment Stephen heard it, he wanted to make her laugh again, just to savor that sound one more time. "I was going to ask this pack of deer," he went on, trying for a lame joke, "but they all just stared at me like *I* was the crazy one for being lost in their woods."

She did laugh again, and he felt a warmth rise up beneath his ribs, a happiness which transcended the evening's wanderings and the joyless box of Hamburger Helper awaiting him. As he neared the porch steps he could see her face, oval-shaped and creamy in the porch light, and he immediately wanted to see the rest of her.

"You're actually really close," the woman told him. "But it's cold out here. Come on in and I'll draw you a little map."

Stephen couldn't believe his luck. Not shot, a woman with a pretty laugh, *and* she lived this close to his father's house? Maybe things were turning around. Maybe the rest of his time here in Catoctin Creek would be enjoyable, after all.

Chapter Three

Rosemary

As soon as she welcomed Stephen inside, Rosemary regretted her words. What was she thinking, inviting a stranger into the house late at night? Well, not late. It was only eight thirty. But still. She was basically asking to be murdered.

That's definitely Gilbert Beckett's kid though, she reminded herself. *The New York accent gives him away. And Gil was a good guy. His son won't be the murdering type.*

That was the best reassurance she could do for herself on short notice, but she decided it would be enough. Gil Beckett had been a stranger when he'd come to Catoctin Creek, but he hadn't stayed that way. He'd assimilated to life here, become a part of the community, and everyone had eventually stopped making fun of the way he said his *r*'s. His Fourth of July parties had entered into Catoctin Creek mythology, filled with food and fireworks and fun, and open to everyone. Hopefully, this apple hadn't fallen too far from that tree. Although she supposed the parties were probably a thing of the past.

As he came closer, the porch light started to illuminate all sorts of things about the Beckett boy. Chit-chat from the Blue Plate, filtered through Nikki, had merely said he was tall and decent-looking, like Gil must have been when he was a young man. What Nikki hadn't mentioned was the confidence with which Beckett carried himself, or his broad shoulders, or his chiseled chin. He brushed back dark hair as he looked up at her from the bottom step, and she mentally added to the list: strong forehead, piercing eyes, excellent nose.

Oh *damn,* Beckett boy, Rosemary thought. She hadn't bothered with men in years, but if this one was just going to appear on her doorstep . . .

"So, I'm Rosemary," she greeted him, offering her hand. "And you've been marooned on Notch Gap Farm."

"Seems like a nice place to be marooned," Beckett replied pleasantly, taking her hand gently. His skin was soft, reminding her this city boy wasn't from her neck of the woods. She wondered if he felt her callouses and thought the same thing about her. "Maybe I won't get saved for a little while yet." He smiled at her in a conspiratorial sort of way.

She smiled back. *Here's hoping.* "Well, come in, it's freezing out here." She stood back and let Beckett get past her—or rather, she tried to, but he was broad-chested and the old doorway was narrow. Beckett's arm brushed against Rosemary's chest, and despite the sturdy, no-nonsense layers of flannel and wool between her skin and his, she felt his touch ripple through her body like a pulse of electricity.

Take it slow, she warned her body, but her overactive nerves didn't seem to want to listen. She counted to three, breathing in the cold night air, and then closed the door. She glanced down at his feet and the clean wooden floorboards just before he started tramping mud everywhere. "Would you mind taking off your shoes? The clay from the yard gets everywhere."

"Not at all." Stephen leaned down and started unlacing his leather oxfords.

"I'm sorry about your father," Rosemary said, deciding some preliminaries must be delivered. "Everyone in Catoctin Creek loved Gilbert."

"Thanks," Stephen replied, still bent over his shoes. "I loved him, too. We didn't see each much in the last ten years, though." He straightened. Even barefoot, he was still several inches taller than Rosemary. She had to look up to meet his eyes.

She tilted up her chin and met his green-blue gaze head-on. His eyes seemed to hold hers with magnetic force. Rosemary felt that flutter of sensation running through her nerves again, and briefly wondered if she might be getting sick. If this was attraction, it was like nothing she'd ever felt before. This was a full-body experience.

There was a moment of silence while they considered one another. Then he took a breath and rocked gently from side to side. It was just enough movement to bring her back to earth. His feet must be cold, standing on the chilly floor right in front of the door. "Come to the kitchen where it's warm," she urged him. "It's too cold to stand here."

"Of course," he said, in tones of extreme politeness. "Thank you." He looked down at her for a moment. Suddenly, Rosemary felt her old friend anxiety rising up in her throat, pushing aside everything else. Oh, why was she talking to a stranger? Who was this man in her house? Why hadn't she stayed upstairs in her bed until he went away? Why was he staring at her? How long had it been since she had said something? Say something, Rosemary! *Say anything!*

"I'm Rosemary Brunner," she blurted, because her name was the only thing she could trust at this moment.

Then she remembered she'd already told him her name.

Rosemary curled up her toes inside her thick woolen socks, feeling like a fool.

Stephen smiled, his sea-colored eyes twinkling at her. "Proper introductions! Of course! Where are my manners? Madam, I am Stephen Beckett. Late of Manhattan," he added, bending at the waist and giving her a little bow. "At your service."

Rosemary grinned, feeling weak with relief. "Now, now, none of your highfalutin' city manners *here,* sir, we are but quiet country folk."

"I love this," Stephen stage-whispered. "Let's always talk like we're in a British farce."

"I already can't think of what to say next," she whispered back. "I don't think it's going to work out."

Stephen sighed tragically. "Very well, madam. Lead on to the kitchen."

She laughed, noticing as she did how his eyes lit up and his gaze traveled around her face. "Let's get you those directions."

"And a cup of tea? In the metropolis where I hail from, wandering travelers are always offered a cup of tea. It's considered polite."

"Oh, you're still doing *that* tired old act?" She winked to show him she was just joking and he winked back with such joviality, Rosemary was able to force down her uneasiness. She was determined to see this through . . . whatever *this* turned out to be. She wasn't sure what was happening here. All she knew was somehow, she had instantly liked Stephen Beckett—and she never liked anyone. The feeling was as wonderful as it was alien. Add on his magnetic good looks and she was flying higher than she'd been in years.

Stephen Beckett's woolen footsteps followed her past the staircase, down the hall, and into the kitchen at the back of the house. She gestured to a chair at the old wooden table, wherein he settled comfortably and commenced watching her with undivided attention. Rosemary felt a little like a mouse under the gaze of a barn owl. Except, she didn't actually *dislike* his gaze, and she doubted a mouse would have similar second thoughts about the owl's predatory nature.

Then she got hold of herself, picked up the kettle, filled it at the kitchen sink, and put it on the cream-colored stove. The flame hissed up beneath the kettle.

"I could definitely use a cup of tea," she said airily, as if a hot drink had been her idea all along. "It's chilly in my bedroom tonight. The north wind always comes right in under the windowsill."

Then Rosemary froze for a moment, shocked that she'd mentioned her bedroom. It was an old teenage phobia of hers, left over from high school days and the terrifying, enticing, constant implication of sex floating in the air between everyone in her age group—all of which flared right back up when she said the word *bedroom* to this handsome stranger sitting in her kitchen.

Yikes, Rosemary thought, taking down mugs with slow, careful consideration, trying to keep her back to Stephen long enough for the pink to fade from her cheeks. Before tonight, she really hadn't thought about sex in some time. Truthfully, she had essentially sworn off men—too difficult to meet, too annoying to talk to, too impossible to understand—and unless she developed a sudden appetite for Nikki, she wasn't going to find a likely female partner, either. So the sudden surge of interest she felt every time she looked at Stephen was . . . disconcerting.

But exciting.

And a little annoying.

And maybe a bit . . . thrilling?

It was certainly exciting when their eyes met and she realized he was having the same sort of hungry thoughts about *her.*

When the kettle finally whistled, Rosemary told her quivering loins to calm themselves down and put the mugs on the table with as much dignity as she could muster. Even so, her hand shook a little as the ceramic met the wooden top of the kitchen table.

"You hungry?" she asked. "I have some leftovers in the fridge."

Instantly, Stephen's hungry gaze changed to an altogether different kind of hunger. "Oh God, so hungry," he admitted. "I got to the Blue Plate at five after eight. The manager was . . . not amenable to a late arrival."

Rosemary laughed, thankful the atmosphere had lightened, because she didn't know how she'd be able to carry on a conversation with all of that desire weighing on them. Although, truth be told, as soon as the sexual tension dissipated between them, she missed it. *Ah well,* she told herself. *It was probably just a fluke. I'll bet he has a hot Manhattan girlfriend waiting for him back at his penthouse.* After all, who was to say if Stephen Beckett was even staying in Catoctin Creek? He was probably selling the house.

"I'll heat you up a plate." Rosemary winced inwardly. The words made her sound like someone's mother. But Stephen looked appreciative as she pulled a covered Corningware dish out of the fridge, doled out a heaping helping of the chicken and broccoli casserole she'd had for dinner, and put the plate into the microwave. Then she noticed he hadn't touched his tea, so she placed the sugar bowl onto the table in front of him. Everything felt so domestic, she wondered if she'd just imagined the charged atmosphere of a moment before.

Stephen spooned a truly astonishing amount of sugar into his mug. "It's cold out there," he said neutrally. "I don't drink much tea as a rule, but it feels right in a place like this." He looked around the kitchen as he spoke. "It's very homey. Nothing like my apartment in the city."

Rosemary smiled at him, but she really wanted to scream. The Notch Gap farmhouse kitchen was unchanged from her mother's time, and her mother hadn't even changed much about it when she'd come here as a bride, thirty-five years ago. Consequently, the plastered walls were a faded yellow, trimmed around the white ceiling with a once-cheerful, now faded wallpaper border printed with drooping daisies. The cabinets were of an indeterminate brown-stained wood from the nineteen-seventies, and the counter tops were almost brown-stained, too, they were so far removed from the original white. The sink was a relic of another age, a porcelain beast standing on its own sturdy legs, with a frilly curtain of faded gingham hiding the cleaning products crouching underneath. Only the refrigerator was of a recent vintage, and its relentlessly shiny metal face seemed to cast everything else into the room still deeper into shabbiness.

Rosemary had always liked this kitchen, liked feeling a connection to her mother and her grandmother as she stood at their old countertops whisking batter for a cake or washing dishes in their antique sink. Now, though, in front of Mr. Manhattan, she felt unbearably fusty, a farmhouse relic in a house that was practically a roadside antiques mall.

"It's very old," she managed to say.

"Well, I like it," Stephen declared, nodding appreciatively. "It feels like a TV show from the fifties."

The microwave beeped, sparing Rosemary from having to think of a reply. She put a steaming plate of casserole in front of him, and sat down at the chair across the table.

"None for you?" Stephen asked. "I have to eat while you watch me?"

"I have to make sure you clean your plate," Rosemary teased. Maybe adopting the down-home farmer mama persona was the way to go. It was the only option open to her, anyway. "Waste not, want not. If you finish that, you can have some pie."

"Pie, you say? Well, I assure you, I'm not going to waste a bite of this," he said happily, digging a fork into the mass of food. "It looks amazing, and I am literally dying of hunger. Forgive me if I'm lacking in sparkling dinner conversation." He filled his mouth with casserole and closed his eyes in appreciation. *"Mmmm."*

Rosemary sipped her tea and let him eat in peace. She had to admit, there was a satisfaction in watching Stephen plow through the food she'd made, and it wasn't the same as the pleasure she took in feeding her elderly neighbors every Thursday night. *That* was motherly, a doting feeling of caregiving as she watched Aileen and Rodney Kelbaugh smile over the dinner she'd prepared for them. This was more . . . *satisfying,* somehow, as if she'd been waiting all day for the chance to cook for a man who couldn't fend for himself.

This thought was so un-feminist that Rosemary felt she had to stop her line of thinking altogether. *New subject, hmmm.*

"So, how are you liking Catoctin Creek?" she burst out suddenly.

Stephen looked up, chewed, and swallowed, all rather laboriously. He'd had quite a lot of food in his mouth. He cocked his head, thinking. "It's . . . quiet?" he finally offered.

Quiet sounded as if it was the nicest thing he could think to say, and Rosemary didn't like what this implied. "Well, yes. We're far away from all the traffic and noise down in D.C.," she agreed, rather pointedly. "It's quiet in a good way, if you've ever been down there in that mess. My English teacher in high school had a bumper sticker on his desk that said *Frederick County: far from the maddening crowd.* Of course, it was supposed to be *madding* so he crossed out the extra letters with a Sharpie."

"Nothing like a good English teacher correction. I have admit, I'm not used to quiet," Stephen said, working in the words around another mouthful. "I have to use a white noise app to get to sleep at night. And sometimes it shuts off and I wake up in the middle of the night to total silence . . . it's terrifying. I tend to think, I don't know, that I've died or something. I always wonder if that's what my dad felt like when he first moved here. I never asked him. I wish I had. I don't know why he came here to begin with. I never asked, and then he passed away, and now I'll never know."

Stephen took another large bite of casserole, but he looked thoughtful.

Wow, Rosemary thought, shifting uncomfortably. *A lot of death in that statement.* "Your father was a nice guy," she said hesitantly, not sure where to take the mention of his departed dad, but pretty certain the opportunity for a condolence and a compliment could not be overlooked. "We don't get a lot of newcomers in Catoctin Creek, but he seemed to fit right in."

"But, here's the thing. I don't see how that could be," Stephen said, putting down his fork. He looked perturbed. "He was a cop from Queens. He had never been out to the countryside for more than a couple of days in his life. How could he have come *here?*"

The confusion in Stephen's voice surprised Rosemary. What was there to question about a body wanting to live in Catoctin Creek? It was perfect here. Anyone could see that. Just take a look out at any window. Well, during the day, anyway. Not much to see at night if there wasn't a moon.

"Maybe he just needed to slow down," Rosemary suggested, shrugging. "Take in some beauty. Maybe he drove through here once on a trip and saw one of our amazing sunsets. You've seen them, you've been here long enough. You know how beautiful they are. His place has some of the best views." *Not as good as mine, of course.* "Anyone would fall in love with Catoctin Creek."

"I can't even imagine how he ever found this place," Stephen insisted. He picked up his fork again. "Let alone, decide to live here. I'm telling you, he was a city boy through and through. Like me."

"Have you ever tried living in the country before?" Rosemary asked, suddenly deeply curious. Stephen's life must be the polar opposite of hers. What would that be like? She tried to imagine herself in the New York City of sitcoms and movies, and failed utterly. There were far too many people there. Cars and lights and tall buildings certainly, but ugh, the people.

"Oh, just the past month! And that's been enough, thanks. I can't wait to get home. I can't believe I've been here this long." His tone grew harsh, as if this was an offense he'd been brooding over for some time. He picked up his fork again and took a savage bite.

Figures, Rosemary thought. *First guy I'm attracted to in years, and he can't wait to get away from me.* Well, maybe not from her, exactly . . . but, away from Catoctin Creek, anyway.

And wasn't that the same thing? Rosemary wasn't going anywhere. She knew where her home was.

She'd lived in it her entire life.

Suddenly, she couldn't bear having him in her kitchen any longer. All of that attraction, and where would it get them? Nowhere, that was where, because he was going back to Manhattan just as fast as his legs could carry him.

"Well, let me get you those directions!" she announced, pushing back from the table as if Stephen's departure had suddenly become urgent and time-sensitive. She picked up the legal pad she kept beneath the old wall-mounted telephone and started drawing a little map. "You're very close, just a couple of miles. You must have taken the wrong turn at Clancy Farm Road; happens to the best of us when it's pitch-dark out like this. Mr. Clancy had put a big wooden sign at the fork once, years ago, and he'd painted on it *'All Through Traffic Turn Left'* but the state came out and took it down. If you turn right you end up driving alongside all Mr.

Clancy's cattle pastures and then you come out on Routzahn Road, near the . . . "

She shut her mouth suddenly, realizing she was rambling and that her map was sprouting all sorts of forks and detours Stephen would never need. He had come here just long enough to settle his father's estate and head right back home. He didn't have to learn the neighborhood or its folklore. She slapped the map in front of him as he pushed his empty plate aside. "It's all right here," she finished, her tone short.

"Have you ever been to my father's house?" Stephen asked, sounding impressed.

"Of course I have," Rosemary snapped. "Everyone goes to his Fourth of July party. He has some of the best sunset views around, plus no animals, so we can light off fireworks from the yard." She paused. "Well, we did. He did. Sorry."

"It's hard to remember to think of people in the past tense," Stephen said.

"I know," Rosemary sighed, thinking of her parents. Four years into this version of life, and she still stumbled on the tenses. "Sometimes it's better to not even try."

"Hey," Stephen said suddenly, "do you live alone out here?" It was as if this startling thought had just occurred to him.

"Almost alone," Rosemary said. "I have eight horses and a cat."

"All alone in the middle of nowhere." He shook his head wonderingly.

"I have the Kelbaughs."

He looked up sharply from the map. "You know the Kelbaughs?"

Rosemary was startled. *"You* know the Kelbaughs?"

He nodded, looking back down at the map as if he didn't want to meet her eyes. "A little."

"Well, they're my next-door neighbors. And they're not that far away." She paused. He was still bent over her little map as if it was a vast parchment filled with wonders. She wanted his attention again. "Do you want to see their place from here?"

Eyebrows raised, but evidently up for a little bit of mystery, Stephen looked up again. "Lead the way."

Rosemary led Stephen down the hall, then climbed up the creaking stairs, listening to the wood groan as Stephen clumped up behind her. She turned right in the upstairs hall and hesitated just a moment at her bedroom door, then pushed inside. She turned off the light on the way in.

Stephen paused in the hallway behind her. "You want me to come into your dark bedroom? What are you going to do to me? Rosemary, if you're going to murder me you have to tell me. That's the law."

"I'm pretty sure it isn't," she laughed. "But I just want to show you the view out my window." She went over to the tall, narrow window with its warped glass, shivering a little as a gust of wind hit the house and slid beneath the leaky sill.

"Your view, in the dark?" Stephen sounded mystified, but to his credit, he came and stood beside her.

Through the dark, bare branches of the trees along Catoctin Creek and Notch Gap Run, past the open field where she knew Long Pond sat invisible beneath the moonless sky, a little golden light glimmered like a tiny star fallen to earth. Just the sight of it made Rosemary feel grounded and safe. She put her fingers to the glass.

Stephen stood beside her, a solid and warm presence she knew she'd miss as soon as he left. *Not just tonight, but forever,* she thought, then mentally chastised herself for being so dramatic.

"What is that light?" he asked softly.

"It's Aileen Kelbaugh's kitchen night-light," she explained. "And it's been lit every night for as long as I can remember. It's only been out when there's been power outages . . . and then she tries to light a candle for me."

There was a moment of silence while he took it in. She waited, watching the light with a dreamy pleasure.

"How did you end up here alone?" Stephen's voice was wondering. "You're not a ghost, are you?"

"Take your pick, I guess . . . I'm a ghost or I'm a murderer."

"I choose ghost, but please don't ask me to avenge anyone. I'm a lover, not a fighter." He chuckled softly, and bumped against her.

Rosemary let herself lean into him ever so slightly, her heart racing, her skin tingling. Too bad they were both wearing thick layers of flannel and wool, because she got only the slightest impression of what his chest felt like beneath all those winter clothes—but it was enough to let her guess what he looked like. Stephen had a gym membership, even if he had soft hands.

"What if I haunt your dreams?" she asked him, and immediately wondered if she'd ever said anything so flirtatious in her life . . . and if she would ever manage to follow it up.

"I think you will for sure," Stephen whispered, pressing his lips close to her ear, and Rosemary felt herself melt against him.

Chapter Four

Stephen

S tephen felt as if he'd tumbled down a well, and he would have been glad to keep on falling forever. Rosemary just might be a ghost, but she was a little bit of a vixen as well. He didn't know what he was doing here, in this stranger's house, but he wasn't going to stop and ask questions. He was just going to take this moment for whatever it would give him.

Life was short, and brutal, and unpredictable. He'd learned all of that the hard way. He'd thought his entire life was figured out, and then he'd come here to visit his sick father and his world tumbled like dominoes behind him. Stephen wasn't sure he could ever take anything for granted again. So when Rosemary leaned in against him, he didn't ask questions, didn't pause to think about the world of permissions and politeness which had come to dictate his behavior with the opposite sex. He just took the gesture for what it was: a moment of sweetness, a moment of clarity.

Stephen buried his face against the soft skin behind Rosemary's ear, breathing in the smell of soap and something sweet—lavender? Violets? He'd never been much for the names of flowers, but he could already see she had a thing for purple. With the light spilling in from the hallway, he could see her bedroom had little touches of the color everywhere, from the pot of deep purple flowers on her simple white desk, to the delicate tint of her sheets—which were rumpled where she'd been lying in bed, reading, before he'd shown up in her front yard. Her book was resting on a pillow, face-down.

For some reason, Stephen found that abandoned paperback incredibly arousing. He'd wonder about it later. Why on earth had he reacted like that? It must have been the whole tableau: the pastel sheets, the forgotten romance novel, the dim starlight shining serenely on the frozen countryside outside the wavy glass of her bedroom window.

Stephen's lips were on her neck almost before he realized what was happening, not hungry and wolfish but tender and gentle, pressing a kiss that was more longing than lust just below the curve of her left ear. She sighed, so softly he barely heard it, and then he felt her start, as if she had just realized what was happening. Her sharp motion broke the spell.

Stephen nearly leaped away from her, absolutely horrified. Had he really just embraced this woman he'd known all of twenty minutes? And kissed her neck? Jesus, he'd kissed her neck. She must think he was some kind of . . . well, he didn't want to go down that route. She was turned away from him, her face hidden in shadows, and Stephen took another step back, feeling the only way to show his regret was with physical distance.

And words. Good Lord, he'd better say something.

"I am *so* sorry," he gasped, trying to think of a stronger word and coming up short. "That was incredibly inappropriate. I didn't mean—" he stopped, trying to think of a way to explain himself, but he didn't have anything. He'd simply felt compelled to touch her, to kiss her, and he had. "I am sorry," he said again, his voice catching. "That was wrong."

She turned, and he was treated to a view of her graceful profile which he couldn't possibly deserve. The hall light lit her face, and he saw a point of pink high on her cheek. Anger, fear, or embarrassment? Her eyes were too dark to show him. She lifted a hand to push back her waves of dark hair, and he thought her fingers were trembling. His heart clenched with shame.

"I'll go," he said quickly. "Thank you for everything."

He was in the doorway when she spoke. "Don't go."

Stephen's hands clenched the doorframe; he tried not to squeeze, tried not to look like a crazy person. He turned around slowly. Rosemary's lips were pressed together, she looked as if she were trying to find the right words. She ought to be throwing that little flower-pot at his head, not trying to make him feel better. Stephen could name at least three ex-girlfriends who would have called the cops on him for a stunt like this. He knew he should go . . . but he waited. She had told him to stay.

"You don't have to leave," she repeated, her voice low. "I think . . . I think we both had a moment. Something with the starlight . . . " she chuckled lamely, and looked at her feet, her hands still clenched in front of her. Then she looked up again, facing him resolutely. "Please don't feel bad. I'm not upset. But maybe . . . maybe we should go back downstairs?"

He took a deep breath. She wasn't kicking him out. He was getting another chance. The phrase tumbled through his confused mind, and he wondered what it meant. *Another chance for what?*

She was looking at him, a question in her gaze. He had to pull it together.

"Of course," he agreed. "I am sorry. Really."

"You said that." Rosemary smiled crookedly.

"Right. Well . . . after you," he said, with an attempt at gallantry, and stepped to one side to clear her path through the doorway. In doing so, he stepped on something soft and squashy, which sent him stumbling backwards, and he ended up leaning heavily against her antique chest of drawers, smiling idiotically. "That was a perfect follow-up, right?"

Rosemary burst into laughter, that bubble of pleasure he'd fallen for when they'd first met, just an hour—or a lifetime—ago. Stephen was captivated enough to not mind she was laughing at *him.*

"Sorry about the beanbag chair," she chortled. "It's been there forever. Since I was a kid."

Stephen shook his head at her. "That's why you're not afraid of strangers. You have booby traps."

"I just like to have comfy places to read! And the beanbag wedges up against the wall next to the radiator really nicely. Okay then. Let's just . . . let's go finish our tea before something else crazy happens."

Stephen followed her downstairs, taking care this time to look where he put his feet.

"So you've got an apartment in New York City, plus your father's house, plus your father's *car,* and you're trying to decide which ones to keep, is that right?" Rosemary asked. She was sitting across from him at the kitchen table now, with a luscious-looking, cinnamon-flecked apple pie still in its tin resting between them. Stephen was endeavoring to finish the last few bits of his casserole portion so she'd pick up the serving spoon and start dishing out pie, and so he answered her with his mouth still half-full.

"I'm keeping my apartment in the city," he responded, unhappily aware that *city* came out *shitty*. He chewed and swallowed. "That's where I live. This is just a temporary stay. While I do some business and figure out what to do with it all."

"Hmm." Rosemary looked down at the table. "You *really* don't like it here? I know you think it's too quiet, but the people are nice. The air is clean. The views are spectacular. I'm surprised you wouldn't, I don't know, keep it as a vacation home or something?"

Stephen compressed his lips, trying to hide his grin. A vacation home, in the rural farmland of western Maryland? Was she out of her mind, or simply that sheltered? "I don't know that I can afford a place in the country," he said with a little shrug, as if it would have been a great idea if he could just find the money.

"Of course," Rosemary agreed. "Who can afford two houses? And New York is so expensive."

"Have you ever been there?" Stephen spotted an opportunity: women from out of town tended to love hearing about his glamorous city life. The subways! The restaurants! The parks! He never mentioned the endless struggles of mice in the kitchen cabinets or clanging radiators in the middle of the night or the piles of garbage blocking the sidewalks every trash day. That wasn't what they wanted to hear.

"Oh, no." Rosemary shook her head dismissively. "I wouldn't want to go to New York."

Well, so much for that. Stephen couldn't help but feel a little offended, as if she was attacking him along with his birthplace. "Why not? New York is an amazing place."

She looked at him with one eyebrow arched. She looked so artlessly beautiful, he wanted to push both plate and pie aside and climb over the table to get at her. "I live alone on a farm in the most beautiful place in the world," Rosemary said simply. "Why would I want to go to a crowded city?"

"For the change?"

"I don't need a change," she told him seriously. "I have everything I could possibly need right here."

Stephen sat back in his chair. He couldn't think of a single argument to *that.*

He couldn't even imagine feeling so content in life.

Rosemary leaned forward and pushed the serving spoon into the pie. "Let's eat some dessert. These apples came from Aileen Kelbaugh's own little orchard. You can have a little taste of Catoctin Creek's finest."

Stephen pushed his dinner plate aside, more than ready for pie. And really, if he was going to continue behaving like a gentleman with this eccentric but lovely loner, he was going to have to take whatever crumbs she would offer him.

Chapter Five

Rosemary

They'd finished their first slices of pie and were both eyeballing the tin between them, considering seconds, when Rosemary's phone buzzed. She pulled it out of her pocket, not really surprised by the late call. It was just past nine thirty, about when Nikki would have gotten home from a closing shift at the Blue Plate. Anytime Nikki had some interesting gossip from her shift, she saved it up to tell Rosemary at the end of the night.

"You just go ahead and eat another piece," she told Stephen. "I'll take this call and be right back."

Rosemary went down the hall and into the living room, then considered the possibility of being overheard from in the kitchen —what if the gossip was about Stephen?—and went up the stairs to her room, stepping as lightly as possible so Stephen wouldn't hear the floorboards creaking. She wasn't used to having anyone else in the house, and the lack of privacy for her conversation made her feel uneasy.

"What's up, Nikki?" she said, answering the call just before it would have gone to voicemail.

"You let the phone ring long enough!" Nikki declared. "I was going to drive over there and check on you if you didn't answer. You could have choked on a fishbone or something."

Rosemary sat down on her bed. "Oh, please don't worry about me. Didn't I promise that if I died you'd be the first person I'd haunt? You'd know *immediately.*"

"So helpful."

"How was your night?"

"Slow. Even for fried chicken night. But Aileen and Rodney were here, and . . . " Nikki paused for dramatic effect, a moment which Rosemary always felt compelled to fill in with some dull joke of a reason, just to dampen the suspense.

"It's Wednesday. They always show up for fried chicken night."

Nikki's sentence continued as if Rosemary had not spoken. "And they told me they're considering selling the farm."

Rosemary opened her mouth, but found she had nothing to say. Nikki's drama would have to win this round.

She turned to look out the window, to the little night-light burning in the Kelbaugh kitchen window. The Kelbaugh's bedroom was on the other side of the house, or she probably would have seen that light on as well, but the kitchen light had always been her constant.

"Rosemary?"

She found her voice, a little scratching croak. "I'm here."

"They told me not to tell you, but . . . I had to. Obviously."

"Thank you." She took a deep breath, to remind herself she was not drowning. Things would be fine. She would figure this out. "They'll probably tell me tomorrow night when I bring over dinner."

"Maybe. They were being pretty cagey about it. Aileen asked me if I knew anything about a guy named . . . hang on, I wrote it down." There was a fumbling as Nikki put down the phone and Rosemary knew she was rummaging through the black waitress apron she always wore at the diner. Rosemary could picture her now, dressed in tight jeans and a flowered blouse, curly hair piled on top of her head and straggling a little bit in auburn corkscrews behind her ears, frizzing after a steamy night in the kitchen. "Ah! Here it is. Stephen Beckett. From New York."

Rosemary was rendered quite dumb.

"Yeah," Nikki went on, misinterpreting her silence. "Gilbert Beckett's son, if you can believe that. He's been around since the funeral. Beforehand, I guess, not that anyone met him at the hospital. So anyway, he called Rodney up and said he was interested in Long Pond, just completely out of the blue. Said it looked like a pretty piece of land."

Well, that was the understatement of the year. If there was any place on earth—or at least in western Maryland—which was as pretty as Notch Gap Farm, it was Long Pond Farm. Rosemary thought of the symmetry of the graceful stone farmhouse with its double front porch, its green front lawn running down to the sparkling lake formed by Notch Gap Run. The pond narrowed back into a babbling brook again just before entering the woods running along Rosemary's property line, and the noisy influence of Catoctin Creek took over. The hills rising up behind the farmhouse were gentle swells topped by fir trees; farther out, the mountains rose above it all. Their view of Notch Gap was just as nice as Rosemary's. Long Pond was exquisite, historic, and irreplaceable.

It was unimaginable to think Rodney and Aileen would even consider selling the farm. The Kelbaughs had lived at Long Pond for two hundred years.

Well, not Aileen and Rodney, specifically, but Rodney's Kelbaugh ancestors. They had come to Maryland sometime around 1800, or thereabouts, and, to hear Rodney tell it, those insightful pioneers had hightailed right out of bustling Fredericktown in search of glorious isolation below the Catoctin Mountains. They'd found perfection here in the Maryland woods, where the creeks were ice-cold and crystal-clear, the trees were tall and ramrod-straight, and the grass grew knee-high all summer long. They'd been founders of the town of Catoctin Creek. There was even a little road—really an alley—a block behind Main Street called Kelbaugh Lane. It was just a few hundred feet from Brunner Crossing.

The farm was just a tiny loss, though, compared to losing the Kelbaughs as neighbors. If Long Pond was a constant lynchpin of Catoctin Creek, Rodney and Aileen were two of the most important people in Rosemary's life. She'd been raised with the elderly Kelbaughs as unofficial aunt and uncle, and after her parents had died, they'd become sort of stand-ins when she needed advice or support. Rosemary loved riding Rochester over to Long Pond for a chat with Aileen, letting the horse graze on the lawn while they talked over tea or lemonade and Rodney banged on things in his workshop.

Then there was Thursday night dinner, when she took over a meal and they sat around the kitchen table together, often dining on a rich stew she'd made in her slow cooker and some delightful pie Aileen had baked that day. It was a touchstone of her quiet life, those Thursday night dinners.

Rosemary didn't want to imagine life on Notch Gap Farm without the Kelbaughs next door. Things got lonely enough already. Why would they want to leave the farm—leave *her?* She grasped at the first explanation she could think of.

"I can't believe they'd sell. Do you think they're hard up for money?"

"Must be," Nikki said grimly. "Once I heard Aileen say she'd rather die at Long Pond than live in London, whatever that meant."

"It was an old joke of ours," Rosemary confessed, smiling despite her unhappiness. "When I was little Aileen would ask me where I wanted to live when I grew up. I was obsessed with *Mary Poppins* at the time, so I always said London. Aileen never stopped teasing me about it . . . I guess it just became part of her life." That was the way of it when you knew people forever, she thought. Little inside jokes slowly became folklore.

"Well, you've been warned. I don't know what to think about any of this. Have you met this Stephen Beckett?"

"I think I have." She wasn't about to tell Nikki that he was down in her kitchen eating Aileen's apple pie. She could barely process the information herself. *You know the Kelbaughs?* he'd asked, looking up from the map she'd drawn, and she had been so captivated by his expressive face, in the warmth of his interest in her, she hadn't even thought to notice the alarm in his voice. Even now, she was trying to think of some explanation which would exonerate Stephen. She didn't want him to be the villain in this story.

"Well, the next time he comes into the Blue Plate, I'm going to make sure his mashed potatoes are cold," Nikki vowed. "Although he probably *likes* them that way."

"Some people do," Rosemary said weakly. She herself was not entirely opposed to cold mashed potatoes.

"Only an *animal* would eat cold mashed potatoes," Nikki insisted. "Well, let me get going. I need a shower. I smell like fried chicken night, which is horrifying."

"Go clean up," Rosemary replied, relieved the call was at an end. "Talk later."

When Nikki had hung up, Rosemary sat on her bed in the dark for a few minutes more, straining her ears against the silence. It was so quiet she thought Stephen might have left while she was talking, and that awful thought finally sent her skipping back down the stairs, afraid she'd missed him. She wasn't sure what to think of him now: a few minutes ago he'd been a devastatingly attractive man with whom she'd been seriously considering making some mistakes, and now he was being cast as a deceptive land-grabber. What was a girl to do?

Just ask him, Rosemary thought, standing in the chilly hall of her house. He didn't get to sit in her house and pretend he was someone he wasn't. She would get the truth out of him, or kick him out.

She took a deep breath, summoning her courage for a confrontation, and went back into the kitchen.

Stephen put his hands into his lap the moment she walked into the kitchen. "I wasn't eating a third piece of pie," he declared.

The fork was in the pie-plate, so *that* was a lie. Rosemary stalked past him, picked up the pie, and put it back into the fridge, fork and all. He didn't get to eat her dessert anymore. He didn't get to taste Aileen's delicious apples anymore. Not until he owned up and gave her a good explanation for what Nikki had told her.

"Did I do something wrong? Were you saving it? I'm sorry."

His voice was so contrite, she almost felt bad. Then she steeled herself. A lie by omission was still a lie; he owed her the truth.

Rosemary put her hands on the back of the chair she'd been sitting in and faced him across the table. He looked back at her with a startled expression in his sea-blue eyes. Rosemary knew she couldn't beat around the bush on this one; it would have tried her resolve to stay angry with him . . . those eyes were just *too* compelling. Ugh! This charming man. *Out with it, Rosemary.*

"Are you trying to buy Long Pond?" she demanded.

His eyebrows went up for just a moment, and then a guarded expression swept over his face. "Where did this come from? The phone call? Who was that?"

"You're in Catoctin Creek, Stephen. We all know each other. It could have been anyone."

"It was the waitress, wasn't it?"

"She's the owner."

Stephen leaned back in his chair and sighed as if she was being very unreasonable. "Look, nothing's certain yet. I talked to your neighbors about selling because it's a nice piece of land, and they were interested in my suggestion. I'm not going to coerce them or something. It's not like that. But if they want to sell, it could be a very nice development, with high-end homes, children playing in yards, the whole American dream. And the old couple could move to Florida, and live in a nice house without stairs, and stop shoveling snow and slipping on ice all winter. Wouldn't you like that for them?"

Of course she would. If that's what they wanted. Rosemary would drive them to Florida herself, if that's what they wanted. But she knew they didn't. The Kelbaughs were a part of this place. "They would *never* sell Long Pond."

"They're old, Rosemary. I know that's hard to hear, but it's true." Stephen's voice turned gentle, sympathetic, and it was almost more than she could bear. She turned around and began to drop dishes into the sink, clanging them as loudly as she could. Over the noise, she heard Stephen push back his chair and walk across the kitchen. He stopped behind her, and she froze, her body longing to feel his hands again, but her mind fiercely angry at the thought he might presume to touch her now. That moment upstairs had been a mistake. It wouldn't happen again. Certainly not with the knowledge she had now.

She ran out of cutlery to throw into the sink and leaned her hands against its cold porcelain rim. "They won't leave Long Pond," she said stubbornly. "They wouldn't leave . . . the farm."

They wouldn't leave me.

The selfish thought came rising, unbidden, from her aching heart. The Kelbaughs had no children, but they'd never spoken of the reason. They just lived with their disappointment. Farmers of their generation would have wanted big families to help run the place, to inherit the land, to keep the name going, but Rodney and Aileen had simply wound things down as they grew older, and bestowed all of their parental love on Rosemary. How could parents leave their only child all alone?

She took a long, ragged breath.

"Rosemary," Stephen said from behind her, his voice low and gentle, "why do you stay here alone? Why live out here in the dark countryside?"

Rage came flooding back. Her fingernails clawed into the porcelain. "Don't question it just because it's not how *you* would live."

His sigh was a warm breath that just barely touched the skin of her neck. So close, again. "I'm only questioning it because I think you could do better than this. Alone out here—and the Kelbaughs are elderly, they won't be with you forever, no matter what you think—"

"You don't know anything about me."

"I feel like . . . " he paused, then chuckled, a sweetly self-deprecating sound that made her loosen her grip on the sink. "I can't explain it, but I feel like maybe I do."

She felt that way too, she realized. She never spoke more than a few passing words to new people; it took months to get past her defenses, and most people never would. Stephen had walked into her house and sat at her table and they'd talked as easily as if she'd known him forever.

She'd taken him to her *bedroom*.

He'd kissed her neck and she'd arched into it like a purring cat.

Rosemary shook her head slowly, still looking into the deep bowl of the antique sink. "We don't know each other."

Stephen was silent now. But he didn't leave. She could feel him there, right behind her, so close that if she turned, her chest would brush against his. The knowledge flitted through her brain and her nerve endings fluttered a quick response. She almost did it; she very nearly spun around to face him. And then what would happen? His face would be a few inches away, his chin would dip down, his gaze would lock onto hers—

She was clearly going crazy. She should have listened to Rodney when he'd told her to keep a shotgun by the front door. She should have answered the door with it. She'd do better next time.

She drew four slow, deep breaths, counting them out the way a long-ago grief counselor had shown her, and when she spoke at last, her voice was low and steady.

"You're right, Stephen Beckett of New York City. It is dark out here, and it is a crazy place for me to live, all by myself. I don't *want* to feel alone out here. But I also don't want to live next to a couple dozen suburban families who don't understand our community, either. And I *also* don't want the Kelbaughs to be unhappy if they're ready to give up the farm and move somewhere warm."

Stephen was silent for a long moment. She heard him take a deep breath. "Well, Rosemary, what do you want me to do with this information?"

She sighed. Why did men always need everything spelled out for them? "I want you to remember that what you do here, before you go back to the city and never come back, has real consequences for real people."

"People like you," he said, his voice soft.

"People like me," she agreed.

The tension which had surrounded them in the kitchen was back now, buzzing in the air, tugging at Rosemary's hands and feet, urging her to turn around. She resisted every impulse but one; she turned her head slightly and looked up at him with one sidelong glance.

Stephen looked back down at her. And although she couldn't read his gaze, she thought she knew what he was thinking. She thought she knew what he was feeling.

She turned all the way around just as he took a cautious step back, flooding her with a strange disappointment. They watched each other warily. Rosemary pressed her fists back against the sink, waiting. It was his turn to speak, and she could be silent all night. It was one of her lopsided gifts.

Stephen finally rubbed at his chin as if she was a problem he could not solve. "Rosemary Brunner," he said finally. "Tonight has just been one surprise after another."

"That's certainly true," she replied tartly. He'd have to do better than that.

"Not bad surprises." He lifted his eyebrows. "Not *all* bad surprises, anyway."

The air in the kitchen was electric, crackling. She'd swear the hair on her forearms was standing on end. Her nerves were certainly tingling.

This has to stop, she thought. Whatever they were doing, their stories would only intersect for a little while. He wasn't staying here, and she wasn't leaving. He was taking away Long Pond, and she would never forgive him. Gilbert Beckett had been a nice man, but who was to say what his son really was? Maybe Stephen really was some greedy vulture swooping in from the city to take what he could: land, lonely spinsters. Just two random examples, of course.

What was attraction compared to a lifelong enmity, anyway? Rosemary steeled herself to tell him to leave. The moment came, and went, and returned in a few thuds of her heart.

"You'd better get going," she told him at last.

"I guess I'd better," he agreed, watching her a moment more. Then he turned away and headed down the hallway.

She swallowed hard, feeling the connection between them stretch and thin. Did it snap? She didn't know. She couldn't tell. She wasn't that experienced. But she didn't think so.

Finally, she followed him down the hallway and handed him his coat and hat, waiting for him to bundle up before he went back outside. "Remember to watch for the turn at Clancy's place," she reminded him. "Or I don't know where you'll end up."

"I'll try," he assured her.

He looked fine, she thought angrily. He didn't look hurt at all.

"And Stephen?" Her voice went up an octave, preparing for a final blow. He ought to go away feeling punished. He ought to go away knowing what he'd lost.

"Yes?" He looked attentively at her.

"I'm not going to let you do anything that hurts the Kelbaughs *or* Catoctin Creek. You got that? You can't show up here with your money and your investments and start treating us like part of your portfolio. We won't stand for it. *I* won't stand for it." She ran out of breath and nerve at the same time and had to resist the urge to grasp the coat tree for support. Instead, she clasped her hands behind her back and stiffened her arms, to give her spine a little extra stretch.

Stephen was staring at her now as if he'd never seen her before, as if the past hour of light banter and good food and sexual tension was all a strange dream he'd just woken up from. "Where is this coming from?" he asked finally.

"It's coming from Rosemary Brunner," she told him, opening the front door to show him out. "You think I'm a quiet little sheep, all huddled up alone in the dark, but you don't know me at all, Stephen Beckett."

When he was gone, she went into the kitchen and took out the pie again. His fork was still there, the metal cold now, and she tossed it into the sink with the rest of the dishes. She took a new fork from the drawer and dug it into the pie.

Apples. Brown sugar. Cinnamon. Butter. Rosemary had been eating Aileen's apple pie since she was just a little girl in pigtails. She'd eaten it at birthday parties and at her graduation celebration, warm and topped with ice cream. She'd eaten it after the wake for her parents, cold and straight out of the tray, just like this. Apple pie wasn't her favorite—*that* was lemon meringue—but it was special to her nonetheless. It was a constant in her life. A touchstone, she supposed, if pie could be a touchstone. Something she associated with good, bad, and everyday.

She wondered if she could make pie as well as Aileen, or if this flavor, this feeling, this moment which spanned all of her twenty-seven years, would simply disappear one day, never to return.

It was the first time Rosemary had seriously considered that the quiet life she had spent her past four years putting together was destined for change, whether she wanted it to or not. As permanent as life in this old house could feel sometimes, the people around her would shift, move on to new things, vanish altogether . . . and she would have to rebuild every time.

Well, she'd rebuilt her life once. She could do it again.

"I'll have to bug Aileen for baking lessons," she sighed to the empty kitchen. "And soon."

Rosemary went upstairs and glanced around her bedroom. There were no signs Stephen had been there, and yet she felt his presence as keenly as if he was standing in the center of the room. Just lonely, she told herself. She hadn't had a man around the house in years; she had nowhere to meet them and no inclination to go looking for them. She went over to the window, kicking aside the beanbag chair as she went, and gazed out into the night.

Through the darkness, the night-light glowed. Rosemary pressed her fingers against the cold glass.

Chapter Six

Stephen

He wasn't going to let it bother him. He *wasn't* going to let it bother him.

It was bothering him.

Stephen sat on a bench in Baker Park, a bucolic village green in the center of Frederick's pretty historic district, and watched some kids feeding the geese in the pond. Their little fun was going to end in tears, as feeding geese always did, but these kids seemed ready to deal with the challenge when it eventually arose. The older one, a tough-looking boy of maybe eleven or twelve, was armed with a very long stick. He held the stick resolutely at his side, looking like a goose shepherd, while his younger brothers tossed bits of bread at the honking birds in what Stephen reckoned was nothing short of a dance with the devil. Some of the geese were already looking mutinous about their portions and were beginning to eyeball the little boys' bread supply.

The impending bird bread riot was almost enough to distract Stephen from the nagging feeling he was doing the wrong thing with his life, and he very much needed the distraction of avian versus child battle, as anyone would. So, he leaned forward, elbows on knees, waiting for the birds to rebel.

As he waited for feathers to begin flying, another man approached from the direction of Bentz Street and sat down next to Stephen, sighing heavily. He was an average sort of man, dressed much like Stephen in khakis and a plain black dress shirt, a black wool coat left unbuttoned over the uninspired ensemble. His chin was pointed, his green eyes were kind and, at this moment, looking very tired. His hair was what really kept the man from being a less dramatic version of Stephen: a full head of rich, fox-colored locks which fell into his eyes when he tipped his head down.

Stephen glanced sideways at the tired newcomer.

"Kevin," Stephen said. "Where have you *been?*"

"I've been walking in circles for half an hour. Your directions are terrible." Kevin ran his hands up and down his thighs. "Pretty town, though."

"It is pretty," Stephen acknowledged. He looked back at the geese—he was pretty sure the tide of avian opinion was about to turn against the kids—but he felt as if a balloon of anxiety in his chest was finally collapsing, giving him room to breathe again after weeks of struggle. Kevin was one of his oldest friends.

Finally, Stephen would have someone around this place who was on his team.

"So what are we doing?" Kevin asked, scraping his hair behind his ears. "This is how you spend lunchtimes now? Watching geese in a park? That's very unemployed of you."

"This is how everyone in Maryland spends lunchtimes," Stephen explained earnestly. He chose to ignore the crack about unemployment. Most people couldn't get away with that, but

Kevin wasn't most people. Not to Stephen. "This is an entire state of birdwatchers. Everyone here carries around binoculars and bread. I'm surprised you didn't know that, Kev, honestly."

Kevin shrugged. "Well, now it all makes sense. I mean, knowing that now, I can see why you stayed. We all thought you'd be gone two weeks, tops, and the months start to go by and people have been asking what happened to you, but now it all comes together. *Birds.*" Kevin leaned forward and craned his neck, trying to get Stephen to make eye contact. "Seriously, what happened to you, man? What's going on down here in the hinterlands?"

Stephen pressed his lips together. He hadn't yet said the real reason he was here, not out loud. *Let's feel it out.* "You mean, besides my father dying unexpectedly?"

Kevin wasn't as bowled over as Stephen had expected. He rubbed his hands together and sighed. Then he squeezed Stephen's knee, a brotherly sort of gesture which Stephen found surprisingly gratifying. "I'm sorry, man. Everyone was so sorry to hear that." He paused. "Still. That was a blow, I get it, but it wasn't enough to have kept you here for a month. Not when all your friends are in New York. Not to mention your *job.* You gonna come back to it? We haven't heard a peep out of Ernie Rogers since you left. A startup like that with no Stephen keeping the books? It worries me. Ernie's a spender."

No time like the present, Stephen thought. *Out with it.* "There's no job, Kev. I got *fired.* Confluence Reality already ran out of money. Ernie shut it down while I was down here. I was getting ready to come back. I was *packed.* Ready to get in the car. Locking the front door of the goddamn house. And he calls. 'No rush,' he says. 'Stay there and enjoy the countryside.' Like I had some deep need to hear cows moo for another ten minutes. That was three weeks ago. More, even. He says he's going to get more capital and reopen but, come on. We both know that's not happening. So, I've been trying to figure out my next move ever since."

Stephen tore his gaze away from the geese and looked over at Kevin, searching for his response to the news. Kevin looked morose . . . but not exactly surprised. "I guess you knew a virtual reality start-up was a bad idea all along," Stephen sighed.

"I'm not going to say anything about it."

Another thing to appreciate about Kevin, who had always played it safe: he would never fault a man for taking a different path than the one he would have chosen. This was an incredible quality in a friend, one Stephen thought was under-appreciated. But having Kevin for a friend was something which could hardly be appreciated enough.

They were old work friends who had become closer than brothers, a true rarity in life. They'd worked together for nearly ten years, cubicle mates and lunch buddies from right out of college. Then Stephen had left his nice, secure investment job for the siren of a start-up called Confluence Reality, which made . . . well, never mind what they'd made, or rather, what they'd *said* they were going to make. It was all over now. Tech start-ups had something like an eighty percent failure rate, he'd read that somewhere. He'd just always assumed the failures would belong to someone else.

With the job loss and his long absence, Stephen had lost all of his momentum in Manhattan power circles. At least, thank goodness, he still had Kevin.

"Thanks for that, man," Stephen said softly.

Kevin nodded. "But, I have to ask: why I am in Maryland, Stephen? Not that it isn't very pretty. Or entertaining." He gestured to the path along the pond, where the rebellion had begun and the geese were gathering around the children. The boy with the stick was beginning to wave it around defensively. There was an ominous honking. Kevin eyed them appreciatively. "I wonder if the ducks in Central Park are this bloodthirsty."

"I told you why on the phone. I found a nice piece of land, and I want to bring you in on it."

"So you did. One hundred and fifty-three acres, as I recall. Even if you do estate lots and allow for watersheds and conservation pads, you're thinking what, fifty houses?"

"Maybe a little less. Thirty, I'm thinking. There's some steep slopes in the back, some water in the way. Still, it's a great site. There are some hoops to jump through, but we can make it work."

"How far from D.C.?"

"About an hour and fifteen minutes. More in rush hour, obviously, but . . . "

Kevin nodded slowly. "Seems doable."

"That's what I think. It's a pretty little gold mine."

"I could use a gold mine," Kevin reflected. "Did I tell you my new building sways in storms?"

Stephen shook his head. Kevin had invested in several condos in a new building overlooking the East River, one of those slim needles which were popping up all around the city. He'd moved into one of them just last month. "That sounds terrible."

"It's unbelievable. I get seasick in my own bed."

"So you need a win, so you can get out."

"God, yes. What are the neighbors like at this place? Amenable to a subdivision? Not too much manure smell wafting across the property line, is there?"

Stephen was quiet for a moment, thinking of the neighbor he'd met last night.

"Or haven't you talked to them yet?"

"Not formally. But . . . the idea is out there. It's percolating, let's say." He thought of Rosemary's fierce parting words to him the night before. It was percolating, all right. It was percolating into a cup of brew so strong, neither of them would be able to drink it without plenty of sugar. What would she want? A buffer of trees seemed doable. He could turn the woods between the two properties into a conservation lot to prevent her from having to see the new houses.

Or the loss of her night-light.

Stephen felt a sudden sadness.

He hadn't wanted it to bother him, but it was going to anyway.

"Well, okay." Kevin stood up. There was a clatter of shoes as the boys recognized they'd lost and rushed past the park bench, closely followed by the hissing geese. They watched the cavalcade gallop off through the park towards the relative safety of the street. "You want to show this place to me?"

"Let's get lunch first," Stephen said. "I have reason to believe the manageress of the one and only restaurant in Catoctin Creek is also a mole."

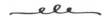

An hour later they were on the road, Kevin and his overnight bag packed into the old beige Toyota Stephen had been bequeathed, heading out of Frederick on their way into the rural hills beyond. The historic brick and clapboard homes of Frederick's pretty downtown quickly changed to strip malls and subdivisions, and eventually to farm land, interspersed with nondescript little ranch houses like Stephen's father's house—well, like *Stephen's* house, now—and oversized McMansions with huge, glaring windows. As they drove farther into the countryside, the hills became more rolling and the bare-branched forests between farms grew more thickly. The rounded blue humps of the Catoctin Mountains slowly drew closer, the bare branches of trees on their slopes becoming more and more defined.

"This is nice, Stephen," Kevin remarked. "Very rustic. Very, I don't know, classic Americana."

They drove past a steeply slanting pasture inhabited by a herd of black-and-white cows, grazing amongst sharply pointed boulders which stabbed from the earth like spikes, and then through a tiny settlement of no more than a dozen old houses, leaning crazily together as if they were holding one another up, their porches and cellar doors so close to the road they were practically on the asphalt. The crumbling house at the far end boasted a Victorian turret at the corner and an old Coca-Cola sign over the door. Faded letters beneath the classic logo read: *Brunner's Grocery.*

Stephen had managed to distract himself for most of the drive, but the sign brought his discomfort back. Rosemary's last name was Brunner. He remembered it because she'd told him twice. It might as well have been her face up there on that faded sign, so completely did her name distract him from the tidy cul-de-sacs of middle-class wealth he'd been building in his mind. He frowned back at the nameless little town as its leaning buildings grew smaller in the rearview mirror.

"Much farther?" Kevin asked, stirring restlessly in his seat, clearly bored with Classic Americana once he'd had to spent more than ten minutes in it.

"Five minutes," Stephen promised. He was growing familiar with this commute. He'd been driving in and out of Frederick nearly every day for the past few weeks, conferring with real estate agents and contractors and lawyers—lining up everything so neatly, Kevin wouldn't possibly find a reason to say no to joining up with him and buying the Kelbaughs' property as soon as possible.

Speed was the goal here. The sooner this deal was set in motion, the sooner he could go back to New York and his real life.

Long Pond's driveway was nearly hidden by overgrown sumac trees, and only the Kelbaughs' rusty mailbox, its green coat of paint long since chipped away, served as a warning of the rutted trail back to the farm. Notch Gap Road curved sensuously right about where this mailbox stood, making matters slightly worse. Stephen had to turn left without really being able to see if a car was approaching from the northbound lane, which was worrisome to a person accustomed to grids and leveled streets.

"Awkward entrance," Kevin observed.

"I have a firm working on the layout, and the road straightens out at the other side of the property. We can make the entrance there if this doesn't work out. But just wait until you see the way this opens up. It's worth the trouble."

Kevin nodded and leaned forward, interested.

They drove up the bumpy lane, the leafless trees falling away on the left, rising on their right. When the land leveled out again, the driveway broke free of the trees, and the sparkling expanse of Long Pond dazzled both men's eyes for a moment.

"Wow," Kevin breathed, blinking dramatically. "Now *that's* a view."

Stephen put his foot down on the brake, and they looked at the prospect before them: the wintry shimmer of Long Pond, the wide sweep of grassy lawn, and the historic farmhouse with its broad front porch looking over a little slope. Old gray fieldstone glinted through the house's fading white paint. Pastures spread out to the right, sunny fields of winter-dry grass carved by fences overgrown with brush and small trees. Behind the house, a steep hill covered with thick forest began the slow climb up into the Catoctin Mountains.

"How did you find this place?" Kevin asked, his voice astonished.

"Satellite view."

"Are you serious?"

"It gets boring up here. I was fiddling around with Google Earth one night, and I just had this idea to look for a nice open piece of land. The pond caught my eye, so I found the address and drove up."

"You're a lucky fool," Kevin said admiringly.

"So listen." Stephen pointed north, past the pond. "We *could* move the entrance over to the far right, to fix that blind spot. Then we wrap the drive back around to right here, and we keep the farmhouse as the sales office and community center." Stephen paused, considering. "Most of it. There's a newer addition on the back that can probably get torn down. We wouldn't need all those bedrooms."

Kevin slapped his thigh with appreciation. "Stephen, this place is a gem. Yes. I want in. My goodness. Who *wouldn't* want to live here?"

Stephen was laughing at Kevin's over-the-top enthusiasm when something caught his eye in the woods off to their left, in the spot where Long Pond narrowed back into a creek and disappeared amongst the trees. After a moment of scanning the gray, bare trees, he realized there was a dirt trail running along its banks. And on that trail, looking like the beautiful ghost of an angry Amazon, rode a woman on a huge black horse.

Rosemary.

"Oh, shit," Stephen whispered.

"What?" Kevin turned and saw the apparition. "What the hell is *that?* Is this place haunted?"

"No . . . that's the neighbor."

He almost wished she *was* a ghost. He remembered calling her one the night before, standing in her bedroom beside her, nearly coming to pieces with desire. A ghost wouldn't be out here in the January sunlight, reminding him of everything which had passed between them . . . and everything which had not.

Today she was bareheaded despite the chill, her dark curls caught up in a long braid falling over one shoulder. The effect of that smoky knot of hair against white cheeks and a cherry-red winter coat was nothing short of stunning.

The horse wasn't bad, either, Stephen had to admit. He'd never seen such a big horse in his life.

Kevin was mesmerized, leaning forward until his forehead nearly touched the windshield. "Is she riding that monster *bareback?*"

Stephen squinted. "I think so."

"On an animal of that size," Kevin muttered. "Well I'll be damned."

"Don't get smitten with her," Stephen warned, and then he wondered what on earth had led him to say it.

Kevin looked at him curiously. "That sounded possessive. Wait! You said *not formally* when I asked about the neighbors. You dog! How well do you know her?"

"I was not being possessive. And . . . not very well. I met her last night, actually. That was the first time."

"How late at night was this meeting?"

"She gave me supper." Stephen grinned. "And a slice of apple pie. And then she told me to get out."

"I could do better than that," Kevin said reflectively, still studying Rosemary with obvious appreciation. "Whoops! She sees us!"

"Oh, no." Rosemary was definitely riding towards them now. She had turned that big black horse's nose in their direction and it was walking their way with an energetic gait. Stephen resisted the nearly overpowering urge to throw the car into reverse and back all the way down the winding driveway behind them, onto Notch Gap Road, and drive off into the winter's day.

"So is she a problem, then?" Kevin was still grinning; Stephen could see his stupid face in his peripheral vision. He was *loving* this. What a jerk! He had no idea how tense and awkward things had gotten with Rosemary last night . . . or how tense and *interesting* things had started out.

In an all-too-brief period of minutes, the horse had reached the car, and Rosemary was peering down at them from her perch high above the car.

"Stephen?" she called. *"Seriously?"*

Stephen opened the car door slowly and climbed out. The horse snorted at him and backed up a few steps, as if he hadn't realized any humans would be involved in this encounter. The horse's off-balance reaction made Stephen feel, however irrationally, like he had the upper hand. So he smiled winningly at Rosemary.

"Hello again!" he replied cheerfully. "Fancy meeting you here!"

He would have liked it if she'd looked a little pleased to see him, but in this, alas, Stephen was to be disappointed.

Chapter Seven

Rosemary

Rosemary kept her seat as Rochester took a few anxious steps backwards, but his broad back was a slippery place, and she would have liked the security of a saddle if he was going to bounce around. She had a little loop of his thick black mane wrapped around three fingers of her left hand, and she felt a sharp bite of pain as the coarse hair tightened around her skin. "Whoa," she murmured. "Relax, bud."

Rochester steadied himself, and had the grace to duck his head with apparent embarrassment. *Whoops,* he seemed to say to her. *My bad, thought that guy was a demon.*

You'd be excused for thinking that, Rosemary thought wryly.

She surveyed Stephen Beckett uncertainly. He was smiling at her with a sunny grin, as if last night's confusing moments had never happened, as if they were old friends who were just bumping into one another. He certainly looked like he hadn't lost a wink of sleep over her. Must be nice!

She had been utterly exhausted after he'd left last night, wrung out from the unaccustomed effort of talking to a stranger. Yet she'd also been so anxious over the thought of the Kelbaughs moving away, she hadn't been able to catch more than a few hours of sleep.

She'd woken before the late winter dawn and gone to the window to look for the night-light, but the elderly couple were up already and she saw the warm, cheerful light above their breakfast table instead. Just the sight of that yellow glow was comforting. She didn't need to be sitting at their table to feel as if she was safe in their company.

After getting through the morning farm chores and poking at a solitary lunch in her kitchen, which felt more empty than usual after Stephen's strange visit, Rosemary decided to ride to the Kelbaugh farmhouse early and check in with her neighbors. She'd be taking over dinner in just a few more hours, but suddenly she didn't feel like she had any time to waste. If they were really going to leave, she needed to soak up as much time with them as possible.

Now she looked down at Stephen and wondered if she could square up how much she liked him with how much she wished he had never come here, putting ideas in her old neighbors' heads and turning her careful little life upside-down.

"Why are you over here today?" Rosemary finally asked him.

"No hello?" His broad smile faltered just a little, a sure sign it was a false front.

He was just as confused about her. She felt a little rush of triumph.

Happy to have found she could needle him, Rosemary sighed and shook her head at him impatiently. "Why, *hello*, Stephen! *What* a surprise! Why are you over here on private property today?"

"Hello, Rosemary!" Stephen replied cheerfully. "I just wanted to give my friend Kevin here a little look at Long Pond. Show him what a beauty of a place it is. You surprised us. I knew your place was close, but I didn't realize you could just appear out of the woods like that."

Suddenly another man, with a wide, cheerful grin and an impressive head of fox-colored hair, popped out of the passenger side of the car. "I'm the Kevin he meant," he explained. "That's a nice horse."

The nice horse side-stepped beneath Rosemary, his wandering attention suddenly fixated on a sprig of early grass growing in a sunny patch along the driveway. She let the reins slip through her fingers so he could reach it without too much fuss. Nothing could really come between Rochester and a bite to eat. She nodded at Kevin. "This is Rochester." That was it for introductions. "Are the Kelbaughs expecting you?"

"Oh, we weren't going up to the house," Stephen demurred.

"Too bad! That's where I'm going." Rosemary shrugged and started to pick up the reins again, tugging at Rochester's head. The big horse tugged determinedly back, enticed by still more tufts of new grass. "I'll tell them you said hello," Rosemary went on, panting a little as she tried not to show she was struggling.

"That's not necessary," Stephen replied quickly.

Too quickly. Rosemary nodded, her suspicions confirmed. "Mmhmm. You're not supposed to be here, are you?"

"We only came up the driveway. And we know the owners— well, I do. That's hardly trespassing."

"You're in the country now, Stephen," she informed him, highly amused by his back-pedaling. "The *backwoods*. If you show up unannounced, you better at least bring something to eat."

"I have a box of Tasty-Kake in the back seat," he offered.

"Hey, I had my eyes on those!" Kevin quipped.

"Rodney has diabetes," Rosemary said regretfully. "And Aileen will eat all of them by herself, just to protect him. Better give them to Kevin."

Kevin heaved a dramatic sigh of relief.

"You'll have to come back another time," Rosemary assured them. "Stop at the Blue Plate and pick up the sugar-free berry pie —Rodney loves it, and Aileen lets him have a whole piece, which is more than she'll do with her apple pie."

"The Blue Plate, where your spy awaits my latest intel, you mean?"

"A girl has to have her lookouts. What if someone handsome comes to town? I'll want to be the first to know. *If* that ever happens." She laughed as Stephen scowled at her.

Rosemary had to admit to herself: she having a wonderful time picking on Stephen. She hardly recognized herself! Where was silent, shy Rosemary? When Stephen was around, she seemed to bloom.

No, that couldn't be it. She wouldn't give him that kind of credit. The difference had to be Rochester. Sitting six feet above them on a large-boned horse clearly freaked both men out quite a bit. She imagined a world in which she was always a-horse and always in control of every situation. She would have made a very good knight, she thought wistfully, or a lady of the manor.

On that note, Rosemary decided, it was time for a dramatic exit.

"Come on, Rochester," she declared masterfully, tugging at the reins and giving the big horse a solid shove in the ribs with her heels. She expected him to pick up his head, turn around, and shove off at his usual ambling walk. He wasn't a dramatic horse in any way, so when she insisted on compliance, she usually got it.

Unfortunately, she had underestimated the romance between a once-neglected horse and the first tender shoots of early grass. Rochester was in no hurry to leave this little patch of heaven he'd found along the Long Pond driveway. And so instead of resigning himself to Rosemary's will, the big horse did something totally out of character: he uttered a petulant little squeal, tucked in his tail, hunched his back, and gave a fussy little buck.

The buck wasn't so bad itself—it was the *surprise* which unseated Rosemary. She gasped, heard herself say *"oh,"* in an unusually high-pitched voice, and then she felt herself slipping sideways and forward, right over Rochester's massive shoulder. She had a glancing vision of his black coat passing her face, and then she put out her left hand to block the rapidly approaching gravel of the driveway.

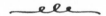

When Rosemary opened her eyes again, Stephen was so close she nearly screamed. Then she winced at the pain in her temple and was glad she hadn't—she was pretty sure the noise would have blown the top right off her skull.

"Jesus Christ, Rosemary!" Stephen exclaimed, seeming to lose his control when she opened her eyes.

"Shhhhhh," she hushed him urgently. "Quiet."

"Sorry," he muttered, his face falling. "Are you okay?"

Rosemary considered all of the parts of her that hurt. Hip, hand, elbow, temple, pride. Then she moved everything which included a joint. They all worked. "I think mostly, yes. Nothing feels broken or anything."

"I don't want to tell you how to do your thing, Rosemary, but I'm pretty sure you should have been wearing a riding helmet."

She wished she had a retort for that, but for one thing, now that she was on the ground she'd lost her powers of repartee, and for another, he was absolutely right. She'd considered putting on her helmet, but the sun had felt so good after several straight days of winter gray, she had decided to risk riding without it. She was just riding steady old *Rochester,* after all. Speaking of whom . . . where the hell was Rochester?

She moved to get up, but Stephen's hands were on her shoulders, keeping her firmly on the ground. "Let me up," she insisted, though without much fire. "I have to go find Rochester."

"Kevin went after him. He's . . . " Stephen looked up and she saw his eyes searching the distance. From below his chin, she could see a fine dark stubble, and she wondered if he'd skipped shaving today, or if he was the sort of man who always had a bit of a shadow. She hadn't noticed any last night, though. And his chin had felt pretty smooth against her neck . . . "He's chasing him around the side of the Kelbaughs' house."

"He's never going to catch him," Rosemary sighed. "That horse was abused by his last owner. He doesn't trust anyone but me."

"I guess I should call him, and tell him to get back over here." Stephen went on watching, and made no move to go for his cell phone. A slight smile played on his lips. Rosemary realized he was enjoying the chase Rochester must be leading Kevin on. Boys were such jerks. "Whoops! He almost had him, would have definitely caught him if he hadn't slipped in that mud. Well, he's not getting back in this car without a change of clothes, I can tell you that much. My car isn't much but it's been kept very clean."

Rosemary smiled despite herself. "That's mean."

"I'm a terrible person," Stephen said, dropping his eyes back to her. "I mean, really awful. Also, I don't have any idea how you clean up a car, so I can't let it get dirty for practical reasons."

His eyes were really the most beautiful blend of green and blue, Rosemary thought. Like Long Pond on a summer's day when the reflections of the trees and sky blended together in the watery ripples. Was that cheesy? Yes, it was definitely cheesy, but it was true. She would go on thinking it, then. There was no one to stop her. No one would ever know.

"I should think about getting you to a hospital," Stephen sighed.

"No." Rosemary almost shook her head but thought better of the movement. Still was the way to be right now. "I'm fine here."

"On the driveway?"

"For a few minutes. And then I'll get up extra-slowly, and you can help me walk back to my house, and I'll sit very quietly and promise not to fall asleep."

"How can you promise something like that?"

"I'm very good at not sleeping," Rosemary said truthfully.

He studied her for a long moment, and she took the opportunity to admire everything about him—really, *everything* about his face was very nice, she thought, feeling a measure of disgust in herself for not simply abandoning her attraction to him —and then he shrugged his shoulders. "If that's what you want. The hospital is an hour away, anyway."

There was a shout in the distance. "Oh," Stephen said, looking up. "Kevin has caught your horse."

"He must be exhausted." Rosemary thought of Rochester's big frame and infrequent workouts. "He doesn't do much running."

"Yes, I'd say Kevin looks very tired from here."

She couldn't help it. She started to giggle, and then she started to laugh, and then the pulse in her temple began to hurt terribly and a few tears slipped out, and just when Stephen was starting to look really alarmed and she felt the threat of the hospital rising up again, she heard a storm door slam.

"Here come Rodney and Aileen," Stephen said, sounding chagrined. "Now we're all in trouble."

Rosemary sniffled, trying to pull herself together. "*You* are, anyway," she murmured.

Chapter Eight

Stephen

Stephen had been on the verge of telling Rosemary he'd stay with her to make sure she was all right. He had to, right? There was no way to just abandon her in that lonely farmhouse with a head wound, for God's sake. He couldn't force her to go to the hospital, but she was definitely concussed and needed to be looked after.

He'd already decided he would give Kevin the car, mud and all, and give him the map back to his house, the one Rosemary had drawn for him last night. It was right there in the car's cupholder. There was a key under the flowerpot next to the front door. Kevin would be all set for a little getaway at the Beckett house. Yes, Stephen had things all figured out.

Now, however, there was an elderly farm couple, a pair of people who frightened him just a little bit, walking slowly across their front lawn towards him, and he felt his plans evaporating away. No doubt *they'd* want to take charge of Rosemary. They might even have strict attitudes about emergency rooms, for all he knew. Somehow, whole minutes before the slow-moving Kelbaughs arrived, Stephen knew he'd lost control of the situation.

Then there was Kevin, who was dragging the black horse in his direction, wearing mud on his jeans and an alarmed expression on his face. The Kelbaughs caught up with him first and there was a quick exchange of conversation. Then, Kevin was turning to the right and following the creekside path into the woods. He must be taking the horse back to Rosemary's farm, Stephen realized, but what on earth would he do with him once he got there? Kevin had never taken care of anything larger than a cat.

Rosemary was struggling to sit up, and he moved to help her, recognizing she would want to be as much in control as possible when her neighbors arrived. He didn't know much about their relationship, but he knew her parents were gone and she'd come to rely on these two, which probably meant they had, in turn, begun to boss her around a little bit.

"Rosemary Brunner, you lay right back down!" Aileen Kelbaugh's voice was like iron.

Maybe more than just a little bit, Stephen thought.

"I'm fine," Rosemary protested in a raspy voice, but she put her head down as instructed. Stephen put out his hand to catch it and give her a pillow. She smiled up at him, a true smile without a hint of irony, which stretched all the way to her emerald eyes. He swallowed hard, truly alarmed at what her smile did to his composure.

"Rosemary, I cannot *believe* you came over here riding without a hard hat on," Aileen said gruffly, standing over the two of them with her hands on her hips. She was a slight woman, her skin gone wrinkled and fragile with age and outdoor life, and yet there was nothing frail about either Aileen or Rodney. They were bundled up in plaid flannel and woolen hats and duck boots, but even so, Stephen knew underneath there would be hard muscle and ropy sinew covering their old bones. When they'd first met to talk about the property, Rodney had told him they'd only just gotten rid of their dairy herd and their pigs a few years before. "I was seventy-eight," Rodney had said laconically. "Felt like time."

"I know," Rosemary was telling Aileen now. "I'm really sorry."

"Not as sorry as you're going to be in a few hours when that knot on your forehead shows up," Aileen told her brusquely. "Rodney, go and get the truck. We'll bring her back to our place to keep an eye on her."

Rodney turned to do his wife's bidding.

"No," Rosemary protested, slowly sitting up again. "Please don't, Rodney."

Rodney glanced meaningfully at his wife, who had pursed her lips and wore a forbidding expression on her face. "Rosemary, let's not make a fuss, now," he suggested.

"Exactly," Aileen announced. "Come on, girl."

Stephen was ready to pack it all in and hand the reins to the formidable farmwife, but Rosemary was apparently made of tougher stuff than he was.

"No, I need to go home," Rosemary said, her voice thin. "I'll be fine. I have compresses, I have soup, I have everything I need there."

"Who will keep an eye on you? I'm not leaving Rodney at home alone, and we're not packing up and moving over to your place tonight. It makes much more sense for you to stay with us. Heaven knows you've done it before."

Rodney just waited, watching, while the women battled it out. Stephen met his eyes and flashed a quick smile. The old man gave him a nod and a wink, then looked meaningfully at Rosemary.

How interesting, Stephen thought. Rodney had his money on Rosemary!

"Nikki can come over," Rosemary said. "I'm sure she'll come over. As soon as she closes up. I can keep myself alive until then."

"I don't think so," Aileen decreed. "She won't be done until after nine o'clock. With *that* kitchen staff? Maybe later. She needs to fire every one of those girls and start fresh. I told her that last night, I told her, 'Nikki, you need to fire every one—' "

"I'll stay with her until Nikki can come back," Stephen burst out. He spoke the words without thinking, but immediately knew there'd be consequences. Aileen was looking at him sharply, her eyes narrowed. She had eyes green as jade, paler than Rosemary's but unfaded by age, and they could skewer a man who didn't know when to keep his mouth shut. Feeling stripped bare now by that gaze now, Stephen glanced nervously at Rodney, who had taken to studying the empty blue sky overhead, a benign look on his face.

"Fine," Aileen decided eventually. "But don't let anything happen to her." She looked back at Rosemary with a sudden fondness softening her features. "And don't let her push you around."

Rosemary proceeded to push Stephen around the moment her feet were back on her own property. "There's Kevin with Rochester," she said urgently as he helped her out of the car. "He's going to let him loose in the barnyard with his bridle on! Let *go* of me—" this last line was delivered to Stephen with the spitting rage of a provoked kitten. "I have to go fix things."

"I will *help* you walk over there," Stephen allowed, "if you will promise to keep calm. I think Rodney probably told him to take the bridle off. Look! He's doing it now."

They watched Kevin stand on his tiptoes in an attempt to lift the bridle's crown-piece over Rochester's ears. The mission was in vain. Kevin hopped in the air, hoping an extra inch or two would get the job done, but his attempts fell short. Finally, he stood still and stared at the horse's immense height in what Stephen could only assume was quiet desperation. The horse looked off into the middle-distance, his gaze impassive, but Stephen got the impression the whole situation was giving the horse great pleasure.

"He can't do it," Rosemary hissed. "Rochester is always a pain about things like this, even with me."

"Just wait," Stephen told her. "I'm interested."

After a lengthy pause, Kevin went for a stealthy attack, waiting for Rochester to show some interest in a few tufts of grass growing near the fence. He slowly slipped his hand up the horse's neck, behind his ears, and suddenly had the leather grasped in his hand. He whipped the bridle over the ears and tugged it down just as Rochester threw up his head again.

"That was good," Stephen said. "Bravo, Kevin."

"It actually was." Rosemary sounded impressed.

Kevin began to do a little dance of triumph, then yelped as Rochester turned away from him and bolted across the little barnyard, his hooves thudding like thunder on the half-frozen ground. He darted around the fence-lines, snorting and kicking like a colt in clover.

Stephen tensed, ready for Rosemary to take off for the barnyard, but instead she shrugged. "He's just showing off. Leave him alone. We can bring him in later."

"So you'll go inside and behave yourself?"

She gave him an exasperated look. He admired the way she could make her eyebrows meet between her eyes when she was annoyed. Not everyone could do that.

"I mean, can we go inside and put a nice, cold compress on your head?" He smiled angelically.

"Yes," she agreed, and for just a moment he could see fatigue in her features. "A compress would be nice, actually."

"Lean on me a little. You don't want to get dizzy."

Rosemary obligingly pressed up against him, and Stephen caught his breath at the feel of her. Maybe this afternoon would be a good thing, he thought hopefully, wrapping an arm around her shoulders. Maybe they'd manage to put all of this Long Pond business behind them. Not that he was about to seduce a woman with a concussion; and anyway, Stephen couldn't quite explain it, but this attraction went deeper than sex. He wanted to get to know her, and he wanted her to *like* him.

He felt like he'd give anything to avoid being her enemy.

Kevin had caught up with them by the time Stephen had Rosemary up the porch stairs, and was chattering about his epic capture of Rochester. Pushing open the front door, Stephen wondered if Kevin would just automatically figure out he was a third wheel and vanish, or if he would need a little help catching on.

Judging by the way Kevin hustled ahead of them into the kitchen and started opening cabinet doors, he was going to need some help. Stephen sat Rosemary down at the kitchen table. It was odd being in this space again so soon. Last night he'd left here never expecting to see this old kitchen again, and now here he was, less than twenty-four hours later, putting her kettle onto the stovetop and turning on the flame.

"What are you doing?" Rosemary demanded of Kevin, who was still rummaging in cabinets. "Stop that before you break something."

Stephen thought she sounded even more tired now, as if coming indoors had been a drain on her energy.

"I was looking for towels," Kevin replied contritely. "To make you a compress?"

"Towels, in the cabinets? The closet is in the hall," she said. "Just next to the kitchen door. Ice in the freezer." She rested her chin on her upturned palm, tilted her head, and closed her eyes. "Why would there be towels in the kitchen?" she asked no one.

"New York City apartments," Stephen explained. "They do strange things to a person."

She didn't open her eyes. "Clearly."

Stephen picked up a likely-looking bottle from the counter and gave it a shake, rattling the pills inside. "Headache meds?"

"Yes, please." She held out her hand and accepted the pills he shook out, then swallowed them before he could get her a glass of water. She caught him staring and smiled wearily. "Yeah, I know. It's a bad habit."

"Here's water anyway." He put the glass down in front of her. "I can't do that without choking. You're pretty impressive."

Kevin had returned and was pulling ice from the freezer with crashing sounds, pouring it into a plastic bag he'd dug out of a drawer. Stephen waited until he'd finished and handed the bag, well-wrapped in a towel, over to Rosemary. Then he fixed Kevin with a practiced look of entreaty. "Listen, bud, could I get you to do me a favor?"

"Yeah, of course."

"There's a stack of papers in my car that were supposed to get faxed up to the contractor's office. Would you mind running up to my house and getting those sent out? The number is by the printer in the back bedroom. You'll see it."

Kevin smiled uncertainly. "I would be happy to, but I haven't *been* to your house. I don't know where it is."

"The directions are in the cupholder. It's ten minutes away. Couldn't be easier." *In daylight,* Stephen added mentally. He glanced at Rosemary and saw the tiniest of smiles on her tired face.

"Well, okay then." Kevin looked down his side as if he'd just noticed how muddy he was. "Guess I could get cleaned up, too."

Stephen considered the future state of his car's upholstery. "Guess so," he agreed after a pained moment. "Take your time, though, buddy. No rush."

"Sounds like a plan," Kevin decided. "Well, feel better, Rosemary. Call me if you want me to bring anything over."

"We sure will."

Kevin went off down the hall. Stephen heard the front door shut behind him, and allowed himself a small sigh of relief. That was one obstacle out of the way, he thought, and then: *out of the way of what, exactly?*

He hadn't been planning on a fling during his last weeks in Catoctin Creek, and even if he had, keeping a concussed woman awake because she was too stubborn to go to the hospital wasn't the stuff of great sex. Sure, he wanted to get to know her better, but what was the end goal? He was leaving. He had no future here.

Still, Stephen *wanted* to be here right now. If for no other reason than to be around her.

The kettle whistled with shrill authority, and he got up to make tea, happy for something else to think about.

Chapter Nine

Rosemary

H er headache wasn't that bad, but it was nice to have someone around to take care of her.

Rosemary lay across the living room sofa with her feet up on one end, a fat lump of pillows lifting her shoulders at the other. On the antique table next to her sat a mug of lukewarm tea and a plate of sandwich cookies. The curtains were open to the bright winter afternoon sky, and Stephen was sitting in her grandfather's old easy chair across the room, watching her with a serious expression.

Maybe too serious.

"I'm not dying," she informed him for the third time in the past hour. "I can manage alone until Nikki gets here."

"How can I be sure?" he asked, lifting his eyebrows. "No, I think I better keep watching you, just in case."

"What good is watching me going to do? What's the plan here? I don't think you have one." She couldn't resist picking on him. He *needed* it, she thought. He was just desperate to be mocked. She could tell these things.

Also, she didn't really care to be the subject of scrutiny. She wished he'd take care of her by turning on the television or reading her the news off his phone or something. Anything besides just this constant, unnerving surveillance. Her typical desire to hide in a corner was emerging, replacing the unusual pleasure she'd taken in his company last night. She liked Stephen, really liked him with an intensity that was foreign to her, but even the mysterious forces of instant attraction couldn't atone for the annoyance of being stared at for an hour.

"I don't have a plan," Stephen sighed, steepling his fingers together. He looked up at the ceiling and then back at her. "The moment I met you, all of my plans went out the window."

They stared at each other for a moment, and then they both laughed. Uncomfortable laughter, Rosemary knew. Because what the hell did he mean by *that?*

Apparently, Stephen thought he'd said something over the top as well, because he looked out the front window and didn't say anything else for a while.

A long while.

Rosemary yawned.

"Nope, none of that," Stephen commanded, turning back to her. "There will be no napping on my watch."

"Let me do something, then." She pushed herself upright, tossing the soggy compress to one side. "I feel much better. I'm going to go take care of Rochester, and then feed the horses. Look, it's getting late."

"*I* will take care of Rochester," he announced. "You can supervise. Quietly. From a seated position nearby."

Rosemary considered him for a moment. She *could* just let him go out and get trampled into the thawing ground by Rochester. It might be a good lesson for him about what could happen to proud city boys when they came out to the country. Roam around on farms, find out the hard way what can happen to you on a farm . . . that was an effective and time-honored way of handling people with over-inflated egos, like Stephen.

But she liked Stephen despite all of his flaws, and she didn't want him to get into trouble while he was trying to catch her troublesome Percheron. She had no doubt Rochester would cause him grief. Kevin might have managed to get the horse home without issue, but she wasn't going to trust the horse to behave himself twice in one day, for two different strangers. Rosemary had worked hard to build a relationship with Rochester, but he was generally distrustful of the rest of the world.

"I don't think so," she said finally. "I will go so far as to let you *help* me with him."

"How kind of you. And supposing you drop dead because you won't be sensible and stay nice and relaxed on the sofa? What do I do then?"

"If I do, please feed everyone their dinners. The feed is in the old dairy, there is a chart with how much each horse gets." Rosemary got up slowly, stretched. Her elbow was a little sore, her shoulder was aching. But her head wasn't too bad at all, since the painkiller had kicked in. Well, thank goodness for that. She should have worn a helmet, she knew that. Next time, she would. Since she'd been given a next time, and all.

They pulled on coats at the front door and she gallantly lent Stephen a pair of her father's old boots, still leaning together like old friends in the back of the hall closet. The mud of winters past were caked to the soles.

"It's getting soft out there, I can tell just from looking," Rosemary said, peering through the door's window. "When the afternoon temperature gets up above freezing on a daily basis, we'll know we're about to enter mud season."

Stephen eyed the heavy red clay on the boots. "Do I want to be here for mud season?"

She laughed. "Nobody does. But it's the price we pay for all of our pretty sunsets."

They walked out into the yard side by side. Rosemary shivered a little, and she felt Stephen move closer to her.

"These sunny winter days are so deceptive," she said with a dry chuckle. "It looks warmer outside then it is."

"It's still warmer than it was yesterday," Stephen replied blandly.

"That's true," Rosemary replied, wondering if they had anything real to talk about, or if constant back-and-forths about air temperature were the best they could do. If so, silence would be better. Rosemary had a horror of small talk. It took so much effort, and for what?

"There's Rochester," she said pointlessly, because there was no missing that big black horse. The moment he entered a person's field of vision, his pure majesty seemed to blot out the rest of the world.

Rochester was watching them with his head held high and his ears pricked. His long black forelock fell over his right eye, giving him a dashing, piratical look. Rosemary knew he would be lonely after an afternoon stuck in the barnyard while all his friends were out on the back pasture behind the barn. But that's what made this such a good punishment for him, she thought. He didn't get to dump her, run away, and then go straight back outside to play with his mates. Where was the lesson in that?

"Did you miss us?" Rosemary called, and he whinnied back to her with his surprisingly high, lilting voice.

"That horse sounds like a girl," Stephen guffawed, and Rosemary mock-punched him in the arm.

"Don't make fun of my Rochie! He's been through a lot."

"You must be kidding me. Who would mess with a horse that size?"

"A very small man." She walked up to the fence, where Rochester was waiting for her, and tugged on his chin. The big horse leaned down to lip at her fingers. From the corner of her eye, she noticed Stephen was keeping a prudent distance. *Newbie.* "He came from a farmer with a very bad reputation up in PA. When I got him, you couldn't catch him in the field unless you had five pounds of carrots and a couple of hours to kill."

"Damn," Stephen replied soberly.

"And he bit," Rosemary went on, tickling Rochester's nose until his nostrils fluttered, "and he kicked, and he ran away under saddle. Of course that wasn't his fault, I didn't find out until later that the auctioneer had lied to me and he wasn't actually saddle-broke. He was literally a plow horse. A big, *beautiful* plow horse!" she sang to Rochester, who shoved his head against her shoulder, nearly knocking her down. She steadied herself against the fence.

"So how did you get a plow horse?" Stephen sounded genuinely interested now. "What made you bring him home?"

Rosemary walked along the fence to the little wooden gate her grandfather had hung decades before. She opened it and beckoned

Stephen to follow her into the yard. With one finger, she hooked the bridle Kevin had left hung on a post earlier that day and slung it over her shoulder like a handbag. "I had room for horses, and nothing to do. The farm was empty and it seemed like I should fill it up again. I found Rosita from an ad at the feed store. She was my first rescue, just a cheap purchase from a guy who didn't know how to take care of her, but then I went up to this auction over the state line. This particular auction has a reputation. Not the nicest place. So I went up there to see who needed saving. Bongo and Rochester weren't even going through the auction-ring. They were out back, waiting for the under-the-table meat sales. Skin and bone then, but draft horses are easy to fatten up quickly." Rosemary shook her head, remembering the sight. "And they're fat and happy now. Aren't you, buddy?"

She walked up to the barn doors with Rochester following eagerly, his platter-sized hooves sinking an inch into the soft ground with every step. Rosemary shook her head at the sucking sound. She was already dreading the muddy clay of March and April. "I almost wish it would freeze solid again just to avoid the hell that is coming."

At the barn doors, where the building's shadow fell darkly over the ground, the earth abruptly turned rock-hard again. "Ah," she sighed. "That's better." But she couldn't help but shiver. She tapped the thermometer on the wall: thirty-two degrees, precisely, in the shade. "It's going to be cold again tonight." Then she shook her head at herself. *More weather-talk, Rosemary?*

She shoved on the door handle, and the barn door slid open with a rumble, revealing the cozy little stable within. Stephen looked in with surprise. "That's what's inside these hill barns? Is this like, a basement?"

"*Bank* barns," Rosemary corrected him, "and kind of, yes. The lower level is good for animals, the upper level is for storage. This is where my great-grandfather kept his couple of dairy cows and his plow horses. Now, my grandfather built a whole dairy barn, but it collapsed in an ice storm about ten years ago. No cows were in it," she added hastily, seeing the shocked expression cross Stephen's face. "We'd already gotten rid of the dairy business by then. My dad didn't love cows. He preferred crops that didn't make manure."

By now Rochester was right on top of them, pushing his nose against her back. "He wants to go in and eat," she laughed. "Want to help me feed?"

Without waiting for an answer, she stepped back, tugging on Stephen's arm to pull him out of the horse's way, and let Rochester charge past them into the barn. The big horse went straight into his stall and started rattling the empty buckets inside, reminding Rosemary she needed to fill everyone's water buckets before they came in from the pasture. She beckoned Stephen to come inside. "How about you grab that hose and pull it around to each stall, fill the buckets inside?"

"I can do that," Stephen agreed. "And what are *you* going to do? Nothing strenuous."

"I'm just going to set up their evening feed. Pour grain into buckets," she amended, seeing his confusion. "I'll add some meds and supplements. Like, tablespoons of vitamins. I swear it's not going to over-exert me."

"Well, okay," Stephen grumbled. "If you say so."

Rosemary left him to his water buckets and went down into the dairy to start doling out grain. She smiled to herself as she pulled down tubs of vitamins and supplements for the horses. It wasn't so bad, having Stephen trip around after her like a big watchdog. He wasn't much of a nursemaid, but he knew how to make a decent cup of tea. Now they were out of the house and she didn't feel so pent up, she even found she didn't mind his constant scrutiny of her. Which was funny, because usually Rosemary couldn't bear to have anyone looking at her, ever.

A fluffy apparition appeared in the dairy's doorway and leapt down the stairs, padding up to her and twirling around her Wellington boots. "Hey, bad kitty," Rosemary crooned, leaning down to stroke his soft head. "Did you kill anything for me today?"

"*Meow,*" Smoke explained earnestly, his tail twitching for emphasis.

"Oh, I see. Excuses, excuses." She gave him a handful of dry food. "I should just move you into the house and get a new barn cat."

Stephen's face appeared in the doorway. "Are you hallucinating? Who are you talking to?"

"My *cat*, Smoke." She laughed up at his scowling face. "Less spying, more bucket-filling, if you please!"

"I'm filling, I'm filling." He disappeared and a moment later she heard the roar of water rushing into a bucket.

"That's better." She went back to her feed set-up, a process she loved. Rosemary lined up the little buckets along the rough floor of the dairy, then went about scooping in the sweet-smelling, molasses-rich grain and adding everyone's various powders. Some of the horses, like Bongo, were on permanent joint supplements due to hard farm labor in their youth. Kiki got an anti-inflammatory for an old injury in her left hind leg which had left her permanently unsound. Everyone got electrolytes and trace minerals.

When she'd mixed up the grain with all of the supplements, she carried the buckets up the steps, four at a time, and emptied them one by one into the feed bins in each stall. Rochester nickered appreciatively. She had to push him off her so that she could get into his stall to drop the feed. "Dummy," she told him affectionately. "You make everything harder than it needs to be."

Stephen was still filling water buckets. He looked at her suspiciously as she stacked the empty feed buckets. "Rosemary . . . did you just feed seven ghost horses and one real one?"

"Yes," Rosemary said gravely. "I love all of my ghost horses."

He cocked his head at her, looking so concerned she couldn't keep a straight face and burst into laughter.

"They're outside, Stephen! My God. First I'm a ghost to you and now you think my horses are spirits? They're in the upper pasture behind the barn. As soon as you're done watering, we'll let them in."

The horses were waiting at the gate, their furry coats catching the slanting light of the coming sunset and making them look like fluffy plush toys. When Rosemary led Stephen around the side of the bank barn, picking her way carefully up the flat slate stones her great-grandfather had placed into the hillside, she couldn't help but glance back at him to see if he appreciated the pretty scene.

The winter sunset from this hillside, looking up to the tree-dotted upper pasture and beyond to the dark, forested heights of

Notch Gap, was one of Rosemary's most beloved views on the farm.

This evening was shaping up to be breathtaking, with just a few long, narrow clouds in an otherwise crisply blue, clear sky. In a little while the sun would begin to sink towards the mountains, and light up those unassuming little clouds into golden majesty.

"It's nice out here," Stephen commented.

Rosemary's mouth turned down. Just *nice?* "This is the nicest place in the world," she declared.

She found Stephen had nothing to say to that. Well, it was early. In another quarter-hour, when the sunset turned on its full charm, he'd know what she was talking about.

Their boots crunched on the flat gravel driveway running in front of the barn's upper story. The horses were clustered against the fence just a few dozen feet away, turning in tight, excited circles at the prospect of dinner.

"Those are my ponies." Rosemary gestured with a flourish of her fingers. "Are you ready for the rodeo?"

"The what-now?"

"Did you notice I left the barnyard gate open?"

"I assumed we were going to be walking right back through it."

"Oh, we are."

"So what's the rodeo?"

"That's what I call it when I let these fire-breathing beasts go running down the hillside and into the barn."

"By themselves?" Stephen stared at her, then back at the horses. "Won't they run away?"

"With dinner on the line? Hardly. Horses are just little kids, Stephen."

He looked skeptical.

"And anyway," Rosemary went on, "how do you think one woman would get eight horses into the barn every night? Back and forth, back and forth?"

"I guess I would assume so, yeah?"

She laughed. "I'm too lazy for that, buddy."

They reached the gate. The horses were milling around, nipping and squealing at one another, hot with anticipation. She gave everyone a quick look over, checking for blood or swelling or anything else obviously wrong. She'd give them a more thorough check-up inside the barn, but for now, upright and moving soundly on all four legs was good enough. Rosemary nodded, satisfied, and put her hand on the pasture gate.

Then, she paused and glanced back at Stephen. A smile played around her lips as she considered the thought that had just come into her mind. From the barn, Rochester whinnied plaintively, and a few of the pastured horses neighed in reply, stirring restlessly behind the gate.

She decided to go for it.

"Come on, guys!" she called, rapping the chain on the gate. "Let's go, let's go, let's go!"

The horses turned in tight, anxious circles.

"Are you ready? Let's *go!*"

"They're already here," Stephen said, clearly confused.

Rosemary grinned and reached for the gate chain. "You'll want to stand back, Stephen."

Chapter Ten

Stephen

He couldn't believe the noise they made.

Stephen was used to a certain constant level of noise; he was from a city, after all, where trains and buses and trucks and cars and sirens all combined to create a constant din. But city sounds were more or less white noise, a regular hum punctuated occasionally by momentary additions: someone shouting on the street beneath his open window, a Mr. Softee ice cream truck playing its twinkling tune on summer evenings, a barking dog meeting another barking dog to have an impromptu barking dog convention.

The noise of twenty-eight hooves slamming against barely-thawed clay was something else altogether, a rumble like thunder rising up from the earth. He jumped backward in surprise as Rosemary threw the gate open and the horses launched themselves forward, mud flying up from their hooves as they went. They shoved through the gateway in ones and twos, then galloped up the gravel road before turning in one smooth curve, looking for all the world like a flock of birds, to run down a smooth section of hillside and through the open barnyard gate.

Stephen was rather impressed by the choices they made, heading for a less-severe slope rather than just plunging headlong down the hill next to the barn. Pretty intelligent, he had to admit. Who knew horses were capable of judging grades? He wondered what else they knew. Maybe all of these horses could count, like the one he'd seen at the Big Apple Circus as a kid.

When the last flying tail had disappeared behind the stone walls of the barn's lower story, he turned back to look at Rosemary. She was smiling at him. That was a bit of a coy smile, he thought. She was looking for his reaction.

Had she done this to try to *scare* him?

Oh, Rosemary.

There was something about this woman he just couldn't pin down. She kept to herself out here on this farm, clearly placing a lot of value on her solitude, but then she clung to a tiny night-light in her neighbors' kitchen. She told him she didn't want him around, but then smiled at him so provocatively, he didn't know how she could ever expect him to leave. She looked strong-boned and tough with her layers of coats and Wellington boots, but he'd seen her eyelashes flutter against her cheeks as she lay on the ground, as delicate as a floundering butterfly. Now she was teasing him with her herd of horses, making her cozy little farm as intimidating as she possibly could.

He was tickled by her. There was no other word for it.

So Stephen put on his broadest smile for her. "That was quite a show! Do you put on that kind of circus every night, or was it for my benefit?"

One slanting eyebrow arched upward. "It's more or less like that, although I admit I gave them a little extra riling-up for you. I wanted to show off how nice they are when they gallop around. Are you impressed?"

"Extremely." Stephen was mostly just pleased she wanted to show off for him, but the horses *had* been impressive. "And where are they now?"

"Each one in his or her own stall, eating their dinners. But I have to close their doors before they finish, or the quickest ones will go and steal from the slow eaters."

He followed Rosemary down the slope, keeping close in case she needed a hand. But she was moving confidently on her own, without any sign she'd recently taken a tumble from a tall horse onto cold, hard ground.

Stephen wondered if she'd insist he leave after they'd finished with the horses. She was clearly too independent to want him hanging around for no reason, and if her head was feeling better, she might decide she didn't need babysitting any longer.

Of course, if so, she'd just have to wait to kick him out. Kevin still hadn't come back with his car. His absence was getting a bit worrisome.

With Rosemary's direction, Stephen started closing stall doors and shoving sticky latches home. He noticed she took more than half—mostly because Stephen fumbled with all the latches, and only a little because the black-and-white miniature horse in the back corner charged at him when he came up to the open stall door, ears flattened back against his skull, making the tiny horse look like a terrifying snake.

"Oh, sorry about Mite," Rosemary laughed, rushing over and closing the comically short door on his stall. The miniature horse had already gone back to his feed bin and was ripping into his grain with the force of a killer robot. "He doesn't know how little he is. Or he *does* know, and it makes him crazy. I don't know which."

Stephen took a deep breath to steady himself. For a moment he'd thought that tiny horse was going to kill him . . . or maybe just bury his teeth in Stephen's crotch, which was about as high as the vicious little creature could probably reach. Either one would be terrible. "It's fine," he said finally. "No one died."

"Another successful barn evening!" Rosemary declared. "I just have to throw down hay." She walked down the little aisle along the front of the stable and Stephen assumed she would go down into the dairy. Instead, she started to climb a set of wooden rungs fastened into the wall.

Stephen looked up and realized there was a trap door in the low ceiling. He started forward, pretty sure she shouldn't be climbing to high places, no matter how much better she was feeling.

"Rosemary, let me," he said hastily, reaching for her waist, which was rapidly ascending away from him. "Don't—"

Rosemary paused and he thought she was listening to him. Then she listed, gave a little cry, and fell backward.

She was only a few feet above him, but even so, Stephen was knocked backwards when he caught her. He staggered a moment, his arms beneath hers, automatically locking into place to keep her from hitting the ground. For just a few breaths, she was limp as a rag doll, and he was absolutely terrified. Why had he told Kevin to take his car? Where the hell had that man gone, anyway? How was he supposed to get help now?

Then she moved just a little, life coming back into her limbs. Stephen felt shaky, as if his bones were dissolving.

"Rosemary," he hissed urgently, "are you all right? What happened?"

"Got dizzy," she murmured, trying to put her feet on the ground. She was already less limp in his arms. "I'm all right, I'm fine. Let *go* of me."

He marveled at how quickly she could go from a dead faint to impatient and anxious to be on her own. "You fainted," he insisted, refusing to let her free. "You could have fallen flat on this hard ground and hurt yourself even more. I'm not letting you go until you promise to sit down."

"Fine," she huffed. "Sit me down, then. But you'll have to throw down a couple of hay bales."

"I feel capable of that," he assured her, helping her over to an old wooden chair near the dairy door. "It's just upstairs?"

"You'll see the hay when you get up there. Three bales, please. Just drop them through the trap door. Straight down, or they'll bounce and break apart."

Stephen obediently put his borrowed boots onto the rungs of the ladder and clambered up, shoving the trap door open with one hand when he was close enough. The wooden door clacked on the old beams of the barn ceiling, and he shoved his head and upper body through the opening.

Now he was on the upper barn floor, a vast open space like a warehouse. He hauled himself the rest of the way up and looked around, impressed with the scale of the place. The floor was built of old planks which creaked under his feet, their splinters padded with a generous layer of dust and chaff from the hay stored up here.

The walls soared to a high roof, with occasional gaps where the timbers had pulled apart from age or weather. Across from him were the tall barn doors which he'd noticed earlier, when he'd been standing by the pasture gate. They were tightly closed, but slanting golden rays of sunlight found their way through innumerable gaps and knotholes, lighting up the drifting dust with sparkling motes, floating through the sunbeams.

For a moment, Stephen was so taken with the fairy-tale quality of the old barn, he forgot why he was there.

"Do you not see the hay?"

Rosemary's voice still sounded a little weak, in his opinion. She'd been doing far too much work. He decided he'd better hurry up with the hay, then get her inside to warm up. "It's fine," he called back. "I'm getting it."

The tall stack of hay bales huddled against the far wall, near an antique tractor and several pallets' worth of horse feed. Walking across the dusty floor, Stephen guessed he was looking at the tail end of a years' worth of hay. He wondered when it came back into season, how expensive it was, what kind of grass it was. He knew absolutely nothing about farming, something he had been realizing with just a touch of embarrassment as he'd been dealing with the Kelbaughs. For his entire life, food had come from restaurants, delivery guys, carts, and the overpriced Food Emporium at the end of his block, or the cramped Associated Market by his dad's apartment. Anything actually grown in his sight was a novelty, like tomatoes on a girlfriend's fire escape, or a community garden with earnest do-gooders spading away at the imported dirt in the raised beds, a necessity to keep any potential edibles away from the tainted, formerly industrial earth of the city.

Here in the mountains and valleys of western Maryland, food actually existed in its raw state. Cows were milked, corn fields were planted, eggs were plucked from the nesting boxes of chickens. If Stephen let himself admit it, he found the whole thing fascinating.

Now he located a wheelbarrow and climbed onto the hay stack, reasoning that if he pulled away the bottom bales, there'd soon be no way to get the ones from the top, and Rosemary would be left with a tower of hay fifteen bales tall—not exactly useful. He made his way to the top, climbing up the ziggurat steps she'd already constructed as she'd thrown down earlier bales, and did his best to lift a hay bale and drop it straight down, as instructed. It wasn't as easy as it looked; he winced as his dry, cold fingers interlaced under the thin plastic hay strings. He wouldn't have admitted it to Rosemary, but his skin was city-soft; absolutely nothing in his current life would have toughened his palms for any degree of heavy labor. The hay string cut into his hands like dull daggers.

He lifted, he winced, he shifted, he dropped. One by one, the bales plunged to the cushion of the first layer of hay below. He took one final look around the massive barn from this lofty position, then jumped down after it, nearly turning his ankle in the gap between two bales.

"Here it is," he called, having finally gotten the hay onto the wheelbarrow and over to the trap door. "Watch out below!"

"I'm ready. Remember, straight down!"

He tried, he really did, but the strings were absolutely sawing through his soft fingers. The first bale went down relatively straight, which made him smile. Sadly, he lost the second one halfway through the trap door and it went down nose-first. He leaned over just in time to see the bale bounce on its end and break apart, the string flying loose and the bale splitting into sections. The sensation he felt was not unlike watching a fine china dish shatter into pieces.

Rosemary groaned.

Stephen felt like a jerk. "I'm so sorry."

She looked up at him and shrugged. "It's fine, Stephen. I break bales too. Just drop the last one and come on down."

Stephen dropped the last one as carefully as he could, then swung himself down through the trapdoor. He thought it would be cute if he bypassed the ladder and just lowered himself into the stable area with his own brute strength. It wasn't a far drop, after all.

He nearly knocked Rosemary down.

"Ow!" she cried, staggering sideways and nearly toppling into the pile of loose hay. "Why would you *do* that?"

"I'm so sorry—" Stephen was floundering on the uneven floor, trying to catch his own balance without grabbing at Rosemary and dragging her down—but he failed. One flailing arm caught her around the shoulders and as she fell backward, he went with her.

They landed in a heap on the broken hay bale. Stephen found himself nearly nose-to-nose with Rosemary. He should have been embarrassed. Instead, he just felt appreciative.

This close up, he found he could truly appreciate her vivid green eyes, flecked with tiny brown chips. He could appreciate her smooth brow and arching eyebrows, especially if he ignored that smudge of a bruise at her hairline. He could appreciate her creamy little shells of ears and her wide, humorous mouth and her full, rose-colored lips and—

"What are you doing?" she whispered, her emerald eyes narrowing.

Stephen paused to appreciate her long, smoky lashes before he replied.

"Kissing you."

Chapter Eleven

Rosemary

For just a moment, Rosemary gave in.

There was something so solid and reassuring about Stephen, and it became much more real when he was pressing her down into the soft bed of scattered hay. She hadn't been kissed in years—hadn't *wanted* to be kissed in years—and the sensation of lip on lip, arms against arms, body against body, was so richly delicious and fulfilling, she had shivers running up her spine. Rosemary couldn't quite believe how good she felt. How good this kiss felt. How good *Stephen* felt.

Finally, Stephen picked up his head, just enough to separate their lips, and looked into her eyes. He was so close, she felt at her leisure to admire him. He had such long lashes, she thought drowsily, and such smooth skin, *ridiculously* smooth city skin, and the unfurrowed eyes of a man who never squinted into the sun, because he always had on designer sunglasses and he always kept a back-up pair nearby in case he lost the first ones.

A moment passed, and then another, and Rosemary slowly stopped feeling so liquid and content, and started feeling anxious

—which was a much more normal feeling for her. Luckily, she knew how to handle her anxiety around other people: she would simply make jokes and play things off as silly.

"Well, that was a fun roll in the hay," she began, a fake grin twitching her lips.

"Rosemary," Stephen murmured, his voice husky, "You're more than just a roll in the hay."

His eyes glittered and she had a feeling she knew where he wanted to take this party next. *Slow down, cowboy,* she thought. They hadn't even hayed the horses. Also, she was about to have a panic attack if he didn't stop gazing into her eyes so meaningfully. All of this had felt easier in the dark, in her bedroom, and even then, they'd both stopped and ended this madness before things went too far.

They'd had the good sense to know this attraction was going nowhere.

Most importantly of all, Rochester was going to tear the barn down if he didn't get some damn hay. He'd been staring over the stall wall at her ever since the first bale fell through the trap door, ears pricked and eyes bright, ready to start kicking walls if he didn't get what he wanted in a timely fashion.

Rosemary made up her mind: time to get up.

"This is good hay," she told Stephen firmly. "Too expensive for fooling around in. And we have to get it into the stalls. Which is going to be tough, since the bales broke," she added coolly.

That did it. Stephen pushed himself up. He hesitated a moment, his arms pressed into the hay on either side of her, and from the open look on his face, she thought he was going to stay something sweet and tender . . . but he seemed to think better of it.

His features closed off again, and he settled into the hay at her side. "I can take care of this mess for you," he said gruffly.

Rosemary felt like she'd pushed him away farther than she'd intended. She'd just needed her space! And to get the horses fed! She didn't mean for him to retreat completely.

But there was no explaining that to men. They wanted all or nothing. She bit back a sigh. "If you just help me hay everyone, we'll be done in a few minutes," she offered. "Then we can go inside, maybe have another cup of tea?" *Tea,* she thought witheringly. *The sexy nighttime drink!*

Well, this wasn't going to be about sexytimes with Stephen. She wasn't in any condition to get involved with some transient guy— not emotionally, and not physically, either. She touched her forehead without thinking, brushing the sensitive skin around the little bump at her hairline.

Instantly, Stephen's expression softened. He pushed himself to his feet, and held out his hands to help her up as well. "Let's find you a comfortable seat so you can order me around," he suggested, smiling companionably. "I don't want you to exert yourself anymore tonight, got it?"

Still feeling frustrated—and mad at herself for feeling that way —Rosemary allowed Stephen to help her out of the hay. She tripped on a loose coil of hay string as she got to her feet, and his hands tightened around her wrists, drawing her close to his chest.

She looked up at his face, saw his brows drawing together in a frown that seemed directed somewhere internal rather than at her, and was just about to make a joke, something about going twice in ten minutes, when the barn door behind her began to slide open. She turned her head quickly.

Stephen was slower to react; he still had his hands gripped around her wrists, holding her hands up to her shoulders to stop her from falling.

That pose, Rosemary reflected later, was probably what made him look very dangerous and suspicious to Nikki.

Nikki was in proud possession of a shriek like a banshee haunting an ancient castle, and she unleashed it with full force when she saw Stephen gripping Rosemary's arms. The horses all shot back in their stalls, hooves banging in protest against the walls, but Nikki didn't spare the spooked animals a single glance. She came charging up the little aisle, her boots slapping on the packed clay and old slate, and very nearly decked Stephen in the eye before Rosemary was able to open her mouth and stop her.

"Nikki, it's nothing, please stop, Nikki, he's a *friend!*"

Nikki lowered her hand, but stood her ground. She glared at Stephen, who by this time had let go of Rosemary and retreated several steps. Too many, unfortunately—his back was against the stone wall by the dairy door. His face was expressionless, but Rosemary could sense his alarm. Well, he should be afraid of Nikki. She was a dangerous enemy.

Nikki's corkscrew curls seemed to vibrate with outrage. She was ready to murder Stephen if Rosemary just gave the word. She'd always been like that, Rosemary's fierce protector ever since grade school. Nikki's rages had gotten her sent to the principal's office more than a few times in their school days. It had never been more than pulled hair, maybe a shove, always in defense of Rosemary, and if Nikki had known she *shouldn't* be violent, she had also felt incapable of holding back when other kids bullied her shy best friend.

These days, though, a thrown punch could land her in jail. They were adults, with real consequences to watch out for. Rosemary knew she had to take charge of the situation, or there'd be hell to pay. She put her hands out, blocking Nikki from getting any closer to Stephen.

"Nikki, *stop!* Listen to me—"

"What the hell's going on here? Why did he have you by the wrists like that? And why are you covered in hay?" Nikki's gaze took in the split bales, the Rosemary-shaped depression in the pile of hay, and the guilty look on Rosemary's face. Realization swept over her, and she nodded slowly. "Oh, I see," Nikki said, in a much more quiet voice. "Oh, I have interrupted."

"No," Rosemary insisted. "We were just going to throw hay, and I tripped on the hay twine, look—" she pointed at the loop of orange string from the broken bale, "and Stephen caught me before I fell. Before I fell *again* today," she added, with a laugh that sounded as fake as it was. *Oof,* she thought. *Try harder.*

Nikki rolled her eyes. "I thought the first fall would be enough to keep you in bed. I came over to feed the horses, and you. And I left the diner to *Kathleen* to run."

Rosemary winced. Kathleen was seventeen and largely incapable of making a decision, but she was not as helpless as some of the other teenagers who worked dinner at the diner, none of whom had become servers because of their future high-flying careers in restaurant management. "I am feeling a lot better than I expected, or I wouldn't have called you earlier. I'm sorry."

"Humph." Nikki shrugged. She cast her gaze back at Stephen, still trying not to cower against the wall. "Well, *Stephen,* I suppose I will leave you in charge while I take the food in and get dinner set. You're staying for dinner, I assume?"

She marched out of the barn without waiting for an answer.

Rosemary watched her go, then turned around. Stephen raised his eyebrows at her. "I'm *really* sorry—" she started, but he held up his hand.

"Don't be. When you told me you lived her alone, I thought: *without a big dog? She's crazy.* But it turns out you do have a guard dog, a very loyal one. I'm glad about that."

"She's just really protective of me. When I was in school . . . well, I wasn't well-adjusted, let's say. Nikki handled all of the difficulties for me."

Stephen knelt to gather up some of the loose hay. He dropped it into the little wheelbarrow Rosemary kept by the dairy door. "Everyone should have a friend like that. I wish *I* did."

Rosemary took the manure fork and started to scoop hay up. She tossed it into the nearest stall. "So Kevin wouldn't fight for you? I guess it would be the other way around."

Stephen chuckled. "Oh God, Kevin. He's a nice guy, really. I can count on him. But . . . you saw him with your horse. I'm honestly shocked he managed the sneak attack to get the bridle off, or that would have been hours of fun. And don't think I haven't noticed that he was supposed to drive up to my house ten minutes away and has been gone for hours. Who knows where he ended up? Kevin is just a little . . . " Stephen cast about for the right word.

"Bumbling?"

"Perfect word. Nice guy, a little bumbling, tends to come out on top but no one is really sure how. That's Kevin."

"Would you beat up someone for him? Like say, if you guys were in school together and he was getting bullied, would you get out there and fight?"

"I never thought about fighting anyone, honestly. There wasn't a lot of fighting at my schools. Not that I'm aware of, anyway. Maybe some of the sportier kids got into fights, but me and my friends just went home to play video games. Is that what you do in the country for kicks? Beat each other up?"

"We did in high school," Rosemary said thoughtfully. "Not *we*, you know, but like . . . things could get physical. And I guess since everyone here has known everyone else since high school, maybe it still feels like that, like those lines still exist. You can see it at the diner. The old football teammates will still sit close by each other, even though now they're with their families. There are still teams and rivalries even when they get old."

"That's actually kinda nice, minus the physical stuff." Stephen proffered the wheelbarrow to her. "Hay, madam?"

She took it to the other aisle and started doling out hay to the horses there. "Well, dinner should be interesting, anyway."

He made a face which she could see from two stalls away.

"You *are* staying for dinner." It wasn't a request. She wasn't ready for him to leave, even with her guard dog at the table, ready to bite.

"I have to stay," Stephen said, shaking his head. "Like I said, Kevin hasn't come back with my car yet. God only knows where he ended up." He gave her a twinkling smile which made her skin prickle deliciously. "I might just live here now."

Chapter Twelve

Stephen

That Nikki was still circling him like a rabid wolf, and Stephen was not enjoying the attention.

Outside the farmhouse windows, the early winter night had fallen. Stephen was still waiting for Kevin to show up. He'd called the guy three times, and each time the call had gone straight to voicemail. Stephen was starting to worry, wondering if he should be organizing a search party. Would Rosemary lend him her truck? Probably. From what he knew of Rosemary, she would definitely be generous to a fault.

Now she was in the kitchen, sitting reluctantly at the old table while Nikki bustled around her, putting out plates while the dinner she'd brought over from the Blue Plate was heating in the oven, pouring iced tea and placing silverware on folded paper napkins. Stephen had been sitting across from Rosemary at first, trying to catch her eye so they could resume whatever it was they had going on, but Rosemary seemed captivated by Nikki, keeping up a steady flow of questions about the diner staff, about Nikki's parents, about the regular customers. As Nikki answered her, the curly-haired woman kept casting a look through her lashes at Stephen—an expression which could only be described as the *opposite* of a come-hither look. Feeling hunted, Stephen had finally left the kitchen and settled in the living room where he could watch, with increasing desperation, for car headlights.

When Stephen wasn't mentally berating Kevin, he was berating Nikki instead. Why did that creature have to come storming in here like a hurricane and take over right when he and Rosemary had actually been, you know, *getting somewhere?* Where they'd been getting, he didn't know, and he didn't much care, either. Stephen just knew he'd been hungry for the touch of Rosemary's lips on his, he'd gotten it, and now he wanted more.

So here he was in the front room, sitting amongst the chintz and lace of what must have been Rosemary's grandmother's furniture, while the women gabbed in the kitchen. Stephen felt like he was in some pre-war black-and-white movie. Probably a slapstick comedy, judging by all the physical mayhem that had gone down today, and the threat of more violence every time Nikki caught him looking at Rosemary.

A shadow fell across the room and he looked up. Nikki was standing in the doorway, her frizzy hair silhouetted against the yellow light in the hall. "Dinner's ready," she announced flatly. "Come on down."

He stood up, pushing his hair back from his face in a nervous gesture he instantly recognized from his school days. This woman did *not* have a good effect on him. "Yeah . . . thank you. I'll be right in."

Nikki shrugged and disappeared down the hall.

"Dammit, Kevin," he muttered. "What a time to leave me stranded!" Now he had to go sit at the same table as that terrifying woman and listen as she bossed around Rosemary.

At least Rosemary threw him a sympathetic smile as he settled into the chair opposite her. "Nikki's meatloaf is really amazing," she said, pushing a platter of dark slabs at him. "You've got to try it."

Stephen raised his eyebrows. He was pretty certain he'd never actually had meatloaf. It had not been on the menu at the Beckett apartment. But he wasn't about to turn up his nose at Nikki's food. She might stab him with a bread knife. So he took up the serving spoon and dislodged a slice of the stuff, sliding it onto his plate where it sat, brown and confusing, while Rosemary plied him with green beans and mashed potatoes and a sumptuous pour of thick, brown gravy from a styrofoam container. Stephen found himself confronted with what looked a bit like Thanksgiving dinner gone wrong. He stole a glance at Nikki and saw her watching him.

"Dinner look alright?" she asked sweetly.

"Delicious. Thank you so much," he gabbled. "I can't imagine where Kevin is . . . he'd hate to miss this."

Rosemary was pushing meatloaf into the gravy spilling from her mashed potatoes. "Mmm," she said. "I might need more gravy."

"There's plenty." Nikki turned to her own plate, stirring gravy over her own meatloaf.

Gravy went on the meatloaf! That seemed fine. Gravy could fix a lot of problems. Stephen picked up his fork and raided his own gravy supply. He popped a bit of meatloaf into his mouth before he could think twice.

This was . . . delicious?

Sure, a little weird if you really thought about what you were eating, a mushy slice of ground beef and bread, but definitely delicious. Suddenly aware of how hungry he was, Stephen gratefully dug into the meal, letting the ladies do the talking.

"So the spring fundraiser registrations showed up in my mailbox," Nikki was saying between bites. "Are you going again this year?"

"Yeah, I am." Rosemary sighed. Stephen glanced up, concerned by the resignation in her voice. She smiled at him, explaining: "There's a non-profit fair at the high school gym every March. Last year was hell on my nerves, but I made enough money to cover my hay bill for the entire year. Feels like the more people move up from D.C., the more they feel guilty and want to contribute to the farms. And hay's getting more expensive every year."

"Maybe you could get some volunteers to man the booth for you," Stephen suggested. "Avoid the public altogether."

"I wish. But honestly, I think I made so much because it was just Nikki and me. I bring Mighty-mite for a mascot and we look pathetic and helpless to all the concerned out-of-towners. I'm a little afraid if people thought I was doing really well, they'd just donate elsewhere. Does that make sense?"

"It sounds like you're just going for the sympathy vote," Stephen said. "Which no one could blame you for."

"I mean, yeah. That's what an animal rescue survives on, right? Sympathy? It's not like I'm giving back to the community. I'm just rescuing horses and then keeping them here." Rosemary sounded even more glum. "I saw Caitlin Tuttle at the feed store last week, and she told me they're adding therapeutic riding at Elmwood. She said she didn't know why I'd never tried something like that, with all of my big, quiet horses here."

"Well, you could," Nikki said, shrugging. "But then you'd have people here and that's never been your thing."

"It wouldn't be good for the horses," Rosemary insisted. "I don't ride any of them except for Rochester as it is, and he's a giant! And not the most predictable horse in the world. I don't have any horses who could be safe enough for therapy rides."

"They do stuff on the ground," Nikki said. "I think. But it's your business. Not Caitlin's."

Rosemary looked at her plate. "Caitlin really made a big deal out of giving back to the community. She made it sound like I was just taking up space and money here."

Stephen thought Caitlin Tuttle sounded like someone who needed a punch in the nose.

"Oh, she's very charitable," Nikki snorted. "Charitably looking for tax savings. I know for a fact she can't keep students past the beginner stage. She's definitely not her mother."

Rosemary giggled, a bubble of sound Stephen found as charming as her laugh. He wondered how he could get her to do it again. "Remember when we rode at Elmwood? Stephen, we were thirteen years old. I'm telling you, we would have jumped the arena fence if Caitlin's mom told us to. She was the craziest riding instructor in the world and we all loved her."

"She got results," Nikki agreed. "You could ride any horse in the world, if you wanted to. And I learned just enough to stop riding before I killed myself."

"You were a fine rider," Rosemary chided her. "Just . . . not the most balanced person in the world." And then she giggled again.

Stephen forgot himself, enchanted by Rosemary's mirthful little bubble of laughter. He leaned forward, grinning. "Rosemary, maybe you *could* teach some kind of horsemanship here. If you're as good as Nikki says, and I'm sure you are. How bad could it be, having some horse-crazy kids around?"

Rosemary smiled at him, but her cheeks were flushed and he realized his mistake immediately.

"I'm sorry," he said quickly. "I didn't mean to pick on you. I don't know anything about it."

"It's fine," she replied softly, and looked at her plate. "I just don't like the idea. I *do* feel silly about it, but at the same time . . . you have to know what you're good at, and I'm not good with lots of people around."

Nikki was looking daggers at him and Stephen was desperate to change the subject. Frantically, he went back to their first topic. "When did you say the spring fundraiser happens?" he asked, as casually as possible. "Maybe I'll still be in town."

Rosemary's fork screeched across her china plate.

Nikki's eyes flitted between them, and Stephen watched her square her jaw for a moment, considering. Finally, she said: "The fundraiser's the third weekend in March, at the high school gym. It's a really big deal, with a carnival and food outside, every kind of church group and school club and local charity inside. It's kind of like a spring warm-up for the county fair in September. Everyone goes. People come up from the suburbs. Those are our victims." She grinned at Rosemary. "We make puppy-dog eyes at the doctor's wives until they get out their wallets."

Stephen considered the idea of a small-town fair. It sounded fun, like a street fair in the city, but with more manure. March, though . . . in two months' time, where would he be? Still sorting out what to do with his father's house and dealing with the Long Pond purchase in person? Or would everything be tied up neatly, with investors all in line and money in his account, allowing him to go back to New York and put his life back together?

He sometimes woke up in the night thinking he had to rush back to the city or he'd be fired. For some reason, he kept forgetting he didn't have a job anymore, and there was no office waiting for him, no colleagues anxiously awaiting his return so they didn't have to pick up his slack any longer. Every time he remembered it was all gone, the realization was like a jerk on a chain around his neck, as if he was that big horse of Rosemary's, pulling too hard and getting yanked back to reality.

Now though, he considered the possibility of simply staying here a little longer, not worrying about rushing back to the city. What would he be missing by skipping the city during the dreariest months of the year, anyway? His clanging radiator, garbage-filled ice on all the street corners, ordering in dinner because sleet was rattling against the windows and it was too bleak to consider leaving his apartment in search of food and humans? The misery of a job hunt during the slowest time of year?

Instead, why shouldn't he stay here, perhaps get to know Rosemary better, and enjoy the spaciousness of his father's house for a little while, the silken silence of the furnace heating all of those vast, empty rooms?

"I *could* still be here," Stephen said aloud, testing the possibility. "If you want, I could stick around. I could even come help you out."

Rosemary looked resolutely at her plate. "I don't think so, Stephen. Nikki and I should do just fine. Thanks, though."

He raised his eyebrows, surprised and a little hurt. He'd thought she liked him. He'd really thought—

They all looked up at the sound of car tires crunching on gravel outside. Nikki took the napkin from her lap, but Stephen was already pushing back his chair. "That'll be Kevin," he said. "I'll get going. Don't get up—" this to Rosemary, who was arising, her face pale as lilies, the little lump at her hairline seeming to bloom pink. "You stay put. I'll call and check on you tomorrow."

There was a ringing knock at the front door. Stephen hustled down the hallway, trying not to feel too triumphant about the disappointed look on Rosemary's face when he stepped away from the table. She wanted him to stick around . . . she just didn't want to admit it. Well, he could play that game, if that was what she wanted. He could leave her wanting more.

Kevin pushed inside as soon as Stephen opened the front door. He tried to wrestle his friend back, hoping for a quiet word on the porch, but Kevin was oblivious. "It's *cold* out there!" he huffed, shoving the door closed behind him. "Wow! It was nice and warm back at the house. Warm in here, too," he added appreciatively, looking at the old wooden trim around the doors and baseboards, the shadowy antiques lurking in the living room. "Nice place."

"Where have you been?"

"All over. I was in Pennsylvania for a while. The sign for Gettysburg tipped me off. But I made it back to your place and sent off the faxes. I'm not really sure how I found it." Kevin laughed. "But at least I got it done. Then I showered and nosed around in your stuff for awhile. And now I'm here!"

"Well, I'll drive you back now," Stephen said. He started to pull on his coat. "Let's head out."

"What smells so good?" Kevin asked, stepping around Stephen. "Rosemary? You didn't cook dinner, did you? Stephen, you shouldn't have let her make dinner."

Rosemary appeared in the hallway, looking so vulnerable Stephen wanted to run and wrap his arms around her. "I didn't make anything, Kevin. My friend Nikki did. Do you want some dinner? There's plenty." She looked past Kevin and her eyes met Stephen's. "If that's alright with Stephen."

Stephen had been hoping to avoid introducing kind, bumbling Kevin to terrifying, razor-sharp Nikki, but now he was out of options. Kevin was already slipping off his muddy shoes and bouncing towards Rosemary. He looked like an overgrown schoolboy.

Nikki was going to eat that innocent boy alive.

But Nikki seemed to have reserved her worst growls for Stephen. She had already set a place for Kevin by the time he was pulling out the chair next to hers, and was settling a big chunk of meatloaf on his plate. "Have you had meatloaf before?" she asked. "Do they eat that in the big city?"

"I've had it at a diner in the Village," Kevin told her eagerly. "But there they serve it with ketchup. You eat it with gravy?"

"It's amazing with gravy," Nikki assured him, dousing his meatloaf with a ladleful of that delicious brown gravy. "Honestly, just mix it with your mashed potatoes, you won't regret it."

Rosemary smiled at Stephen from across the table as he sat back down to his abandoned plate. He shrugged and picked up his fork. "I guess there's no rush," he said, winking at her.

Rosemary blushed. "I'm sorry if I was hasty about the whole fundraising thing before," she said softly. "And the riding lessons. I just get very nervous even talking about it. I . . . don't like a lot of people around me."

"Anxiety?" Stephen asked offhandedly. Everyone in the city had anxiety. At least, everyone Stephen knew. They talked about their anxiety the way they talked about hunger before dinner, or thirst after a run. It was part of their vernacular.

"Yeah," Rosemary sighed. "Extreme anxiety."

Something about the way she said it made Stephen feel Rosemary did not deal with her anxiety in the same way as his friends back home. "Well, I'm sorry to hear that," he said, his tone more gentle now. "If you decide I can help you at that fundraiser, well, I'll try to keep the worst of the people away from you."

To his surprise—and gratification—she actually giggled again. "Thanks," she chuckled. "I could use a second guard dog. One I can take out in public."

He raised his eyebrows and she nodded very slightly in the direction of Nikki, who was listening to Kevin talk about diner food in New York: "And so you get this giant menu with like, eight pages worth of food, and half of it's Greek and the other half is like, cheeseburgers and omelettes and stuff, and you can get cottage cheese with *anything* . . . "

"That sounds so bizarre," Nikki said admiringly.

Stephen tilted his head at Rosemary. *What's with those two?*

She shrugged and gave him a secret smile. Then she tugged at her own dark hair, and nodded toward Kevin, her eyes widening expressively.

Stephen looked at Kevin for a moment before comprehension washed over him. The red hair! He covered his mouth to hide a grin and turned back to Rosemary, who nodded enthusiastically, then filled her mouth with mashed potato as Nikki looked over.

"What are you two giggling about?" she asked suspiciously.

Rosemary pointed to her mouth to show it was too full to answer.

*

"So, Nikki's obsessed with gingers," Stephen said later, as they walked through the cold night to the barn. Rosemary had said she needed to do a night-check on the horses, and Stephen had immediately insisted he escort her about her duties before he left for the night. Kevin was happy to stay inside and work his way through the lemon meringue pie Nikki had brought for dessert.

"She's got a thing," Rosemary shrugged. "I wouldn't call it an obsession. Now, these babies of mine? I'll admit it. Fully obsessed." She pushed open the barn door.

Stephen was surprised by how warm it had gotten in the little stable. With all those big animals beneath a low ceiling, half-insulated by the hay upstairs, the rise in temperature was enough to make him unzip his coat. "Comfy in here," he observed, glancing meaningfully at Rosemary, but she was already walking between the stalls, looking into each one with a critical eye.

"These guys could use some water," she said. "Would you mind?"

Again with the water buckets, Stephen thought, but he willingly started pulling down the hose. It was like he had his own appointed task in the stable, he thought. It was like he belonged here, with Rosemary.

The thought drew him up short.

What exactly did he think was going to happen here? Rosemary had made her interest in him clear earlier tonight . . . but she'd also mentioned an anxiety so severe, she didn't want him around at a crowded event, even to support her.

He had to wonder if she was really the sort of girl who could just have a fun fling and move on without getting her feelings hurt. If he pushed her for more right now, he had no doubt she'd respond, but what happened after?

She'd expect him to stick around.

And that just wasn't going to happen, even if he settled in for the rest of winter, even if they fit together as perfectly as he suspected they would. No matter what happened, he would have to go home to New York eventually. Rosemary might be the nicest girl in the world, but she lived in the middle of nowhere, with eight large animals totally dependent on her. This was a strange interlude for Stephen. It was a life-choice for Rosemary.

There would be nothing long-term happening between them. And he'd be happy to plow forward regardless, but not if this would all end in Rosemary's tears.

Stephen pushed the hose over the Dutch door of the closest stall and unkinked it, letting the water flow into the bucket hanging on the wall. The horse in the stall, a red-colored one with a big white stripe running down the middle of its long face, blinked over at him curiously, but didn't step away from its pile of hay.

"I'm Stephen," he told the horse. "Don't bother getting used to me."

"What was that?" Rosemary called from the other side of the stable. "I can't hear you over all that water."

He kinked the hose and moved down to the next stall, where Rochester was chewing his hay with lordly disregard. "It was nothing," he said. "Just talking to the horse."

He filled the rest of the buckets in silence.

When he'd finished spooling the hose, Rosemary was waiting by the barn door, her hands deep in her pockets. A gray cat was weaving around her legs, his fluffy tail brushing her knees provocatively. "Have you been formally introduced to Smoke?" she asked.

"Hi, Smoke," Stephen said dismissively. He didn't want to meet Rosemary's cat. He didn't want to get to know any more of her animals. He didn't want to lead her on another minute. Well, that wasn't true. He wanted to lead her right back into the house and up the staircase to that pretty little bedroom and—

No. That wasn't in the cards. If he decided to stay and play, he'd end up hurting this girl. And Stephen was a man who liked to play, but he wasn't a heartbreaker. His earlier visions of a winter fling were disappearing, replaced with the renewed desire to get back to New York and his real life as quickly as possible. He'd been crazy to think he could stay, lured into delusion by the homey meal and the quaint kitchen and that beautiful, *beautiful* girl sitting across from him.

"I better collect Kevin and get going," he said, edging past her and sliding open the door. The cold air rushed in and the cat meowed once, quickly, before ducking deeper into the warm barn. Rosemary looked at him with surprise, but he just stepped outside and crossed to the yard's little gate, opening the latch and waiting for her politely on the other side.

She passed through the gate and started to walk towards the house, then stopped, seeming to reconsider. She came back, turning her face up at him. In the soft yellow light spilling from the farmhouse windows, he thought he could see the question she was asking him.

Stephen didn't want to answer it, but at the same time, he was aware he'd kissed her first. This was on him.

Still, he had to look away from her hopeful gaze. He let his eyes wander through the dark woods beyond the barnyard, toward the distant farmhouse where he hoped he'd have a sales office and a community center for an exclusive subdivision someday, and he said, softly: "I'm not going to be here when the fundraiser comes. I don't know why I said that. I guess I thought maybe I would, but the truth is, I'll be back in New York by then."

He heard her sharp intake of breath. He focused on the shadows, because if he turned around, he'd see what he'd done, in the span of one foolish evening, and he'd feel even worse.

Rosemary sniffed.

Oh God, she was going to cry. Stephen turned around, prepared for a white face and glistening cheeks, but Rosemary was looking at him with her jaw set, and he realized, with some shock, that the sniff he'd heard was one of derision.

"Hustle back to the city, so you don't see the damage you've done," she snapped, her voice icy as the night air. "Will you come back when the bulldozers are rolling over the pastures and crushing the grass into the clay? Maybe when the chainsaws are cutting down the orchard? Oh! I hope you come back for the first night the streetlights block out the stars. Look up before you go, Stephen. You don't have a sky like this in New York."

Rosemary spun and stalked away, her boots silenced by the thatch of last year's grass. Stephen watched in stunned silence as she climbed the porch steps and went into the house, closing the door behind her without so much as a glance in his direction. And then he did as she said.

He turned his head up, and looked at the stars shimming over the dark mountains beyond the farm, and Stephen knew she was right: he didn't have a sky like this in New York.

Chapter Thirteen

Rosemary

March wasn't Rosemary's favorite month of the year, but it came awfully close.

The best month, to Rosemary, would always be June: the month of escape, the month of *"school's out!"* and the first heady days of freedom from teachers, bells, crowded cafeterias, being singled out. The sense of release had been engrained into her, so that no matter how long ago school days became, she'd still feel a strange sense of relief once summer arrived.

But, March was pretty nice, too.

In March, Catoctin Creek slowly began to bloom and bud. The mountains, left drab and gray with leafless trees for so many months now, began to alternately blush pink with redbuds and turn pale with dogwood blossoms. The roadside ditches began to sprout long green leaves as the coming summer's daylilies prepared for another showy season. The pastures themselves took on a fresh green shimmer as new grass began to poke up through the tired brown thatch of last year's growth. Every day which wasn't filled with gray rain made up for its stormy sisters with an azure-blue sky, clean and fresh and filled with promise.

Today the creek was high from a spring storm which had raged all weekend, and Rosemary could hear it roaring over the rocks as she worked in the barnyard. She was trying to clean up Mighty-mite for the approaching spring fundraiser, but he was not the most cooperative of subjects. The mini horse was tied by a short rope to a fence-post in the sunny yard, but everything south of his little head was wiggling all over the place, side to side and back and forth, testing the rope constantly, while Rosemary worked feverishly to get the worst of his shedding winter coat under control.

"Would you—stop—*moving*—" she panted. It was hard enough grooming a horse so small she had to bend at the waist just to reach; a moving target was entirely unfair on her back.

Eventually there was a small pile of black-and-white hair on the muddy ground, and Rosemary decided to call it a day. She leaned back on the fence and watched Mighty-mite bounce around at the end of his rope, tossing his head and occasionally squealing with indignation.

"You're a brat," she decided eventually. "There's just no other word for it."

"He's a good mascot, though," a reedy voice said from behind her.

"You're right, Aileen," Rosemary sighed, turning around. The elderly woman was gingerly making her way down the porch steps and across the new green grass of the lawn. "If he didn't get me so much attention at the fundraisers, I might be tempted to give him away. To someone shorter. Some little kid."

"He's not a pet," Aileen Kelbaugh scolded. "He's barely civilized enough to be considered livestock."

"I know. But he could make a 4-H project or something. Anyway, it doesn't matter. The brat isn't going anywhere. Because I love you, that's why," she told the mini. "I love your stupid bratty face and your awful bratty ears and your nasty bratty little butt."

Mighty-mite pawed at the mud, digging a hole which quickly filled with water. Rosemary knew she should turn him back out in the pasture, but something schoolmarmish in her wanted to make him stay tied a little longer, as if he'd magically learn manners, so she let him stand and stew.

Aileen leaned on the fence beside her and sighed. "I think you're all set for pies now," she said. "And biscuits, besides. But, Rosemary, I want you know I hate leaving you like this."

"You're only going for two weeks. And I want you to know," Rosemary added affectionately, "coming over here and baking for me was completely unnecessary, but deeply appreciated. Every night will feel like I'm over in your kitchen, feasting."

"Just don't sneak over and into the kitchen," Aileen chuckled. "I'm sure Rodney has set up some kind of booby trap for all of the intruders he thinks will come creeping in the moment we're gone."

"Nothing will happen to the farm. I'll ride over and peek in the windows everyday, tell him that."

"I'll tell him." Aileen was silent for a moment, looking across the yard and through the trees, their boughs just beginning to bud. In another month, her farmhouse would be invisible from this spot, but right now both women could see its white paint shining in the spring sunlight. "Rodney's brother Wilmer has a few places lined up for us to look at," she said eventually. "One of them is right by the beach."

Rosemary imagined Aileen and Rodney traipsing down to the beach in Victorian bathing costumes. "That could be nice," she agreed cautiously, barely trusting her voice. The idea of the Kelbaughs moving to Florida was still hard to stomach. But in the middle of February, after a particularly vicious blizzard dropped more than two feet of snow on Catoctin Creek, they'd decided: it was time to go.

The Kelbaughs signed papers with Stephen and his attorney —"*stacks* of papers," Aileen had assured Rosemary—and then they'd made arrangements to visit with Wilmer, who had lived in Daytona Beach since he'd retired twenty years earlier.

"I don't think I'd like to live in Daytona Beach," Aileen went on, "but there are other places that aren't so wild. I don't want to live where there are a lot of hotels and people vacationing. I don't see how that could ever feel like home."

Rosemary nodded absently, her thoughts still on Stephen's abrupt departure, now a full two weeks ago. He'd been on her mind a lot, even though she'd barely seen him after those two days he'd been at the farm: the day she'd met him, and the following day he'd spent with her. The day he'd kissed her.

She still couldn't believe he'd come to Catoctin Creek, spent a day and two nights flirting with her, and then not come near her again. Even worse, that he'd stayed on long enough to buy Long Pond and then gone straight back to New York City. His presence was too vivid in her mind for him to be gone; still, someone who had been in her life for the equivalent of thirty-six hours should not have taken up permanent residence in her thoughts. Especially not now, weeks after their heated encounters.

Nikki had told her over emergency pancakes a few days ago that this was how city men were, they came and they went, a bunch of assholes if you asked *her,* and then she'd gone into the kitchen of the Blue Plate and slammed a lot of pots and pans around in the dishwashing sink. Nikki told Rosemary nothing had happened with her and Kevin, either, but just saying the words seemed to make her furious. Of course, Kevin was gone, too.

It was like they had never been here, and yet what a trail of destruction they had left.

"Are you looking forward to the fundraiser? We'll be back just in time for it." Aileen asked.

Rosemary realized she had been silent for quite some time. "Of course," she replied, flustered into lying. She leaned over to untie Mite and let him loose in the yard. The mini went galloping away, bucking and squealing. "I'm used to it now."

"Last year you were a little tense."

Tense was an understatement. She'd had a panic attack while Nikki had gone to lunch and had to rush out the back doors of the gym, Mighty-mite trotting at her side, after a group of suburban women started quizzing her about the care and maintenance of her little herd of horses. Aileen had found her in the parking lot, gasping into Mighty-mite's shaggy mane, and called Nikki to come and rescue her. With Nikki's support, she'd managed to finish out the day and make several thousand dollars in the process, but it had been painful.

She wasn't looking forward to doing it all over again this year.

"It will be fine," Rosemary said now, putting as much strength as she could into her voice. "Nikki will be with me all day. I want you and Rodney to go enjoy Florida and get a nice tan to show off when you get home. And then we'll have fun together until you move." She smiled bravely.

"I never thought I'd move," Aileen said softly, her eyes flicking back to her house in the distance. "I thought I'd die at Long Pond."

"I guess God wanted you to warm up your bones beforehand," Rosemary joked. "Have a little taste of the good life."

"I guess maybe so," Aileen agreed. "I guess maybe so." Her voice was meditative.

Once Aileen had driven home—she said the walk back through the woods was too long for her some days, and this was one of them—Rosemary caught Mighty-mite and led him back up the hill to the pasture. He went skidding through the new grass and thundered up the slope to join his friends, who looked up from their grazing to watch the tiny beast come rocketing towards them.

Rosemary walked over to the south pasture and surveyed the new grass on its slope, which was coming in nicely. Another month and she'd move the horses to this field, giving the north pasture time to rest after their hooves had been carving it up all winter. It would probably need seeding and fertilizing this year . . . another big expense which the spring fundraiser dollars could help pay for, if she could bring them in.

Sinking into farm planning and plotting was Rosemary's favorite pastime. When she was thinking about hay and fertilizer and fencing, her thoughts were too busy to dwell on anything else. This was important, because Rosemary was a textbook dweller. She was terribly prone to sitting in a rocking chair and thinking out all her most dark thoughts. She wasn't a dark person by nature . . . she was just the sort of person who was very good at coming up with worst-case scenarios.

And, right now, her life was feeling an awful lot like a worst-case scenario.

That's ridiculous, she chided herself, heading back down to the house. *You have the farm, and the horses, and the backing of the community. You have friends, even if you don't see them much. You are loved.*

These were all true statements . . . and yet they didn't quite feel like enough. Which was, Rosemary concluded, just a sign of what a crazy old farm spinster she was turning into. Pretty soon she'd be throwing fits at Trout's Market when the deli clerk didn't slice her ham as thin as she wanted it.

Rosemary walked past the house and down the gravel driveway, crossing the little culvert bridge over the rushing waters of Catoctin Creek, and through the gray trees of the little wood between the farm and the road. At the end, she opened her rusty mailbox and found three advertising circulars, a seed catalog addressed to her father, and the mailer for the Catoctin Creek Spring Community Fundraiser. There it was, in glossy cardstock: time and date and place and parking information. This invitation would be in every mailbox from Catoctin Creek to Emmittsburg.

There's no escape now, she thought, and then had to remind herself such bleakness in the face of what was essentially free money was terribly unbecoming.

She leaned on the mailbox for a few minutes, listening to a pair of cardinals chirping in the trees around her, watching the empty road for some sign of life. A bunny hopped out of the woods across the road, and nosed around the grass in the roadside ditch. "Don't eat those daylily bulbs, now," she called, and the bunny stood up on his hind legs and observed her, nose and ears twitching, before he went back about his business.

Rosemary smiled and shook her head. There were always more than enough daylilies blooming in the ditches come May and June. The bunny could have a few. She began to turn back up her driveway, thinking she might sample one of the pies Aileen had baked for her, when she heard the low hum of a car coming around the curve in the road. She paused, just in case it was someone she knew.

An unfamiliar white sedan appeared, and Rosemary began to turn away. Then, the driver seemed to slow. She took a cautious step back towards the road, thinking it was a neighbor in a new car who might want to say hello, but the car's engine suddenly throbbed back to life as the driver accelerated.

Shocked, Rosemary jumped back, and as the car went past she was astonished to see Stephen in the driver's seat, looking grimly and determinedly over his steering wheel, as if he'd never even seen her.

Or, Rosemary thought, as if he didn't *want* to.

Chapter Fourteen

Stephen

H e shouldn't have driven past the farm. He *knew* he shouldn't have done it. So why did he?

Well, it was easier to head north out of Catoctin Creek to visit Long Pond, rather than go all the way around Clancy's farm and then turn south. And he wanted to check on that damned tricky curve and blind entry again—the one he figured he'd have to get replaced if the development went through.

If, if, if.

Long Pond was bought and paid for, Stephen's problem now, although he was in no hurry to take possession. There were a thousand boxes to be checked and a thousand hoops to be jumped through before he'd be allowed to turn the farm into a housing development, and he wasn't about to hustle the Kelbaughs out of the farmhouse where they'd spent most of the twentieth century and all of the current one. His investors were sound, he had top people on the job, and there was no reason to believe the state of Maryland and the county wouldn't eventually let them build there. But the waiting still had him nervous.

And, well, kind of broke.

With no job waiting for him back in New York, and most of his network a bit leery of anyone or anything with the reek of failure floating around, Stephen had spent the past few weeks in the city feeling bored to death. He'd gone out with a few friends, and seen a few women, and congratulated himself on his good fortune in being a New Yorker when he finally got a proper slice of pizza. But his attempts to set up meetings for anything besides the development were met with silence. He wasn't sure what sort of gag order that idiot Ernie had placed on his email address when Confluence had gone under, but it was looking like no one in the city wanted anything to do with his resumé right now.

Finally, sick of looking at the bland white of his apartment walls, he'd decided to go back to Maryland.

After all, he reasoned, he needed to be close at hand for the zoning board meetings which would be coming up. He really should be available for meetings with his attorneys, and he'd wanted to start talking to architects about tasteful, traditional-yet-modern designs which would please the aspiring-country-gentry types he was hoping to market to in a few years' time. His father's house had better heating than his city apartment anyway, and who knew? Maybe Maryland was nice in spring. Might as well find out while he had an empty house just sitting there. The car was there, too. Everything he needed, paid off and insurance current.

So, Stephen rented a car he could return in Frederick once he'd gotten his father's car, and set off for Maryland.

He'd set just one rule for himself: avoid Rosemary.

Because yeah, after all these weeks back in New York, Rosemary was still on his mind. There was something about that girl which he couldn't shake. She had gotten under his skin the moment he'd met her. Soft and tender-hearted with her little farm of unwanted horses, fierce and protective the moment she felt her kingdom was threatened. She was a passionate little introvert who preferred animals to people, which Stephen thought he could understand. Had people actually gotten *louder* while he'd been in Catoctin Creek? The city's usual white noise had turned into absolute clamor since he'd come home.

He wanted to see Rosemary again, that was the bottom line. She wasn't like anyone he'd ever met before.

Those dark curls and long eyelashes weren't too bad, either.

Too bad Rosemary wasn't the kind of girl who could just have a good time. That was the problem with the passionate types. They meant everything they said.

elle

When she'd seen him, she'd recognized him. That much had been obvious. He'd seen her eyes widen with shock, and he'd faced forward, setting his jaw fiercely, as if he could ward off her gaze with sheer willpower. But of course it was too late by then. When he drove past, he could practically feel her eyes on his back.

Well, *this* was a disaster. The trees were much greener than when he'd seen them last, but he knew if she went upstairs she'd still be able to see the farmhouse at Long Pond. She'd see his car and know what he was up to. She might even come over and take the opportunity to berate him for buying the farm.

He didn't want to take that risk. What good would it do him, do either of them, to be so close when there was so much enmity between them? He didn't want to fight with her. He wanted to . . .

never mind that. Stephen tightened his hands on the steering wheel. He would *not* think about Rosemary's emerald-green eyes, or the way she blushed when he looked at her, or the bubbling mirth of her laugh . . .

He would go home.

Better to unpack and regroup before he marched on enemy territory, he told himself.

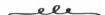

By the time Stephen got up the nerve to leave his father's hilltop house and visit Long Pond, three days had passed, all of them rainy and cold. The sparkling promise of the blue sky on the day he'd arrived had all been a lie. Maryland was just as deceptive as New York in spring, never forthright about which season it would commit to. The little brick rancher weathered the storms just fine, and the furnace was enthusiastically up to its job, but Stephen grew so weary of the beige walls and mismatched flea market furniture, he went on a little bit of a drunk online shopping spree and spent far more than he should have on a redecoration splurge. When he saw the receipts piling up in his inbox, he realized he'd been subconsciously planning for a long haul at this house. Maybe it was time to stop thinking of the place as his father's.

Maybe he'd even find a sublet renter for his New York apartment, and just stay here through the summer. It was nearly mid-March. June was just around the corner, if you thought about it. New York was so hot in summer. What would he really be missing, if he skipped out on Manhattan until a more temperate season, like September? There was no one waiting for him in the city; there were no opportunities beating down his door. He thought of the tight confines of his apartment and his inbox filled with automatic replies, and could see no reason to go back.

"Would you stay, Dad?" he asked aloud.

The tatty old furniture didn't reply, but he knew the answer. His father had chosen Catoctin Creek over New York for a reason, and Stephen was starting to think he knew why. Not to say it was the right choice for *him,* but there really was something about this place.

Yes, Stephen thought, looking out the kitchen window at the mist-shrouded Catoctin Mountains. Maybe this time he really would just stay here for a while. *However,* he would still avoid Rosemary. That was definitely a non-starter . . . especially now that he'd actually bought Long Pond.

With this resolve in mind, Stephen put on some boots which would withstand the astonishingly gluey Maryland mud— Rosemary *had* warned him—and went out to his father's car, which had been snugly waiting in the old carport while he'd been back in New York. He'd returned the rental and taken a ride-share back to the farm; the cost had been astronomical. Now, he cheerfully backed out and drove down the asphalt driveway, turned onto the country road, and steered without much thought to Long Pond.

He was a little astonished to see how high the water had gotten. The creeks seemed to have turned into rushing rivers, and the calm waters of Long Pond had swollen to take up most of the front lawn. The little lake had to be at least three acres now, maybe more. Stephen drove gingerly over the creek bridge, not liking the sounds the hurried water was making underneath, and pulled up in front of the farmhouse.

The place looked unusually dark and quiet. He stepped up onto the front porch and tried the doorbell.

There was an echoing of chimes within the house, then silence.

Odd, he thought. He had never known the Kelbaughs to be out during a weekday. Even though their fields were leased and their herds were sold off, they'd gone on living as farmers, doing their shopping on a weekend and limiting their dining out to an occasional dinner at the Blue Plate. He peered through the lace curtains dimming the living room and dining room windows. No one was moving inside the house.

Stephen had a sudden, horrible thought: the Kelbaughs had died and no one knew it yet. Not even Rosemary. He looked over his shoulder, to where Rosemary's white farmhouse was just visible through the new leaves on the trees, and had a sinking new realization.

Today was Thursday, the day Rosemary had told him she brought the Kelbaughs supper. She was going to come over here, casserole dish in hand, and find the house dark and cold. She'd use her key to get in, because of course she'd have a key, and when she opened the door, she'd know at once. The casserole dish would slip from her hand—in Stephen's fevered imagination, it was her mother's casserole dish, a treasured relic of Rosemary's lost family —and shatter on the shining wooden floor.

Stephen couldn't let that happen. He raced back over to the front door and ran his fingers over the handle and lock. He nearly laughed when he saw it was nearly as ancient as the Kelbaughs themselves. "You couldn't have made this easier, old friends," he muttered, pulling a credit card from his wallet.

Chapter Fifteen

Rosemary

T hree days of spring rain had caused nothing but trouble around Notch Gap Farm, and Rosemary had never been so heartily sick of mud in her life. Granted, she'd been in a terrible mood *before* it had started raining. Seeing Stephen was back in the neighborhood and still determined to ghost her hadn't done her self-esteem any favors. The fundraiser was coming up and she couldn't help but remember how he'd suggested he come and help her, and within the hour reneged on the offer. The heavy rain matched her attitude, and then some, but really, she thought, enough was enough.

"I can't take it anymore! This mud! It's *everywhere,*" she moaned to the farrier, a round-bellied older man named Gus Heintzler, and Gus, who had been bent over muddy horse and mule hooves for the past month, was inclined to agree.

"And it took off that shoe right quick enough, didn't it?" he observed in his blurry mountain accent. "I sure can fix him up, but you oughter keep him outter mud if ya can."

Gus called all horses *him*.

Rosemary sighed as she looked at Rosita's long, dished profile. The horse was an uncommonly feminine Thoroughbred, with slim legs, a narrow chest, and a dainty head that was almost Arabian in shape. She looked flighty and nervous most of the time, with wide eyes and a way of fluttering out her nostrils into broad black circles, but the truth was the little chestnut mare just liked to be aware of everything, all of the time. She wasn't afraid of much, but she was the definition of hot-blooded nonetheless. She'd been a poor riding horse due to a variety of owners who didn't know how to handle her, and when Rosemary had first brought her to the farm, she'd been a skeletal, nervous wreck who couldn't get through a meal without having a panic attack.

Now she was full-fleshed and gorgeous, although still scared of her own shadow, but she couldn't keep on shoes to save her life. Rosemary didn't keep her horses in shoes as a general rule, but Rosita's thin, shelly hooves wouldn't last two minutes on her mountainous pasture. The clay was studded in places with hard, flinty bits of shale, and of course in winter the ground froze; in summer, it turned rock-hard. Rosita went lame almost immediately without some steel between her feet and the ground.

That was how Rosemary had known immediately this morning that she'd come in from pasture without her right front shoe. The mare had been limping like she'd broken a leg.

"Any chance you found the shoe?" Gus asked, pulling his rolling toolkit closer. Rosita was standing cross-tied in the barn's narrow front aisle, watching the rattling tools come closer with big eyes and flared nostrils. Rosemary gave the mare's neck a reassuring rub. "Or are we making a new one today?"

Oh, that was the other fun (expensive) thing about Rosita. Her hooves were oddly shaped, so Gus had to use the portable furnace in his truck to heat a standard shoe and then use an anvil and a hammer to reshape before it would fit. Some horses could just take an off-the-shelf shoe size and with a few bangs of the hammer, it would pop right on. Not our dear Rosita. She was custom all the way.

"Nowhere to be found," Rosemary sighed. "I looked this morning, too."

"You'll find it when you don't want to," Gus assured her comfortably, bending over and swinging Rosita's foreleg up. He tucked her hoof between his leather-clad knees and went to work with a file, sanding down the ragged areas. Rosita pressed her nose against the buckle of his chaps and sighed. She loved Gus, who moved slowly and spoke in low tones.

Confident in the mare's ability to stand still while she was being worked on, Rosemary went to the doorway and looked out over the farmyard and the woods beyond. She was startled to see a flash of light through the trees. Had that been sunlight on a car driving up the Long Pond lane? But no one should be there now. The Kelbaughs had been gone for days and—

Stephen, she thought, her heart pounding in her ears. That son of a . . . *now* he showed up, after they were safely out of the state! He would avoid her, and apparently the Kelbaughs as well, but he wasn't afraid to go poking around the property without them.

Well, he didn't belong there. Maybe he owned Long Pond now, but it was still the Kelbaughs' property until they moved to Florida. Aileen had told her he'd said as much. He wouldn't lift a finger on that farm until they were out of the picture.

Did he think vacation didn't count?

Rosemary looked back at Rosita and Gus. She was contentedly rubbing her upper lip against the strap of his chaps, pulled low against his waist, and Gus wasn't bothered by the mare's affections. But as much as Rosita enjoyed Gus's attention, Rosemary couldn't leave the two of them completely alone while she stalked off to confront Stephen. It would be a major breach of farrier-horse owner etiquette.

So she went back into the barn and picked up a pitchfork. Rosemary spent the next three-quarters of an hour ruthlessly taking out her anger on her horses' dirty stalls, while Gus lit his forge, beat a horseshoe into submission, and then tapped the nails into Rosita's fragile hoof walls. When he was finished and had packed up, she turned the mare back out, closed the barn door, and went marching down the path to Long Pond.

◦◦◦

The creek was roaring above its banks, the water loud and angry after days and days of rain, but the path itself was still above water. Well, mostly. Rosemary had to track through the woods a few times to avoid some caved-in banks. This happened nearly every year, the trail to Long Pond shifting again and again to accommodate the ever-changing creek.

When she emerged from the trees, the size of Long Pond itself made her pause. She'd seen the pool in flood before, but now it was nearly up to the front porch of the house. Rosemary was thankful the weather forecast was dry for the next few days, or she'd have to go into the house and check the basement for flooding. After all, who else would? Stephen? Hardly. She doubted he was interested in the farmhouse. All he wanted to do was build cookie-cutter McMansions around custom-designed winding roads.

Rosemary cultivated her anger against Stephen as she marched up the lane, water lapping inches from the hard-packed clay. She was just about to go up the porch steps when she heard a strange sound—an unearthly moan, not to put too fine a point on it. Rosemary stood still for a moment, rattled, and then she swallowed, clenched her fists, and went on around the side of the house.

The first thing she saw was Stephen's beige sedan, the one he'd inherited from his father, parked close to the house, as if he'd been hiding it from her view. The *nerve* of that man . . . Rosemary surveyed the car with a simmering rage. Afraid to face her, was he? She'd give him something to be afraid of.

The second thing was a pair of hands, trying to wrench up a reluctant window from inside the house—the living room, to be exact. She frowned—Rosemary had a ferocious frown when she was angry, although she didn't know it—and stomped up to the window. The sash was a few feet above her head, but that just made it easier to see Stephen, looking down through the glass at her. She watched his eyes widen with shock.

"First of all," she declared, "that window doesn't open. The frame is warped and it hasn't opened more than two inches in ten years. Second of all, what the hell are you doing in the Kelbaughs' house?"

"I'm trying to get out," Stephen hissed, looking around wildly. "And don't be so loud, there's someone upstairs!"

Rosemary looked around at the empty yard beside the house. "Do you see any cars? There's no one here but us. Aileen and

Rodney are in Florida."

"There's a goddamn *intruder* upstairs, Rosemary, I'm telling you! Does *that* window open?" He slowly retreated from the broken window, and she realized he was tiptoeing towards the next one in the room. She left him there, a suspicion brewing in her mind.

Rosemary walked into the backyard and then tipped her back to look into the upstairs windows. The sun was glaring against the distorted old glass, but she could just see the shadow of a man inside the back bedroom. The shape of his cap told her the man was facing the doorway. The perfect spot, she knew, for a view down the stairs.

Rosemary smiled.

Smirking, she made her way back over to the window Stephen was trying, with more success, to open. He had just put a leg over the sill and was waving at her to get away. "Put your leg back inside," Rosemary told him. She rolled her eyes at his panicked expression. "There's no intruder. That's just Colonel John."

Stephen glared at her, his leg still hanging out of the window. "Colonel Who?"

"Colonel John Kelbaugh, First Regiment, Maryland Cavalry. The Potomac Home Brigade, they were called." Rosemary smiled sweetly as she delivered the killing blow to Stephen's self-esteem. "That's a dummy wearing the mothballed old uniform of Rodney's great-grandfather."

Stephen put his other leg over the window-sill and sat there for a moment, leaning forward, his face slowly coloring red with embarrassment. "So . . . he put a dummy at the top of the steps to scare away burglars."

"He hasn't done it in a while, but the other day Aileen said she thought he was booby-trapping the place. I guess he thought it was a good time to bring out Colonel John. He used to pull him out to scare us local kids at Halloween." Rosemary shook her head, remembering how much Rodney had loved putting on a haunted hay-ride for the children of Catoctin Creek. Those holidays were still sorely missed. When he'd sold off the farm's livestock, the big Halloween parties had stopped. Even though she'd offered Rochester and Bongo to pull the old wagon, he'd turned her down, saying he was too tired to have all those kids around any more.

Rosemary had a sudden hankering to visit with Colonel John once more, even if she was pretty sure he was held together entirely with camphor.

"Go back inside and I'll introduce you," she told Stephen, but he was already jumping to the ground, his boots squelching in the mud.

"We can go in the front door," he said wryly. "It's open."

When Rosemary opened the door and stepped into the front hall, she laughed immediately: Colonel John, backlit against the bright light streaming through the upstairs windows, was a very menacing presence indeed. "Oh, he even has his rifle!" Rosemary exclaimed. "And he's turned to the side so that it's not suspicious if he doesn't see you at once. That's clever, Rodney."

Stephen nodded, a crooked smile on his face. "It *is* clever. And I'm . . . about as embarrassed as I've ever been in my life."

"You can be more embarrassed and tell me why you broke into the house," Rosemary told him. She kneeled and picked up his discarded credit card. "What is this to you, a heist movie?"

Stephen took the credit card. "I don't know if I can handle that level of embarrassment. What say we go and meet the colonel?"

"Fine, but you still have to tell me." Rosemary shucked her boots and started up the stairs. "Or he'll haunt you forever. Colonel John is *very* protective of me."

As Stephen shambled up the steps behind her, explaining the reason for his visit and his subsequent worry that the Kelbaughs had died, Rosemary felt a smile curving her lips. The silly fool! As if anyone could die alone and forgotten in Catoctin Creek! These old farmwives were on the phone back and forth all day long, and forever checking up on each other, cloth-covered pies in hand. She smothered the urge to remind him, once again, that he wasn't in New York City anymore.

"Did they both die at once?" she asked, unable to keep the amusement out of her voice.

Stephen sighed. "You know, I hadn't really thought about that."

She laughed.

But when he faltered over his fear that *she* would be the one to find them, Rosemary's mirth faded. He'd been worried about her? After all these weeks of silence, he was still worried about her?

What right did he have to even *think* of her?

She stopped in front of Colonel John, propped up on a spindle-backed chair in the bedroom doorway. "Well, here he is," she announced, waving a hand. Her pleasure in the proceedings was gone. And the camphor smell really was enough to choke a person.

She watched Stephen take in the worn old uniform, the dull brass buttons and the badges of John Kelbaugh's company and rank. If he could have read the story there, he would have been impressed. Rosemary might have told him all of it, if she'd a mind to. Rodney had told her Colonel John's tale so many times: how young John had ridden down to Frederick to join the cavalry in autumn of 1861, and how he'd come home a tired but handsome hero. After the war, he married his schoolhouse sweetheart, Charity Crawford, and they'd lived out the rest of their years at Long Pond. It was a favorite story to tell on winter evenings by the fireplace; theirs was one of the great romances of Catoctin Creek.

"He rode away on a horse named Winter," she recited now, Rodney's favorite lines still fresh in her memory, "but he came back limping on his own two feet."

Stephen glanced at her, his eyebrows lifting. "That sounded like poetry."

She shook her head. "Just part of the story."

His gaze seemed to intensify, and Rosemary felt a blush sweeping over her cheeks. "I better get back home. And you—you'd better skedaddle before the ghost of Colonel John comes for you."

"You told me he'd leave me alone if I told you the truth!"

"I didn't say that. I just said he'd haunt you for sure if you didn't." She stepped past him, intent on the staircase, and felt her shoulder brush against his chest. She tried to stiffen against the sensation, shoving through it, determined to get back outside. He made her too crazy . . . angry and infatuated at the same time. She couldn't deal with him.

In the fresh air and the sunshine, she'd feel less crowded by him, and less likely to do something she'd regret.

He was coming down the stairs after her, Colonel John forgotten, and she shoved her feet back into her boots and rushed out onto the porch. After the shadowy house, the sunlight shining on the swollen expanse of Long Pond dazzled her eyes and she had to stop. Stephen was so hot on her heels, he bumped right into her.

"You have to go," she said softly.

"Rosemary, listen, I—"

"You have to *go,*" she insisted. "This isn't your house. Not yet."

"I don't want to talk about the house," Stephen said, his voice rough. "I want to talk about *you.* Come on, can we—can we get a cup of coffee or something?"

She burst out laughing. "Coffee? Do you think we're in Manhattan? Where do you expect to get coffee? Maybe we'll go to the Blue Plate and Nikki can serve us, would you like that?"

He was silent. She felt bad for mocking him.

Almost as badly as she felt for turning him down.

"Go home, Stephen," Rosemary told him, keeping her voice low with an effort, and then she forced herself down the porch steps, heading for the path back to her own farm, swiping angrily at her own tears.

Chapter Sixteen

Stephen

Stephen's phone buzzed incessantly the entire way back to his house, and there was nothing he could do about it. He'd left the damn thing in his pocket and there was no way to wiggle it free with the seat-belt buckled; plus, he needed two hands and all of the attention he could muster to keep between the lines on these wiggly-waggly country roads. Damn, but driving himself around was annoying! He missed subways and cabs and Ubers, other people doing the tedious work of weaving in and out of traffic and sitting at stop-lights while he went on with his life in the backseat.

Still, his surroundings were nice, and when he wasn't thinking about the vibrating phone against his thigh (not as pleasurable as one might hope) he was able to take in the beauty of Maryland in spring. The road to his father's house—to *his* house, he reminded himself over and over, although it was still hard to think of it that way—wound up through some fairly high foothills, and at the top of each one he was granted a birds-eye view of Maryland's farm country. Silver-capped silos and red-walled barns, black-and-white cows and green-and-beige fields, chalk-white farmhouses and pale-green orchards: the colors, scattered beneath an azure sky, were as rich as a child's paintbox. The city he'd left behind had been brown and gray, with a faint wash of green in the budding London plane trees, and the occasional brave tulip blooming from tree-pit garden or a window-box.

Stephen thought there was something about springtime in the country that couldn't fail to lift a heart—*anyone's* heart, even his urban version.

Maybe that was why his father had settled here. Maybe Rosemary had been right, and he'd come here on some project or driven through these mountains on some road trip, and the place had made a home in his heart. Judging by how quickly Gilbert Beckett had hightailed it out of New York after his retirement party, that almost certainly had to be the case.

He drove up the winding driveway, then sat in the car for a moment, looking at the house.

"This place is nothing to look at, Dad," he said out loud. "All these pretty farmhouses, and you buy a brick rancher from the seventies?"

Stephen shook his head. And then, first from the corner of his eye as a blip but then as the whole picture, he saw it. The red bricks and cream-colored mortar were the same color as the building he'd grown up in. He remembered the Sunnyside apartment house with its view of nothing, with its sparse hedge just barely managing to hold back the concrete of the sidewalks ringing it. He remembered, more like a dream than a proper memory, his mother pulling back the checked curtains to see what was going on down on the noisy boulevard. He remembered when the three of them went down to two as he left for college, and then just to one when his mother passed away.

They were in no way alike, these two places, and yet there was a resemblance, here: a kinder and gentler version of the place where the Beckett family had once lived, a little trio in a big city.

Stephen got out of the car slowly and looked at the house with new appreciation.

"I didn't know, Dad," he said softly, feeling a strange squeeze in his heart for the father he'd never really mourned. They hadn't been close by the time Gilbert had left New York, and moving to the backcountry of Maryland hadn't made them any closer. Stephen had always known he loved his dad, but not with any demonstrative show of affection. Now, he felt tears pricking at the backs of his eyes. This had been his father's chosen place, and he'd been living in it and making fun of it without ever really recognizing how significant it must have been to the man.

Now, how was he going to live up to that?

A cool wind whipped up the bare hillside and ran its fingers under Stephen's collar. He shivered and the vision of his old building faded. *Time to get inside.* He paused at the concrete stoop to slide off his boots, wincing at the orange mud they were leaving everywhere, leftover from stomping around the Kelbaughs' front yard after Rosemary had walked away from him and he'd tramped around his purchase to try and simmer down.

The thick Maryland mud he was forever tracking into the house didn't really mesh with this new view of his father's house, nor did the rather ragged hedge which ran along the front of the house, its branches just touching the sills of the tiny fuel-crisis windows. He sighed at the straggly landscaping as he kicked his boots against the concrete step in front of the door. He should trim that up, and maybe plant some flowers, he guessed. What grew every year? Annuals? What even *was* an annual?

Stephen had never planted anything besides a bean-plant in elementary school science experiments. In second grade, his class had sprouted little beans in Dixie cups filled with potting soil, and then taken their budding bean-plants to a nearby park and planted them in a raised planter. There'd been a big ceremony and photos were taken and then he'd never thought about that bean plant again. Now he pulled off his boots and wondered about his single horticultural experience. Had his plant grown up? Had it produced beans? Had someone walked by, said to themself, *hey, free beans,* and plucked them?

Stephen hadn't even *liked* green beans when he'd been a kid. Imagine being a farmer, and every year planting seeds for things you knew children would push around on a plate and make faces about. Stephen couldn't do it. If he were a farmer, he would have to concentrate on the things people liked, universally: grapes, or apples, or maybe a dairy which specialized in chocolate milk and ice cream.

It wasn't until he'd gotten inside that he remembered his phone had been buzzing up a storm on the drive over. Four text messages from—his brow furrowed into a frown—Sasha Binds. What did *she* want? He'd texted Sasha while he'd been in New York, but his former colleague from Obsidian Investments, the same firm he'd worked at with Kevin, hadn't made a move to get back in touch. Just like everyone else.

It was too bad, because Stephen would have loved for Sasha to have replied while he was still in the city. She was a fun girl to have around in a crisis. Nothing got Sasha down, and she was very generous with the people she liked. She used to *really* like Stephen, as a matter of fact. They'd been friends with benefits for years, a casual and thoroughly relaxing relationship which gelled very well with their nonstop career demands. Even after he'd left Obsidian and gone to the start-up—ugh, that *idiotic* start-up!—they'd stayed close. Then Stephen came to Maryland, Confluence folded, and it was like a brick wall had gone up between them.

Or, like she'd blocked his number, not that he was one for texting again after the first message went unanswered. Stephen had too much self-respect to grovel. Be his friend, or don't, either one was fine.

He skimmed through the messages he'd received while driving: Sasha was sorry she'd missed him in New York, she'd just heard he'd been in town and now he was gone again, so crazy, blah blah blah. She finished off by saying she had some meetings in D.C. in a week and wondered if that was close enough to get together while she was around.

Stephen's eyebrows went up at that last suggestion. If Sasha wanted some company while she was in the capital, she didn't need to look too hard. She was well-traveled and well-liked; he was sure she had a few phone numbers to call in most cosmopolitan cities with a spot on the biz conference circuit, from London to Los Angeles.

So maybe this message meant she really wanted to see *him,* and she wasn't just after a familiar face for some chit-chat and a little hanky-panky afterwards. Stephen considered this idea. It felt . . . strange. And not just because she'd effectively abandoned him since January, either. There was another, nagging reason he didn't feel like texting Sasha back. He didn't like it, but he had to acknowledge its presence: Rosemary.

"Dammit," he muttered, heading into the kitchen. He poured himself a cup of cold coffee from the pot on the counter and slowly drank it down, staring out the kitchen window all the while. The green haze on the Catoctin Mountains could have been a thin layer of gauze, so delicate were the baby leaves on the trees. He found it touching. Then he was annoyed; Maryland was making him soft, if he was going to be emotionally moved by a hill full of trees. And the damned silence! He'd almost gotten used to it, but now his ears were buzzing with the absence of ambient noise. How had his father gotten used to the quiet? Had he really found New York too loud just a few days ago?

Stephen wondered, somewhat desperately, if just one thing could make sense for like, thirty seconds.

Then he sighed, picked up his phone, and texted Sasha back.

On Friday evening, Stephen donned a slim pair of brown oxfords below an even slimmer pair of tailored navy pants. He tightened the brushed steel buckle of a butter-soft leather belt, and buttoned up a pale blue shirt of fine cotton. He looked in the mirror and ran his hands over his too-long hair. It was curling just a bit above his collar, not a look he would usually cultivate. He'd gotten a little messy out here in the boondocks. Sasha would just have to get over it.

The sun was already setting as he drove through the hills and over the creeks towards Frederick. She'd decided to drive up from D.C. and stay the weekend in the historic city, saying there were some galleries and breweries she'd like to check out. "It looks like a cool town," she'd texted Stephen. "I can see why you're living there." He hadn't told her he lived nearly an hour away from the cool town, out amongst the farmers and the moo-cows.

Stephen found a parking spot in a vast concrete garage which could have housed five hundred New Yorkers and a half-dozen businesses, and wandered down into the historic district. There was a party atmosphere being cultivated around the Federal-era brick buildings and the Victorian tenements. Colored lights were strung over the concrete-corralled banks of Carroll Creek, and bands were playing roughly every two hundred feet. Their bass lines and guitar solos hummed uselessly into one another, a sonic match-up no one won.

Well, Stephen thought, he could make fun of this place endlessly for not being New York, and it would still be a welcome change from the deadly silence of his hilltop. Since he'd come back, the echoes and creaks in the house had been his only companions, and the ringing in his ears was growing more insistent. Had he really ever thought it was restful? Maybe for a moment, when he was talking to Rosemary, trying to imagine the world in her eyes. Experienced on his own, the place simply felt abandoned.

"Stephen! Over here!" Sasha was waving at him from the patio of a restaurant, which had been built into the first floor of an industrial brick pile looming behind her. "Isn't this place cute? It used to be a warehouse during the Civil War. They stored like, weapons inside. Or grain. Not sure which."

Stephen leaned on the wrought-iron fence separating the diners from the river-walk and gave Sasha a long, appraising look, which she clearly appreciated, laughing and shaking out her ash-blonde hair for him. She was a white-skinned, blue-eyed, red-lipped magazine spread of a woman, at least two sizes underweight by medical standards and just a little heavy by her own. Stephen didn't have to get her naked to know she was a woman of points and sharp edges, but he didn't mind her lack of softness; she was just as hard mentally as she was physically, both brain and body toned to an impossible level of fitness and ready to be deployed in order to get whatever she wanted.

Tonight she was wearing a short, sleeveless black dress with a preppy buttoned collar. It was open to show off her pale breastbone, where a little silver pendant glinted under the fairy lights. "New necklace?" Stephen asked, because he knew she liked to be asked about jewelry trends, her particular hobby.

"Isn't it adorable? It's just a perfect circle of silver, hand-hammered in a Hudson Valley forge. They sell them at this boutique in Millerton—of all places!—and at the Greenmarket in Union Square *if* you can get there in time . . . I had to get up at four a.m. to capture this little beauty." Sasha fingered the circle fondly. "Now get in here and order a drink! I want to catch up."

He made his way around the hostess standing guard at the patio entrance and wound through the tables back to Sasha. She patted his knee under the table as he pulled his chair in closer. "I can't believe you came to the city and then left immediately. I didn't even have time to call you—I just figured you were back for good."

"I thought I was, too," Stephen admitted. "But I'm developing this land and there are a lot of complications . . . historic preservation, watersheds, farmland covenants, that kind of thing. So I'm here to make myself available as soon as hitches come up, to try and push it through."

It sounded like the truth. It almost was. It certainly made more sense than the truth, which was becoming an elusive thing in his mind. Maybe all that *was* why he was here.

"I never saw you as a developer! So . . . *tangible*. It's ironic, really."

"Is that a crack about my last gig?" Working in virtual reality had felt like a genius move when he'd taken the job. He still wasn't sure if the company had been too far ahead of its time to succeed, or just the victim of a poor business plan and Ernie's celebrated inability to control costs.

"I would never! Stephen! But we are investment people. We move money around, make it play. This is . . . this is *land*. This is the *earth*. I'm seeing you out walking your property in boots and a long coat. Maybe one of those little flat caps on your head? Maybe a bird dog?"

"You're confusing building houses with being a country squire," Stephen chuckled. "And the Scottish Highlands with rural Maryland. How many of those have you had?"

"Oh, this?" She picked up her glass and shook the ice. "Sparkling water and lime. You have to *drive* here, Stephen. It's barbaric. But kind of exciting. I'm going to allow myself one beer. I actually have no idea how drinking affects my driving because I've never had to know. But I kind of love driving! Don't tell anyone at home."

"No worries. I don't even know when I'm going back." Stephen watched the surprise register on Sasha's face. She was opening her mouth to interrogate him when a black-shirted server arrived and talked to them for five minutes straight about beers.

Once their orders were in, he leaned back in his chair, letting the chilly spring night wrap around him. The crowds on the river-walk were thinning as people began to pair off, walking into restaurants or heading into bars. A few of the nearby bands gave up the ghost, which came as a relief. Maybe Stephen didn't hate quiet after all. There were limits.

Sasha watched him with a wry smile. "What?" he asked after a few moments of her silent perusal. He forced a grin. "Wondering how I'm making it here? You don't believe I could be a country gentleman?"

"I *know* you're not," Sasha insisted, her eyes sparkling. "And I don't know how long you're going to keep up this little game. If it's because you thought everyone was avoiding you—"

"Why would I think that?" he interrupted smoothly, but Sasha ignored him.

"You just need to wait it out, pay your dues. You went off to play with the wrong crowd and you got hurt. It happens. Someone would have hired you back eventually. Michelle mentioned you at lunch last week, so did Rory, I think Ishawn asked after you at an opening the week before that, so things *are* happening. I've heard rumbles. Maybe it's not on the timeline you wanted, but . . . " Sasha shrugged her thin shoulders. "Good things are worth waiting for, right?"

Her smile was positively wicked. She wasn't talking about work anymore.

Stephen sipped at his beer. He felt a little tired of Sasha already. She could be wearing; he'd forgotten that sometimes her slick go-girl attitude could get on his nerves. He wanted to talk to someone who would treat him like a friend, with gentleness and a little humor, not someone who spoke as if every single move might betray an agenda or, God forbid, an actual emotion.

This place is getting to me, he thought wryly. *If I stick around, I'm never going to acclimate back to New York.*

Well, he didn't intend on staying here forever. He would have to keep friends like Sasha close, even if they were exhausting at the moment. Stephen sighed and made up his mind. He'd play along. He'd follow their rules. "Let's order some food," he suggested. "And then, how about you show me your hotel?"

Sasha gave him an approving nod. "I thought you'd never ask, Stephen."

Chapter Seventeen

Rosemary

All you have to do is get through today.

Rosemary kept repeating the words to herself, hoping they'd get more helpful. She'd been up since three a.m., once a fitful attempt at sleep had turned into literal tossing and turning. Giving up on her bed, she'd pulled a soft-cushioned chair up to the window, looked out at the Kelbaughs' kitchen night-light, and waited for the pink spring dawn to arrive. At least her neighbors had come back before the fundraiser.

A week ago, she'd been afraid she'd be looking at an empty house on this nerve-racking morning. To her surprise, Aileen and Rodney had returned home two days ago, sunburned and excited about the land they'd bought and the house being built for them.

Relief was an understatement. Just knowing the Kelbaughs would come visit her today was going to make the time pass more easily. She was going to have to field visits from old school friends and family acquaintances all day, in between meeting complete strangers and asking for money, and the prospect was unappealing. At least with Rodney and Aileen, she didn't have to explain herself over and over, describe the farm and the horses, say that yes, she was doing really well on her own.

These constant explanations were the single strongest reason she'd withdrawn from nearly everyone in the past few years. The curious glances, the faux-friendly remarks: she hated all of it. When people expressed surprise over seeing her with all of her rescue horses, what they all meant was: no one ever thought she'd keep the farm going with her parents gone. They were just too *polite* to tell her they'd all expected she'd sell the farm and move into Frederick, or worse, into D.C.

Rosemary didn't want sympathy, or attention, or even solidarity. She didn't want to talk about the past as a bygone golden era. She simply wanted to move on, as if nothing had ever happened, as if there was no tragic backstory. She was a woman alone, surrounded by horses rescued from their own sad pasts— this was all anyone needed to know about her, and if it was enough to open their wallets, so much the better.

Nikki understood this. The Kelbaughs understood this. Somehow, she thought Stephen had understood this. He'd certainly asked no questions. But, she supposed, that might have been because he simply didn't care.

Talking to him hadn't felt like that, though.

Rosemary sighed at herself. She *had* to stop thinking about Stephen. She hadn't seen him again since their surprise meeting last week, when he'd broken into Long Pond and been startled by Colonel John. His distance wasn't really surprising, since she'd gotten angry with him and told him to leave in a tone so icy, she'd barely recognized her own voice.

She'd been right to do it, of course. He couldn't just drop in and out of her life that way, acting as if he had some right to care about her feelings after leaving her high and dry for weeks. She had spent much of her adult life searching for stability, and so she knew Stephen was no rock she could cling to. He'd go under at high tide and leave her floundering on her own.

"Get going, Rosemary," she told herself. It was past eight, and the doors would open at nine. She needed Mighty-mite inside the gym and a bright smile on her face when the early birds arrived. She had no excuses to be late, either. Everything at the farm was finished. The horse trailer was hitched to her big red truck and Mighty-mite was already inside, eating hay and whinnying back to his friends between bites. The horses had been fed and turned out in the pasture for the day, and at this point only Rosita was kind enough to occasionally whinny back to him. Everyone was stuffing their faces on the new blades of spring grass.

Rosemary sighed and looked at the truck with reluctance. She didn't drive it very often, preferring the little car she'd had since high school for quick trips to town and occasional forays into Frederick. The farm truck came out for feed store runs, picking up hay, the occasional addition of a new horse to her herd, and this: the annual spring fundraiser, with Mighty-mite as her all-important mascot.

"Okay," she told herself. "Let's do this. All you have to do is get through today. Earn the money for a load of hay. That's the goal. You can do it. All you have to do is—"

"Get through today?" a voice echoed. "I think you can do that, my dear."

Rosemary whirled around. Aileen was walking up from the woods path, bundled up in her long insulated coat, followed closely by Rodney in his overalls and plaid flannel shirt. Aileen had a covered dish in her hands, and Rodney was carrying an old-fashioned Thermos.

"What'd you two do?" Rosemary asked them, delighted they'd come to see her. Just the send-off she needed!

"Just brought you a little lunch," Aileen smiled, holding out the dish. Rosemary took it carefully and inhaled its rich scent.

"Oh! Is this *pie?*"

"Apple pie," Aileen confirmed. "Perfect for snacking on all day. It will keep your blood sugar up."

Rosemary wasn't positive that was how blood sugar worked, but she could see the benefits of keeping a homemade apple pie at her side today, so she nodded.

Rodney held out the Thermos. "And this is tea, for your throat," he told her in his gravelly voice. "Sweetened with honey."

Aileen nudged him. "Sweetened with Long Pond honey."

Rosemary could scarcely believe it. The Long Pond hives had been legendary once. Now all that was left was one white box, which buzzed industriously all spring and summer, sitting back behind the farmhouse. Rodney's honey was still the sweetest in the county, but oh-so-rare! "Thank you," she breathed. "This will really help today."

"We'll come by and see you around lunchtime," Aileen promised. "Nikki's going to be there to help you, right?"

"She's probably already there," Rosemary grimaced. "I better get going or she's going to be all over me."

Inside the horse trailer, Mighty-mite neighed in agreement and then kicked the metal wall for good measure. Rodney laughed, a rusty sound which went straight to Rosemary's heart. They'd bought a house in Florida. They were going to *leave*. But for now, they were still here, still supporting her.

"Thank you," she said again. "Thank you both so much."

Nikki was waiting just outside the back door of the high school gym, her arms crossed and toes tapping. She was wearing tight black jeans and a black cowl-necked sweater, paired with a chunky silver necklace which gave her a rather dangerous look—especially while she was hanging around behind the school they'd gone to, Rosemary thought with amusement. All she needed to complete the look was a rebellious cigarette. But Nikki wouldn't be caught dead smoking, even back in senior year when everyone was doing it. She said it was a waste of money and smelled dirty besides. It was unclear which fault Nikki found more distasteful.

Rosemary led Mighty-mite out of the trailer and walked up, watching Nikki scowl at her royal blue polo with *Notch Gap Farm Sanctuary* stitched on the chest.

"You didn't wear your polo shirt!" Rosemary said accusingly, before Nikki could say anything about her mom jeans and dirty boots.

"I'm not going to ask people for money wearing that old polo of yours," Nikki snorted. "You're just going to make folks feel uncomfortable. Especially anyone you went to school with who might have some money."

"Is that what this outfit is about? Looking like a hotshot in front of old school friends?" Rosemary handed over Mighty-mite's lead-rope. "Hang on a sec. I have some stuff in the truck to grab."

When she came back, toting a canvas bag stuffed with rescue fact sheets, the little rubber keychains she'd ordered to give out as donation thank-you gifts, the pie and the Thermos, she found Nikki had ignored her orders and already gone into the gym, taking the mini horse with her. Rosemary shook her head and shuffled down the rows of card tables and makeshift booths to their little square of gymnasium floor. Last night, she'd come out and set up Mighty-mite's little corral, constructed with dog-kennel fencing and padded by wood shavings poured over a thick rubber stall mat.

Nikki was shutting him inside as Rosemary walked up. The mini horse had found the flake of hay she'd left waiting and was happily filling his face. There was nowhere Mighty-mite would not eat.

"I *said* to hang on," Rosemary huffed, putting her bag down on the table. She started unpacking, placing the pie off to one side.

"Is that a *pie?*" Nikki asked, flipping up the dishtowel covering the pie. "Oh, la la! What a heavenly day."

"That's a pie for helpers," Rosemary said, biting back a grin. "Helpful people only. Not headstrong volunteers who run off with ponies."

"Listen, I can handle this pony." Nikki covered the pie again. "And I can handle this booth. All you have to do is smile and lead kids over to pet Mighty-boy here while I get their parents to open their wallets. Today is going to be easy-peasy."

There was an electric hiss as the loudspeakers came to life. "Exhibitors, the doors will be opening in five minutes! This is your five-minute warning!"

A buzz of conversation went up as the people in the booths began to call instructions and hustle through last-minute prep. Chairs were pulled across the floor, tables were straightened, towers of jars and boxes were re-organized. Everyone tried to get themselves into the most appealing position possible. The spring fundraiser was well-attended by both Frederick County locals and D.C.-area weekenders; for years the event had been making the big city newspapers as a fun outing for people who wanted to see more of the countryside in spring. The same article, with subtle variations, came out every year: combine a trip to the fundraiser, where you can load up with jams and honey and freshly-baked bread to take back to your urban kitchen, with a bite to eat in a local farmer's market cafe and a drive around the pretty farming towns of western Maryland. The perfect March Saturday!

Rosemary might have had some thoughts about their farming community being a tourist attraction, but those thoughts were drowned out by the more immediate prospect of the money flowing in from those well-heeled city visitors and new suburbanites flooding the county. Everyone in the region who ran some sort of non-profit showed up at the fundraiser to set up their tables and sell their wares—plus, there was a craft corner for the local knitters and weavers and painters to show off their creations, and a food fair out front with everyone dishing up local grub, from the Frederick County Farm Women and their famous French fries to a quiet old woman who had been dipping her orchard's apples in sticky red candy syrup for as long as anyone could remember.

"Mighty-mite, are you ready for this?" Rosemary asked the mini horse.

He snorted into his hay.

Nikki was poking curiously around the crumbling edges of the pie-crust.

"Nikki!"

"Sorry, sorry."

"Game faces," Rosemary told her.

"So serious," Nikki laughed. "You can do this in your sleep by now."

All you have to do is get through today, Rosemary thought.

———— *ele* ————

The morning started a little slowly, and Nikki soon had Mighty-mite by the lead-rope, calling to passing kids to come pat his fluffy neck. Rosemary took over the fundraising, her least favorite function, as it was made a bit simpler with Nikki's pet-the-pony hawking. She showed the kids' parents, earnest-looking organic types up for the day from D.C., a binder filled with before-after photos of the horses she'd rescued. The donation jar began to sprout green with currency, the credit card reader attached to her iPhone began to see some use, and the email list sign-up sheet had addresses written halfway down the first page. By late morning, she was beginning to feel like she'd actually survive the day.

"So that's the farm," Rosemary finished up with her latest spiel, turning to the last page of the binder. The final photo was of all the horses turned out in the pasture together, grazing on deep summer grass. "The expenses with rescuing horses are really—"

"Do they *do* anything?"

Rosemary looked up at the couple. She usually avoided too much eye contact when she was making her pitches, trying to stave off the anxiety of talking to strangers, but the pointed way the question was asked, and the weight placed on the word *do,* had thrown her off-guard.

The woman who had asked shifted her weight from foot to foot, as if Rosemary's pause was taking up valuable time. She was well-dressed, in cream-colored linens and woven knits which were designed to look artlessly primitive. Her plain brown purse had a gold logo indicating it certainly cost more than the auction prices for Rochester and Bongo combined.

"They live in peace," Rosemary said carefully. "They've had difficult lives and now they're not being asked to do anything but be horses."

The woman sighed, as if this was what she had feared. Her husband, a man so close-shaven his skin gleamed under the gym lights, simply looked amused. "Must be nice," he chuckled.

"It should be," Rosemary agreed, managing to smile. "The goal is to keep their lives stress-free. It's hard to ask them to do anything without pushing their limits. A lot of times, horses who have been mistreated can act out in ways that are difficult to predict. It can be better for these horses if we just allow them to live out their days in peace, rather than try to wedge them back into careers they might not be suited for. That's what I do. My horses aren't suitable for . . . *doing* things. That's why my farm is called a sanctuary."

"I don't know that I agree," the woman said, shaking her head. She had the astonishing confidence of a person who had never been told to sit down and listen to someone who knew more than her. "I was just talking to another horse farm owner down a few aisles

—her name was Katie? Caitlin? Something like that. She is doing therapy riding of some kind. It was very interesting. Using the horses to help out people with . . . oh, cerebral palsy, I want to say? And maybe autism? Things like that, you know what I mean. Have you ever thought about that? Therapy would be a good job for rescue animals, I think."

Rosemary heard Nikki make a strangled sound and she held up her hand behind her back: *not a word!* She put on her most polite voice for her reply. "I think you must have met Caitlin Tuttle, from Elmwood Farms? I heard she'd added therapeutic riding to her lesson program. She has a slightly different situation. Caitlin's barn is full of carefully selected lesson horses and ponies. They're kind of the opposite of my horses? Some of them were raised right there at Elmwood; Caitlin's mother bred show ponies. So it's great that they're doing that, but for my horses, unfortunately—"

"Well, I think you should consider something like that," the linen-and-knits woman interrupted. She shifted her thousand-dollar purse on her shoulder. "Try giving back to the children of this community. They'd appreciate it. I donated to the other woman already, sorry. Harper! Flynn! Let's go, kids!"

"Awwww!" The chorus of disappointment was always the same, no matter where the parents were from or how the kids were raised. Usually, Rosemary would hand them little trading cards of the Notch Gap horses she'd printed and cut out herself. They were pretty effective consolation prizes for giving up stroking Mightymite's thick mane and forelock, and also helped keep the rescue on people's minds after they'd left. But now she was so taken aback by the woman's presumption, the cards stayed on the table unnoticed, even as the parents dragged the protesting children away.

Rosemary sat down on the folding chair and pulled the pie over to meet her.

"Is it pie time?" Nikki unclipped the lead-rope and left Mighty-mite to his hay. "I'm ready. I've been thinking about that pie nonstop for this entire time."

"It's only been two hours," Rosemary said woodenly. "Six more to go."

Nikki produced a plastic fork from the depths of her purse and stuck into the center of the pie. "It's been longer than that. What's the matter with you? You let that lady get under her skin? She doesn't know anything about you."

"She told me I should be doing more for the community. Like it's selfish to just rescue horses. So what, now I have to rescue people, too? I have to rescue people with the rescue horses? That's not their job, Nikki! They've done enough! It's because of Caitlin Tuttle, I just know she's saying something about me . . . "

"Wait a minute. Is Caitlin *here?* Like, soliciting donations here?"

"Apparently," Rosemary sighed. "And she's closer to the front door than us, if they met her first."

"Crap." Nikki chewed her pie moodily. "Did I ever tell you that I can't stand Caitlin Tuttle? If not, I'm telling you now. I can't stand Caitlin Tuttle."

"You've told me. Since we were thirteen. But she's smart, you have to give her credit. Her mother left her a beautiful farm and no money, and now she has a beautiful farm and people are giving her money."

"I'll bet she's not doing that great," Nikki decided. "She probably just didn't know what to do with the farm when her mom's students figured out she couldn't help them win. She's just turning a failed lesson program into a tax break by calling it therapeutic riding."

"She might actually be doing therapeutic riding," Rosemary pointed out. She reached into Nikki's bag and pulled out another fork; there were always bagged utensils from the diner floating around in the depths of Nikki's enormous purse. "She's certainly down there somewhere telling people she is. And, that now she's giving back to the community and providing a service beyond regular, for-profit riding lessons."

The word *community* rankled the way that woman had used it, as if only doing nice things for humans could matter to the greater good. The horses' interests, it seemed, were not to be taken into account. Nor was what might happen if Rosemary were to put a child onto Bongo's back right before the huge horse had one of his random mental breakdowns, twitching and kicking if anything touched him.

There was a reason her horses had ended up at Notch Gap Farm, and it wasn't because they were useful riding or driving horses. Rochester was the only horse remotely safe to ride, and even he had his moments. Rosemary touched her forehead unintentionally, where a tiny scar at the hairline was a reminder of her fall.

"Caitlin might be a saint," Nikki agreed, "and I'd be the first to tell her she was doing a good thing . . . except we both know she's no horsewoman."

This was an unassailable point. When they'd ridden at Elmwood as children, Caitlin's position as the barn owner's daughter had been the only thing that let her save face. She was not a naturally gifted rider, nor an empathetic horsewoman, and she had blamed every tumble she'd taken on the horse she'd been riding. There had been a *lot* of falls, and a horse blamed for every single one—the sure sign of a poor equestrian. With a moral compass like that, what good could she be doing anyone now? Rosemary sighed and dug into the pie with her fork.

She was savoring the sweet apple on her tongue when she heard another couple walking up the aisle. She looked up automatically, not wanting to miss a single opportunity.

A tall, slender woman with platinum-blonde hair and a sharp face was fingering the wool shawls at the booth next to Rosemary's. "All of these sheep are rare breed?" she was asking. Next to her, rolling his eyes at her question, was Stephen.

The fork dropped from her fingers.

Was this was how it would be now? Was she destined to run into him every week or two, some random meeting when she was at a mental low-point and really couldn't deal with the pressure?

She couldn't help but give him a thorough looking-over, her eyes devouring him hungrily. He looked fantastic, his jeans and black shirt resting on his body with a certain elegance she supposed came from buying tailored clothes, as opposed to off the sales rack at Target, and his strong jaw had a light dusting of close-cropped beard; a look of his that she quite liked.

Just as his incurious eyes wandered towards her booth, Rosemary realized she was staring at him, and she ducked.

Oh Lord, she actually *ducked.* From under the tablecloth, well aware half her body was still visible to the corridor, Rosemary wondered what on earth she was doing and how in hell she could simply vanish. Because there was no coming back from *this.*

Suddenly, Nikki's head was beside hers. She shoved her purse over to Rosemary. "Start rummaging around in there and then come out with whatever you want and say 'a-ha, I found it,' but *do not* look at him, got it?" Her head vanished again.

Rosemary took a breath and reached into Nikki's bag. She shuffled things around—there was a lot in there—and came out with a paperback mystery novel. No, too much of a conversation-starter. What if he'd read it? She dropped the book and dug deeper. Ketchup packets. No, those weren't going to look natural next to a half-eaten apple pie. A handful of tampons. Definitely not.

Starting to feel desperate, Rosemary rummaged into a side-pocket and finally scored a bottle of water. It was cold and sweating, wrapped in a few napkins to keep condensation from getting anything else wet.

Nikki really did keep a lot of stuff in that bag, Rosemary thought, shaking her head at its depths before she came back to the surface.

"Here we are," she announced triumphantly, placing the water bottle on the table.

Nikki's eyes grew round. *"Put that away,"* she hissed.

"What on earth—"

"Hi, Rosemary," Stephen called, his voice washing over her. "I thought we might see you here."

We? Rosemary stood up from her chair, feeling her cheeks flushing dangerously red. "Well, I recall telling you this was an important day for the rescue," she replied, amazed her voice was so tart. Was that what she really felt for Stephen now? Disdain, maybe a little disgust? It would be nice to think so. For just a moment, she let her eyes meet his, let her gaze linger there.

No. That wasn't what she felt at all.

"And who is this?" Nikki asked, trying to deflect attention from Rosemary—she probably saw those crimson cheeks and sensed a panic attack forthcoming. "You brought company."

"This is Sasha," Stephen replied smoothly. "Sasha Binds, a friend from New York. She's been down in D.C. on business a lot lately, and I decided to make things easy on her with a weekend place to stay."

"Too many hotels and take-out dinners, so he took pity on me," Sasha said with a little laugh—a laugh which sounded brittle to Rosemary's ears; well-rehearsed, certainly, but not real.

She watched Stephen's gaze turn sideways to look inquiringly at the other woman and thought: *he hears it, too.* Then his eyes locked back on Rosemary's and she dropped her chin immediately, letting her eyes rove over the contents of the table as if to check all of her collateral was in place.

Sasha looked down as well.

"Keychains!" she squealed, reaching for the basket of rubber horses. "These are so cute, my nieces would love them!"

"They're for a donation," Nikki told her forcefully. "Twenty-five dollars or more."

They were really for ten dollars or more, but Rosemary let it ride. She concentrated on containing her blush, and wishing Stephen would go away—or that he'd stay, alone, and talk to her. Fine, she wished Sasha would go away. But anyone would. The woman was a nightmare—she could just *tell.*

What was she doing with Stephen? He didn't actually like her, did he?

"Rosemary," Stephen murmured.

She was startled into looking up again, and found his gaze intent on her face. A thrill she couldn't help ran up her spine. He put his hands flat on the table and leaned forward, as if to tell her a secret.

Rosemary glanced around: Sasha was still occupied with the keychains, and Nikki was hovering over her, credit card swiper in hand. She'd drawn the other woman to the far end of the table, and Rosemary felt as if she and Stephen were alone.

They weren't, though, and there was no reason for him to be leaning in, acting all seductive, when they'd parted on bad terms not once but *twice*. Or was it three times? She could scarcely recall, now that he was standing in front of her.

But instead of letting him into her space, she stood up and gestured for him to follow her. "Come and see Mighty-mite," she told him. "It's been awhile."

Stephen obediently trailed her over to the pen and they watched the miniature horse nosing through a flake of hay. The cured grass was yellow after a long winter of storage, and he was being choosy about which bits he ate first.

"So, who is she?" Rosemary asked, her voice low.

"A friend from the city, like I said. She tagged along today."

"Why are you always here?" She struggled to keep from shouting the words. "Always popping up? Is this what it's going to be like? Because—"

He was standing very close to her. "Because what, Rosemary?"

"Because . . . because . . . " She felt dizzy, and put a hand to her forehead without thinking about it. "Oh, I don't know! Forget it. I'm being stupid."

Now Stephen was gazing at her with worry. Always worried, always thinking she was going to faint! It was hard to believe she was a tough farm girl. There was something bad luck about him, something that ended up with Rosemary out cold.

"Maybe you should sit down," he said, putting a hand on her elbow. He made to guide her towards the chair, but she shook her head, not willing to play the invalid female for him yet again.

"Three hundred dollars! Our record for the day!" Nikki announced, so loud Rosemary jumped.

She whirled around. "Three *hundred?*"

Sasha was beaming at them as if she'd won a contest. "I think you're doing great work out here, ladies," she told them, scooping up a handful of keychains. Then she coughed. "Oof," she said. "I think I might be allergic to hay." She coughed again. Nikki lifted her eyebrows, then bent down to finish emailing Sasha her receipt.

Rosemary plucked up the water bottle from the table. "Here, take a drink."

"Thanks," Sasha coughed. She took the bottle and put it to her lips. Just as the liquid tilted towards her mouth, her expression changed to confusion, then surprise.

Nikki leapt across the table. "Stop!"

Rosemary had to stifle a shriek. Stephen looked alarmed. Nikki was snatching at the bottle. But Sasha was leaning backwards, the bottle still pressed against her lips, laughing hysterically.

"Oh, you country girls," she chortled as soon as she could get the breath. "Vodka! In your purse! I love it!"

And she took another swig.

Chapter Eighteen

Stephen

Stephen knew bringing Sasha was a mistake.

He knew coming to the fundraiser at all was a mistake.

He did them both anyway.

Was he compelled? Did he have some sort of demon on his shoulder? It certainly felt that way. He knew Rosemary would be in that school gym, and he'd felt drawn to its doors, as if any good could possibly come of seeing her again. There was nothing between them but hot feelings and cold words, and Stephen had never been the kind of person who found conflict a turn-on.

Still, despite all of that, he sought her out. People could change. Maybe a little love-hate *was* hot. He wouldn't know until he'd seen it through.

Bringing Sasha along was a tactic of a different sort. Stephen wasn't sure why he couldn't avoid Rosemary—no, he was sure, he just didn't want to admit it to himself—but since he couldn't, he brought along Sasha to keep things more distant. More difficult. Less: *let's fall into bed together* and more: *oops, I already have someone in there.*

Sasha thought the whole thing was hilarious, from the moment she first found the mailer on his kitchen counter to when they finally pulled up in front of the high school. "What is this, Stephen?" she'd asked, holding up the mailer announcing the fundraiser. "Is this some old-timey country ritual? Will there be dancing? Will there be pies? Will there be quilts? I always wanted a quilt for my guest bedroom."

"You don't have a guest bedroom," Stephen had responded, looking at her in some confusion. "You live in a one-bedroom in Hell's Kitchen."

"*You* have one, country boy," Sasha told him with a sidelong look. "Maybe I'll put my fabulous new quilt in there. And it's Midtown West, now," she added with a snide expression.

"Oh, were you cold last night?" He ignored the gentrifying realtor-speak.

"A little." She'd poured a cup of coffee and sat down at the breakfast table. "I have to admit, this trip isn't going the way I expected."

Stephen had looked past her, gazing out the sliding-glass door behind the table. He'd begun pulling the old vertical blinds wide open first thing every morning. The house might look vulgar and garish on its bare hilltop, but there was a million-dollar view out back, of gold-tipped trees and ancient mountains basking in the sunrise. This morning his backyard was a long slope of dewy emerald, its brilliance still cast in shadow by the house, with a nearby bird-feeder currently in use by a cardinal and several hopping sparrows. The birds were regulars. He'd started calling the cardinal "Carl," but he hadn't named the sparrows. Too hard to tell them apart.

"So take me to this fundraiser," Sasha insisted. "And then maybe I won't tell everyone in the city you've become a hopeless bore now that you live in the middle of nowhere."

"Fine," Stephen had sighed. "We'll go." He made his face look put out, as if he hadn't meant to go, when all the while he'd known there was no way he'd skip this chance to see Rosemary.

But what had he really hoped to accomplish?

Had he counted on watching her face fall when she'd seen Sasha? And had he hoped to make her feel jealous just by parading a long-legged blonde through that gym? A gym where she'd once had high school phys. ed., a gym where she'd probably had to run laps and shoot baskets and do jumping-jacks, some hard-jawed man in gym shorts blowing a whistle at her. No wonder she had anxiety attacks at this fundraiser, Stephen had thought as they walked inside, as he looked around and took in the rubber-padded walls, the tall stack of folded wooden bleachers, the pennants from county and state glories hanging from the high steel beams. If Rosemary had been a nervous student, coming back to the scene of her unhappiness couldn't be easy for her, and yet she dug deep and found the strength to do it each year, to keep her horses fed.

Stephen gave himself a little shake, trying to drag himself back to the present, which was, unfortunately, this bizarre encounter between Sasha and the women of Notch Gap Farm. Sasha was still drinking, actually trying to down a water bottle full of vodka, as if she was going to prove something to the country folk about how big-city women could tip back their liquor. Stephen didn't think this would send the message Sasha wanted it to. He touched her on the shoulder, noticing the laser-sharp focus of Rosemary's eyes on his hand as he did so.

"Oh, you want a sip?" Sasha laughed, holding out the bottle. She had knocked back a quarter of it, which probably wasn't that much vodka when spaced out between several cocktails, but was a lot for one slender woman who hadn't eaten since her morning yogurt. She staggered a little. "Whoa! That hit my legs in a hurry!"

"I'll just give this back to its owner," Stephen said hastily, taking the bottle and setting it on the table. Nikki looked at it, and then him, with barely disguised rage.

"Did you think I was going to want that back?" she asked caustically. Her tight curls seemed to bristle at him.

"Nikki," Rosemary said quietly.

That was all she said: *Nikki.* But it was enough to cause both Stephen and Nikki to look at her. Rosemary shook her head slightly. She had nothing else to say.

Sasha was dangling all of her rubber keychains from her fingers, making the colorful ponies dance like marionettes. "I love these. I love these! You guys take it easy, okay? I need to get some food in my stomach. Stephen, let's go find some lunch."

That was exactly what she needed. Stephen took her arm above the elbow. "What a good idea," he said carefully. He looked back at Rosemary. He had an intense longing to stay with her—as dramatic as those words were, there was no other way to put it. He felt the need to touch her, to wrap his arms around her, like a deep, insistent urge tugging him bodily across the corridor.

But Rosemary wasn't looking at him. Her eyes were cast down, her lips pursed, her fingers curved against the table-top, as if she wanted to claw right through the cheap blue fabric to the veneer beneath. Stephen's jaw tightened, and he turned away.

He'd made her day worse, even though he had already known this would be a terrible day for her.

He was a jerk.

Stephen sat Sasha at a picnic table outside and set about acquiring food for her: French fries doused in salt, a baked potato loaded with broccoli and cheddar, a paper plate filled with fried mozzarella sticks. He put the fair food in front of her and commanded her to eat, not realizing until Sasha had eaten only the broccoli and a few of the fries that she probably hadn't eaten carbs since the early 2000s. Feeling foolish, he scraped the breading off the mozzarella sticks and told her to eat the melted cheese with a plastic fork.

"Can you get me a Diet Coke?" she asked, obediently pulling at a mushy piece of cheese. "Everything's so salty."

He went off in search of the stand with the shortest line, but things were getting backed up as the clock ticked towards noon. Stephen settled in for the wait behind six people at the fried cheese stand, reasoning that fried cheese did not come with multiple customizations and would therefore be the quickest-moving line. He didn't realize until he'd been there several minutes that he was standing behind Aileen Kelbaugh.

Maybe he wouldn't have recognized her small white head in front of him, and that excuse would have been fair enough—there were dozens of small, white-haired women wandering the high school grounds just now. Still, when she turned around and looked at him with questioning eyes, he felt guilty and embarrassed not to have realized she was standing right in front of him. He smiled wanly as she took him in.

"Stephen!" Aileen said, her eyes widening behind a pair of surprisingly on-trend sunglasses. "How long have you been there?"

He looked at the line of people behind him, which had gained seven more followers since he'd joined the cheese queue. "Just a minute," he lied.

"Rosemary's inside," she told him, as if dangling a toy for him to bat at. "You'll have to go visit with her."

"I just saw her, actually." He tried to look as if their meeting had gone well.

"Oh, good. How is she? I haven't been inside yet. Rodney wanted some fried cheese and I only let him have it twice a year . . . here, and at the county fair in September. He's getting us lemonades from the Apple Valley stand, though. That's the best lemonade in the state. Don't get a drink here."

"I was just going to get a Diet Coke," Stephen explained. "But that lemonade sounds good."

"You should go over there. Don't even wait here." Aileen shook her head. "The lemonade here comes from a powder. They *say* it's real but . . . " her tone trailed off darkly, indicating Aileen knew things about that lemonade. "How did you say Rosemary is doing? This place gives her fits, poor girl."

"She's doing okay," Stephen guessed. He hadn't seen her actually having an anxiety attack, after all. "Nikki's with her."

Aileen nodded, satisfied. "I don't know what we'd do if Nikki wasn't here to watch her. We'd have to stay forever. And Rodney's tired . . . heavens, *I'm* tired. This winter . . . the cold is a different thing when you're old, Stephen. And that house . . . I love that house, but my goodness, it's cold." She shook her head, imagining the cold. The March sun was warm, but Stephen thought he could see the winter's chill draped around her thin bones. "The new house will be done by October, did I tell you that? We'll be in Florida by winter. One more county fair and we'll be on our way."

"Well, congratulations." Stephen smiled down at Aileen. He wondered if Rosemary understood how happy the Kelbaughs really were to get out of the northern climate. She probably was, he decided, and that was the only reason she still stomached his presence.

"Ma'am, your order?"

"My goodness, we reached the front of the line!" Aileen turned around and ordered from the teenager leaning out of the service window. "And a Diet Coke for the young man behind me," she added.

"That's not necessary—"

"Too late!" Aileen turned and laughed at him over her shoulder, looking like a little white-haired witch. The cheerful kind, who consorted with woodland animals and made love potions from flowers. "Now you can go back in and talk to Rosemary more. I think you two have more to say to each other."

He took the heavy paper cup from her. It was already sweating from the ice inside, water rolling down the sides and soaking his fingers. "More to say?" he heard himself asking, peering at Aileen curiously. "Why do you say that?"

Aileen went on chuckling, shaking her head as she collected her paper plates, greasy with fried cheese. "You kids think you know everything. But Rodney isn't the old fuddy-duddy you take him for. The minute you went in the front door, his security cameras started recording. We saw everything that went on in there. And," Aileen paused and gave Stephen a piercing look, right over the tops of her fashionable sunglasses, "we were both a little confused about why you didn't kiss her."

Stephen was too astonished to reply.

"You can't let her run the show," Aileen told him, shrugging. "Rosemary doesn't let people get close to her. It's up to you now. Don't let her down. Oh, I see Rodney. Let me go catch up with him before he wanders off with my lemonade."

Chapter Nineteen

Rosemary

Rosemary felt like she'd been hit by a truck, but the day had to be seen out. The hay bill wasn't going to pay itself. With Sasha and Stephen gone, she put Nikki out front to be the spokesperson and took over Mighty-mite duties, hoping lots of rubs on the mini's furry little face would keep her anxiety at bay. As the lunch crowd filed in and began to swell the aisles, warming the gymnasium and filling it with a constant din of conversation, Rosemary could feel her heart beginning to pound ever more insistently against her ribcage. She knelt by Mighty-mite, digging her fingers into his mane, and just managed to welcome the children who came sidling up to pet him.

"He's a baby pony," a little girl announced to her toddler brother. "What's his name?" she asked Rosemary.

"This is Mighty-mite." Rosemary took the little girl's hand and directed it to stroke the pony's soft neck on the left side, away from the more coarse strands of his heavy mane. "There you go. He likes to be pet right there."

"Can we ride him?"

"No, sorry, he's just for loving on."

"I think we can ride him," the girl decided. "I'm not that big, and neither is Mikey."

"Well, you can't," Rosemary said as patiently as possible, although pushy children (usually girls for some reason) made her want to scream. "He's not for riding."

"Ponies *are* for riding," the little girl informed her. "Mikey knows that, too."

Mikey was rapturously stroking Mighty-mite's neck and did not bother to agree with his sister, which made the girl look even more mutinous. Rosemary was fascinated to see the girl's lower lip actually protrude into a storybook-worthy pout. She was less pleased, though not terribly surprised, when the girl opened her sulky mouth and let out a holler.

"Mom! I want to ride the pony and she said no!"

"Oh my God," the woman speaking to Nikki said. "I'm so sorry. Maddy! Mikey! Come here!"

Maddy gave Rosemary one last hard glare, one that proclaimed them enemies for life, before turning back to her mother. Mikey, meanwhile, remained at Mighty-mite's side, blissfully unresponsive. Rosemary gave the woman a little smile to indicate the toddler was welcome to stay with her—certainly for as long as it took for her to give Nikki a donation.

The woman gave her a little nod and smile in return. "The woman at the last horse farm booth said Maddy could come out and ride a pony, and it's been mayhem ever since," she explained.

Nikki's attention was immediately aroused. "The last horse farm booth? Who was that?"

"Oh . . . " the woman scrounged in her purse and plucked out a heavy piece of glossy card-stock. "Elmwood. They do riding lessons? They're here as a therapeutic riding center but I guess they teach everyone. Maddy has her heart set on learning how to ride and I wasn't sure where to take her, but this seems like the right place. It's so important to give back to the community."

"Yes, it is," Nikki agreed nicely enough, but Rosemary could tell her friend's molars were grinding together.

"We have different missions," Rosemary explained, hoping to spare Nikki's dental plan. "The horses we take in at Notch Gap generally aren't able to be ridden due to prior abuse. I have an exceptions, but he's a Percheron, so he's too big for children to ride."

"Oh, of course," the woman said with an understanding nod. "There's room for everyone, right? Sure seems like Mikey's taken in with that pony," she added.

Mikey was leaning against Mighty-mite, his little towhead pressed against the miniature horse's withers. He had put his spare thumb into his mouth and there was a look of utter contentment in his half-closed eyes. Mighty-mite looked pretty happy with the situation himself.

Looking at the pair of them, Rosemary suddenly wondered if there *was* room for something more at Notch Gap.

Almost immediately, though, she felt a tightening in her chest; the idea of bringing people out to the farm, being responsible for them around her horses, was enough to push the breath right out of her lungs. She smiled and let the woman go on talking with Nikki, and she waved goodbye to Mikey (though not to Maddy) when they had finished their conversation. Then, she got up and walked over to Nikki, who was looking critically at their donation log sheet.

"How are things going?"

"Not great," Nikki said tersely. "And I think I know why."

"The bottle of vodka? Which you haven't explained, by the way."

"Hah! That was to dose you with if you went a little crazy. Miraculous curative powers, vodka. No, the booze isn't to blame, just our friend down the hall."

"You're blaming Caitlin?"

"I sure am."

Rosemary sat down and picked at the pie, its half-eaten remains still buried safely under the dish towel. "We can't exactly vilify someone for starting a therapeutic riding program," she said around a mouthful. "Therapeutic riding is a good thing."

"Not the way she's doing it."

"You don't know what she's doing. She could be amazing at it. This could be her calling. Maybe she can't teach show-ring equitation, but she can help kids stay in the saddle." Rosemary shrugged. "It seems dangerous to me, to start attacking someone who is doing charity work, Nikki."

"I'm not attacking." Nikki dropped the clipboard with a thunk. "I am questioning her motives and I'm questioning her qualifications. She's bringing in donations *and* paying clients today and I don't know . . . something about that just doesn't sit right with me. But you're right—for all I know, she's spent the past year mastering the art. Either way, she's extremely convincing at getting people to donate, because we have made exactly half as much as we have previously made by this time for the past two years, and everyone I've talked to has asked if we teach riding lessons, either therapeutic or the usual sort, like Elmwood does. And I've gotten disappointed looks every time I say no. Apparently, like you said earlier, our horses are not allowed to just be." Nikki added this with a touch of bitterness.

Rosemary took another bite of pie. *Maybe they aren't,* she thought. Maybe no one could just be. Not on a donation budget, anyway. She felt like the day had given her a lot to consider. Maybe, she thought, maybe she'd just go down and talk to Caitlin, see what all this was *really* about.

Nikki waited for a response from Rosemary, but when she didn't get one, she turned back to the shuffling crowds, waving and drawing them in to the table with her winning smile. Her curls bobbed around her neck as she turned from person to person, pointing out Mighty-mite and explaining their cause of providing a sanctuary to abused animals. Rosemary watched her absently, fork abandoned in the pie plate, wondering what else they could do, what else the horses could offer the world which would make people find them worth supporting.

Then Stephen came back.

Jesus, Rosemary thought, standing up slowly as his face appeared from amongst the crowds wandering the aisle. *What does this guy want from me?*

"Can we talk?" Stephen asked.

Rosemary studied his face for a moment, as much to buy time as to simply indulge herself. The line of his jaw and the tense muscle above it, flexed so hard she knew he was clenching his teeth; the wickedly short-cropped beard that gave him the look of a pirate; the intense emotion in his stormy blue eyes. His expression made her think of every single private moment they'd shared: the kisses, the meaningful looks, that moment on her back in the hay when he'd devoured her with a single glance and she'd felt warm and safe and wanted—

"We can talk," she agreed, because she wanted nothing more than to escape this crowded place with him, despite everything that had gone wrong between them. "Outside?"

"Not out front," he said quickly. "Is there a back door?"

"This way." He was hiding her from the blonde, but what about it? She gestured and turned, weaving through the crowd until they were behind the booths, in a narrow aisle along the wall which had been left for the exhibitors. She pushed through the back doors and they were instantly out in the fresh spring breeze, the hot gymnasium left behind like another dimension. She breathed in the cool air and looked up at the blue sky, dotted with cottony-white cumulus clouds. The green athletic field stretched out ahead of her before ending in a line of fresh-leaved trees, with the rolling swells of the mountains behind them. Rosemary's heart lifted, and the anxieties of the crowd left her. She could talk out here. "God, this is better," she sighed, turning to face Stephen.

He didn't look better for having left the crowded gym; his face was drawn in anxious lines and his gaze was flicking around, as if he was afraid to look at her. Rosemary thought he looked like a rescued animal, grateful to be out of the fire, but not sure if what he faced now was worse.

"Stephen," she said gently, "if we're going to talk, you have to tell me what it's about."

His eyes focused on hers at last. She dug her fingernails into her palms.

"I'm not sleeping with Sasha," he blurted.

Rosemary blinked at him. She hadn't expect that, but she was hardly surprised. She couldn't imagine him with Sasha. "No," she replied after a few moments of expectant silence. "Of course not."

"I *have,*" Stephen went on, suddenly explanatory. "In the city. Not—recently. Not since I moved here. She's just staying at my house. She thought . . . I thought . . . but I was just lonely. I went to her hotel room but nothing happened. Then I wanted a friend around the place and she hinted that she needed a weekend out of the city, so I told her . . . but we aren't. Sleeping together."

"That's fine," Rosemary said encouragingly. "Thank you for telling me that."

His expression was suddenly desperate. "I think about you all the time, Rosemary."

She felt the pink rising up from her chest, coloring her throat, her cheeks, her forehead. She might as well have been having a hot flash, she thought, irritated with herself. "What does that mean?" she asked him, her voice cracking just a little. *Nerves,* she told herself.

"I think we should see more of each other. I would like it, if we saw more of each other." His words ran over one another, like water falling over rocks in a creek. Rosemary pictured Catoctin Creek in its summer fullness, the trees draped over the water like a green veil, the clay path she would walk with Stephen, their heads tilted close in effortless conversation. It was a pretty daydream, but it came to her with such urgency, she knew it hadn't been buried very deeply in her mind. She had wanted this all along.

"I would like that," Rosemary told him gravely. She folded her hands behind her back to hide their trembling. She wished she could do the same with her traitorous cheeks.

They faced each other for a long moment. The spring breeze caught at her hair, trapped mercilessly in a bun, and began to pull strands loose. A wavy lock flung itself across her forehead, blocking her eyes, and she reached for it at the same time as Stephen.

When their fingers touched, Rosemary felt as if a dam had broken. Unbidden, their fingers entwined themselves, and then Stephen's arm bent, pulling her towards him. She crossed the short distance between them in one sure step, just as he took his other hand and tilted her chin up. He sighed against her lips as they met, and the soft hum of it sent Rosemary's will to love him shoving recklessly through all of her stone walls.

She leaned into him, her hands sliding around his neck and her body tucked against his, giving herself over completely to their kiss. And if he'd felt new and thrilling in the hay that cold winter's night, he felt familiar and adored in the spring sunshine, their embrace a sort of homecoming which couldn't be explained in simple words and phrases. His body felt like she was exactly where she was supposed to be, and she knew he felt the same, and there was no other way to describe it.

ele

Rosemary sat back down behind the table and tried to still her trembling hands. She had initially placed them on the table-top, but their tremors were too obvious, so she sat on them, instead.

This was also very conspicuous. Nikki peered at her. "Where did you two go?" She looked around. "And what happened to

Stephen? Did you murder him behind the gym? Because we're going to have to hide the body. You can't just leave it there."

"He left," Rosemary said simply. "He had to go."

"That only answers one of my questions," Nikki observed. "And really only halfway. Where did he go? To heaven or to hell?"

"He apologized for his friend."

"His girlfriend, you mean."

"No, not his girlfriend. Just a house-guest."

Nikki snorted. *"Legs* there was not just a house-guest. Don't let him sell you a story like that."

"She was," Rosemary insisted. "He told me there was nothing going on. She just needed a weekend out of the city, so she stayed with him."

"Of course! And why would he lie to you about that?" Nikki asked sarcastically, pushing back from the table. "Why would a man with money and a hot blonde at his side ever lie?"

Rosemary sighed. The gym felt unbearably close after the freshness of the spring day outside, and she felt lost and aimless without Stephen nearby. He'd gone back around the side of the gym, promising to take Sasha to lunch and then get her packed into her car and back to New York as soon as possible, while Rosemary had come in the back door.

"Dinner tomorrow night," he'd insisted before they parted. "I know you have the horses to take care of, but we're going out, so feed them early. Do you need me to come help? I'll come help. This can't wait. Not another day."

What could she say? She didn't want to wait another day, either. She didn't want to wait another *minute*. Stephen was in her blood, and every inch of her was given over to craving him, longing for him. It was all she could do not to run out the front door of the gym and seek him out, if only to watch him drive away, see the tail-lights of his car disappearing.

Rosemary realized if she didn't force herself to actually *do* something, she was going to go out of her mind. Maybe not literally, but it certainly felt that way. She had butterflies in her stomach, her hands were shaking, and she couldn't seem to focus her eyes on a single thing for more than a second. She had to pull herself together, for the sake of the farm.

Luckily, she knew of something extremely sobering which would take all of the magic right out of her day. She stood up, shoving her hands into her pockets, and turned to Nikki. "Can you hold down the fort? I'm going to go talk to Caitlin."

Caitlin Tuttle was holding court—there was no other way to describe it—at a booth decorated as if they were at a professional trade fair, not a community fundraiser in a rural high school gym. She was a willowy, slim woman with a chic little pixie cut of golden hair and a small, generously made-up face. Rosemary felt the distinction between their appearances as she walked up; Caitlin had a stylishness which was closer to Sasha's New York aura than Rosemary's country get-up of jeans, polo shirt, and tousled, loose hair—and yet they were ex-classmates, who had grown up riding together.

They were the same age, from the same town, working in what was essentially the same industry, but they couldn't have looked more different.

In a word, Caitlin made Rosemary feel inferior.

As Rosemary crept up to her table, Caitlin looked up from her conversation with a well-heeled out-of-towner, draped in expensive fabric and gold jewelry, and widened her red lips into a broad smile. For her part, Rosemary stopped in her tracks, causing a minor back-up in the crowded aisle behind her.

"Come on, lady," a man muttered, pushing past her, and Rosemary was reminded city manners and country manners were two very different things. *What would Stephen be like in a crush,* she wondered whimsically, and then managed to get her mind back on the conversation at hand.

Caitlin had passed her prospective donor onto a teenage helper and was holding out her hands, fabulously tipped with a pink manicure which Rosemary couldn't imagine surviving a single day on a horse farm. "Come over here and talk to me, girl, it's been forever!" She enveloped Rosemary in a hug. "I can't believe it's you! How are you?"

"I'm just fine," Rosemary said, feeling slightly squeezed by the overly enthusiastic hug. This had to be for show, right? They'd never been close. Especially in that last year of high school, when Caitlin had finally failed to qualify for the state fair's horse show, after five years of squeezing her way into the competition despite questionable equitation, her way paved by a serious of heroically well-behaved horses provided by her disappointed mother. Rosemary had shown and placed third overall; Nikki had quit competing by then, but had attended as her faithful groom and best friend, and Caitlin had sulked at home while her mother coached the team her daughter hadn't made. "It's crazy to see you here! Everyone is talking about your program."

"Oh, it's amazing. It's so popular. I haven't even gotten away for *lunch*. Do you want to grab something? Now that I've got Nadine engaging with everyone I think I can sneak away for a few minutes."

"Sure," Rosemary agreed, thinking it would be easier to talk to Caitlin outside of this warm, crowded place. She was reaching that exhausted point in the day where she could barely think straight, and she wanted to be attentive while she got Caitlin to explain just what she was doing with her mother's old farm.

They pushed outdoors, leaving the hapless Nadine to deal with the hordes of suburban and city moms who wanted to talk about ponies for their precious children, and Rosemary breathed in the spring's fresh air for the second time that hour. "God, it's so nice out," she sighed. "I wish we held this thing outside."

"Can you imagine? But if it rained, that would be terrible." Caitlin dragged her towards the baked potato cart. "I am craving one of those kitchen sink potatoes. Do you remember getting them at the fairgrounds every fall?"

Rosemary did remember—and everything else Caitlin chattered about as they queued for potatoes and then took their paper plates, heavy with potato and cheese and vegetables and bacon, to a free picnic table at the edge of the soccer field. The green grass stretched away to a hedge dividing the school from a corn-field. Rosemary remembered sitting out here at lunch on school days, listening as Nikki lorded over the members of their little group. *Nikki's* little group, to be precise; Rosemary's membership in everything was preceded by Nikki's bold leadership. She wished Nikki could be here now, to effortlessly turn the conversation from nostalgia to the present.

While Caitlin nattered on about the old days, Rosemary's eyes roamed around the food fair and the picnic tables. She spotted Aileen and Rodney in the distance, sitting side-by-side as they did because both had hearing loss. She saw a few old schoolmates milling about in the crowd, some paired up with strangers, some with high school sweethearts, towing around children. No surprises there. She ran into the same couples every year, watching their families get larger as fundraisers came and went.

Then, just as she started to lift a bite of potato to her mouth, she saw Stephen. She froze, her gaze locked onto him, her fork hovering in midair.

He was leaning over a table a few dozen feet away—one of the temporary ones brought in for the fundraiser, not one of the old metal tables where Rosemary had sat as a teenager. For some reason that seemed to make a difference, as if yes, he'd brought that hard-edged woman back to her old school and it was awful, but at least he hadn't sat her down in Rosemary's old spot. Sasha didn't belong here; the least she could do was know her place.

But what were they doing now? She'd thought he was leaving right after they'd talked, but Sasha looked content enough, waving a fork at him and laughing. Rosemary felt jealousy well up inside, even though Stephen had assured her there was nothing going on between them. Well, that was reasonable, though, wasn't it? You couldn't just look at the man you were obsessed with and not mind watching him smile down at another woman!

"Rosemary?"

Caitlin was looking at her inquiringly.

"Hmm, what's that? I'm sorry, Caitlin, I didn't hear you."

"I asked what your rescue is up to?"

"Oh." Rosemary tried to tear her gaze away from Stephen. She smiled weakly at Caitlin. At least their conversation was on the right track now.—*if* she could focus on it. Damn Stephen! "I'm all full, now. I have eight horses and that's as many as my barn can hold."

"Right," Caitlin said, "but what are you going to do with them?"

"Nothing. It's a sanctuary." *It's in the name.* "They've all come from abusive situations. Now they can live at peace."

Caitlin poked her fork into her potato and twirled it around. "That's very admirable," she said, but Rosemary didn't think she meant it at all.

"They're not suitable for therapeutic riding, if that's what you mean. You need bomb-proof, sane horses for that; not horses who have been through the wringer and come out damaged on the other side."

Caitlin offered Rosemary an apologetic smile. "I don't think anything's wrong with what you're doing. Don't get the wrong idea. You're absolutely right about therapeutic riding, and I happen to have a lot of good, bomb-proof ponies." Caitlin shrugged, looking unhappy for the first time. Her discontented expression was one Rosemary remembered well. "And yes, the publicity I get here brings in new students, so one program helps the other and vice versa. The model is working for me. It's not for everyone."

"I don't know how to make people believe that," Rosemary said, feeling defeated. "I've been taking criticism all day. People want to know how my horses are giving back. They don't want to hear: *well, they aren't.*"

"Well, if you don't mind my saying so . . . horses *do* have a lot to offer. Even beyond riding them or whatever. There might be something your horses can do that resonates with people. It's competitive out there, looking for donation dollars. But I don't think we're competing against one another. We're doing different things. What you have to do is find out what compels people to give. If simply feeding a horse isn't enough, I mean."

"I don't know what that would be," Rosemary admitted. She felt like banging her head against the table, but that probably wouldn't help. "What the horses could offer, I mean. Everyone wants to ride. No one wants to show up and pet them, or learn to clean stalls. Riding is the big pay-off for most people."

Caitlin shrugged. "It takes time to evaluate your operation and find a new direction. I didn't just look at my business and decide to change it to non-profit overnight. It took me a long time to get here. But I'll help you. I'd like to help you figure it out." She gave Rosemary a bright smile. "We can do this!"

Rosemary smiled back, nodding appreciatively, then dug into her potato, suddenly aware of how hungry she was. Just eating apple pie probably hadn't been the most sound decision she'd made on this stressful day.

Still, things were looking up a bit, and that knowledge made her baked potato even more enjoyable. Caitlin wasn't as awful as she remembered, and Stephen wanted to take her to dinner, so even if they didn't make their hay fund today, maybe that wasn't the end of the world.

As they took their trash to the nearest bin, Rosemary glanced back to the table where Stephen had been leaning over Sasha. They were gone, replaced with some other couple she didn't know. She felt a stab of longing, and for a moment she stood still, looking around the grounds, hoping to spot him before he left.

"Rosemary?" Caitlin was watching her, a puzzled look on her face. "Are you okay?"

"Fine," Rosemary replied, shaking it off. She'd see him tomorrow. Sasha would go back to New York. They could move ahead with . . . whatever this was. "I'm fine, Caitlin. This has been nice. Thanks for your advice."

"Oh, any time, Rosemary! Seriously. Any time."

They went back into the crowded gym together.

Chapter Twenty

Stephen

Stephen was sweating.

He'd been sitting in the car for half an hour, long past when he'd planned to leave. Rosemary wouldn't wonder where he was, not yet. He'd come out to the car planning to leave early, and he'd expected to drive slowly, maybe turn a few circles down winding country roads, in an attempt to quiet his nerves. Instead, he'd just sat, his hands on the wheel, waiting for the right moment to turn on the car and strike off into the darkening evening.

What was stopping him from pressing the start button, putting the car in reverse, and heading off down the driveway? Was it the way Sasha had sneered at him the day before, as she threw her suitcase into her rental car? Once she'd sobered up and realized he really was sending her on her way without the afternoon delights she'd been counting on, things had turned ugly. Sasha had railed at him for a solid hour after she realized he really did want her to head back to the city without him, and without exercising their old benefits.

He had to admit she had a point in one thing: Sasha was not a woman who men turned down. In doing so, especially after their long friendship, he'd insulted her to her very core. Her rage hadn't been about wanting his body. It had been about his behavior, and how it made her feel. He had no vain illusions on that point.

But Sasha wasn't the woman he wanted, and *that* point was where their differences became irrevocable.

"You're turning into a boring country boy," she'd finally spat at him. "And no one in the city is going to wait around for you. If you want a chance at a new job and your old life back, you better get over this girl really quick."

"Therein lies our problem," Stephen now said to his steering wheel. "Rosemary belongs here."

If he wanted anything real with Rosemary—and at this point, Stephen couldn't even lie to himself anymore, this was not an idle attraction—then he was going to have to stay in Catoctin Creek . . . indefinitely.

And that had never been the plan.

The sun had vanished behind Notch Gap by now, and even by Catoctin Creek's high standards, Stephen had to admit tonight's sunset had been a stunner. There were still wisps of bubblegum-pink cloud glowing against the cerulean blue sky, even as the first vibrant twinkles of Venus began to glow above the mountains. He decided to pretend to himself that he'd just been watching the sunset, not dealing with nerves. He'd pretend that to Rosemary, too, if she asked.

The clock turned over another minute, and he couldn't wait anymore. *Time to go.*

His house's steep driveway was a dark tunnel of newly-leafed trees; it seemed to exist in another time zone where full night had already fallen. As he cautiously drove around the little bends in the drive his father had designed himself, Stephen had to slow for a little herd of white-tail deer which stepped daintily out of the forest and into his path. Their hooves were tiny on the blacktop, their ears and eyes huge as they turned to face the car before they continued, without alarm, back into the greenery along the driveway.

He shook his head; someone had warned him that dusk was the most dangerous time to drive out here. Who had that been? Rodney? It must have been; who else would know? Canny Rodney, with his Union officer dummy and his high-tech security cameras, catching Stephen red-handed while he made a fool of himself in the old man's house. Imagine if Rosemary had been the Kelbaughs' daughter! Rodney probably would have flown back from Florida early just to have the pleasure of shooting him, possibly with Colonel John's own gun.

Maybe Aileen would have stopped him, though. Aileen seemed to be on his side. Why else would she have told him he should have kissed Rosemary, that he shouldn't let her run the show?

The miles slipped past in a matter of minutes, but by the time his car pulled up in front of the Notch Gap farmhouse, inky darkness had fallen over the land. Stephen got out of the car slowly, and blinked as the porch light flipped on. Rosemary was in the doorway, a silhouette against the hall light.

"You're running late," she observed. Her breath made a fog in the chilly evening air.

"I was watching the sunset," he lied.

"Oh!" By now he was close enough to see her smile. "It was a good one."

She asked if he needed to come inside, which he supposed was code for using the restroom, and when he demurred, she stepped past him and closed the door behind her, giving it a good tug. "These damp nights make it stick," she explained. "My father used to fix it every spring, but now it's been a few years. I guess I need to hire a handyman."

Stephen wondered, not for the first time, just what had happened to her parents. He couldn't see any way to ask, though. "I'm not much good with my hands, or I'd offer," he said, because he figured any country woman would expect a man to be ready at the drop of a hat to fix a front door or nail up a board or mend a broken toilet. He didn't have any of those skills. He just knew how to dial the super. Would Rosemary think that was weak of him?

Stephen felt a fresh dampness spring up across his chest, and he shrugged out of his coat once he'd helped Rosemary into the passenger seat. Too country for the city and too city for the country; what was Stephen going to be good for in a few months? The *suburbs?*

He barely managed to suppress a shudder as he slid into the driver's seat.

Stephen had picked out a restaurant in the nearby hamlet of Eckerly Springs, an ungainly name for a pretty town with a thriving antiques market, the proceeds of which evidently kept the streets clean and the cast-iron street-lamps hung with baskets of geraniums. There was still foot traffic on the sidewalks, the last hold-outs of the weekend day-trippers, and the town had a pleasant, low buzz. People, but not too many of them. It was a change, anyway.

"Where are we going?" Rosemary asked, gazing out of the window as they entered the town. "I expected to go into Frederick."

"I thought this might be more your vibe," Stephen explained, guiding the car into a parking spot along Water Street. "There's a special restaurant here. The Waterwheel? Have you ever heard of it?"

"Of course I've *heard* of it," Rosemary answered with a little laugh. "Everyone's heard of it. But it's very fancy—the chef came here from Alexandria, I think? He's been in magazines, he's cooked for the President . . . " Her voice trailed off and she looked at Stephen in wonder. "Wait . . . seriously?"

"Tonight, he's going to cook for you." Stephen had been almost indecently happy to find out that Chef William Woodbury was from rural Frederick County and had returned to his hometown to open a boutique farm-to-table restaurant a few years ago. Even better, an old friend from the city was one of Chef William's financial backers, and was only too happy to hustle a last-minute table for Stephen and his date.

Rosemary was clearly startled by his restaurant choice, and the surprised look didn't leave her face as he led her down the sidewalk, past antiques shop after antiques shop, to the old stone mill standing above the river. He could hear the water rushing past in the darkness as they went down a few wooden steps and entered the restaurant's dim foyer. A shadowy figure in a white shirt and black trousers looked up from a rustic wooden desk. "Mr. Beckett?"

"That's right," Stephen replied. "Table for two."

"It will be just a few moments—would you care to wait at the bar?"

"That'll be fine." Stephen thought they could use a nice lubricating drink to get things started, anyway. The host led them along a passage which opened into a snug bar area, complete with a scattering of low chairs and coffee tables. A few other couples looked up from their cocktails briefly, then went back to their drinks and conversation.

Stephen turned to Rosemary, who was looking around the lamp-lit room with a rather peculiar expression. "Would you prefer a table or the bar?" he asked softly. Above his words, he could hear the low notes of a piano being played in another room.

"Whichever is fine," she murmured. Suddenly she smiled at him, her eyes twinkling with mirth. "You're such a bastard," she teased. "You know I've never been anywhere like this."

"No!" Stephen pulled out a bar-stool and took her purse, hanging it from the hook underneath the sloping wood of the bar. "How would I know that? This is when we're supposed to get to know each other properly, so I can avoid mistakes like this in the future."

"So you're saying now that you know the nicest place I usually eat is the Old Route 40 Steakhouse, you'll only take me to places like that?" Rosemary shook her head, but she was still smiling mischievously. Stephen felt an overwhelming urge to kiss that naughty grin off her face.

"I was going to take you to the Blue Plate," he said instead, "but I was afraid Nikki would invite herself to our table and eat with us."

"She'd never dare—she doesn't take a lunch break." Rosemary laughed. "But now you're responsible for me, because I don't go to bars anymore than I go to black-tie restaurants for well-heeled Beltway types, so what on earth am I going to order?"

Stephen noticed the bartender, very natty and *Newsies* in suspenders and arm braces, looking their way. "Let me see . . . simple or complicated?" He picked up the paper menu. "Any one of these should be sweet enough for you."

"What makes you think I like sweet?" Rosemary snatched the menu from him. "I could like something challenging . . . or spicy . . . are those drink things?"

He shook his head at her. "You were eating an apple pie for lunch the last time I saw you."

"Anyone would. Aileen's pies could be used as currency." She put down the menu between them and pointed at a cocktail. "Would I like *that?*"

Stephen scanned the ingredients. "Do you like licorice?"

"Oh, God, no."

"Then no. Do you like . . . strawberries?"

"I love them."

"This one, then."

Rosemary studied his choice, and nodded. "I'll go with that."

"May I order for you?"

"You may," she said, gifting him with another smile. "And thank you for asking."

The bartender busied himself with their drinks, which proved to be very complicated compositions, and Stephen allowed himself some time to gaze at Rosemary. She was looking very different than her usual self tonight—still utterly lovely, but more refined, more elegant. It took him a few minutes to realize she'd straightened the waves in her hair and added tiny wings of eyeliner around her eyes. He was touched to think she'd gone to such trouble to play a sophisticate for him, but surely she knew none of it mattered? He was smitten with the Rosemary he'd tumbled into the hay and kissed while her face was still smudged from barn chores and scraped from falling off a horse. She didn't have to try and imitate anyone to impress him.

It was a real shame he couldn't share any of that mental speech with her, he thought regretfully, but Stephen had learned from hard experience that women did not like to be told their efforts with make-up and hairstyles were completely unnecessary. He tried to play around the edges, instead. "Your hair looks very striking tonight," he attempted. "Very smooth and—er—sleek." Had he just described a well-groomed dog? That might have been a mistake.

Rosemary was resting her chin on her hand, watching the bartender with absorption, but now she slid her gaze over to him, and her lips curved upwards. "That's nice of you," she replied. "I'm glad I treated this like a special occasion, or I would have felt a little too hick for this place."

"You're not a hick," Stephen insisted. "I looked your shoes over before you got into my car and there wasn't one fleck of manure to be seen."

"I guess I clean up good." She straightened up, placing her hand flat on the bar between them. "It's nice to know."

Stephen put his hand over top of hers. Her skin was warm and smooth, and touching her gave him a pleasant tingle, as if he'd already taken a sip from the drink the bartender was now theatrically pouring into coupe glasses. "You really do," he assured her. "But you're pretty nice dirty, too."

He heard what he said as soon as the words left his mouth, but luckily, Rosemary burst into surprised laughter. They were both trying to choke back general hysteria as their drinks were slipped in front of them. "Enjoy," the bartender said, winking at him.

As if he could help it!

"Take a sip," he urged Rosemary as she leaned back, carefully wiping at her eyes. "Let's see how your first fancy cocktail goes down."

She lifted the coupe and sniffed the drink cautiously. "It smells like sugar," she reported. "And alcohol."

"That sounds ideal."

She took a small sip and her eyes widened. "Oh, that burns," she said after a careful swallow. She considered it for a moment. "But it's very nice."

Stephen took a sip of his Manhattan. "Very nice," he agreed. "Do you really not drink at all?"

"Oh you know, wine sometimes, beer sometimes. But I've never really drank, what would you call this . . . hard liquor? Nothing against it, I just don't go to places where you'd order a cocktail before a meal."

Stephen decided to clear up something which was perplexing him. "Now, Catoctin Creek feels isolated, but you're thirty minutes from a very cosmopolitan little city, and another hour from the capital of the United States of America. Why is it you describe your life as if you live in the middle of the prairie?"

Rosemary pursed her lips, considering. "I guess it's because of the farm, mostly. The horses eat dinner every night at five thirty or six. I keep their routine the same to keep them healthy, because they couldn't deal with any added anxiety in their lives . . . not after what they've been through. So that keeps me a homebody. That and . . . " she paused, and took a sip of her drink, a little more boldly this time. "Well, never mind that."

"What?" Stephen prodded. "There's more than just the horses?"

"Well, sure there is," Rosemary sighed, looking into her glass. "I have anxiety. You know that. I get panicky around lots of people. And local people ask questions I don't want to answer. So . . . I stay home. It's easier."

"Why did you come out with me tonight, then?" Stephen was genuinely curious. "You could have told me no, or that you preferred to eat at home. I could have defrosted a nice lasagna for us."

She gave him a sidelong glance. "You joke, but I'd enjoy that, actually. Not that this isn't lovely, of course! But this place is really quiet, and uncrowded, and it's dark, which are all really helpful for me."

"I'll make a note of that. Dark places, quiet, no one around. All of our dates will take place in back alleys or fine dining establishments, sound good?"

"Sounds perfect." Rosemary took a still more adventurous sip of her drink. "It's nice to be out, really. When I don't feel like everyone's staring at me, I can enjoy myself. Honestly, maybe I should be going to darker restaurants."

Everyone *should* be staring at her, Stephen thought. She was utterly gorgeous, and with that strawberry-garnished coupe in her slender fingers, she looked like a Hollywood starlet from a distant, more glamorous era. He found it fascinating, and delightful, that

Rosemary had these two sides, and apparently all it took was a little work with a flat-iron and some eyeliner to bring out her natural elegance. Stephen felt keenly average next to her; he knew he was a good-looking guy, but he was neither an elegant man who looked at home in a tuxedo nor a wholesome homesteader who could model flannel and denim in his spare time. He wore well-tailored clothes because he could afford to and that was what the people he associated with did, but he never pulled them off the way Rosemary was pulling off this simple black dress tonight.

"I'll find more quiet spots for us," he promised, closing his fingers atop hers, and he was just thinking about leaning in a little closer when the host appeared and offered to take them to their table.

Chapter Twenty-One

Rosemary

The table they were given was small, and pressed close to a large glass window which probably offered a romantic view of the river at sunset in summertime. In the early darkness of March, it was just a large mirror, reflecting two youngish people on a first date, wearing their nicest clothes—Rosemary was, anyway; who knew what Stephen had in his closet?—and hoping they weren't trying too hard. Again, Rosemary knew how *she* felt; it was entirely possible the man sitting across from her was utterly at ease.

Rosemary hadn't been on many dates, but she'd done a little bit in her time and she was struck now by the extraordinary awkwardness of two people who already knew something of the worst of each other, and something of the best of each other, trying to figure out what small talk was left to them now. What did they have in common? Well, they'd shared several extremely intoxicating kisses. On the other hand, Rosemary had caught him breaking into her neighbors' house, running around with an ex-lover, and trying to turn her rural neighborhood into a housing development. None of these were great places to begin the conversation.

Luckily, there was bread on the table. Rosemary felt she could have lived on bread, so this was a problem-solver: fill one's mouth with bread and avoid having to talk. She peeled the crusts from soft slices of baguette and dipped them gingerly into the olive oil on the little plate set before her by a waiter of venerable age, a man who wore his black and white ensemble like an army uniform.

Stephen was keen to jump on her olive oil consumption, just as he had asked her about her drinking. It was as if, she thought wryly, he couldn't think of anything to ask about so he just decided to tease her about being a country bumpkin.

"Of course I know about dipping bread in olive oil, Stephen. They do it at Romano's Macaroni Grill," she added with heavy sarcasm. "There's one by the mall in Frederick."

Stephen's eyebrows went up and she lightly slapped his hand. "Enough of those questions! I have the internet and I know how to cook. They put olive oil on bread outside of cities now. We were allowed to branch out from margarine several years ago. Tell *me* something, Stephen, how are you surviving out here without being able to order in food or run down to your closest pizza place?"

Stephen shrugged and laughed. "Not well. I really should get better at cooking. Right now everything I eat is from a box or the freezer."

"Oh, come on. You can read, right?"

"I—of course I can read?" He looked baffled.

"Then you can cook! You just follow the instructions. Google a recipe and make it happen."

"It's that simple, is it?"

"It's that simple." Rosemary dipped another piece of bread. "I do it all the time. You probably think my head is full of recipes like Ma's Favorite Sunday Chicken or something, but that's not the case at all. I'm just excellent at following numbered steps and clearly written instructions."

"But Ma's Favorite Sunday Chicken sounds amazing. Could we have that sometime?"

Rosemary flicked her gaze up at him. Through her eyelashes, which she'd unnaturally elongated with the bottle of high-school-era mascara she'd unearthed in her medicine cabinet and felt very uncomfortable about, she could see him grinning at her. "I'll make you Ma's Favorite Sunday Chicken when you *deserve* it," she told him.

Stephen leaned forward. "So it really exists?"

"A variation on that, yes." Rosemary's mother *had* had a Sunday chicken recipe, for a roast chicken surrounded by carrots and new potatoes, the skin browned with butter, herbs from the garden stuffed rather profanely into the chicken's emptied insides. It had been one of Rosemary's favorite meals as a child, but she hadn't looked at the recipe in years. In fact, she'd only made it herself on one occasion.

Rosemary blinked hard, her vision of Stephen blurring. She leaned down to fiddle with her handbag, hoping she could stop the tears before he noticed something was wrong. It wasn't Stephen's fault—she'd said the Sunday chicken line as a joke, but she'd been thinking of some country restaurant advertisement when she'd brought it up. It wasn't until the words had left her mouth that she'd made the connection with the Sunday meals she'd once shared with her family.

"Rosemary?"

Damn. "Just looking for something," she croaked. "Chapstick."

"Is that all? Are you all right?"

His voice was so concerned. Damn him, that just made things worse. She squeezed her eyes tight and prayed that eyeliner did not become less waterproof with age. It had been sitting unused in her bathroom for such a very long time.

A few moments of silence spread across the table, which Rosemary used to take some deep breaths and think of happy things: galloping Rochester across the summer pasture, feeling the cold nip of Catoctin Creek around her ankles as she went wading, the sight of a dramatic white egret fishing in Long Pond. Some years back, a counselor had suggested she try this simple tool, and of everything she had learned about controlling grief, this had proven to be the most useful for her. Rosemary visualized her happy places, and the happiness flooded over into her reality. If it wasn't enough to make her smile, it was at least enough to stop the tears.

"Must have forgotten it," she announced, swinging upright again.

Stephen was looking at her with concern. "Did I say something?"

She sighed. He was handsome and kind. Why did he have to be perceptive, too? "No . . . it's nothing. I'm fine, I promise."

"You ducked under the table for a solid three minutes."

"I had my reasons." Rosemary tried to smile but ended up doing something which felt uncomfortably like a smirk. She flattened her expression again to get rid of it. "You did nothing wrong. I just . . . had a moment."

She tried to play it off, but Stephen was convinced there was an issue, and she could feel his concerned glances as the rigidly elegant server somberly set their dishes before them, offered them crushed pepper, and then made his stately way back through the lantern-lit dining room. It was a large, high-ceilinged space, with heavy beams overhead and reclaimed wooden floors beneath their feet, but the quaint lighting and the spaces between the tables made their table uncannily intimate. Sitting so closely together within their own little pool of flickering light, Rosemary knew she couldn't hide from Stephen. The darkness had drawn them together.

"It was the chicken," she sighed, just as he put the first bite (of duck, locally-raised) into his mouth. She saw his lips close around his fork and stop cold, as if he'd been startled into stillness. She regretted her timing, but plowed ahead—it was now or never. "My mother's roast chicken was our Sunday dinner. I made it on . . . the last Sunday we were together. The next morning . . . " She took a deep breath, letting Stephen put his fork by his plate.

His hand came across the table to rest on hers. For the second time that night, she felt a leap of affection accompanied with a twist of longing she couldn't quite explain. "There was an ice storm the night before, but my father needed to get to the feed store. My mother didn't trust his driving on the slick roads, so she went along to help him spot slippery patches, but it wasn't the ice . . . it was a big delivery van. It pushed their truck off the road." Her words came in a rush now. "The hillside was so steep, almost like a cliff dropping off. It couldn't have happened in a worse spot, but it was quick. I think. They *said* it was."

The worst out, Rosemary took a breath and bowed her head. All she could feel was Stephen's hand on hers, squeezing and squeezing with all of his might. She thought she'd be content if he never let go.

The rest of the dinner was quieter than she had hoped, but theirs was a silence she felt comfortable with. Rosemary understood long stretches which passed without talking, and the significance of certain glances, tilts of the head, slow nods. By the time dessert had arrived, a understated confection which seemed to start as simple baked apples and melted into a spiced enigma on the tongue, she found she was smiling freely, and when Stephen felt brave enough to make a joke, she laughed without the faintest need to force it.

The truth was, she'd never spoken to anyone besides the Kelbaughs, Nikki, and that kind counselor about losing her parents. She'd thought it would be too awful to share with anyone else. But having told Stephen, she felt a closeness with him which transcended her old sorrow. He knew her now. He'd known part of her before: the bold side, the young woman who ran a farm on her own and rescued huge horses from bad ends, but now he'd seen her vulnerable side as well—and she was glad of it. She felt like she had someone else on her team now, and she was going to need new team members, what with Aileen and Rodney so eager to escape before the next winter, they'd practically moved out already.

"I've truly never had a dinner like this in my life," she told him as they scraped up the last luscious bits of pastry. "I'm afraid you've spoiled me on the first date . . . now I will be impossible to please."

"That's too bad, because on the next date we are definitely going to Route 40 Steakhouse," Stephen joked. "And you're having ice water to drink."

"Actually, I do feel a little parched from all of this alcohol," Rosemary mused, looking at her empty wine glass with a little regret. She'd gone from whatever had been in that cocktail—gin, plus some other things she hadn't recognized—straight into half a bottle of red wine, and now her mouth was dry and her eyelids were heavy. She thought she might fall asleep on the car ride home.

"Coffees," Stephen told the stern server, who had just arrived with an expectant look. "Please and thank you."

"Coffee at eight o'clock! I'll be up all night. Then I'll sleep through my alarm tomorrow morning. The horses will tear down the barn."

"I think you won't," Stephen promised, his eyebrows gesturing towards the empty wine bottle. "I'm just sobering you up enough to get you home and into your bed."

"Bed, hmm?" Rosemary waggled her own eyebrows back at him, feeling very daring. "Going to put me to bed?"

"And pull the covers up to your chin," he said. "And turn out the light and close the door before you start snoring and the magic is gone."

"What! I don't snore." Rosemary was offended.

"Wine makes snorers out of the best of us," Stephen informed her gravely.

She sighed. She supposed it might be true. Stephen would have more experience with that; Rosemary hadn't shared her bed with anyone in a good five years. Half a decade! That was really something. That was too long. "Are you sure you don't want to risk it?" she asked him, leering.

Stephen just laughed and shook his head. "Rosemary, tonight was a night to talk and get to know each other better. There's plenty I want to risk with you," he added, lowering his voice, "but I'm not going to try anything tonight."

She closed her eyes and felt a wave of sleepiness wash over her. He was probably right about that, but Rosemary couldn't help but feel a little disappointed. They'd already covered the issues of mutual attraction, already had a first kiss, already felt the charging rush when their bodies were pressed close. Damn all of that wine! She opened her eyes again, gazing at Stephen with a sudden revelation. "You got me drunk so you wouldn't have to sleep with me," she accused.

Stephen nearly yelped with laughter. "That's it," he agreed, his face crumpled with mirth. "We do things opposite in the big city."

"Your coffees," the server announced, placing the cups in front of them and eyeing the both of them with distaste. Clearly this level of hilarity was not countenanced in his section. "And . . . the check?"

Rosemary detected his hopeful tone and just started laughing harder. She now felt as devoted to laughter as she had felt to sleep just a few moments before. Her moods were shifting very rapidly, but she rather liked it.

"Yes," Stephen chortled, his hand covering his mouth. "The check, please."

Chapter Twenty-Two

Stephen

He thought he'd had her all figured out, but Rosemary surprised him by sobering up on the drive home. His little country mouse certainly had supernatural powers of recovery, he thought with amusement and a little wonder, watching her perk up as the car drew closer to the farm. By the time they'd turned up the driveway, she was talking animatedly about the stars, pointing out constellations he pretended to see as well as she seemed to.

"Of course, the Pleiades are my favorite," she told him as he parked the car in front of her house. "Let me turn off the porch light and I'll show them to you. The glare would hide them."

Stephen watched her run up the steps and unlock the front door. She reached inside and turned out the light, and he drew in his breath sharply at the sudden darkness. It was as if someone had dropped a bag over his head.

"You can't look directly at them," she said, coming back to him —he felt her presence near him more than he saw her. "You have to look *next* to them. You have to see them out of the corner of your eye."

"And why are they your favorite?" Stephen asked. That seemed like a lot of work for a sky full of stars—he thought one of the brighter ones might make a better favorite. Like that big, pulsing star to the south—was it orange, was it yellow, was it white? It seemed to be a different color every moment. He wondered what its name was, what stories it represented, who was looking up at it, full of adoration, right now. Bright and shiny, *that* was his kind of star.

"They were in one of the *Mary Poppins* books," Rosemary explained, her voice dreamy with memories. "The youngest of the Seven Sisters came down to earth . . . they're the Seven Sisters, in mythology. And she was a little girl in the book who came down to play with Mary Poppins and the children."

Stephen tried to remember any star-children in the Disney movie but could not. "I never read the books," he admitted. "I'm not sure I realized there *was* a book."

"Books. There were . . . four, five? They're so good. I read them over and over when I was little. Now do you see them?"

Stephen thought he saw a pale gray patch of sky which teased his vision. He turned his gaze slightly, and they appeared in his peripheral vision: a little clutch of stars gleaming merrily. When he tried to look directly at them again, they vanished.

He imagined a group of mischievous children, peeking out at him and darting back into hiding every time he looked their way, and Rosemary's story made sense. The Seven Sisters, huh. Funny how ancient stories tended to get things right. "I saw them," he said. "Just for a second. They're tricky, aren't they?"

"They *are*," Rosemary agreed. "I used to lay in the grass on summer nights and try to look straight at them. I pretended if I could see them properly, I could tell them to come down and play with me." She laughed, still looking up. "I must have been a really gullible child. I tried all sorts of things I read in books. Trying to get through wardrobes, wishing paintings would come to life, all those storybook tricks."

Stephen gazed at her, the white outline of her profile in the starlight, which seemed to grow brighter all the time. She'd been a lonely child, no doubt about that, even with a friend like Nikki and plenty of ponies to console her. Lonely and full of imagination, full of dreams. Stephen's own childhood had sometimes felt positively crowded; living with his parents in their tiny two-bedroom apartment, family on every block in the neighborhood, the neighborhood school spilling over with local friendships and enmities. The sheer density of his life couldn't be matched out here in a far-flung country district where yellow school buses covered huge territories every day. He hadn't read much, he supposed, but he hadn't *needed* to; he hadn't needed a dream world when the real one was so full he could hardly keep up. He wondered what other fantasies she'd dreamed up for herself, what dreams she still indulged in, with her face turned up to the stars.

He wondered if he was in any of them.

Then, Stephen had to wonder why he would ask himself such a question and then he knew, with the kind of full-body shock of realization which only comes to a person a few times in their life. At the most important moments, when the truth comes rushing in like a rogue wave, and the whole world tilts for one crazy, exhilarating, terrifying moment.

He took a step closer to her warmth and he felt Rosemary turned to look at him. He saw her eyes shimmer in the starlight, her gaze questioning. Without hesitation, Stephen leaned down and kissed her, his hands sweeping beneath her hair and meeting at the nape of her neck, her soft, lovely, swan-like neck, and she pressed close to him, their bodies melding together, and he knew, and he wasn't afraid.

"Rosemary," he whispered, savoring the old-fashioned flavor of her name. "I was supposed to go home."

"But you're not going to go." Her voice was confident.

"I'm not going to go."

"But, Rosemary?"

"Yes?"

"Can we go inside? Aren't you *cold?*"

She laughed, that delightful burble of sound which had first hooked him on the night they'd met, an expression of perfect happiness, and he had to kiss her again, immediately, his fingers twining in her hair. But then he stepped back, and let her take him by the hand, leading him up the steps of the old farmhouse.

Chapter Twenty-Three

Rosemary

They kissed on the porch steps and they kissed in the front hall, as they fumbled with their shoes and tossed their coats on the shining old floorboards.

They kissed as they climbed to the second floor, and they kissed in the doorway of Rosemary's bedroom. They kissed as they unbuttoned one another's shirts, and they kissed as they unzipped pants and dresses and let their clothes fall to the soft rug in front of Rosemary's bed.

Rosemary's lips already felt rather sore by the time she'd pulled away, just long enough to pull the shades down over her window and flip the duvet back on her bed. She touched her face while her back was still to Stephen, feeling her lips' swollen curves and wondering if they'd look plump and full in the mirror. She supposed they must have looked alluring enough to Stephen, because when she turned back around, he was completely unclothed and coming right for her.

"Oh!" she cried, laughing as she fell back against the bed. It was still made up with her thickest flannel sheets, warding away the unpredictable chill of these early spring nights, and the homely fabric was soft and comforting against her bare back. Rosemary always slept in pajamas, and the sensation was new and pleasant. She almost had a moment to contemplate it before Stephen's lips were on her bare breasts, and then she had a whole other cycle of sensations to think over.

His hands and lips were everywhere, moving over her body like a man possessed, and Rosemary wasn't sure how to keep up with him—she could barely keep up with her own thoughts. One moment he was running his lips up her ribcage, raising goosebumps across her arms and chest; the next he was burrowing close to her pelvis, his fingers playing with her nipples while his tongue did a little tour of investigation elsewhere. She gasped and she sobbed and she laughed, one reaction right after another, and occasionally he gave her a devilish grin right before he made a dive for her lips again, pulling her into a rapturously deep kiss.

But when he finally went for the main objective, brushing himself against her, Rosemary knew exactly where her mind should be. "Stephen," she said softly, "do you have . . . you know?"

He looked down at her with a wry grin. "Good God, Rosemary," he replied. "I certainly hope so."

He was off the bed in a flash, and she watched his white bottom go high in the air as he bent over his slacks and wiggled his wallet free. *How crass,* she thought with amusement, as he pulled out a foil square and waved it at her. *What a player.*

"Well done," she said aloud. "What a good planner you are."

Stephen raised his eyebrows at her as he tore the foil neatly. "I bet you thought city boys couldn't be Boy Scouts."

"Could they? Are there Boy Scouts in the city?"

"Maybe," Stephen said. "I dunno. I never was one. But I am always prepared." He was back on the bed, his hands sliding up to her breasts once again, and she sighed, struck speechless.

Rosemary shifted her pelvis with what she thought was a neat little trick of movement, pleased a lifetime of horseback riding had taught her plenty about controlling her hips and tailbone, and Stephen certainly did look impressed.

I've got that going for me, she thought, right before she stopped thinking altogether.

Chapter Twenty-Four

Stephen

When they were still again, when she was asleep, her hair spilling over the lavender pillowcase, her full lips parted gently, Stephen found himself wakeful. He was like this in new beds and strange surroundings: he didn't sleep well in hotels, he never closed his eyes on red-eye flights. He had barely slept for his entire first week at the brick rancher on the hill, the house he now thought of, though still with gentle astonishment, as home.

So he didn't expect to get much sleep tonight, as relaxed as his body felt now, as spent and satisfied and deeply joyful as his mind was. There were questions to mull over, of course; he had plenty to think about while he lay here sleepless, listening to Rosemary's even breathing. The question of what he was going to do with this relationship, now that he'd gone and started things, now that he'd pushed the ball down the hill, now that it was rolling irretrievably into the murky distance.

He sat up a little, moving carefully in case she was a light sleeper —there was so much he didn't know about her, so many practical things they'd skimmed over in favor of deep, dark confessions about lonesomeness and loss, and he'd never done that before, never passed over the light-hearted and easy in favor of the heavy and hard, but she was different—*this* was different.

There was a shade over the window; he pulled it up and brushed his fingers across the curtains. They were thin and white, the sort which would ruffle in a cool spring breeze with cinematic good looks. Even in the darkness, they evoked visions of matching heartland home accessories: gingham table cloths and cooling pies on windowsills. He pulled them aside and peered through the wavy old glass of the four-paned window, eyes searching the night.

The trees were harder to see through now than they had been in January, when Rosemary had brought him up here to see the Kelbaughs' night-light, but a gust of wind and a tossing of leaves revealed it at last: the little golden star in the distance, as bright and constant as the Pleiades were dim and retreating. She said her favorite stars in the sky were those fickle Seven Sisters, who wanted to play hide-and-seek but always did the hiding, never the seeking. Yet her favorite star in the night was really that little yellow light in her elderly neighbors' kitchen.

He couldn't take that from her.

Stephen didn't know where things went from here—not with Rosemary, not with his plans, not even where he'd be in a few days, a few weeks, a few months. He had never been at such a loss. Even when his father had died and his boss had told him not to bother rushing back to Manhattan, to stay and grieve awhile because the company was closing down anyway, he'd been able to make a plan. Stay. Tidy up affairs. Look for an opportunity. Leap upon it. He'd managed all of that, but he hadn't counted on falling in love.

Chapter Twenty-Five

Rosemary

"So let me tell you something," Rosemary began. They were leaning against the fence of the north pasture, the spring breeze playing in their hair. Rosemary had left her hair down, thinking her waves looked particularly fetching after the night (and morning) they'd spent together, and the loose strands were tickling her cheeks and getting in her eyes . . . but she judged a little discomfort was worthwhile for bed-play beauty every once in a while. Judging by Stephen's *many* appreciative glances her way, she was quite correct in her assessment. She batted a curly lock out of her nose and smiled at him.

"Tell me something," Stephen encouraged her. "Anything. As long as it's not an idea like getting in the car and driving off to find breakfast, because I am never, ever leaving this perfect spot."

Rosemary looked around and felt a fresh surge of exhilaration. From this high patch of ground above the farmhouse, she could see over the trees to the rooftops of Catoctin Creek village in the distance, and the day around them could not have been more beautiful: blue sky, clear air, yellow sun, green-budding trees. The whole thing could have been a child's crayon drawing come to life. If only the sun had been wearing sunglasses and a smile. "I would never suggest leaving here," she said, and she wasn't joking.

"Okay then. What's your idea?"

"Well, it's sort of a long-term thing . . . not like a, what will we do with this gorgeous day kind of thing."

"That's good," Stephen said with a leer. "Because there's only one thing to do with this gorgeous day."

Rosemary laughed and leaned into him, her skin prickling delightfully. "No, this is *serious*. Listen to me. So at the fundraiser, there was that woman, Caitlin?"

"With the other farm."

"Right. I used to know her. Nikki and I both did—we took riding lessons from her mother."

"Small world."

"The smallest. *You* can see. It's all right here in front of us." Rosemary gestured at the farms and houses of the valley. Then she turned back towards the pasture and looked up the slope, where her little herd of misfit horses grazed at the new grass. "So anyway, I talked to her a little about her program, and why she was getting donations, and I was getting lectures."

"You were?" His astonishment was plain to see. "Who would lecture you?"

"Oh, it was awful. Basically everyone met her first, and by the time they got to me, they wanted to know why they should give me money for horses to just eat and get fat, when Caitlin's are giving back to society."

Stephen looked down at her, his brow furrowed. "Did you tell them all to go straight to hell?"

"No, I couldn't do that! I need their money, idiot."

"I would have told them to stick their money up their asses," he grumbled.

"That's why I run a charity, and you run investments," Rosemary reminded him. "You have to be nice to get donations. And make people feel like they're heard, and that you're taking them seriously."

"It sounds awful."

"It can be. But they're worth it." She nodded at her herd.

Stephen looked at the horses, then back down at Rosemary. "So what's the idea?"

"I want to get Caitlin's input on what I *could* do with these horses. To give back to the community." Rosemary took a breath —just saying the words out loud gave her a funny, trembly feeling. A change! She wasn't good at change; she'd been actively avoiding change for a long time. But with Stephen here, suddenly she was thinking there were some changes she could handle. "They're still not riding horses. But there's more to horses than riding them. I wish more people understood that."

"Maybe that's part of what you can teach the community. Is that the idea?"

"Maybe. If I can just figure out . . . oh, I don't know! It's a new idea. Not really hatched." She laughed. "I guess I was getting ahead of myself by telling you. Maybe I just wanted to say out loud that I was doing something."

"Hey." Stephen's voice was soft.

Rosemary looked up. His face was very close to hers, his eyes boring into hers. She felt her heart beat faster.

"I think it's a good start," Stephen said gently. "And I'm touched you would tell me about it. I think you're amazing. You're going to do great things."

"I am?" Her heart wrung in her chest; her voice was barely a whisper. "It's just a little farm."

"Amazing things," Stephen replied, his lips coming closer and closer.

Rosemary closed her eyes . . .

A rumble rose up from the ground, quickly growing nearer, like thunder in reverse. They both jumped. She knocked her forehead on his chin as he swung around, hands clutching her shoulders. "What the hell?"

Rosemary rubbed at her forehead. The horses were galloping in their direction, eyes wide and hooves flying, sending clods of turf into the air behind them. "Dummies!" she shouted. "Stop tearing up the new grass!"

The dummies ignored her, because they were horses and did what they wanted. She shook her head as they came up to the fence, plunging and snorting, wheeling and kicking at one another. Rochester shoved his way to the front of the pack and leaned hard against the fence, making the boards groan as he tried to reach Rosemary's arm. She pushed his nose back and he gazed at her with a bewildered expression in his big brown eyes.

"Oh, good grief."

"What do they want? They were just fine."

"Something must have spooked them, and they knew I was here so they came running for Mummy." Rosemary peered past the horses and up the pasture's slope. She spotted something small and brown moving near the pine tree wood. "See that? Groundhog. That'll be it."

"Oh." Stephen's voice was blank. "A . . . did you say ground*hog?* Like the holiday?"

"You've never seen one in real life?" Rosemary was amused. He really was the most sheltered creature. "Do they have *any* animals in New York?"

"Of course we do! You've heard of the Bronx Zoo, right?" He grinned at her, eyes twinkling.

"Proper animals? North American animals, who don't live in cages? Besides squirrels and rats." Rosemary gave in and patted Rochester on the neck; the big horse was still looking desperate for comfort. "Or horses who aren't afraid of their own shadows."

Stephen considered her question. "I saw a chipmunk once," he said eventually. "But that was in Brooklyn."

Rosemary laughed. "I guess that counts. I don't know how you've been staying up at your dad's house alone, though. When you hear noises at night, do they scare you?"

"Yes," Stephen said, suddenly looking very serious. Rosemary's laughter stilled in her throat. "I hear the noises at night, and I wish . . . I had a dark-haired woman in my bed to scare them away." He grabbed her around the waist and she squealed at him. Rochester bounced backwards, startled by the quick movement, and the other horses moved with him, snorting their alarm.

"You jerk," she laughed. "You had me for a second. Acting like a tortured soul."

"I admit it. I am not tortured. I am a very straightforward person."

Rosemary leaned into him, savoring his strong arms around her. "You can be a little complicated, if you want to be," she told him graciously. "I think that's only fair."

The horses decided there were neither treats nor saviors on the other side of the fence and moved back off to nose the short grass nearby. Rosemary was content to let Stephen hold her closely while she watched her little herd. *This is truly heaven,* she thought lazily. *Let's stay like this forever.*

Stephen moved restlessly behind her. "Rosemary?"

"Hmm?"

"Do you want to start by teaching me?"

She pondered his words. "Teaching you . . . what? About horses?" Surely not.

"Yes, about horses. I look at them and I just . . . I'm amazed that you can do whatever you want with them."

"Not *whatever*—"

"You know what I mean. I wouldn't even know how to get one to come when I call."

She laughed, imagining one of her horses trotting up like an obedient collie when she whistled. "First off, they aren't dogs. I've known like, two horses that came when they were called by name. And even then it was just because they knew there were carrots waiting for them. They would have come for any word you shouted."

"Well, see what I mean?" Stephen tucked his chin against her neck. "Do you really want me to be so ignorant around your beasties? A fellow could get hurt."

Rosemary gave in. "Fine," she laughed. "Do you want to start right now?"

He kissed her cheek. "What about . . . in an hour?"

Chapter Twenty-Six

Stephen

When they finally emerged from her bedroom later that afternoon, the shadows of the little pine forest on the upper slope were slanting across the pasture, and there was a definite chill in the air. Stephen went downstairs ahead of Rosemary, hoping to find some coffee in the kitchen. The pot was half-full and he tipped some into a mug, drinking it cold while he looked out the window. The kitchen was at the back of the house, and the view was of the pastures, with Notch Gap in the near distance. He thought the mountain looked particularly fine this afternoon. He didn't know much about the trees, but the green-leaved ones he thought of as "regular" trees were occasionally interrupted by blooms of magenta and festoons of white blossoms, which looked like spools of lace had been unfurled amongst the trees.

Stephen admired them, his bare feet turning cold on the floorboards, until Rosemary came downstairs and slipped up behind him.

"Is anything wrong?" she asked, and he was surprised by the note of alarm in her voice.

"No, why would there be?" He turned and gave her an inquiring look.

"Well, you can see the pasture from that window. I just assumed the horses had done something." Rosemary stood next to him and peered through the wavy glass. "They all look fine, though. What are you looking at?"

"Those red and white trees on the mountainside." He pointed.

"Oh, the red-buds and dogwoods. I love them. What is that, coffee?" She glanced in his cup. "Good idea."

"Why did you assume the horses had done something?" Stephen looked over the herd: black and white, red and cream. "What would they do? Don't they just eat all day?"

"Horses are always getting into trouble," Rosemary sighed, her voice muffled by the cabinet door. She took down a mug for herself. "They're always sticking their hooves where they don't belong or kicking one of their buddies or slicing their face open on a tree branch . . . owning horses is just an endless stream of problems, believe me."

This sounded worrisome. Stephen had lived a fairly trouble-free life—well, when he was employed, anyway. His biggest problems were generally the endless leak in his bathroom sink and remembering to pick up his dry-cleaning before the shop closed for the day. He tried to imagine having another life to care for and found the idea troubling. Stressful enough sharing an apartment with a woman from time to time, and they fed and bathed themselves . . . mostly. "You know, I've never even had a cat," he told Rosemary, and watched with amusement as her eyes rounded into saucers.

"And you want to learn about taking care of horses?" She sat down at the kitchen table. "Oh Stephen, that's jumping in at the deep end, my friend. That's skipping pre-algebra and going straight into trig."

"Come on, now, that's a little dramatic. They're outside eating grass right now. How tough could it be taking care of an animal that can live outside on a patch of unmown lawn?"

Rosemary chuckled grimly. "Last month one of those simple lawnmowers had a five-hundred dollar bellyache, and we never even figured out why."

"Five *hundred*—"

"Dollars," Rosemary finished for him. "Horses are very delicate. And they get into trouble. Once, Rosita decided she didn't want to be in her stall anymore and climbed out over the front wall. She needed stitches in six different places on her forelegs and chest. I think I actually blotted out that vet bill from my memory."

Stephen was baffled. "But why would she climb out of her stall?"

"Who knows? We never found anything wrong with it, and she didn't have any other symptoms to show she was sick or in pain."

"And this is what horses do? They just . . . get sick and freak out?"

"Basically. Yes."

"Rosemary, have you considered a more restful profession? I hear air traffic controllers have a good pension."

She shrugged. "When you love horses, you love horses."

"Will I love horses?" Stephen smiled hopefully at her.

Rosemary gazed at him for a moment. He felt her judging him, weighing his life against hers, and he wondered how he really measured up to her, this strong and independent woman who really, truly didn't need no man. He wanted to be tough enough for her—yeah, he wanted to be *man* enough for her, even though he knew that phrase had not aged well and didn't belong in his lexicon. Still, he could feel the urge welling up from somewhere deep within: to be the strongest, the fastest, the protector who kept the homestead safe and led the livestock in at night with calloused hands and a firm grip. He wasn't sure he'd ever felt that way before; or at least, it had felt different from the basic, gentlemanly chivalry he had always practiced with women in New York.

This was more than walking on the traffic side of the sidewalk or making sure a woman got her building door safely closed behind her before leaving. This was . . . *primal.*

Rosemary was narrowing her eyes at him. "What are you thinking about?"

He lifted the coffee mug to his lips to hide his smile. "Gender roles."

She stared at him. "Are all New Yorkers this weird?"

"The interesting ones," Stephen replied. "Now come on, drink that and let's go. You promised me horse lessons."

Rosemary led him into the barn. While Stephen liked the barn—this was a good place for kissing, after all—it was missing a key component of his lesson. "The horses aren't in here, Rosemary," he complained. "What are we doing?"

She gave him an arch look. "You wanted to learn about horse care, you said."

"Yes."

"Well, this is the most important part." She picked up a wooden-handled rake-looking thing. "Mucking out. Lucky for you, I was waiting until you left to clean stalls. So we have plenty to practice on! Oh, and here's my extra manure fork. Hang on and I'll get the wheelbarrow." She thrust the rake at him.

The rake—the manure fork, what a name!—was light-weight and he tossed it gently a few times, getting a feel for it. Then he went into the first stall and winced. The box was full of wood shavings which appeared to have been blended with discarded hay, round road-apples (his grandmother's term) and dark patches which looked wettish.

"This is a lot of shit and piss," Stephen said, wrinkling his nose and dropping Nonna's polite verbiage. There was no room for sugar-coating here.

"Smell getting to you already?" Rosemary asked, dropping the wheelbarrow in front of the stall door. She grinned at him. "You get used to it. Well, the manure. Not the pee. That's just nasty. But you'll be okay. Doesn't New York smell like pee?"

"You're enjoying this far too much," Stephen informed her. "I have half a mind to throw you down in some hay and teach you who's boss."

"You're not wasting any more of my hay, Mister. It's too expensive and I didn't make nearly enough at the fundraiser this year. Now, start scoopin'." Rosemary gestured in the general vicinity of the stall. "You have to shake out the shavings, but not too much or the poop will fall through in little bits."

Stephen made an attempt—a valiant attempt, in his eyes—but the manure did, indeed, break up and fall through the tines of the rake. He gave Rosemary an apologetic smile. "I guess it takes practice?"

"You're not born knowing how to shovel shit," Rosemary agreed, picking up the other manure fork. "Just follow my lead." And she proceeded to scoop up a forkful of manure and shavings, gently shake out the clean shavings, and toss the leftover manure in a graceful parabola to the wheelbarrow, four feet away.

"Wow." Stephen was deeply impressed. "You made that . . . artistic, I want to say, although it feels like a weird word for the circumstances."

"It *is* an art," Rosemary said, smiling at him. "Look, it's in the wrist . . . or the elbow, or the shoulder, I don't have any idea. You just . . . you just *do* it." She shook out another pile of manure and gave the road-apples a soaring send-off through the stall door.

Stephen tried to think of anything he'd done in his life which would help him now. Baseball, maybe? He'd been okay at whacking a ball in elementary school. Not so great at catching and throwing it. What else did he do with his arms on a regular basis? Hail a cab? Not so much, anymore, thanks to apps. Pry open subway doors when the conductor was trying to close them? Pretty regularly, but that was brute strength and a flagrant disregard for authority, not much use to him now. Carry groceries up four flights of stairs? Again, just impressive muscles. What he needed now was *precision.* He made an attempt at a manure toss and missed the wheelbarrow by inches.

"Close," Rosemary said, regarding the little mess he'd made in the doorway. "You'll get there. Eight stalls to clean; you're bound to improve."

eee

Stephen had finally accepted none of his city skills were of any use around horses when Rosemary realized the water spigot was broken. "It turns, but nothing's coming out," she complained. "I think the barn well must be broken again."

"What can we do about that?" Stephen did not know how to fix wells, and he had a secret fear of small, dark spaces, so if Rosemary was going to propose he lower himself into a well to . . . well, to do whatever made wells work, it just wasn't going to happen. "Is it a deep well?"

"Oh, I have no idea." She unscrewed the hose from the spigot with a resigned sigh. "It's not like, a wishing well or something. Those are just in fairy tales. There's an electric motor and it makes the water run. The house well is in the basement—I'll have to show you sometime, it's really something—but the barn well is more modern and it keeps burning out for some reason. I have to call someone out to fix it."

Stephen looked in the stall closest to him. The water buckets were empty. "So . . . how do we get water to the horses?"

"We bucket it." Rosemary did not look enthusiastic. "There's a spigot on the side of the house and the hose will reach about halfway here. I ought to have another hose but . . . I don't. Ugh. I *hate* doing this. That damn well needs replaced."

Stephen suddenly knew he had a skill which would apply to this exact situation. If he could tote home two full bags from Whole Foods Market, which was two long blocks and three short blocks away from his apartment, he could certainly carry two full water buckets at a time between the house and the barn, eight times in a row. "I'll handle the buckets. You don't have to do a thing," he told her, feeling triumphant. Finally, something he was uniquely suited for!

Rosemary protested, but Stephen would have none of it. He let her show him the spigot, attached the hose, and dragged it out its full length. There was still another thirty or forty feet to the barnyard gate. Piece of cake! He picked up two buckets and swung them experimentally.

"You're sure you don't want my help?" Rosemary asked uncertainly.

"Trust me. I have to carry heavy things all the time in the city. And I live on the fourth floor of a building with a very finicky elevator. It's about as reliable as your well."

"Gosh, I hope not," she muttered. "I wouldn't wish that on anyone."

"Just take a load off while I get this handled," Stephen insisted, and trotted off with the empty buckets, feeling like he'd won some kind of lottery. Which was a pretty weird way to react to having to carry sixteen full buckets of water up a gentle slope, admittedly . . . but when it came to Rosemary, he was desperate to prove he was more than just a city-bred paper-pusher.

"Stephen, you've got to come see this sunset!" Rosemary called. "Hurry up!"

"I'm coming," he shouted back. "Be right there!" But instead of heading for the barn door, Stephen leaned on Rochester's doorframe, watching the big horse eat his hay. He had helped with everything this afternoon, the stalls and the watering, the hay and the evening feed, even brushing the dried clay and mud from the horses once they'd come inside for the night, and he had an overwhelming feeling of achievement and satisfaction. He could see now why Rosemary didn't mind doing all of this work, alone, day in and day out. The effort was backbreaking, but the pay-off was sensational. Stephen knew people back in the city who would pay a fortune for the peace of mind and feeling of accomplishment he was enjoying right now.

A fortune . . . there was something there, he thought. An idea slowly struggled to find form in his mind, but he was also tired, and felt a little foggy. He realized he hadn't had a hit of caffeine since those few sips of old coffee in Rosemary's kitchen before they'd done all this work, and he was used to consuming at least twenty-four ounces of coffee in the course of an afternoon. Maybe the big idea would have to wait until he'd nourished his brain with some java, he thought, a tired smile coming to his lips. "Okay, old boy," he told Rochester. "I'll leave you to it."

The horse ignored him.

Outside the barn, the world was bathed in golden light. The sight of gilded trees and fence-posts was so stunning, Stephen was stopped in his tracks. Then he saw Rosemary, drenched in the liquid light like a shimmering goddess, and he lost his breath, as well.

She beckoned to him. "Come over here and *see,* silly. It's everywhere."

Stephen found his power of movement again and walked through the farmyard gate to join her in the clearing between the house and the barn. They had a clear view of Notch Gap from here, the twin mountains dark silhouettes against the brilliant shimmer of the sunset behind them. A slim scarf of yellow cloud cut in front of the sinking sun, dimming the light momentarily, and then as the cloud wafted on past, the sun began to dip behind the mountains.

There was a moment when the entire world seemed impossibly orange, and Stephen turned his head to look at Rosemary, her enraptured face glowing with that fiery brilliance, and just as he couldn't resist her another moment and dove to kiss her, the sun vanished and the day changed, in an instant, to blue-gray dusk.

Chapter Twenty-Seven

Rosemary

"I say this once a month, but that was the most magnificent sunset I've ever seen."

They were sitting on the porch in the azure glow of the blue hour, that magical moment between dusk and night when the world seemed to be glowing with its own mysterious light. Rosemary had always thought if the Earth had its own light, like a little sun, it would be blue—the blue of the oceans, of the sky. The hue of everything around them right now was like the depths of the Atlantic: blue trees, blue grass, blue barn and fences and gravel driveway.

"It was gorgeous," Stephen agreed. "But I might love this moment even more. It's very hard to see in the city. We *do* get beautiful sunsets, believe it or not."

"We're known for our sunsets," Rosemary said dreamily, "but maybe we should be famous for our twilights, too."

"Catoctin Creek should be famous, full-stop." Stephen tightened his arm around her, and she leaned into him, filled with contentment. "But I don't think I want anyone else to know about it."

Rosemary looked up at him. "Stephen! What are you saying?"

He shrugged. "I didn't think I was saying anything."

She frowned. For just a moment, she'd thought he was talking about the subdivision, his future plans for Long Pond. And she'd thought he meant he'd changed his mind.

But then, what would Stephen do with a farm? He'd bought the place; the papers were signed and the Kelbaughs were moving. He had to sell the land for *something,* and there was hardly a thriving real estate market for hundred-plus acre farms with overgrown pastures and tumbledown barns. That wasn't how people farmed anymore, anyway. They either had little hobby farms, getaways from the city, or they ran thousand-acre commercial enterprises. Family farms like hers had been, like Long Pond had been, were in their last generations of existence.

"I thought maybe you meant next door," she admitted after a few moments of silence. The blue glow was fading . . . in a moment it would just be night . . . there. It was gone. She shivered suddenly; the temperature was falling fast. "When you said you didn't want anyone else to know about it."

"Oh." He was quiet for a moment. "I wasn't thinking about anything in particular. I'm sorry if that's what it sounded like."

"It's just on my brain, I guess." She sat a little more upright, and his arm fell away from her. "It's cold. Why don't we go inside and find some supper? You're staying tonight, aren't you?"

"I am now." He leaned over and nuzzled at her neck, and a delicious line of electricity seemed to follow his lips. Rosemary arched her back with pleasure, and all thoughts of the farm slipped away. "Mmm, Rosemary . . . I found what I want."

Nikki called while Rosemary was in the shower, and she managed to hop out and pick up the phone with wet fingers just before it stopped ringing. "What's up?" she asked breathlessly, reaching for a towel. The bathroom was chilly; she was going to have to turn the furnace back on tonight. Unless Stephen was planning on keeping her warm . . . Rosemary smiled at the thought.

Nikki didn't sound so amused. "You didn't call me today."

"No . . . I didn't. Was I supposed to?"

"Did you or did you not have a date with Stephen last night?"

"Oh! I did." Last night felt like a very long time ago. "It was good. It didn't exactly . . . it isn't over yet, I guess you could say."

"Heh." Nikki's chuckle was knowing. "Slow service."

"Yeah, it was actually. We went to the Waterwheel. It was nice, and they don't hurry you out like some restaurants I know." Rosemary grinned at her own reflection and rubbed the towel through her wet hair. "And he brought me home, and had every intention of leaving, but . . . I made him stay. And then he stayed all day, and now it's night, and we have got to eat some dinner, so I need to get dressed and make something to eat."

"Dressed! You're not in bed with him right now, are you?"

"No, I just took a shower."

"Oh, thank goodness. So I guess you don't want me to bring you any dinner? I'm letting Jessica close up tonight. She's up for it and I'm tired of being here every night until late."

Rosemary considered the offer. On one hand, she wouldn't have to cook. On the other hand, Nikki would be at her kitchen table making Stephen squirm with questions, and they'd just had the nicest day together . . . she wasn't ready for it to end. "No thanks," she decided. "I really appreciate it, but—"

"No excuses necessary," Nikki told her firmly. "I just wish I'd find a nice guy to come to my place and keep me in bed for days and nights on end."

Rosemary laughed. "Well, we cleaned stalls and everything, too."

"Of *course* you did. Get back to him, girl. I'll talk to you tomorrow."

Tomorrow, Rosemary thought, putting her phone down and getting to serious work on her wet hair. What would tomorrow bring? Would Stephen stay another day, devote more time to working with the horses? She could show him how to groom and tack Rochester, maybe let him get up in the saddle for a walk around the farmyard—Rochester was fairly safe, it was Bongo who was an unpredictable nut under saddle. Rochester just had his occasional moments, like he had at Long Pond that day . . .

"Rosemary?" Stephen was at the door. She wrapped the towel around herself instinctively.

"You can come in," she said. "It's not locked."

Stephen opened the door and eyed her appreciatively. "You look like a mermaid."

"Maybe I'll lure you to your death."

"Promise?"

Rosemary laughed. "If you want to shower next, I'll start supper."

"I'll be quick. Don't go cooking without me. I'll come down and help you."

"Oh, I don't mind."

"No, really—I want to help. I know I said I can't really cook, but I can do things with instruction. I can even make a couple of things all by myself. Just don't ask me to make meatloaf. I have no idea how that happens."

— *elle* —

True to his word, Stephen came downstairs within ten minutes, wet hair dripping onto his collar. Rosemary had given him one of her polo shirts, a comfortably boxy unisex polo she adored and Nikki despised, and his chest and arms had pushed the fabric taut. She couldn't help but laugh at him. "You look like a muscle boy."

He grinned and pinned her against the wall next to the window, pressing his hands gently against her slim shoulders. "What's a muscle boy?"

"Oh, you know . . . one of those guys who is always working out and wears tight shirts . . . I don't know! Stop it!" He was kissing her now, wet smacks on her neck and cheek. She swatted at him, laughing and squirming. "Yuck, you're a gross yucky muscle boy!"

Stephen let her go and she ducked under his arm to escape him. He leaned back against the wall, lounging like a model. "I think I look good in this shirt. This is how we dress in the city, you know. We all have to show off our amazing bodies all of the time, or we can't get dates. Too much competition."

"It sounds very exciting," Rosemary assured him. "But I'll have to pass. I like being comfy." She gestured at her own outfit: dark blue cotton pajama bottoms, a matching long-sleeved t-shirt, and soft leather clogs. "I don't own anything tight. Well, besides riding breeches. Which I don't wear very often."

Stephen swallowed hard and Rosemary realized, with wicked delight, he was imagining her in riding breeches. "So what are we making for dinner?" he asked after a moment, and she thought his voice sounded slightly strangled.

Maybe she'd put on her riding breeches tomorrow, just to see.

"I found ground beef and I have some taco shells," she said, pulling a yellow box out of the cabinet. "We can have a taco night."

Stephen took the box from her hands. "Old El Paso?"

"Don't you have this in New York? It comes with seasoning and everything." Rosemary showed him the packet. "How are you at chopping? There are tomatoes and lettuce in the fridge."

She thought he was on the verge of saying something, but then he just nodded and opened the fridge door. They settled into dinner prep quietly, so quietly, in fact, that Rosemary started to feel a little concerned. Had she done something to put things wrong? She considered everything she'd said since he'd come downstairs, but couldn't think of anything which might have upset him. Did he maybe not like tacos?

Was that even possible? Everyone liked tacos.

"Stephen?"

"Hmm?"

"Are tacos okay? We can do something else."

"Tacos are fine."

"Do you *like* tacos?" Rosemary's anxiety, which had been amazingly dormant for the past twenty-four hours, was suddenly waking, stretching, and looking around. "Because if you don't—"

"I like tacos a lot, Rosemary. Really."

She ripped open the seasoning packet and poured it onto the sizzling meat, chewing at her bottom lip all the while. Then she turned around. Stephen had his back to her, leaning over the table as he cut up a tomato with impressively professional strokes of the knife. "Are you . . . *laughing?*"

Stephen put down the knife and looked over his shoulder at her, his face stretched wide in an irrepressible grin. "I'm sorry, Rosemary, it's just . . . *Old El Paso!* I feel like I'm in a commercial. On network television."

She stared at him, utterly confused. "On . . . network television? Is that an insult? What is wrong with my taco kit?"

"Nothing, nothing, nothing," Stephen said quickly, wiping the grin from his face. "I'm just . . . I'm used to . . . tacos look a little different in the city. If I want a taco I go to a restaurant or a taco truck and get them there. I've never had these kind. From a kit."

"These kind are good," Rosemary said defensively, feeling as if she had to stand up for Old El Paso tacos, her entire family, and a lifetime of taco nights. "I wouldn't give you *bad* tacos, Stephen."

"Look, I'm just being a food snob. I'm ashamed of myself. That's why I didn't want to say anything out loud. I was trying to make myself behave." Stephen crossed the kitchen and put his hands on her waist, pulling her close to him. His eyes were filled with regret. "Sometimes my first response is to tease. I'm used to a more cynical, sarcastic crowd than you are. But I don't want to be like that with you."

She nodded. That was nice. A little insulting, a little bit like saying she wasn't tough enough to handle his New York crowd, but . . . nice. That he was trying, that he wanted to be kind to her. She didn't particularly want to be teased about her food choices, especially if she didn't have things like taco trucks to frequent. "You're going to like these. I mean, all tacos are good. It's like different kinds of pizza, right? Chicago pizza, New York pizza, microwave pizza . . . they're all different, but they're all good."

He raised his eyebrows. "Rosemary, don't make this impossible for me. *Chicago* pizza? Are you serious?"

She laughed. "Kiss me, you snob," she instructed him, and Stephen obeyed.

Yes, she thought. Tomorrow she'd definitely wear the riding breeches. He deserved a little trouble.

Chapter Twenty-Eight

Stephen

The riding breeches were a sight to behold. She was already wearing them when he pulled the car up to the farmhouse, and he'd have sworn she gave her hips a little extra wiggle as she sashayed down the porch steps to meet him.

Stephen had brought lunch, sandwiches wrapped in butcher's paper and a bag of chips from the deli counter at Catoctin Creek's tiny grocery, and now he watched her walk around to the passenger side of the car, open the door and take out the grocery bag, and then shut the door again. In a daze, he stared through the windshield as Rosemary walked away—oh, there was *definitely* a wiggle to her hips—and began to climb the steps. She paused on the second step and looked over her shoulder at him.

Those breeches, that dark hair cascading around her shoulders, that come-hither smile . . . Stephen got out of the car with a growl and went running after her. Rosemary squealed and ran into the house, slamming the door behind her. He had it open and was hot on her heels before she could make it all the way down the hallway.

He wrapped his arms around her from behind, pressing his chin into her shoulder. "Stop it, wench."

Rosemary giggled outrageously. "Let me go! I have to put down this food or it will fall and all the chips will crush."

"I love crushed chips."

"Are you crazy? Crushed chips are the *worst.*"

"I'll eat any kind of chip. I'm like you with your disrespectful pizza opinions."

His chin was still against her shoulder and he turned his head to kiss her neck. Rosemary stopped giggling and started sighing, but she was still clutching the lunch bag pretty tightly. He decided it would make more sense to put the sandwiches in the fridge first, *then* work his way down to those skin-tight breeches of hers . . .

"Hang on, these heroes should go in the fridge," he said, letting go of her reluctantly.

"Those are hoagies," Rosemary informed him.

"*Hoagies?* No, Rosemary. They're heroes."

"They're hoagies. You're in Maryland now! Give in! Accept it!" And Rosemary took off down the hall, racing for the kitchen.

Stephen sighed, watching her go. He'd do a lot for Rosemary, he thought resolutely. But he wasn't going to call a hero sandwich a hoagie.

"I give in," he sighed. "Hoagies. God help me." *Anything she wants,* he thought, feeling like a desperate man. *It's hers.*

Rosemary stirred beside him. "Where did the day go?" she asked, sounding surprised. "I swear it was just the middle of the day."

Stephen rolled over. They were sprawled across the soft spring grass beside the house, and the late afternoon sunlight was warm on his face. They'd enjoyed some seriously charmed weather for the past few days, he thought. A little chilly at night, but not a drop of rain, not a cloud in the sky . . . perfect for cavorting with Rosemary, this wild country girl on her quiet country farm. He wished he could stay here with her; he wished he could know for sure if this feeling would stay with him when he left.

Because he had to go.

He was going to have to get back to the real world, at least for a little while. Stephen just hoped New York didn't suck him back in. Right now, all he wanted was to be *here,* with Rosemary. But would that feeling last when he was back on his native soil . . . or pavement, as the case might be?

"I think we played the day away," he said, regretful it was over. "Is it time for chores?" The constant of farm life, he thought, was chores. Advantage: city.

"Yes," Rosemary sighed, pushing herself up onto her elbows. She looked past him, towards the horse pasture. "Everyone's waiting for us."

"They probably thought you were going to take one of them for a ride today," Stephen suggested. "The riding breeches and all."

"Oh, I just wore those for you," she said with a rueful laugh. "I wanted to see what you'd do."

"Did you get what you expected?"

"And then some."

There was an expectant neigh from the pasture. "We've been spotted," she said, stretching luxuriously. "Work awaits. Do you want to help me feed? Are you sticking around this evening?"

Stephen wanted to say yes, but he had a feeling it was time to go home. If he was going to find a way to sort out Long Pond to his and Rosemary's mutual satisfaction, he'd have to get busy. He'd had a few vague thoughts about what else to do with the property, but nothing was really coming together. He needed a plan, and he knew a lot of very smart people. If he went back to New York, even for just a few days, he could sit down with some friends and try to spin up some ideas.

So he put his hand on Rosemary's shoulder and squeezed it gently. She turned her head to look at him, her hair spilling over the grass, and Stephen felt a wave of fresh longing for her. He tamped it down. "I wish I could. But I have to get some work done, talk to some people."

Her smile faded. Her disappointment wrenched at his heart.

There was a long pause while Rosemary considered him, then she sighed and shrugged. "Well, I have to do laundry anyway."

Stephen exhaled, a little nervous laughter bursting free. "I see! That's very practical. Admit it, you were hoping I'd leave so you could get back to your normal routines. I know you're a creature of habit. What else have you skipped while I've been in your way?"

"Not much. I mean . . . I usually scrub out the pasture water trough on Mondays. And go to the feed store. And update the rescue website with new photos." She grinned ruefully. "I guess I am kind of behind on everything now. You better go before it gets worse."

Stephen hopped up. "Right, I'll just get out of your hair."

"Stop!" She clutched at his leg, and Stephen looked down at her hopefully, waiting for what she might say. An impassioned declaration, perhaps? "Don't go, Stephen. I want . . . "

"Yes?" He was expectant, nearly breathless.

"I want your help cleaning the stalls."

Stephen put his head back and laughed. Of course she did, he thought. Why else had she taught him how to muck out the barn? Rosemary was a clever girl. "Is that all?" He reached for her wrist and tugged her upright. "You don't want *anything* else?"

"That's all," she told him firmly. "Hard labor, and nothing else."

"I should have seen this coming."

Chapter Twenty-Nine

Rosemary

T hey cleaned the stalls. And then, instead of bringing the horses inside for dinner, they ended up back in Rosemary's bedroom once more.

When Rosemary finally lifted her head, drowsy and disoriented, Stephen shifted beside her and gave her a momentary fright. It took her a few seconds to remember why he'd be at her side, why his head would be sharing her pillow. Then she smiled. Damn him, but they were spending too much time in bed . . . and she enjoyed all of it.

Well, if he'd wanted to give her a few good reasons why she shouldn't kick him to the curb before he had a chance to make good on all those random promises he'd spouted the day before, well . . . good on him, he'd succeeded.

Rosemary reached down and picked up her phone. She squinted at the time and sighed. They'd been asleep for nearly an hour. It was almost five. She had to hustle if she was going to get the horses in before dark. The clocks had changed for the season, but sunset was still early. She pulled back the curtains and looked out at the barn. The old timbers were shining in the golden evening light, the stones of the lower story warm and yellow. She felt that little surge of love and joy her farm always gave her at particularly pretty moments. Did Stephen see its beauty the way she did? Or did he dream of going back to the city? Rosemary wondered what was coming next for them, and then she tried to push the thought from her mind. There weren't any answers, so she wasn't going to spend time speculating.

Well, she was going to *try* not to speculate, anyway.

She got up and started to dress, pulling on her discarded clothes from the little pile where they'd been tossed on the floor, and then she folded Stephen's jeans and shirt over a chair so they wouldn't wrinkle too badly. Her fingers caressed the clothes, savoring the feel of them. He always wore such nice fabrics! Too nice for helping her with the horses, really. She ran her hands over the black cloth of his shirt, thinking it had probably cost more than anything in her closet, and then reached into her closet for a hanger.

"Don't steal my shirt, Rosemary."

She turned around, clutching the shirt to her chest. "It's too nice for you, really. It should be mine."

"I'll bring you back a nice shirt from the city if you want." Stephen was getting up, reaching down for his boxers, and she dropped her eyes back to the shirt in her hands. She wasn't *quite* ready for the two of them to parade around nude in front of each other. "Just like that one, with the buttons on the wrong side for you and everything, or maybe I can sneak into the women's department and maybe find you one there. But for now, I'm going to have to beg you for that one back. I can't wear your polo shirts in the city."

"You're really going to the city *now?*" She didn't mean it to sound as if the next words were *after we had sex?* but that was how it came out, anyway. She'd known he was going, but she couldn't help but feel a little abandoned. They'd spent the past two days nearly inseparable. She'd gotten used to having him around in record time. And even last night, sleeping alone after he'd gone home, hadn't been lonely because he'd just been a few miles away. New York was a different story. The farm was going to seem terribly empty with him so far away.

"I have to," he sighed, and at least, she thought, he sounded genuinely regretful. "But I will be right back. You won't even notice I was gone. Hang out with Nikki. Gossip about me, if you want. Tell her I said *hoagie* like a real Maryland hick."

She threw his shirt at him, but now she was grinning, an idea stirring in her mind. "Will you see Kevin while you're there?"

"Hmm? Kevin? I suppose I might."

Rosemary furrowed her eyebrows. "Might? I thought he was a partner on Long Pond. Aren't you working on that?"

"Well, he is, I just think he might be busy with work. It's the middle of the week. But I'm going to try and catch him. I have a few people in mind to see." Stephen busied himself buttoning up his shirt.

"I really think Nikki liked Kevin," Rosemary mused. "Remember? Back when he came down before? They really hit it off. Do you think you can get him to come back down?"

"Maybe sometime." Stephen's voice was absent. "I really don't know what his schedule is like."

He clearly wasn't paying attention to her. Already back in his city brain, she thought, annoyed. She shook her head at him. "Fine. Be secretive about your little work friends in New York. I'm going to get the horses in for their dinners. It's getting late, and apparently I'm doing chores alone now."

Stephen put his hand on her shoulder before she could walk away. She let him spin her around, let her body melt against his. Sure, he was an annoying guy, but he was *her* annoying guy. At least, that's how things felt. Was it too soon to feel this possessive?

He pressed a soft kiss on her lips. "I *want* to stay with you, you know. Let me go and get this done so I can come right back."

Rosemary had no choice but to trust him. After all, he was obsessed with business. That was how they'd landed in this mess with Long Pond. If he was going to fix the Long Pond situation for her, she was going to have to let him go back to New York, conspire with all his business-y friends. "Are you going straight there? Tonight?"

"I'm going home tonight. And I'll go in the morning."

"Good," Rosemary said. "No rush, so you *can* help me feed." She smiled and plucked a plaid shirt from her dresser. "Cover up that pretty shirt before you get hay all over it."

Chapter Thirty

Stephen

Stephen stopped by Notch Gap Farm on his way out the next morning. He knew he shouldn't, knew he should get on the road and head out without distraction, but it was impossible to drive past the farm without turning in and seeing her. And his route out of Catoctin Creek happened to go right up Notch Gap Road.

Rosemary was in the barnyard, grooming that big black horse she loved so much, and he paused before he got out of his car, watching her as she gazed steadily at him from across the lawn. He wanted to drink her in, his pretty farm girl with her honest eyes and her retreating ways, before he went back into the guile and pushiness of the city.

When he finally got out of the car, Rosemary had given up trying to groom her horse and was leaning on the fence, watching him. "You're back awfully soon," she teased as he approached. "Are you supposed to visit a girl every single day? Aren't I supposed to be kept in breathless anticipation for a few days while you gallivant through the city without me?"

Stephen ducked through the fence-boards and reached for her, pulling her up against him. Her eyes were bright and he felt a stirring that made him want to take her right back into that barn, find a nice soft pile of hay, and—

Rochester gave him a nudge in the side which nearly knocked him over. Rosemary, still in his arms, staggered sideways with him. They righted and looked at one another for a wild moment, startled into laughter, and then he leaned down and put his lips on hers.

She sighed and melted into him, giving in to a long and luxurious kiss which made Stephen's knees go weak. He wrapped one arm around her back, fingers pressing against her spine, and drew his other fingertips up the nape of her neck, feeling the soft tendrils of hair which had escaped her severe ponytail. She arched against his touch, her head tilting backwards, and her eyelashes fluttered as he slowly broke off the kiss and opened his eyes to drink her in again.

"Stephen," Rosemary whispered, a hint of mischief returning to her eyes, "not in front of the horse."

He laughed. "Is this old boy an innocent?"

"I'd like to think so."

They regarded Rochester for a moment. The horse looked back at them reproachfully.

"I think you're right," Stephen said after a moment. "He does seem pretty troubled by the whole thing."

"He's troubled, all right." Rosemary reached out and gave the horse a pat on the neck. She turned back to Stephen. "He has many troubles. So, did you drive here just to kiss me?"

"I did," he admitted. "I didn't realize it until it was happening, though. Is that okay with you?"

She shrugged, but her eyes were dancing. "I can deal with it. Anything else you'd like to do this morning? I'm free. After I'm done with this wretch, that is. He got into a briar patch the minute I turned him out, and I've been pulling brambles out of his mane for the past half hour. But I think they're gone . . . I can turn him back out, and we can go inside." Rosemary's gaze was inviting.

Stephen had to stop himself from licking his lips with anticipation. He had to get on the road. "I can't stay . . . I have to get on the road."

"I was kind of hoping you'd changed your mind."

"I know—I'm sorry. Maybe I shouldn't have stopped by."

It was the wrong thing to say. She looked up at him with a stricken expression. "You didn't want to see me?"

"I just didn't want to give you the wrong idea."

Rosemary's jaw set in a familiar fashion which told him he wasn't improving the situation. "Well, go on then, business boy." She picked up the brush she'd been using on Rochester's mane. "Make those deals."

He felt her retreat from him. He wished he could tell her he was looking for an alternative to subdividing the farm, but without any idea what that might look like, he knew he had to keep his mouth shut. For now. He'd go back, talk to some people, get some ideas. Then, he'd include her.

"Rosemary, I didn't want . . . " he began, but he wasn't sure where the sentence was going. He didn't want what? To ruin her life? To give her false hopes?

Both things were true; neither would get him anywhere.

"You can't just want things," Rosemary said with a little shrug. "You have to mean them, too. How do I know what you really mean?"

Stephen felt as if she'd slapped him. "Rosemary, please don't."

"I have to turn this horse out." She tugged at Rochester's rope, untying the knot in one smooth motion, and began to turn him around. Stephen had to jump to avoid being trodden by Rochester's dinner-plate-sized hooves.

Stephen trailed Rosemary's icy progression out of the barnyard and up the hill beside the barn, all the way to the pasture gate, where Bongo was waiting for Rochester, his big head hanging over the fence. She shushed Bongo out of the way as she hauled open the gate, and Stephen marveled again at the way she fearlessly pushed these huge animals around. If she wasn't afraid of them, why was she so afraid of humans? He knew there was no real comparison, but the contrast still fascinated him.

She certainly wasn't afraid of *him;* she made that clear as she stalked past him again once the horses were reunited and the gate securely latched. He scrambled to keep up with her as she stomped down the stone steps beside the barn. "Rosemary, listen, can we talk about this?"

She whirled to face him, hand on the barnyard gate. "What is there to talk about? You have to go. You have business to attend to. It's all been said."

It shook him, how quickly she could go from warm and loving to cold and severe. Was the only key to softening her a kiss? He considered and discarded this option. She looked as if a kiss might turn her angry simmer into a full-on volcanic eruption.

"I can't go with you mad at me," he said quickly. "I know this is about Long Pond, and I'm sorry, but I'm going to do everything I can to make sure that whatever happens here doesn't ruin what you have here. At the very least, I'm going to make sure all of the front lawn, and the house, looks exactly the same for you." He hadn't even considered this step until this very moment, but he knew he could do it. "The farmhouse will be preserved and brought back up to code—there's got to be a million violations in there, Rosemary, it could burn down any day of the week. I'll save it. Then the lawn, the barn, the pond: I'll keep it all. I'll do everything I can. I promise you, it's going to be beautiful. Even if. . ."

Even if he couldn't save the farm.

He couldn't say the words out loud. Idle promises would go nowhere with this woman. It had to be action, or nothing.

Rosemary looked past him, biting her lip, and he thought he could feel her wavering. He had a chance, he thought, he was going to get through this on top—

"Who will live there?" Rosemary asked softly.

"Where?" It was an idiotic answer, but what else could he say? No one, if he could find a miracle? A hundred government-agency types, if he couldn't?

"Who will live in the farmhouse? When I look over there and it's all the same as before, whose house will it be?"

He hadn't thought that far ahead. He opened his mouth, but no answer came to mind. He'd only planned on making it a sales office, or a community center. But if he preserved everything as it was, all of those plans, from parking lots to a picnic pavilion, would be impossible. *Dammit, Rosemary, I'm not there yet,* he wanted to shout. Instead, he said: "Just let me work on this."

She shook her head, turning her back on him. He watched her back go rigid, her arms fold over her chest. The points of her elbows showed through her light sweater. "What are we doing right now? We want different things. You can't even figure out what to do with a beautiful farm right next to mine—any other man in Catoctin Creek would have no problems right now. Why are we even trying this?"

The words jolted from him, the only ones left to him: "Because I'm in love with you."

Rosemary spun around, her mouth falling open, and Stephen had a grim little feeling of triumph. At least he'd managed to surprise her out of her anger.

Chapter Thirty-One

Rosemary

"Because I'm in love with you," Stephen said, the words running together as if he couldn't get them out of his mouth fast enough, and Rosemary felt her lips part in surprise even as she fought to maintain control of her expression.

She wanted to be angry with him, dammit, she wanted to dig up the courage to finally put an end to this pointless flirtation, this long dance sequence which would not, could *never*, lead to a happy ending. One minute she was telling him her deepest secrets and feeling completely safe in his company, and the next he was running off to New York to keep working on the project that was going to ruin her life, this tenuous little happiness she'd built for herself with her farm and her horses and her beloved neighbors. How could they continue this relationship, or whatever this was, when he was about to make a fortune on destroying the life she held so dear?

He needed to get out, that was all, he needed to go once and for all, and stop coming around here, distracting her, *kissing* her, and she needed to stop wanting him to do it.

That was what she *had* been thinking, when he'd blurted out he loved her, shattering any chance of coherent thought she'd had left.

Now his expression looked so desperate, his hands outstretched and grasping nothing, she knew it wasn't a game to him. He meant it, and Rosemary had an awful, wonderful suspicion she would mean it, too. *If* she said it.

She didn't want to say it; didn't want to give away her secrets quite yet, not when things were so uneasy, when her rational mind was telling her this guy had to go.

But she wasn't just a person of rational mind. She was also a person of passionate heart, and so when she gave in to her desires and stepped into his arms, filling the empty space he looked so anxious to fill, and let him wrap her up in his embrace, she had that terrifying, dizzying, delightful feeling of belonging once more. It was a feeling only he could give her, and she gave herself the go-ahead to enjoy it . . . for now, anyway. She tilted her face up to his. Stephen gazed back down at her, and she felt he was hardly breathing, just waiting—waiting for her to speak, to give him permission, to tell him he was wanted.

Rosemary sighed, half-content, half-furious at the inevitability of it all, and then she smiled in resignation, shaking her head at him. "You're an idiot," she told Stephen. "But I love you."

After all those declarations of love, after the passion, white-hot and fast, which followed, Rosemary expected to feel listless and lonesome in her empty house. But after a few minutes spent wandering around the quiet rooms, she realized she had more energy than ever. She felt oddly confident—odd for her, that is—

and less like retiring back into the shadows. Rosemary decided she wasn't going to sit around and wait sadly for her boyfriend to come back to her. She was going to *do* something.

So she did the unthinkable.

She picked up her phone and made a call.

Not a text, not an email, not a tentative thought of contacting someone later—oh no, Rosemary scrolled through her contacts, found Caitlin's number, and pressed *call.*

This sort of forward momentum was unprecedented, she thought with a self-deprecating smile. Next thing she knew, she'd be cleaning out the entire barn.

Actually, that wasn't a half-bad idea. Rosemary looked out the living room window at the barn. *Hmm.* She'd need a load of shavings, but she could strip out the stalls, scrub down the floors and walls, and—"Oh, hello! Caitlin? Is this an okay time to call?"

"Rosemary!" Caitlin was an extrovert, and her phone voice was accordingly enthusiastic. "It's so nice to hear from you!"

"Yes!" Rosemary agreed, then realized how that would sound. Phone calls were impossible! "It was great to run into you the other day," she amended, keeping her tone bright. "I really appreciated our chat."

"Of course! I meant what I said. *Any* time! So this is as good as any. What's going on? You want to talk about your farm? Let's make some magic happen!"

There were so many exclamation points. Rosemary already felt winded. She plucked at the living room curtains with her free hand and tried to draw herself up as tall as she could stand, to muster up all of that burning energy she'd felt a few moments ago. "I do. Can

I ask you a question? Do you think there's any point in teaching people basic horsekeeping skills?"

"You mean like, instead of riding lessons? I love that idea. Yes! You should do that!"

"But like . . . who does that help? That's the part I'm not sure about. I was showing Ste—I was showing a *friend* how to clean stalls and feed and all of that, and it was fun, but is that really something people will want to know? Or will it be all about riding all of the time?"

There was a slight pause. When Caitlin spoke again, her voice was lower. "Who did you say you were teaching?"

"A friend," Rosemary said hastily.

"Because I've heard you're seeing Gilbert Beckett's son . . . "

"Who told you *that?*"

"Jessica Cross."

"Jessica Cross? Oh, at the Blue Plate. The girl who has been closing for Nikki." Rosemary sat down on the sofa, feeling deflated. "That means everyone in town knows."

"You can't keep secrets in a town this size," Caitlin said matter-of-factly. "I went in for dinner a couple of nights ago and Jessica overheard Nikki talking to you on the phone and then . . . well, Jessica is not great at keeping things quiet."

"No. She's like, eighteen. If that." Rosemary sighed. "Okay, fine, it was Stephen Beckett. That's who I was teaching. And we had fun, and I liked doing it, so I thought . . . maybe that's the ticket. But then I wondered, who will actually want to do all the dirty work with none of the riding?"

"Besides boyfriends who want to impress you."

"Besides them," Rosemary agreed, accepting her fate with bad grace.

Caitlin laughed at her tone. "I don't know why you'd want to keep it quiet, anyway, Rosie girl! Stephen Beckett is absolutely gorgeous. And loaded, I hear. Big Manhattan boy."

Rosemary had her doubts about the financials, but she let it go. "I just don't want everyone talking about me."

"Yeah, that sounds like you. I can't really relate." Caitlin chuckled. "Anyway, there are a lot of ways you could spin this. It could be great for people who want to rescue horses, for example. You could put on seminars. Lots of liberal-type do-gooders move up here from D.C. and they don't know what to do with their extra space, so they go to the auction and see the skinny horses and feel bad. But they do more harm than good, so they end up colicking the horse or something. I could tell you at least half-a-dozen times that's happened in the past two years alone. Right around here!"

Rosemary considered having a lot of women wearing expensive knits and colorful Hunter boots in her barnyard while she went over the basics of horse care. It wasn't the most appealing vision she'd ever had, but since her idea of heaven was being left alone, this wasn't surprising. What was more important was that it didn't seem *unbearable*.

"I could possibly, maybe, do something like that," she said slowly. "Just like occasional weekends, one-day classes or something." That way, she'd have plenty of time to mentally prepare, and wouldn't have to deal with people coming in and out of the farm every day like Caitlin did with her lessons and therapeutic riding sessions.

"That's a fantastic idea," Caitlin agreed. "And you could do a series, different topics on different weekends. And charge a few hundred per session, obviously."

Rosemary considered the gaps in her hay fund and realized this had stopped being conjecture already. If she'd found a socially acceptable way to fundraise, without having people constantly in her hair, she was going to have to try it . . . despite her misgivings about having to stand up in front of perfect strangers and teach them *anything*. "Where do I find the people who want to do this?"

"Oh, online. I have all kinds of groups and mailing lists . . . I'll send you some ideas, how does that sound? We'll get you fixed right up." Caitlin paused, and Rosemary heard someone talking in the background. "Hey, I have lessons arriving. I'm going to email you, okay? Is that your email on your website? Good. Don't worry about a thing. Caitlin will get you all set up. You'll just have to be ready for the response you're going to get!"

Rosemary put the phone down on the windowsill and looked out at the quiet farm. The yellow-and-blue morning was turning into a cloudy gray afternoon, with a spring storm brewing beyond the mountains. She thought about Stephen on the road north to New York, hopefully keeping well ahead of a change in the weather.

He was heading back to the city to try and solve the problem of Long Pond's future for her; the least she could do for her own farm's problems, she supposed, was try and suck it up once or twice a month for some do-gooder women who just wanted to put a rescue horse in their backyards.

She shook her head a little to try and clear her mind, put her phone back into her pocket, and pulled her jacket off its hook by the door. She'd better get stalls cleaned in case a cold rain set in and the horses needed to come inside. On her way out, she plucked up her earbuds from a side-table and stuffed them into her pocket as well. She'd need to listen to a podcast or something to stop from worrying constantly about this new plan. She'd set Caitlin on it, now there was nothing to do but wait and see what happened.

She wished Stephen were here to distract her.

She'd obviously gotten used to having him around far too quickly.

Rosemary smiled ruefully at her reflection in the hall mirror, then shrugged and headed outside. Time to get to work.

Chapter Thirty-Two

Stephen

S tephen guided his father's old car into a miracle spot just a half-block from his apartment near Riverside Drive, and unlocked the building's front door with his backpack slung over one shoulder. A neighbor he didn't recognize passed him in the tight little vestibule, wearing running pants and dragging a small dog on a leash; he watched the woman's profile pass him from less than a foot away, noting that she never turned her head or acknowledged his presence. Even the dog ignored him.

He was truly back in New York, Stephen thought wryly.

He'd had his mail forwarded to Maryland again, so he passed the bank of metal mailbox doors without pause and got to the elevator just as it began a laborious, groaning ascent. Sighing, Stephen ducked into the tiled stairwell, huffing his way up four flights. It was a steeper climb than he remembered, and he was holding his side against a stitch by the time he pushed open the fire door and entered the dim landing. The elevator was still sighing ever upwards, probably going all the way to the tenth floor, where an elderly woman lived in stately solitude in the penthouse. Stephen flicked the polished metal doors as he walked past, heading for the door at the front end of the hall.

His apartment was dim and smelled a little dank, and there was a new intensity to the bathroom sink's steady drip which made him relieved water was included with rent. He made a mental note to call the super about the leak as he opened the blinds, trying to let in a little light. But only having two front windows in the living room, an airshaft in the bedroom, and a chic exposed brick wall in the kitchen did not allow for much natural light, especially as the late March evening drew in. He flung open the windows to let out the damp smell, and cool, sooty air blew in. Stephen sneezed.

Stephen found the apartment's normal darkness unbearable after just a few minutes, so he flipped on all of the lights and then paced back and forth along the narrow hall between the living room and the bedroom, feeling like a caged animal. He was here, now what? At last, he threw himself down on the chair nearest the front windows and peered out onto the street, hoping the sight of traffic and pedestrians might cheer him up a bit.

No use. Even with the window open and the chilly night air flowing in, he felt all pent up. He missed his father's house, with its view of the mountains and the evening quiet, punctuated by birdsong. He'd always loved streetlife, but now the sounds of honking cars, racing engines, and even idle laughter from people on the sidewalk felt intrusive.

And he missed Rosemary.

Well, one thing was for certain, Stephen decided, he couldn't spend the whole evening in this place alone. He picked up his phone and started firing off messages to friends he hadn't seen in months. He needed a dinner date to keep him from going completely crazy. Surely *someone* was free tonight.

—— *ℓ ℓ* ——

"Melinda Fairfield," Stephen announced formally, straightening up from the lamppost he'd been leaning on. "It has been too long."

The woman approaching him on the sidewalk was round-faced and solemn, with owlish glasses and dark hair in a messy bun, but she countered her grave expression with cherry-red lipstick and a similarly-colored scarf over her black sweater and pants. She held out her arms as she came up to Stephen and they folded into a hug. Stephen breathed in the scent of her shampoo and thought how reliable Melinda was. She hadn't changed in years.

"You look fabulous, Stephen," she told him, stepping back and looking him up and down. "Rustic life agrees with you. I'm not surprised."

"You're not?"

"No. In school you were always happiest on the playground."

"That's true, but that was just because I hated sitting in a classroom all day."

"So you went to sit behind a desk for a career?" Melinda smiled with the air of a woman who has won her argument. "You should have been a park ranger."

Stephen pulled out a chair for her. The restaurant Melinda had chosen was a cozy old Broadway bistro just a few blocks from his apartment. In true Manhattan style, the dining room was crammed with at least twice as many tables as comfort would allow, and he was relieved when the hostess led them to a table against the wall. At least he could lean one elbow on the rough bricks instead of putting it into his neighbor's soup. The soup, he noted, did look good.

"I haven't been in a room this small in months," he told Melinda, grinning. "My apartment didn't have room for me to turn around. I think I've grown."

"You didn't grow, the city shrunk. You'll want to be careful of leaving too often, or you won't fit anymore." Melinda turned to the server and ordered a martini. "And a Manhattan for the gentleman," she added, and winked at Stephen.

"Thank you, ma'am."

"It's time for a drink and a catch-up. Tell me what you're doing."

Stephen explained, in short-hand, about his father's house, Long Pond, the development, and even Rosemary. At least with Melinda, he thought he could share his confusion and perhaps get back some good advice. He'd known Melinda since elementary school; they'd grown up a few blocks apart. She'd become an academic, immersing herself in university library collections while he jumped into the business of collecting money, but they'd stayed in touch despite their differing paths. Nearly five years before, they'd actually dated, but they'd eventually decided they were dating more out of proximity and comfort than any real desire to mesh their very different lives into one, and decided to go back to being friends. Now, Melinda listened with the attentiveness of an old friend, sipping gently at her martini and nodding at the sticky parts of the story.

"Well, you're in a pickle with that farmhouse, aren't you?" she said when he'd wrapped it up. "What on earth will you do with it?"

"I really don't know. I'd thought maybe it could be a community center and a sales office, but . . . I don't think she'd want that, either."

"She wants what she can't have," Melinda told him warningly. "She wants to keep the past intact. Maybe you should just help her face the facts and move on. Be a comfort."

"It's hard for me to be the comfort when I'm the cause."

"True. Even if you're a help to the old couple, she'll have a hard time seeing it *only* like that. Her feelings count, too." Melinda looked thoughtful. "How set in stone is this whole development? Like, permits are pulled and land is being cleared?"

"Nothing like that," Stephen sighed. "It's at least a year from land-clearing, the way the lawyers are talking. A lot of easements and zoning to work through."

"So the money sunk into it is . . . "

"Mostly mine." Stephen looked moodily into the amber depths of his Manhattan. "But Kevin is involved—you remember Kevin. He needs a pay-out at some point. The rest of his assets are tied up in this awful residential tower in Queens, and he was hoping this would get him free of that. So he wouldn't mind a quick turnaround. But I can't just sell it as a farm, because it's not worth anything as agricultural land."

"Oh, heavens no. Small farms like that are dead," Melinda agreed. "But I might have an idea for you."

"Anything," Stephen said, leaning forward. Deep down, he'd hoped Melinda would have the solution. Initially, he'd just been happy she'd been free for dinner tonight, but now he knew it wasn't coincidence. It was pure destiny. Melinda was a doer in the most Manhattan way—she willed people and places to do her bidding. "What are you thinking?"

The server appeared with lifted eyebrows. Melinda was immediately distracted, flicking her eyes over the menu. "The soup," she decided, "and the filet, medium rare."

"Excellent," the server replied, turning to Stephen.

"The same, please," Stephen said, wanting only to get back on topic. "What have you got for me?" he asked Melinda.

"A project of mine. I'm working part-time with a girl's school, very select and well-established, on the Upper East Side. I'm working on the new boarding location, in the country. I need a historical setting and room for outdoor pursuits . . . sports, hiking, landscape painting. Sort of an old world vibe with a healthy feminist glow. There's still plenty of appetite for that in wealthy families. From everything you're saying, this farm is the place. And I could make it happen."

Stephen's jaw dropped, and for a moment he couldn't even speak. "I could kiss you," he said finally. "Melinda, are you serious?"

Melinda laughed indulgently. "I think I deserve a kiss. One now, and one when you close the deal. But you have to get past the headmistress, and she's tough."

Stephen leaned across the table and placed a kiss on Melinda's cool lips. She chuckled and cuffed him under the chin like a forties movie star. "I miss you when you're not around, kid," she told him. "But something tells me I'm going to see a lot more of you after this."

Chapter Thirty-Three

Rosemary

Rosemary woke up on the following morning with her sense of purpose still in overdrive. Her energy from the day before hadn't abated, even though she'd worked well into the afternoon in the barn, knocking down cobwebs and greasing hinges while she waited for the rain to begin. Once the storm had moved in and the horses were inside, comfortably eating their hay, she went into the house and proceeded to clean out the pantry and refrigerator.

She'd fallen asleep the moment her head hit the pillow, after exchanging a few quick texts with Stephen to make sure all was well in New York—he'd had dinner with a friend, that was nice— and here she was, eight hours later, with the sky already clearing of last night's clouds and the rest of the barn waiting to be cleaned.

The morning air was cool and still, fog hanging over the burbling creek, and she hustled through barn chores, getting the horses fed and turned out in record time. Then she called the feed store, getting Louisa on the line before the store was even open for the day.

"Rosemary? It's eight thirty. Can a woman not count out her register till in peace any more?"

Rosemary laughed. She'd known Louisa, a rosy-cheeked contemporary of her parents, for her entire life. The feed store in Catoctin Creek had been in Louisa's family for three generations.

"I wanted to see if I could get a load of shavings delivered today."

"Today?"

"Well, this morning."

"Good grief, Rosemary!"

"I'm sorry. I just decided that today would be the perfect day to strip stalls. You know how gross a barn gets after winter. It's been shut up for months and I can smell the mildew, and there's that whiff of ammonia, you know what I mean . . . I just want to clean it out, right now. I did the cobwebs yesterday, which was a great start. You should see the place."

"Well! This is quite a boost of energy for you. Something going right with that New York man, hmm?"

"What?" Rosemary was momentarily flustered. Oh, that *Jessica!* Louise and Porter must have gone to the Blue Plate for dinner this week and gotten the low-down from her. She was probably telling everyone in town. If Nikki wasn't thrilled to have a competent manager in training, Rosemary might have told her to fire the girl. "I don't know what you mean," Rosemary said weakly, making a feeble attempt to play it off.

"Sure, Rosemary. There's nothing going on if you say so! But there's something about a good date or two that sets a woman cleaning. I can't explain it. My mother would have said it was nesting." Louise chuckled.

Rosemary writhed with embarrassment, dancing around the kitchen in agonies. *Nesting?* Oh, that really had to be the worst thing anyone had ever said to her. What was *wrong* with Louise? She wasn't nesting; she was just trying to get the barn cleaned up before the hot summer set in and everything got ten times more disgusting. "Do you think you can manage the shavings, Louise?" she asked finally, her voice straining to keep out her impatience.

"Oh, I'll talk to Porter," Louise said comfortably. Her feelings were not hurt at all by Rosemary's abruptness. A good feed store manager knew how to start gossip and when to stop. "I'm sure he can manage something. He's not in yet—it's his pancake day, and you know how he is about breakfast."

Rosemary knew. Louise's husband was in a decades-long love affair with the Blue Plate's pancake platter. He'd been eating them three mornings a week—studiously maintaining an every-other-day breakfast of eggs and toast at home so as to maintain prime health—for as long as Rosemary could remember.

The very thought of those pancakes made Rosemary's stomach rumble. "You know," she said, "I think he has the right idea."

"Don't *you* go eating pancakes three days a week," Louise advised her. "Not yet, anyhow. You've got a man to lock down."

Rosemary considered shrieking at the top of her lungs, but decided there was no use in it and forced a laugh instead. "Thanks, Louise," she said, managing to keep the sarcasm out of her tone.

Phone call ended, Rosemary decided there was no use starting to strip stalls until she was certain she'd get her load of shavings. She'd go into town, find Porter, and then have breakfast at the Blue Plate herself.

Nikki lifted her eyebrows as Rosemary walked into the diner. She was topping off coffee while the retired farmer before her beadily eyed the level in his cup. "There you go, Mr. Heiler," she told him, and he nodded grimly as she stepped over to the little hostess stand where the menus and silverware were kept in shining stacks.

"Miss Rosemary, fancy seeing you here on a Monday morning!" Nikki picked up a menu in her coffeepot-free hand and waved it at Rosemary. "What brings you out into the world?"

"I didn't realize you were doing breakfast hours." Rosemary was startled. She was used to Nikki working the dinner service, keeping an eye on those high school girls who waited tables at night. Breakfast was reigned by Doris and Phyllis, two gray-haired waitresses who had been pouring coffee at the Blue Plate for decades before Nikki took over the diner. They didn't warrant a manager; they much preferred to be left alone.

"Phyllis called in sick," Nikki explained, sighing in a tired manner, "and when I say she called in sick, I mean that she called Doris and told her she was sick, and Doris called me and told me I had to come in and help her this morning. Jessica will close for me tonight. She's becoming pretty reliable, thank goodness."

"Wonderful Jessica," Rosemary murmured, then she smiled and waved to Doris, who was stalking across the dining room carrying twin platters of bacon and eggs to a booth by the front windows. The Blue Plate was a square box with plate glass windows overlooking Main Street; the front two-thirds was a small tiled sea of padded booths and four-square tables, while the back third was reserved for the steaming, sweaty world of the kitchen. Its decor had not been updated since the seventies, but at this point, Nikki argued, the awful old cross-stitch flowers and oil paintings of farm scenes lining the wood-paneled walls were so old, they were coming back into style. A Catoctin Creek write-up in the *Capital District* magazine had called the Blue Plate "so vintage-sweet your teeth will ache" and Nikki had taken this copy as confirmation she was doing the right thing.

"But why are you asking why *I'm* here?" Nikki went on, settling Rosemary into a corner booth where she could sit mostly unseen. "I figured the fundraiser was the last time you'd be seen in public before summer."

"It was a lot," Rosemary admitted. "I couldn't have managed it without you."

"Especially with your boyfriend hanging around with blonde bimbos." Nikki looked around the sparsely-populated dining room, then shrugged and slipped into the booth across from Rosemary. She tipped the rest of the coffee into the two mugs waiting on the table. "So what happened? Did he stick around or has he vanished again? Did you tie him up and leave him in the barn? I've been dying for updates."

"You could have called me and asked," Rosemary suggested.

"Too needy. I don't want to be that person. You should have *wanted* to call and tell me immediately."

Rosemary took a cautious sip of her coffee, which was just the right side of scalding, and considered how much she wanted to tell Nikki. On one hand, there was a delicious pleasure in telling one's best friend everything about a budding relationship. On the other, there was the fear of embarrassment if it all went south. Rosemary had to suppress a shudder at the very thought. She and Stephen had both moved very quickly, slipping from their state of constant attraction into dinner, sex, and *I love you* in dizzying quicktime.

What if it didn't all add up in the end? What if he came back from New York with the realization he'd said too much, gone too far, made a mistake? Or simply *didn't* come back? Rosemary suddenly felt as if she'd swallowed a stone and it was sitting in her belly, lumpy and painful and weighing her down.

"Oh God," Nikki said, peering at her face. "What did I say?"

"Nothing," Rosemary demurred, sipping more of the steaming coffee. She could blame her pink cheeks on the heat.

"Was he a jerk? Is it over? Is he at his house? Should I go up there and kill him? At least let me rough him up."

"No, he was fine. He . . . " she fumbled over the right word. *He was a gentleman. He was sweet. He was wonderful.* "He was fine," Rosemary finished. "We had a good time, and then he had to go back to New York."

Nikki narrowed her eyes. "Oh he did, did he?"

Rosemary put her hand on Nikki's. "It isn't like that."

"Why did he have to go? Did an uncle die? Did his apartment building burn down? Wait, no, I know. Did an old friend desperately need his help? That's a classic."

Reflexively, Rosemary thought of Sasha's hard-edged beauty. Surely he had other friends in New York, though. "He said he to meet with some people about business," she said defiantly. "About Long Pond." She didn't mention he'd said he would save the farmhouse and front field for her. Against the larger picture of a hundred houses next door, it would look like a very minor victory. Maybe even just a scrap thrown to keep her quiet.

"Oh," Nikki said. "Well, that makes sense, I guess."

They both looked into their coffee cups. Rosemary thought about Long Pond and the weight in her stomach grew heavier. "I should be more angry with him," she said eventually. "I'm trusting him, instead. Maybe I shouldn't. I feel like I'm doing the right thing and like I'm being naïve, simultaneously."

Nikki nodded. "I know what you mean. But you're in love with him, I guess. So that doesn't leave you a lot of options."

Rosemary looked up through her eyelashes. Nikki was gazing at her with . . . sympathy? Resignation? Neither was preferable to the other. She didn't want to be pitied, even by her best friend. Rosemary straightened her spine, rolled her shoulders back, put her chin up. "Well, either way, the farm comes first. And I'm neck-deep in spring-cleaning. I'm going to strip stalls after breakfast. Is Porter still here?"

Nikki took a quick glance over the dining room. "No . . . I think he just left. Why, is Louise looking for him?"

"Yeah, she's going to ask him to take a load of shavings over to my place."

Nikki raised her eyebrows. "Well, girl, that *is* serious. Let me grab you some breakfast and get you fueled up for that. And—hey, I'm leaving after lunch today. I'll bring something over and make you take a break with me."

———— *ele* ————

Rosemary savored the rest of her breakfast at the Blue Plate in solitude, as Nikki was called away to deal with some sort of delivery disaster behind the kitchen door. But in Catoctin Creek, even a solitary meal had its conversations. A few people, mostly older men and women who had known her parents, or even her grandparents, stopped to say hello to her as they headed out to get on with the rest of their days. A cool breeze blew in each time the front door opened and closed, ruffling the paper placemats on the Formica-topped tables, reminding Rosemary of the pretty spring day waiting for her once she'd cleaned up her pancakes and sausage.

"Rosemary." An elderly woman paused at her table. "You're looking fresh as a daisy today."

"Hello, Mrs. Dawson. I *feel* fresh. That's exactly the word I was just thinking about. It's such a pretty day."

"So how are things? I hear you're going with the Beckett boy." Mrs. Dawson revealed a set of gleaming dentures.

Rosemary sighed dramatically and shook her head. "Mrs. Dawson, who told you that?"

"I get around." Mrs. Dawson shrugged and wound her scarf around her thin neck. "I hear things. Gilbert Beckett was a nice man. We all liked him, even if he was from New York."

Rosemary decided there was nothing left to do but embrace the gossip. "His son is just as nice, I'm happy to report."

Mrs. Dawson chuckled in a knowing sort of way and moved on.

Left to the remains of her breakfast, Rosemary poured more syrup on her last few bites of pancake and considered the pleasures of living in the same place one's whole life. She had to admit, it *was* nice to have someone like Mrs. Dawson stop by her table and check in on her. Even if Rosemary felt mostly chagrined at the idea of everyone in town discussing her over coffee at the Blue Plate, she couldn't help feeling a bit warm and fuzzy as well, knowing so many people cared about her.

The hardest part of living here, of course, was seeing her hometown change at all. Catoctin Creek was so far away from the bustle of Frederick, and even more so from the chaos of Washington and Baltimore, that sometimes it was easy to go months without noticing any changes. Then a farmer would sell off a pasture, or even their entire property, to a developer, and the new lines of houses rising over the landscape would remind them all that Catoctin Creek would continue to change, perhaps eventually beyond recognition, as their lives went on here.

Stephen was one of those changes. Not just because he'd bought Long Pond and was the source of coming houses, new people, new traffic and new views, but because he was changing the way she thought about her future.

Rosemary was beginning to understand she'd been thinking of the future as an unbroken string of similar days. She had set up her life to run in a quiet, stress-free fashion—well, as stress-free as any life with horses in it could be. She would live at the farm where she'd always lived, she would talk to the people she'd always talked to, she would bring in new horses when old horses passed on. Perhaps she might add more capacity—she certainly had the pasture space for more rescues. But beyond that?

Rosemary had stopped thinking of the future as a limitless, wondrous place years ago. When her parents had died and their future vanished, to be exact. That had been change enough for anyone to deal with, she thought. So she had organized her life so it would not present any more changes.

So there would be no surprises.

Stephen was a man of surprises, and his presence had made her wonder again, and the wondering itself was nerve-racking. Rosemary had a very good imagination. She could wonder constantly and at length, building a million scenarios out of the most simple of questions.

She was doing it already, undoing all the good of four years of a quiet mind as she puzzled over Stephen. Would he really ever be happy here, or would he go back to New York for good? Would he try to dance between the two places like he was now, stringing her along until she was more fed up than in love? Or would they get closer and closer, until he decided to stay? She knew he'd never ask her to go to New York; there was no version of her life which took place in the city . . . not even one with him, and he knew it.

Most of all, she wondered now, what on earth would her life look like in a week, in a month, in a year? She had thought she'd known. Now, there were no certainties. Just calling Caitlin and asking for help with the farm was a change she never could have predicted.

The strain of it all was enough to make Rosemary add even more syrup to her last bite of pancake. There was hardly any left in the bottle; Nikki would notice she'd gone overboard on the sugar. Well, she needed the comfort. Things were confusing. Stephen was the first new person she'd allowed into her life in years, but in some ways, he'd *forced* his way in, and she truly didn't know what to do with him now that he was part of her world.

And of course I'm in love with him, she thought wryly, accepting a top-off of coffee from grim-faced Doris. It couldn't just be a few dates with a convenient guy, some sex, a little fun to shake up her quiet life. It had to be big, overwhelming, real.

Real.

This was the first real emotion she'd felt for anything besides horses in need of help for years. Was it real for him? Had he meant it? When he'd said he'd loved her, had that been in earnest?

She'd certainly thought so at the time. With him gone so quickly, though, it was hard to tell.

And this, she reminded herself, was why she needed to engage in some hard, hard work. She checked the time—it was past ten already. She'd better get a move on and head over to beg Porter to bring her shavings. The barn wasn't going to clean itself.

Work was the only thing that was going to keep her sane.

Chapter Thirty-Four

Stephen

K evin was eager to pursue the idea—almost too eager, Stephen thought, shaking his head slightly as he put down the phone. He acted as if Stephen had been keeping the Long Pond project all to himself, and insisted they sit down with Melinda to work out the boarding school details immediately.

"This could be a slam dunk," Kevin announced. "A *slam dunk!* We sell the place, they preserve the house, I get to move, everyone wins."

"What about the houses we were going to build?" Stephen heard himself asking, perhaps to be as contrary towards himself as possible—he didn't know anymore. "You were pretty set to make a mint on those houses. A girl's school, even one this fancy, won't pay us a fraction of what we'd make on the subdivision."

"Well, you could argue this would be a much quicker pay-off," Kevin reasoned cannily. "One sale, instead of three years of construction and fifty or a hundred small sales after years of permitting, construction delays, contractor problems."

"True, but the difference is still in the millions. What's your rush *really* about?"

"Oh, I just don't want to see Rosemary unhappy," Kevin replied. "Also, I hate my condo more than the fiery pits of hell and regret buying into that tower. The usual. The last time it stormed I felt like I was on the North Atlantic in a rowboat. And anyway, why are you trying to talk me *out* of it? Aren't you glad I'm on board?"

"Sure, sure. I just . . . I thought it would be tougher? I thought you'd raise more objections for me to think about. Different perspectives—"

"Just make the meeting happen!"

"I will . . . I will."

Stephen put down the phone and looked out his front windows. From the fourth floor, he was looking directly into the London plane tree in front of the building. The tree's mottled branches were still leafless, but at least they were dotted with green buds, a promise of things to come. When he looked down, he could see bright red tulips, bravely sprouting skyward from the dirt around the tree. Spring was on its way, although New York felt weeks behind Maryland. Who knew it would be so much colder here? April was just a few days away, but he was pretty sure the heavy sky over New Jersey was threatening snow.

"Let's finish this and get back to the sunny south," Stephen muttered to himself. He picked up his phone again and sent a quick text to Melinda: *Kevin's in. How soon can we meet?*

Melinda came through for Stephen with admirable swiftness, laying the ground work and then setting up a lunch meeting to talk business with the school's headmistress. Thinking he had a little time and already missing Rosemary something fierce, Stephen had decided to make a quick trip back to Catoctin Creek, but when Melinda called late on a Tuesday night and said their lunch meeting would be the next afternoon at one o'clock, he had no choice but to agree. It was too late to call Rosemary, but on Wednesday morning he sent her a text to tell her he wouldn't be there that afternoon, after all.

He was surprised when she didn't respond. He sent a couple more, just to test her read receipts, but either they weren't turned on, or her phone was switched off. Feeling foolish, Stephen called her number, but it went straight to voicemail.

He hung up the call and told himself not to worry. They hadn't talked outside of a few texts back and forth anyway; she'd said she was throwing herself into spring cleaning and working on some ideas with Caitlin, and he hadn't wanted to be a distraction. She was probably just too busy to get to her phone, or she'd left it sitting somewhere. Rosemary wasn't glued to her phone the way most people were.

That was all it was, he decided, and then he took off the shirt he'd chosen for the meeting and put on the black one she'd liked so much instead.

Melinda was waiting for them in the lobby of a Soho hotel, sitting stiffly upright on a luxuriously cushioned sofa while she tapped very seriously at an iPad. A tall woman with short black hair sat next to her, staring into space. That must be Barbara Young, the headmistress. Stephen raised his eyebrows as they approached, a little startled at the sight of her. With a name like Barbara, he'd expected someone a little older, but this woman was probably their age . . . or ageless. She just had one of those blank, perfect faces which didn't give away a date of birth.

Melinda stood as they approached. "Gentlemen, this is Barbara Young." She put her hand on Barbara's elbow as the other woman stood. "Barbara, this is Stephen Beckett and Kevin McRae."

"Stephen, Kevin, it's so good to meet you," Barbara announced coolly, betraying precisely zero emotion which would back this statement up, and then she turned away from them, gesturing for the restaurant's hostess. "Let's go get some food. I'm starving."

Melinda gave him a lopsided smile and trotted after Barbara.

Cool, Stephen thought. *She seems . . . fun.*

Kevin hung back alongside Stephen as they walked through the restaurant. It was the first time they'd seen each other since he'd come back to the city, and they hadn't really caught up on the phone. "Hey listen, how is Rosemary?" he whispered. "I wanted to ask the other day, but I got distracted with this whole deal."

"She's good." Stephen glanced at him and grinned. "We've started seeing each other."

"Weren't you seeing her before?" Kevin looked surprised. "I just assumed, while you were down there for so long . . . "

"No! I was actually avoiding her . . . over this whole land thing, you know. But we just kept running into each other. I took her to dinner last weekend and . . . yeah." Stephen smiled "It's working out."

"Even the land piece? She's not still mad at you?"

"I'm here trying to save that place from myself, so what does that tell you?"

Kevin snickered. "You're lucky I'm all in for ya, buddy. Listen, when can I come back down there with you? I'd like to see the place now that it's probably greening up and so forth."

"You want to go back down to Maryland with me?" Stephen remembered Rosemary asking him if Kevin could come back down—probably to see what would happen if he and Nikki were together in the same room again. He hadn't expected Kevin to make the suggestion first.

"Well, yeah. I'd like to go back. Are you going soon?"

"I hope. Depends on this meeting."

Stephen took a seat across from Barbara and Melinda, and Kevin settled in alongside him. The restaurant was modern, high-ceilinged and spacious, sort of the antithesis of a typical, tight New York spot, and Stephen was glad of the extra room. He didn't like being shoved up against competitors in a business meeting.

Especially with a whisperer like Kevin on his team.

"So, can I?" Kevin hissed, heedless of the stares from across the table.

Stephen saw Melinda's eyes widen slightly at him.

"I guess, man. I don't know. This weekend?"

"Perfect." Kevin accepted a menu from their server. "Can't wait."

Stephen reserved a glare for the menu, knowing Barbara's curious gaze was on him. He was hopeful Melinda hadn't told his whole story to the other woman, because he suspected she wasn't the sort to take pity on a guy trying to make a land deal just because he was in love. She'd use a weakness like that ruthlessly against him.

And Stephen had to admit that he respected that.

———eee———

"This is going to be some weekend," Kevin announced happily. "Can't wait to get down there and see those sunsets again. Can I have that back bedroom this time? The last time I stayed, I was in the front and it was nice, but I really love that view from your backyard. Those mountains! Man, sometimes I think I could live somewhere like that. Leave the city. Just . . . just leave it all behind."

Stephen was staring down at the sidewalk as his friend chattered. They were walking up Broadway from the subway station at Eighty-sixth Street, and the sidewalk was crowded with shoppers and pedestrians, shoving along in the constant whirl of city life. Those mountains had never felt so far away, and the crush of people, the slapping of shopping bags against his legs, the audible assault of engines revving, horns blowing, music blaring, subway trains rumbling: it was all becoming too much to take. He was starting to think he'd have to turn off Broadway and take some quieter back streets for a few blocks, then cross it again when they reached his block . . . if he didn't go nuts from Kevin's eager chitchat in the meantime.

"You can have any room that isn't mine," Stephen said when Kevin stopped talking for a breather. "Just . . . stop talking until we get off Broadway. It's too loud."

Kevin did him one better and stayed silent until they had climbed up the echoing stairwell to his floor and opened the apartment door. Once inside, his friend went straight to the kitchen and opened the fridge, pulling out two beers. He waved them at Stephen alluringly. "You seem stressed, man. Let's have a drink and relax. Things went really well."

Stephen was unconvinced. The conversation with Melinda and Barbara *did* seem promising . . . but there was no point in getting excited yet. "It's a big deal to push through, Kev, and there's a ton of complications."

"Which will be easier to work out once you've relaxed," Kevin persisted. "It's warm in here, right? The radiators are hot." He put the beers down on the coffee table and made to open the windows.

"Oh, please don't." Stephen bent down and turned on the air conditioning unit instead. "The white noise will drown out the traffic. I've been living with it on since I got back."

"Really? Even with your heat on?"

Stephen shrugged. "I don't pay for heat." The heat in this old building was steam, and ran automatically, regardless of the outside temperature, between October and April.

Kevin shrugged and settled onto the sofa. "Steve, man, I don't know if you're stressed about Rosemary or this sale or if it's something else, but you're worrying me. You're not acting like yourself at all. Touchy, quiet . . . what's going on?"

Stephen gave him a strained grin. "Ain't love grand? This is why I've been avoiding it all these years. I'm certifiably freaking out over Rosemary at this point."

"It's that bad?"

"It's that bad." Stephen sat down and rubbed his face with his hands. "And if I don't fix this farm situation, we'll be dead in the water. She'll never forgive me if I put houses on that front lawn. She seems to think she can handle houses she can't see, but I have my doubts. A school that buys *all* the land would literally save my life here." He didn't mention the other fact bothering him: she hadn't yet responded to his texts or phone call from earlier in the day. Rosemary was absolutely ignoring him, and he had no idea why . . . or what to do about it.

But he wasn't ready to talk about that yet.

Kevin was nodding over his beer. "Okay. I can see the stress levels you might be dealing with here."

"This wasn't in my plans when I brought you in on this farm. I hope you're not mad about it."

"Mad? No, I get it. Love is crazy. I was in love with my girlfriend junior year." Kevin's face went dreamy in a way which made Stephen deeply uncomfortable. "Ashley Houlihan. I took her to Homecoming. We kissed, we did the pictures, we spiked the punch. It was the perfect night. It didn't last. She was actually in love with a guy on the football team, not me. That part . . . yeah, I would call that stressful."

"Because he tried to kill you?"

"Oh, no. He didn't mind me at all. They didn't date until senior year. But I thought about her all the time, *all* the time, and . . . I don't know, the idea that she wasn't thinking about me, that I was in it all alone, that just consumed me. I was miserable. Lost like thirty pounds, scared my mom, it was a whole thing." Kevin chuckled. "I haven't been in love since, not really. But . . . I'd do it again."

Stephen grimaced and picked up the beer Kevin had put out for him. "When does the weight loss portion of love begin? I feel like I've hit all the other marks."

Kevin grinned. "I just got lucky, I guess. Your mileage may vary."

They quieted then, both men drinking their beers silently, listening to the hum of the air conditioner, lost in their own thoughts. Stephen thought about all the ways Rosemary would break his heart if he lost the chance to save the farmhouse for her. He thought about coming back to this apartment full-time, going back to work in investments or at another start-up, about selling the Catoctin Creek house and giving up the peace and quiet he'd been slowly falling for as surely as he had been falling for Rosemary. *I can't do it,* he thought desperately. *I've got to go back.*

He'd lost a version of his life, but it wasn't the one he'd expected to shed. He'd given himself over to the country, and the girl who lived there.

Chapter Thirty-Five

Rosemary

The stalls were cleaner than they had ever been.

Now, Rosemary was cleaning out the horses' brushes, just trying to pass the time until Stephen came back. When they'd texted the day before, he'd said he would be back today, and he'd come to the farm in the afternoon once he'd checked in at the house and made some calls. She was hopelessly excited about seeing him again. He'd only been gone a few days, but they'd been long ones, the time passing impossibly slow while she thought up more and more cleaning she could do around the farm. The place was positively sparkling.

She had just dumped all of the brushes into a bucket of soapy water when Nikki pulled up in her blue SUV. Rosemary was surprised to see her. Nikki had been planning on running errands down in Frederick all day, but it was barely lunchtime and here she was back already, striding across the lawn with her face full of thunder and her frizzy curls nearly standing on end.

"Good heavens, Nikki, what happened?" Rosemary asked as her friend drew near.

"Stephen is what happened. That no-good, untrustable—you have to tell him to get out, the minute he shows his face here—if he *does,* which maybe he won't, can't imagine why he'd show up again . . . "

"Nikki, you're rambling. What did Stephen do this time? I talked to him last night, and he said he'd be here after lunch."

"Well, he should just *stay* in New York, because he hooked back up with his old girlfriend and I hear they're thick as thieves."

"What the—who told you *that?*" Rosemary stared at Nikki in shock. Obviously it couldn't be true—Nikki didn't even know anyone in New York, so who would have told her that Stephen was seeing someone else? But at the same time, she felt a stab of real fear. How much did she really know about Stephen? She certainly didn't know anything at all about his city life, or the women he'd left up there. There'd been that whole sordid situation with Sasha, after all . . . friends with benefits, she supposed it was called, but that wasn't how things were done in Catoctin Creek. What *else* did they do differently in New York?

"Oh, you won't believe who told me. Laney Gotter, of all people! You remember Laney, she works in the zoning office down in Frederick! She said she talked to some contractor from up in New York who is coming out to look at Long Pond, and while they're talking about the place of course Stephen came up, and then the contractor apparently told her Stephen got back together with his old girlfriend. Like, the *moment* he got back to New York, she said. That *he* said. Apparently Stephen had dinner with this woman and kissed her, and this contractor has another New York client who was there and saw the whole thing. And I just won't stand for it, I'm not going to see anyone treat you like this. I will *kill* him if he drives up that lane right now, I swear—"

"No, you can't kill him," Rosemary interrupted, her voice gone cold. "That would deprive me of the pleasure. If it's true."

Oh, it's true, her mind interjected. *Why would anyone lie about it?* She swallowed, wincing at the painful lump rising in her throat, and tried to be logical for a moment. Something was puzzling about Nikki's story. There were too many people in it, and they were in the wrong places. "What's this about a contractor from New York? I thought he was working with people from down in Frederick."

"That's your takeaway from this?" Nikki actually sat down on the ground, cross-legged, and bent over at the waist, resting her forehead on her ankles in a surprising display of stretchiness. Rosemary couldn't help but wonder if she was doing yoga in her spare time. "Lord grant me strength," Nikki murmured into her legs. Then she sat upright again and fixed Rosemary with a stern glare. "Do *not* give him a pass on this. I wouldn't even take his answer as gospel. I'd get some references and make some phone calls. Have any of us properly vetted this man? Or we just all decided that since he was Gilbert's son and Gilbert was such a nice guy, he would be, too? That was stupid. We let our guard down on this guy, big time."

Rosemary's heart was pounding, her fingers trembling. She hoped she wasn't on the brink of an anxiety attack. She crouched down by the bucket and began sloshing brushes around in the soapy water, trying to fool her body into thinking everything was fine. "I can't just believe some gossip saying that he's seeing his ex-girlfriend," she said. "And from such a random source. I mean, he'll be here any minute, anyway, so what am I supposed to do? Confront him the minute he pulls up?"

Nikki narrowed her eyes. "When did he say he was coming?"

"After lunch. Why? He would have told me if he wasn't." She lifted her phone from her back pocket and saw, to her astonishment, that it wasn't turned on. "What's going on here?"

"Did you break your phone? Are you kidding me?"

"I don't think so . . . " Rosemary could never remember how to turn an iPhone on or off. Something with the buttons on the side and swiping . . . she fiddled with it for a moment, holding her breath, until the white apple finally appeared on the screen. "This is so weird. I wonder how long it's been off."

The text messages flooded the screen as soon as the phone had properly loaded—hours-old messages, full of apology and questions. There was a missed call, as well. All from Stephen. Rosemary flicked through the messages, and every last bit of emotion in her seemed to dry up. She didn't even have the means to feel angry, or sad, or betrayed.

"He's not coming," she said flatly. "He messaged hours ago to say he couldn't get away yet. And then he messaged four more times asking why I hadn't answered. And I guess that's what this call was about, too."

Nikki looked up at the sky, her jaw set in a way which announced she was unwilling to say anything out loud.

"But why would he send all of these messages, and call, if he didn't want to come and see me?" Rosemary asked her. "This doesn't prove anything."

"Maybe he wants you both. A girl in every port."

Nikki's words were like a kick in the gut. Rosemary looked back at the messages. She had to reply, or he was going to think something had happened to her. But what could she say now, when Nikki had her soul so rumpled up and filled with doubt? He gave no reason for staying in the city. He just said he couldn't get away. Things needed taking care of at the last-minute. General statements, used when someone didn't want to give away the truth . . . or be bothered making up a convincing story.

But he *couldn't* just be seeing someone else! He'd said he'd loved her.

"He said he loved me," she murmured, looking at his name on her phone's screen.

"He did?" Nikki's tone was sharp. "When?"

"Right before he went back," Rosemary replied.

"And what did you do when he said that?"

Rosemary put her phone into her pocket, suddenly weary of being bossed around by Nikki. Her friend's domineering personality had always felt like a gift to Rosemary, because it stood as a barrier between her and the world . . . but just now, Nikki's steely exterior grated on her raw feelings. With slow, deliberate movement, she picked up the bucket and dumped the soapy water over the fence, letting the brushes fall into the clean grass, and then picked up the hose to start rinsing them free of suds. Nikki, caught in the splash zone, jumped up with an outraged yelp.

"Come on, now, Rosemary," she chided. "Don't blame me for this."

"I have work to do, Nikki," Rosemary said tonelessly. "If Stephen's not coming, I'm going to finish cleaning out the tack room. This place isn't going to spring-clean itself."

Nikki shook her head in annoyance. "Are you telling me to go away?"

Rosemary nodded, her eyes on her job. Work was all she was capable of right now. She wanted to send a message to Stephen, but she couldn't think of a single thing to say. Her mind, shrinking away from the potential for hurt, simply wasn't going to let her think about it.

It wasn't the prettiest coping mechanism, but Rosemary had been alone long enough to know how to work with what she had.

The tack room was sparkling clean by the end of the day, and Rosemary ached from head to toe. Spring cleaning was always an adventure which left her sore, tired, and deeply satisfied—and she'd been more thorough this year than ever before. As the sun set in a fiery furnace between the twin mountains of Notch Gap, she left the horses to their hay and went into the house, thinking only of a hot bath and a quick supper from whatever leftovers Nikki had stuffed in her fridge.

She hummed a little as she climbed the creaking staircase, her eyes falling lovingly on the family photos lining the wall. The photos aged as she climbed, the colors fading as the captured moments kept unwinding into the past. By the upstairs landing, she could see her great-grandparents sitting on rocking chairs on the farmhouse front porch, a toddler version of Grandfather at their feet, his fingers a blur as he reached for a passing barn cat. She loved these photos on days like this, when her heart was sore, because it helped remind her that she had a place in the world. Even if she was the last one in it.

Rosemary smiled at her curious little grandfather and padded into the bedroom to strip off her dirty jeans and t-shirt. She was proud of her family and their long history here at the farm. Sometimes she wondered how such a big family had come down to just her. Such a cast of dozens had run the farm in earlier years. Her grandfather had been one of five; her great-grandfather, one of seven. But Rosemary's parents had both been only children, as she was. Oh, there were cousins out there somewhere, but they had their own histories and their own families. The Brunners of Notch Gap Farm had somehow dwindled down to Rosemary, and the idea had troubled her a little in the past. Now it rose up and confronted her, head-on.

Was she the end of the line?

What brought this on, Rosemary? she asked herself. *You don't have enough to worry about?*

No, her brain wasn't stressed enough, apparently . . . she needed to put on some antiquated show about heirs and succession as well. Rosemary dropped her clothes in the laundry basket and crossed the chilly floorboards to the hall bathroom. Thinking about Stephen must have flipped this switch in her brain. Thinking about him all day while she scrubbed and swept, her hands busy, her mind free to roam. She should have listened to a podcast. She knew better than to work alone with her thoughts.

Rosemary leaned into the bathtub and turned on the faucet. Stupid Stephen. She still hadn't replied to his texts, and her phone had remained silent for the rest of the afternoon, so apparently he wasn't too worried about hearing from her, after all. Maybe he'd been planning on breaking up with her over the phone. Would it actually be a break-up, or were a couple of days of love-making, and a strategically-timed *I love you,* classified more accurately as merely a passionate fling? Maybe this was like those movies where two people had a weekend of tempestuous love and then never saw one another again.

Rosemary hated those movies.

The water grew hotter and the bathroom mirror started to steam up. She flipped on the shower and stepped over the side of the bathtub. Maybe she'd thought Stephen would stay, and they'd get married and she would have babies, raise a family in the Brunner farmhouse, more Brunners for Catoctin Creek. Maybe she'd thought she'd keep her last name, or hyphenate it. Rosemary Brunner-Beckett? Rosemary Brunner and Stephen Beckett? What last names would the children have? And was she really playing this game, *her?* A stalwart and strong single woman, a self-identified spinster, daydreaming of marrying a man she'd been half-fighting, half-loving since January?

Rosemary tugged open the little window at shoulder-height to let in some cool evening air. She felt like her pores were filled with dirt and only a good steaming-out would clean them. "You're mooning about this guy like a teenager," she told herself aloud, watching the steam billow up around her as the breeze met the hot water. "Why don't you go find your journal and write your name next to his a couple hundred times until you see which way you like it best?"

This felt like a really good pastime, which told Rosemary all she needed to know about her current state of mind. She rested her arms on the window-sill, gazing out over the back pasture and the dark outlines of the mountains beyond. The sun was nothing but a fading orange glow, but the fiery light was enough to let her pick out the leaning fences, the grass-grown farm lanes, and the overgrowth of pines on the hillside. The *barn* might be perfectly clean, she thought ruefully, but now the pastures needed attention.

"I love you, farm," Rosemary sighed. "Even when you're looking a little rough. At least the work never ends." She'd never want for a purpose as long as she had this farm to care for.

The hot water beat down on her back, and for a moment Rosemary was perfectly comfortable and utterly content. She closed her eyes, letting the warmth chase away her fears, her foolish worries. Babies? Who needed them? Heirs? A silly remnant of the past. What Rosemary needed to sort out was her legacy as a *human,* and that was why she was going to work with Caitlin on creating those seminars. She was almost looking forward to the idea . . .

A rambunctious gust of wind came rushing through the open window, and the sudden chill raised goosebumps on her shoulders. Rosemary shivered and straightened up. "Fine then," she announced, closing the window with a little thud. "I guess it's still *early* spring. Maybe you can be a little cold, still."

April was almost here, though—then May, then June and summer heat. Rosemary loved Catoctin Creek in every month, each one greener and more charming than the last until everything turned golden and red in late September. She wondered if they would be different this year—if things would be changed, somehow, because of Stephen, because of her new ventures, because of the Kelbaughs' leaving . . . or if the changes would only be in her mind. Surely the sun wouldn't just go on rising and setting, the world wouldn't just keep on turning, the leaves wouldn't grow lush and full and finally fall, while her life turned upside-down?

Rosemary laughed at herself again. Sometimes, it just seemed like the best, maybe the only, answer.

When she got out of the shower, she picked up her phone, swiping at it with wet fingers. There was a text from Stephen. She opened it, barely registering the thumping of her heartbeat in her ears.

Are you okay?

That was all.

Rosemary bit her lip. She supposed that was fair. She had ignored a good half-dozen texts from him today. She tapped out a quick reply.

All fine here. I was cleaning the barn all day. You didn't miss anything.

The words glowed back at her. She tried to think of something else to say. Questions she should be asking him. *Where were you, where are you, why didn't you.* A moment passed. He had asked, though. He had reached out. She was the one who had been silent.

What if Nikki had just heard some stupid gossip? What if the guy in New York had gotten it wrong?

Rosemary picked up a towel, wrapping it around her before she opened the bathroom door and let in the cold air of the hall.

She had padded back to the bedroom and was sitting on her bed, rubbing at her wet hair with the towel, when her phone chimed with a reply. She snatched up the phone so quickly, she nearly dropped it. She blinked at the screen.

I missed you.

Rosemary's heartbeat quickened.

A full email from Stephen arrived while Rosemary was sitting at the kitchen table, ready to dig into a freshly heated bowl of Nikki's restorative chicken soup. The noodles were wide and flat, and one splashed back into the bowl while she was opening the email, dotting her phone screen with salty broth. She sighed and rubbed at it with a paper towel, noticing as she did the words *coming back Friday*. "Oh, thank goodness," she muttered, scrolling back up to top of the email.

The paragraph those words were in made her tighten her lips.

Today Kevin and I met with someone who might help us preserve the farm, so we are coming back Friday to meet with her agents and look at the place. Can you take the Kelbaughs to lunch on Friday so we can go through the house without them around? It's a little awkward having them as residents while we are talking about new uses for rooms and such.

There wasn't much more to the email besides instructions, and it was hardly the love letter she might have hoped for. Rosemary finished her soup without much pleasure. She opened up her notebook after dinner, ready to make some notes about the horsekeeping seminars she was plotting with Caitlin, but no ideas came to mind. Instead, she thought about Stephen, and when he texted again later, she knocked the notebook off the table in her excitement to read whatever he had to say to her.

I've been waiting for a downtown 2 train for thirty minutes and the air smells like hot dogs, miss you. Miss everything.

Rosemary sighed. Maybe she just had to accept his writing style might not lean towards poetic epistles.

Or perhaps he just didn't have those sort of feelings for her, the feelings which could make a man into a bard, either because he was an essentially emotionless male—these things were not unheard of —or because he didn't *really* love her.

"Honestly, Rosemary," she said aloud. "This again?"

Yes, her brain insisted. *This again. It's important.*

Very well, she'd think about it. Yes, it was possible he'd just said he loved her to get the response he'd wanted.

Heaven knew he'd gotten it.

Stop that, Rosemary chided herself. Hadn't he said he loved her with his heart in his eyes, hadn't he reached for her with an achingly evident need, hadn't he wrapped his arms around her with an embrace that went beyond mere sex? At that moment, at least, he had definitely been in love with her. Whether those feelings had survived the trip back to New York, the bustle and trappings of his old life, so far removed from what she could offer and what she might represent here in Catoctin Creek, was anyone's guess.

She tapped back a text: *maybe you just want hot dogs?*

She had just leaned over to pick up her notebook again when her email chimed. Stephen was *emailing* her now? She snatched her phone back up, and her eyebrows came together. This email was from someone she didn't know. Someone named Barbara Young.

Hello Rosemary, we haven't met but I think our mutual friend Stephen has mentioned my interest in the property adjoining yours. He said you'd be able to take the residents off our hands for a few hours and I just wanted to share my appreciation. I understand you have rescue horses and that is something I'd like to speak with you about while I'm in town—perhaps we can set up some time later on Friday?

When I met with Stephen and his girlfriend, I found they are very keen on this property already, so I'm hopeful it will contain everything we need to make a great location for our new venture. I look forward to meeting with you!

So it was true.

Rosemary put down the phone as if it had suddenly grown eight legs and a lot of eyeballs.

Chapter Thirty-Six

Stephen

Rosemary had been damned quiet the past two days, but at least she'd come through for him with the Kelbaughs.

He'd felt like a chauffeur all the way from New York. Kevin sat in the passenger seat, playing games on his phone; Melinda and Barbara made themselves comfortable in the backseat of his car, chatting companionably and occasionally making requests for different music, bathroom breaks, and snacks.

They'd quieted as he'd driven through the Maryland countryside, growing ever closer to Catoctin Creek, looking out at the farms and forests, taking in the twisting country lanes. Now, they were gazing out of their windows attentively as he drove up the lane to Long Pond. There was a flowering apple tree in the front yard he'd never noticed before, and its white blossoms reflected on the pond's still waters. The effect, along with all of the fresh green leaves on the trees behind the house, was practically movie-worthy. He heard the women draw in their breath with appreciation.

While he enjoyed the tree, what Stephen was actually most appreciative of was the empty spot where Rodney's truck usually sat—the confirmation of Rosemary's promise to occupy the Kelbaughs all afternoon. She was taking them down to Frederick to do some shopping and have lunch, promising Stephen he would get at least four uninterrupted hours with Barbara, Melinda, and her contractor from the city, who would be meeting them there since he'd driven down already to talk with the zoning board.

He was relieved Rosemary wasn't around, but found it still felt like a betrayal to be here without her next door. The week had dragged on and on, every day wasted without her face, her smile, her laugh—even her tendency to lecture him felt like a long-lost favor he would do anything to get back. He knew she hated the phone, or he'd have called her every single day, sometimes twice, just to tell her she was on his mind. He was terrible at texting, he knew it, but he'd tried to send her little messages to let her know he was thinking of her. The responses he'd gotten had been a little stilted, and Stephen was starting to wonder if he'd done something to make her angry.

But that was ridiculous. He was showing Long Pond to Melinda and Barbara *for her*. She knew that . . . didn't she? She must.

He found himself stealing glances every few minutes at the trees between Long Pond and Notch Gap Farm, but they had grown lush with spring leaves, and he couldn't see her house or barn. Still, the pathway along the creek was obvious, and it beckoned to him even as he opened the front door of the house and ushered his guests inside.

Colonel John was nowhere to be seen this visit, and the ladies flanked Eli, the New York contractor, as he roamed the house, tapping the walls and bouncing on sagging floors and doing mysterious builder-things which Stephen couldn't translate.

"This house was built to last five hundred years," he announced at one point, which Stephen found a bit hyperbolic, but judged to be a point in his favor, anyway.

Barbara nodded carefully, her face expressionless. They were in the upstairs hall, a short corridor connecting two bedrooms on either side of the house, a bathroom in the middle, and light from the hall window shining in, casting the old woodwork in a buttery mid-afternoon shine. It was beautiful, and Stephen didn't see how anyone, male or female, could be immune to its charms. At this point, he didn't even see how the Kelbaughs could leave this place behind for Florida. All the warm winters in the world wouldn't make up for giving up this gorgeous farmhouse. Had he ever really thought he'd just gut it for a sales office? Jesus, what a bastard he'd been. No wonder Rosemary had hated him.

Barbara peered out the window at the end of the hall. "The pasture back there, with the horses in it—that belongs to the neighboring farm?"

Stephen had to stop himself from rushing. He hadn't been up here long enough before to realize Rosemary's farm was visible from the upstairs windows—he'd been too busy falling for her while she made fun of him for getting spooked by Colonel John. He looked past Barbara's sleek dark head and saw the steep hillside of her pasture reaching up past the border treeline.

"Yeah, that's Notch Gap Farm," he confirmed. "Rosemary Brunner's farm."

"I'm talking to her later, I hope," Barbara said offhandedly.

"You're . . . talking to Rosemary?" Stephen was baffled.

"Yes, we made an appointment to talk about how her horses can be involved in the program. I emailed her . . . oh, Wednesday. Right after we made arrangements to come down here."

Stephen watched Barbara go back into the front bedroom, a dusty guest room with antique furniture and a beautiful view of the lawns and pond, while his mind raced. Barbara had been talking to Rosemary? And Rosemary had been strangely quiet, barely responding to his texts and emails, ever since. The two things couldn't be connected . . . but nothing else matched up quite so well.

They were roaming around Long Pond's cavernous old bank barn when Stephen made his escape. Leaving them to exclaim over the hand-hewn rafters in the lower section, he went searching for a little quiet.

He found a secluded spot beneath the blossoming apple tree and took out his phone. He looked at the screen for a long moment, its blank glass faintly reflecting the pink glow of the flowers around his head, and then he hit Rosemary's number and pressed *call.*

The phone rang three times and he was preparing himself for voicemail when Rosemary answered. "Stephen?" Her voice was worried. "Is everything okay?"

"It's fine," he said quickly. "They love the place. They're in the barn right now."

"Good," she replied. "So . . . why are you calling me? I'm just taking Aileen and Rodney to lunch."

"Did something happen with Barbara?"

"What?" An edge came into her tone. "Did she say something?"

"Not to me. Did she say something to you?"

"Something? Stephen, I don't understand what you're asking me." Rosemary's tone was frigid. "And Aileen is coming back right now to see why I'm not coming with them into the restaurant. What do you want? Be quick."

He hadn't been prepared for her voice to go cold like that. Something inside of him deflated. Maybe Barbara hadn't been the cause of her quiet this week. Maybe it was him. Maybe Rosemary just regretted moving too quickly over the weekend. Maybe she'd said too much, and gotten more than she wanted. Had telling her he was in love with her been a mistake? It had felt right at the moment, and he'd been certain she felt the same. But now he wondered if he'd been a fool, if he'd been grasping at something which simply wasn't there. She'd said she'd loved him . . . but people had done worse under the pressure of the moment and the influence of a spring morning.

"Nothing. Just—she wanted to confirm what time you were meeting her," he lied.

"At six, at my farm." There was a pause. "Am I going to see you after that?"

"I have to drive them back to New York . . . but I'm driving her over to meet with you, I guess, so I'll see you then."

"Why did you drive them down here? They couldn't drive themselves? That's hours and hours of driving you wouldn't have had to do otherwise. You could have stayed here."

"They don't have cars, Rosemary. Just like I didn't have a car before I inherited this one from my dad."

She blew out through her lips. *"Puh,* of course. New Yorkers. You all live in your own world. Listen, Stephen, I have to go. I'll see you at six, since you're driving her over."

The call ended abruptly.

He stared at the blank screen of his phone, astonished. Had he ever had a phone call go so badly? Well, yes. He'd broken up with several women over the phone. None of those had ended well. But he'd never felt so wretched after a bad call as he did at this moment.

No wonder Rosemary hated talking on the phone. There was no context afterwards, just emptiness.

Chapter Thirty-Seven

Rosemary

R osemary thought she'd like Barbara, if it weren't for the circumstances. The tall woman was no-nonsense and so devoid of humor it was almost alarming, but she was intelligent and asked good questions. She was interested in Rosemary, in her life and her farm and her horses, and Rosemary found herself telling Barbara more than she usually shared with outsiders, even when she was soliciting donations for the farm's hay fund. The woman's extraordinary reserve and lack of emotion made her an ideal confidant, like talking to a robot with excellent speech patterns.

It was such a comfort to Rosemary, she had almost forgotten she had no idea why Barbara was even there . . . or that Stephen was sitting on the porch near his supposed girlfriend, Melinda, tapping emails on his phone. Their greetings had been brief and rather formal, either out of deference to Barbara, or because he really didn't want to talk to her. Rosemary swallowed hard every time she saw him, but otherwise she was able to comport herself professionally.

"So some of them can be ridden, but all of them can be handled safely, is that right?" Barbara asked. They were standing in the barnyard. The barn doors had been pulled back and the lights were pale against the encroaching dusk, while they looked in at the horses eating their hay.

"That's right," Rosemary replied, still unsure where the conversation was headed. "I ride Rochester regularly, and I have gotten on a few of the others just to see how they go. But some of them are too traumatized from their past lives to even be saddled up, and I'm not interested in trying to push them through that. They've done enough. Every single one of these horses was worked hard and got no thanks for it. Now, they're retired." She remembered the derisive tone of the woman at the fundraiser: *try giving back to the community.* As if giving back to horses weren't enough, as if everything on earth had to be measured by its value to humans and humans alone! Rosemary was so annoyed by the memory, she almost forgot she was working to do exactly that.

Steady there, she warned herself. *Barbara isn't picking a fight.* Yet.

"I'm working on a program," Rosemary continued, "to teach equestrian skills to adults. Not riding, but horse care. We get a lot of people up here who want to put a horse on their property. Rescues, like these guys."

Barbara cocked her head. "Interesting. That's almost what I wanted to talk to you about. I have girls in my school who could use some occupational therapy, so to speak. I'd like to set up a program for them, with animal care. Riding wouldn't be necessary. Are you interested?"

"Interested? In . . . what, exactly?"

"Running the program. You'd set up a curriculum for daily lessons. It would be one of their classes. Grooming, bathing, cleaning up . . . they'd learn all about horse husbandry from you. Absolutely no riding lessons required. If we have any budding equestrians, we'll send them to a local stable. This is about girls who need . . . " Barbara considered her words carefully. "A little bit of help learning to love, let's say. Loving themselves, loving others. Some of these families, their lifestyles are . . . it can put a lot of pressure on a teenage girl. Bringing them here, I hope, will let them turn back into real people."

Rosemary was too astonished to answer at first. "That's . . . I . . . *how* old are these girls?"

"Teenagers," Barbara replied, gazing at the horses impassively. "Thirteen and up."

Rosemary nearly took a step backwards. The thought of having teenage girls coming to her farm every day, bringing their cliques and judgement right to her barn door, was absolutely terrifying. She felt like she could already see their sideways glances and hear their vicious whispers, interrupting her with derisive little giggles as she tried to explain how delicate and special her horses were. They'd never respect her. Rosemary knew this as well as she knew the sky was blue.

Barbara sighed, a breath of sound which was doubtlessly meant as a little reminder to Rosemary that her time was very valuable and she wanted to get back on the road. "What do you think? It will help me get this passed by the board. They love equestrian programs, but the expense of running our own just isn't in my budget right now. Having you next-door, practically on-site, would be a big boost."

Rosemary wished she could say yes. She wished *so much* that she could say yes. She thought of the half-empty hay storage with no money to fill it up, and the lonely days ahead with the Kelbaughs gone. And Stephen—whatever *that* was seemed to be over as quickly as it had begun. She could see him now, in the blue glow that suffused the farm after the sun was gone, moving restlessly on the front porch. Nearby, sitting on the porch steps, was that woman Melinda—the one Barbara had called his girlfriend in the email. The one he'd kissed in New York. So many women surrounding Stephen, and all of them beautiful and well-dressed and self-assured! Rosemary felt her heart beginning to pound and her lungs beginning to tighten, and she knew an anxiety attack was on its way. She needed to get everyone out of here.

Anyway, what Barbara wanted was impossible. This wasn't bringing in a group of women for occasional Saturday seminars. This was a five-day-a-week job teaching teenagers, presumably rich girls from Manhattan, right here in her own barn.

"No," Rosemary said to Barbara. "I'm so sorry. I couldn't possibly."

Barbara gave her a *look*. A look which said Rosemary was being ridiculous, childish, and completely foolish.

"I have to—feed the cat—" What Rosemary really needed to do was get away from this woman, from all of them, immediately. She darted into the barn and flung open the feed room door, ignoring the startled reactions from several of her horses.

The feed room felt safe and snug, and she leaned against one of the trash cans where she kept feed, hugging her arms to her chest while she struggled to get her breathing under control.

Smoke came twirling around her legs, happy to corroborate with her lie, although he'd already eaten. His long tail was fluffed out to the max, and she leaned over to let him push his face against her trembling hands. She had done this all wrong tonight. She shouldn't have let anyone come over without having Nikki here as a buffer. There was too much here for her to deal with alone. She would have done better even if she'd just had Aileen nearby, but the Kelbaughs had gone home on their own while Stephen had brought the New York delegation over to see her.

That was another thing she didn't want to think about: the girlfriend. *Melinda.* A lovely woman, completely gorgeous in a chilly, sophisticated way, who had given no sign that she saw Rosemary as a rival. In fact, nothing about Barbara's careless use of *girlfriend* nor of Nikki's story of the New York kiss seemed to make sense; Stephen and Melinda had barely looked at each other since they'd gotten here, while Rosemary had felt Stephen's gaze on her every time she'd walked through his line of sight.

But they must have done *something* to make Barbara see them as a couple! They must have done *something* for a tale of a kiss to make it all the way to Maryland!

Rosemary swallowed a sob.

She slipped down to the cold stone floor, and pushed her forehead against Smoke's. She felt his purr rising rapturously up from his throat. Humans were insane, she thought. She never should have let anyone into her life. The sooner these crass New Yorkers left her alone with her animals, the better. She would take five deep breaths and then she would go out and tell them to leave. One . . . two . . .

"Rosemary?"

She looked up, her traitorous heart racing again at the sound of his voice. Stephen stood at the top of the feed room stairs, blocking the yellow glow of the barn lights. She resisted the urge to open her arms to him.

"I'm here," she said instead, scooping Smoke up into her lap. "Are you leaving?"

He came down the stairs. "I'd like to get them back and find my bed before midnight. But I haven't seen you at all . . . hey, are you all right?"

She bit her lip. "I'm fine." She *would* be fine once he was gone. He could go back to New York and her life could go back to normal. Work with the horses. Cuddle with Smoke. She could get another cat to help him with his mousing duties. She'd teach her weekend courses to her rich new clients, help them find horses in need, spread the love. Maybe she'd get some chickens. Plant a vegetable garden. Learn to weave. Really lean into the spinster homesteader lifestyle.

It was all that going to be left to her.

And really, shouldn't all of that be enough? Why did she need Stephen, when she had Notch Gap Farm, and Catoctin Creek? She could sit out every evening and watch the sunset and know she was the richest woman in the world. Even without him. Even without *him*.

"Rosemary, you're not fine." Stephen was coming down the stairs. She felt herself shrinking back against the wall. He was going to undo all the good she'd just done for herself, all of the plans she'd just made to see her through a lifetime without him. She knew she could forget him if he'd just *leave*.

"I'm *fine,* and you need to take them home."

"Come on, Rosemary, we have a minute to talk. Tell me what's going on."

She sat upright. Fine. They'd talk. She opened her mouth to tell him what she'd heard, to tell him what she thought of him. *Two* sources, for God's sake! Two different people, unrelated, telling her he was seeing Melinda!

And then there she was: Melinda herself, appearing in the doorway. Rosemary ground her molars together and looked down at Smoke again.

"Stephen, are we heading out? Barbara's already in the car."

"Just a minute," she heard him say lightly. "I'll be right there."

"Perfect, thanks. Bye, Rosemary! Thank you!"

Rosemary concentrated on holding her body together. Melinda had said goodbye to her with breezy confidence. She knew Rosemary was no rival of hers.

"Rosemary?" Stephen's voice was questioning. "Can we please talk?"

"Just go," she managed to say, grinding the words out between clenched teeth. "Go back to New York."

There was a moment of silence, and she looked up. In the dim light, she could see the shock on his face.

That's right, she thought viciously. *You've been found out.*

"I'll text you when I get home," he said faintly.

Rosemary started to tell him not to bother, but the idea of escalating this confrontation was too much for her. She just nodded instead. She looked down at Smoke as Stephen slowly turned and went back up the stairs. She heard him pause once more in the doorway; then his footsteps continued as he left her. She listened to his progress through the barn as if she'd turned on a radio show. A car engine started, doors slammed, tires crunched on gravel, and then there was nothing left but the sound of horses chewing their hay.

Smoke wriggled free of her tightening grip, and Rosemary slowly got up from the cold stone floor.

She'd managed without him before; she would manage just fine when he was gone.

It would only hurt at first.

Chapter Thirty-Eight

Stephen

The drive back to the city began with a rather celebratory vibe, the women in the back seat congratulating Stephen (and each other) on Long Pond's seemingly perfect setting for a girl's school.

"So charming," Melinda sighed, gazing into the night. A yellow moon was rising, playing hide-and-seek with the black-limbed trees between the fields. The dark countryside was dotted with the twinkling stars of farmhouses. "Barbara, remember how you offered me a live-in position at the country school, and I turned it down? I might have to rethink that."

Barbara nodded, a faint smile crossing her ordinarily expressionless face. "I'll accept your new answer, if you do change your mind. You'd be the perfect librarian for us. And I think the farm is a good fit for our needs. But, Stephen, I'm going to drive a tough bargain. Don't think I'm just going to give you your asking price. The board would never forgive me. They're a bunch of investment vultures in their day jobs. Like you."

Stephen winced. "Unkind, Barbara! I'm just trying to preserve a farm, here." *For a girl who apparently doesn't want me around anymore.*

What had happened back there? This entire week? A few days ago, they'd been deliriously happy in one another's company. He went back to the city for all of four days and came back to a woman who didn't want him anywhere near her.

The conversation was still going on around him.

"Heh," Barbara snorted. "Preserving that house and land is just a bonus. You want to get back what you invested."

Kevin, sitting up front in the passenger seat, squirmed around to face the women in the back. "Come on, Barbara. Ignore Stephen. Think of *me*. Your new pal Kevin, who needs a solid recoup on his investment so he afford to get out of his nightmare condo."

Barbara looked startled; Melinda just burst out laughing.

Stephen shook his head. "You and your condo. No one told you to buy in that stupid glass tower. It looks like a pencil. Was their architect just chosen on his ability to draw a straight line and fill it in with windows?"

"I think he also had to make it sway as much as possible in thunderstorms." Kevin closed his eyes, clearly feeling ill just thinking about it. "I would be better off living in an abandoned barge on the Hudson. Barbara, imagine getting seasick in your own apartment, thirty-five floors up. That is the position your dear friend Kevin is in right now! Help me out, kind lady."

Barbara and Melinda exchanged a look.

Stephen gave up on conversation and tried to concentrate on the traffic. Friday night was not the best time to travel anywhere, and once their rural route had joined up with the interstate, a million of their closest traveling friends were also merging onto the roads, flowing in fits and starts towards their weekend getaways. The brown-and-green of Frederick County's remaining fields and forests were quickly replaced by concrete barriers and garish roadside signs, and his eyes grew tired. He spotted a Starbucks mermaid rising above a cluster of fast food joints and moved to exit.

"First coffee break," he announced.

"First of *many,*" Kevin predicted. "And bathroom breaks, too."

In the Starbucks parking lot, they stood outside of the car and breathed in the chilly, sooty air, clutching warm paper cups in their hands. Kevin was lingering inside, having said something about wanting a warm pastry which apparently threw the baristas into chaos, and no one wanted to sit in the car waiting when there were hours left in the drive. Stephen sidled over to Melinda, who had just taken Barbara's cup for her so the other woman could go back inside and use the restroom.

"This was a good day," Melinda told him brightly. "I can't believe it's all coming together so quickly. A week ago you weren't even back in New York! And now we're solving your Maryland problem *and* my school problem. I wasn't serious about moving there, though." She laughed. "Rustic life is good for getaways, but I couldn't live that way all of the time. Who would deliver my groceries? Could I get Thai food at ten at night? Are there good jazz clubs in Catoctin Creek? I doubt it."

Stephen smiled as best he could. "The two lives sure are different."

"But you—you've spent a lot of time there this year." Melinda lifted an eyebrow inquisitively. "And the ravishing Rosemary was nothing like what I expected. I thought you'd fallen for some Daisy Mae in overalls and a gingham shirt . . . you could bring this girl back to Manhattan and she'd fit right in."

"Not quite. I can't really see Rosemary in Manhattan."

"Oh, put her in a black dress and some good heels and she'd turn heads anywhere. You should bring her up for a visit."

"It's true. But she'd hate that," Stephen said. "Trust me."

"Well, you know her best."

"I thought I did." Stephen paused. He'd have to bring it up now. "But listen, Melinda, I have to ask you something—is there any reason Rosemary wouldn't . . . ugh, how do I say this . . . wouldn't want you around?"

Melinda's smile faded, and she looked at him confusedly. "Rosemary? The woman I met for half-a-second when we arrived and waved to before we left? I don't know anything about her besides what you've told me, so I'm not sure how she could have formed an opinion of me. She didn't *say* something about me, did she?"

"No, no . . . " Stephen hesitated. "There was just something in her face. She was angry at me. She told Barbara she didn't want to help with the school, and I thought that was why she was being so stiff with me, but when you came over to say it was time to go, I saw her expression. She just got . . . *hard*. And then she told me to leave. She didn't want to talk to me. And I just have no idea why."

Melinda leaned against the car, and looked up at the fast food signs lording over the night sky. When she spoke again, her tone was dry. "So she doesn't want a subdivision next door, but she also doesn't want a school that preserves the property; sounds pretty hard to please. I don't suppose *she* is going to make an offer to keep it a decrepit old farmstead forever, is she?"

"She's not like that, if she doesn't want to deal with the school, there must be a reason—I just don't know what it is."

Melinda huffed. "And you think it's my fault? You know this because of . . . what were your words, exactly? Because of her *face?*"

"Well, when you say it like that . . . "

Barbara suddenly materialized next to them. "What are we talking about?" she asked with her customary blandness. The brief moments of amusement she'd shown in the car earlier were wiped clean from her face. "Someone's mad at Melinda? That can't be right. Everyone loves Melinda."

Melinda shrugged elaborately. "Apparently our dear Rosemary doesn't think our school is good enough for her neighborhood. And it's *my* fault."

Barbara looked at both of their faces in turn. "Well, that makes sense," she said finally. "I think she has a crush on Stephen. She was watching you the whole time I was talking to her. And since you're his girlfriend, Melinda—"

"His *what?*"

"Hold on a moment—" Stephen held up his hand, sloshing his coffee.

"I'm not his *girlfriend.*"

"Well, you don't have to be that indignant—" Stephen looked pained.

Barbara was still looking back and forth between them. She raised her eyebrows in clinical apprehension. "Oh, I see. I misread the situation, didn't I?"

A suspicion rose up in Stephen's mind. "Barbara, you didn't . . . did you say anything?"

"To Rosemary? I don't think so. We kept things pretty businesslike." Barbara put her finger to her chin. "Well now, wait a minute." She reached into her purse and pulled out her phone. She flicked the screen a few times and then nodded briskly. "Ah, I did actually. I referred to Melinda as your girlfriend when I first emailed her. On Wednesday night."

Stephen leaned heavily against his car. On *Wednesday*. And all day Thursday and today she'd been so cold to him . . .

Barbara frowned at her phone. "I'm sorry. I thought you and Melinda seemed very close . . . I just assumed . . . and it's not like me to assume, I assure you. This is a terrible mistake."

Just then, Kevin reappeared, holding aloft a greasy paper bag. "I have achieved warm danish," he announced triumphantly. "They said there were no more, but lo, I bade them look in the back and yea, they found danish and . . . what happened, guys?"

Chapter Thirty-Nine

Rosemary

The darkness fell over the farm like a quilt, a still night which had started out moonlit, but was soon layered in clouds. Rosemary looked out at the heavy sky and shivered.

There was no use trying to stay home alone tonight; she felt all rumpled up, like an unmade bed after a sleepless night, and the idea of pacing around the empty farmhouse was utterly unappealing. What she really wanted was someone to talk to, and Nikki was closing at the restaurant. She briefly thought about calling up Caitlin, but dismissed the idea; she didn't want to talk about business, and she wasn't ready to let Caitlin into her inner circle. Caitlin was better than she used to be, but she still wasn't exactly best-friend material.

So she pulled on a coat and went outside. She walked along the creek and crossed the broad lawn of Long Pond. She could see through the windows, with their threadbare old curtains pulled back; Aileen was in the kitchen, checking on a dinner roasting in the ancient oven. Unlike Rosemary's house, the farmhouse at Long Pond hadn't been updated since the early twentieth century.

Stephen had probably been right when he said the whole place would need brought up to code in order to preserve it. The expense would be terrible. Only someone with deep pockets would be able to manage it . . . or some*thing*, like a fancy Manhattan girl's school.

She paused and looked up at the farmhouse, with its peeling paint and its sagging roofline, and she tried to imagine it new and fresh, but she found she couldn't. She realized Long Pond had looked like this as long as she could remember: beautiful and serene, for sure, but maybe just a little too far on the tumbledown side. It needed help to survive, help the Kelbaughs could never have afforded to give it. Just like they needed to get away from its drafts and damp, an escape they never could have afforded on their own.

Things happened for a reason. It was important to remember that. Although she couldn't possibly fathom why she'd had to fall in love with Stephen. There had better be a damned good reason for all of this.

Slowly, Rosemary went up the stairs, noticing a new soft spot on the second tread, and knocked at the door, taking care to thump loudly enough to get through to her half-deaf neighbors. The effort made her knuckles sting, but Aileen came right over to let her in.

"Did you come over for dinner? There's plenty."

Rosemary slipped off her rubber boots and sniffed the air, filled with good cooking smells. "I didn't at first, but now I'd love to. My house feels too empty tonight."

Aileen pursed her lips for a moment, studying Rosemary. Then she stood back. "Come into the kitchen with me."

The kitchen glowed yellow from the old globe light-fixture overhead. Between the antique light and the checked wallpaper, its pattern dotted with roses and hens, which probably dated back to the thirties, the room held a country warmth which Rosemary doubted could ever be duplicated by stylish restorations. The floorboards were splintering at the edges, the wood stained a dark brown and likely soaked through with decades of spilled cooking oil and sloshed coffee, dropped eggs and turned-over glasses of milk. Generations of children, the offspring of Brunners and Kelbaughs and a host of other old Catoctin Creek families, had brushed cake crumbs off the old kitchen table down onto the floor, filling the cracks between the boards while their mothers talked over cups of tea. The kitchen's atmosphere was thick with love and the scent of homecooked dinners.

If they ripped down the wallpaper, tore out the wiring, and replaced the mellow old stove and furiously growling refrigerator, would this still be the same kitchen at Long Pond? Would the night-light even matter, then? Maybe, Rosemary thought, this was going to have to be a clean break, painful and swift but at least not left to fester.

Aileen set a cup of tea before her. It was a thin china cup Rosemary had loved since she was a child, with a pattern of roses and green leaves. The cup had no saucer, no mates; the rest of the set had been broken long ago. "Tell me what's wrong with you while I stir this gravy," she instructed.

Rosemary looked into her tea. "I fell for Stephen," she said. "And it was stupid of me, and now I'm paying for it."

Aileen's back was to her as she stood over the stove. "Mmhmm," she prompted. "And what else?"

"He's going to sell this place to a girl's school and the principal . . . or whatever she is . . . wanted me to teach the girls horsemanship, but I turned her down."

Aileen nodded. "And what else?"

"I'm a failure."

Aileen turned around, her mouth drawn in grim lines. "And why would you say that?"

"Because I can't get anything right. I tried to make the farm a rescue, but now I don't have enough money to buy hay for the year. I got offered a job, and I turned it down because the idea of it gave me a panic attack. You know, Louise and Porter offered to buy the place back when . . . after the accident. They wanted it for Porter's nephew Matthew. But I said no, it was home and I had to keep it, and now how am I going to keep it going, if I can't even accept work when it's offered to me?" The confession spilled out of Rosemary almost faster than she could process the thoughts. "And Stephen will go, and you will move away, and there will be nothing left. I have to make this plan work with Caitlin, but Caitlin is *exhausting,* and sometimes I'm afraid even that will be too much for me, and . . . "

"Stop." Aileen rapped her spoon against the battered old saucepan. "Now you're just wallowing. Rosemary, you think too much."

Aileen had said this before, many times. Rosemary nodded obediently.

"You think until you're all tied up in knots, and there are no more answers because you've made too many new questions." Aileen took down the china gravy boat from its shelf. "You'd rather think than do."

Rosemary took a sip of tea, considering this. She supposed the mere act of thinking about Aileen's words could be construed as just one more example, but she wasn't sure there was a physical action she could take instead.

"I suggest you stay to dinner, and then you go home and go to bed, and tomorrow you write down everything you'd do with a group of teenagers from Monday to Friday, and then you call up that woman and tell her you'd like the job, when it starts. It's at least a year away, you realize that, don't you?"

Rosemary had not actually considered this. But with construction and school calendars to consider, they were hardly going to be moving girls here in midsummer. "You're right."

"And that gives you plenty of time for whatever you're cooking up with Caitlin. Who is exhausting, I'll grant you that, but who is also a master businesswoman. She got *that* from her mother, anyway." Aileen chuckled. She knew all about Caitlin's lack of riding ability. "You just have to stop thinking about how you feel and start thinking about what you are going to do."

"That does sound sensible," Rosemary admitted.

"Sensible!" Aileen crowed, throwing open the oven door to retrieve the roast. "Sensible! I should hope at this point in my life I know how to talk good sense, Rosemary!"

Dinner was a quiet meal; the Kelbaughs had learned to eat rather efficiently as busy farmers, and despite having much less to do with their time these days, some habits were too deeply engrained to change. Rosemary tried not to think *too* much, but there wasn't much else to do while she worked her way through a generously-laden plate of roast beef, new potatoes, and carrots. She tried to focus on what she'd teach in horsemanship lessons. Aileen was right; she was just going to have to suck it up and make them happen. Jobs didn't just get offered every day. She'd sort out the basics for the school and get that lined up, and then she'd finish work on the adult classes. Caitlin was dying to start advertising them for her.

Rodney reached for a roll from the basket. His eyes flicked up to meet Rosemary's. "That young man was here today, wasn't he?"

"He was," Rosemary agreed pleasantly, as much as she didn't want to talk about Stephen. "He's found a buyer who wants to preserve the house."

"Preserve it, hah." Rodney glanced around the old kitchen. "I've seen the way they *preserve* houses nowadays. Granite countertops and pendant light fixtures, just like my mother had, right Aileen?" He laughed huskily.

Aileen gave a little shrug. "They can do what they want. I'm sick to death of this kitchen. That wallpaper! I've never liked it. Stupid chickens."

Rosemary was shocked. "I've never heard you say you don't like the wallpaper!"

"What was the point in complaining?"

"Why didn't you get new wallpaper?" Rosemary countered.

"It wasn't like that, Rosemary," Aileen said simply. "We didn't just replace things because we wanted to."

Rodney grunted in agreement. "If it wasn't necessary, it wasn't new."

"That was exactly what your father used to say."

"I remember."

The elderly couple smiled at one another. Aileen shook her head and went back to her carrots. They were very soft; Rosemary noticed all of their food was soft these days.

"Everything in the new house is going to be brand-new," Aileen announced happily. "Sparkling new. I'm going to have the most modern house in the world. For once in my life."

"Cost an arm and a leg," Rodney grumbled.

"What else is the farm money going to get spent on?"

Rosemary couldn't help but feel an upwelling of gladness. Stephen had done this: he'd given them this money, this freedom to try something new, to feel rich and leisured for the first time in their lives. "I'm so glad this is happening for you," she told them, and she meant it.

"Stephen Beckett changed our lives," Aileen said, tucking back into her food. "I wouldn't be very surprised, miss, if he changed up yours, too."

Rosemary shook her head gently. "I think he's already done everything he's going to do for me. But . . . " she looked back at her plate, considering the changes coming to her life, the progress she'd made in every aspect except love. "Maybe it's enough."

Chapter Forty

Stephen

Stephen was not feeling very gifted in the life-changing department at this moment. He was sitting on a bench in Riverside Park, under some pink flowering tree which reminded him of the apple tree at Long Pond, trying to figure out where it had all gone wrong.

She'd told him to leave in the strangest way. He couldn't stop hearing her words, the way they'd been delivered, so sad and empty of life. So unlike her.

Go back to New York.

And what had he done in response? How had he combated that? Had he gone down and scooped her up into his arms and kissed her silly, until the light came back into her sparkling green eyes and she smiled at him again?

No, of course he hadn't. He'd listened to her. He'd said *I'll text you* and then he'd just left. He'd gotten into his car and he'd driven away and he'd left her like that.

Was he *insane?*

He had to be insane. That was the only reasonable answer. Or just a fool. A fool who wasn't capable of hanging on to a strong woman like Rosemary, a woman who didn't need him, only wanted him for who he was. He'd loved that about her; he wasn't anyone's savior, he knew that. But he'd loved being the someone who could make her life a little brighter, someone who could support her as she grew ever more capable, achieved ever greater heights.

He'd texted her late last night. *I'm home, please call me if you're awake and you want to talk.*

She hadn't replied, but she still had her read receipts turned off. She could have been asleep with the sound turned off, a sensible girl who wouldn't be disturbed by late-night texts from a man who didn't know any better.

So he'd fallen asleep in the wee hours and then woke at nine o'clock in the morning, his air conditioner humming away like a giant white-noise machine, and he'd snatched his phone and checked . . . no messages.

Now he sat in the gray morning under pink flowers, joggers and dog-walkers passing him by, willing himself to call her. He had to tell her Barbara had been wrong; there was nothing between him and Melinda. She needed to hear it from him . . . and yet, on the other hand, there was the disappointment he felt, that she'd believed Barbara, a woman she'd never met, so quickly and so completely. She'd read that email and decided *yes, Stephen is cheating on me* and never once gave him the benefit of the doubt. How could she have so little trust in him? What kind of relationship could they ever have, if this was how she saw him?

Stephen watched a barge move slowly up the Hudson and considered the person he presented in Catoctin Creek. A businessman who arrived ready to broker some land deals. A man who flitted in and out when he wasn't too busy elsewhere, sometimes with a gorgeous blonde on his arm, sometimes wining and dining the local beauty at a restaurant so fabulous the natives had never even been there.

Of course she was suspicious of him. He was lucky she'd ever been foolish enough to go out with him.

The barge disappeared and for a moment there was nothing between him and New Jersey but the rippling gun-metal gray of the river.

"I don't know what to do," Stephen said to the river, and a passing golden retriever cast him a quizzical look, although the dog's human never turned her head. A man talking to himself on a park bench wasn't worth anyone's notice, not in New York.

He would just call her, he decided, picking up the phone. And he would say . . . what?

His mind was a blank. Had he ever called a woman and asked: *baby, what's wrong? How can I make it better?*

Not once. Sasha would have cussed him out, then laughed at him for caring. Melinda would have just laughed and hung up the phone, leaving him to figure it out for himself. The other women he'd seen over the years rose up in his memory: sharp, independent, laser-focused on careers and success. Everyone of them a winner, he couldn't deny that, but they had different edges and curves than Rosemary, they could not be treated or handled in the same way.

He put his phone back in his lap. So he wouldn't call her. *She* should call him, and just ask him! Just say: *Stephen, why did*

Barbara say Melinda was your girlfriend? And he'd answer her . .
. it was all a mistake.

But she would never call him. He knew that. This was a woman
who had already made her peace with living alone. If he wanted her
to change her mind, he would have to do the convincing himself.

Stephen sat on the bench and gazed past the joggers and into the
distant shoreline of New Jersey, lost in an agony of indecision.
Behind him, the cars on Riverside Drive revved and honked and
braked. Above him, sparrows twittered frantically to one another.
In front of him, park life went back and forth, the hum of exercise
as industrious as everything else in New York City: work, play, art,
fitness. They were all subjects to be mastered.

Suddenly there was a new sound, metallic and melodic all at
once. Stephen leaned over and looked down the pathway. A
mounted policeman was approaching, on a big black horse which
instantly made him think of Rochester. He remembered the
warmth of the horse's neck beneath his hand, the girlish eyelashes
over the huge dark eyes. He remembered Rosemary's easy way with
the horse, the way the creature seemed to ache to please her, and he
felt a surge of longing to do the same thing.

As the horse and rider grew closer, Stephen stood up and held
up his hand.

The policeman reined back a few feet away. His gaze was sharp.
"Everything okay here?"

"I'm sorry to stop you . . . I just . . . " Stephen didn't know what
he was saying. "This horse, does he have a brother?"

The policeman raised his eyebrows. Twin lines of quizzical
regard, they met the padded liner of his riding helmet and stayed
there. He crossed his hands over the saddle's pommel in a casual

sort of way. "I assume he would, but we haven't met him. No one invited us to the family reunion, anyway."

"No, I know . . . ugh, you must think I'm an idiot." Stephen felt his cheeks grow hot. Was he *blushing?* He was. He was blushing. Like Rosemary, who hated her blushes. "Sorry, I just know this girl and she has a horse who looks exactly like this one."

The big black horse tossed his head, jingling his bits, and rolled one brown eye at Stephen. "I know," Stephen told him, because it was something Rosemary would say to Rochester.

The policeman regarded him for a moment. "It's a girl, huh?"

"She has eight horses and they all love her. This horse follows her around like a dog."

"What's the other horse's name?"

"Rochester. And he has a . . . a friend, I guess, named Bongo."

"I knew a Bongo once. Not a Rochester, though, that's a long name. This is Noble."

"Noble," Stephen repeated. "I like that name."

Noble nodded his head again.

"It's easy," the policeman said. His nameplate read *O'Hara.* "And it fits him."

"Officer O'Hara?"

"That's me."

"My dad was on the force. Gilbert Beckett. Detective Beckett. He retired more than ten years ago, though. I don't suppose . . . "

"I've only been here about six years," O'Hara said.

"Sure, of course."

"I've been in mounted for a year. Was never around horses before this. Learned it all on the job. And let me tell ya, buddy, horses know things. If they follow a girl around, she's probably worth following."

— ele —

"You're *sure* this is her favorite pie?" Stephen asked for the third time.

Nikki paused in the act of pulling a pie from the glass case on the Blue Plate's back counter. "Stephen, why would I lie to you about this?"

"You're the spunky sidekick that is hellbent on keeping the heroine to herself?"

"What?" Nikki shook her head and went back to the pie. "You're such a weirdo. I shouldn't even help you out. Rosemary deserves better than you."

"Why are you helping me?" Stephen was genuinely curious.

"You came back and you asked what to do. That shows humility. I like humility in a man."

"Do you get a lot of humility around here?"

"From these farmers? I can't even get them to apologize for getting shit on my nice clean floors. I can't believe I'm getting it from a New Yorker, though. You guys are infamous." She expertly clipped a plastic dome around the pie plate. The luscious-looking lemon meringue pie had high peaks, their white crests gently touched with brown from the oven. "But you came back, you asked for my help, you gave me the whole story, I believe you. And if I believe you, Rosemary will believe you. Because *no one* lies to Nikki."

Stephen nodded, doing his best to continue looking humble. He had driven back to Catoctin Creek and gone straight to the

Blue Plate, praying Nikki would be there—the first time he'd ever hoped to run into her. When she finally agreed to listen to him, he spilled everything: Rosemary's coldness, her weird attitude around Melinda, and the truth about Barbara's email. Nikki had shaken her head at him, called him a dummy for kissing a woman who wasn't his girlfriend in a crowded restaurant—"Don't you know restaurants are like maternity wards for gossip?"—and finally agreed to help him make amends with Rosemary.

And to sell him a lemon meringue pie to present along with his apology for being such a dummy.

Nikki had moved on. "Listen, where the hell is Kevin?"

"He can't just come whenever. He has a job and responsibilities, unlike me."

She snorted. "What *do* you do for money, anyway? Answer me that, before I let you go off and snatch away my Rosemary for good. I don't feel like I've put you through the whole best-friend wringer nearly enough. I've been working too hard myself."

Stephen leaned on the counter and considered Nikki. She cut a formidable figure, standing with her hands on her hips behind the yellow Formica lunch counter. Stephen knew Rosemary loved Nikki and he was prepared to love her as well because of this, but he was sure as hell scared of her, too. Nikki held the power of life and death over his relationship with Rosemary, such as it was. If she told Rosemary he was no good, Rosemary would listen to her.

"I used to work in investments," he began, "and then I was a financial manager for a tech start-up called Confluence—"

"So, you throw other people's money around."

"I did." He paused. "Well, I guess I still do. I have an investor in Long Pond, as well."

"Kevin."

He noticed the way her voice softened on the hard consonants of his name. "Yeah, Kevin. Nothing he didn't want to do. He wants to sell out of a big investment he made in the city and he thought this was a way out."

"Oh yeah? Why is that? Does he want to move out of the city?"

"I don't know," Stephen lied deliberately, thinking he'd found a good way to appease her. Kevin had never mentioned moving out of the city. "I suppose it's possible. He wants to come down here and visit more, maybe he'll think about moving eventually. I don't know if that's what he wants right now, though."

"Do *you?*"

He was unprepared for the way she turned the subject back to him.

He was unprepared for the question.

His hesitation was deadly.

Now she pushed the pie to one side, out of his reach. "Do you want to move out of the city?" she repeated, her eyes narrowing. "Because if you're just playing around right now, you and I have a problem."

Stephen was exhausted. He had been driving back and froth between Catoctin Creek and Manhattan for the past forty-eight hours, turning the days into a nonstop blur of turnpike rest areas, blue exit signs, and concrete barriers. He had woken up in his own apartment and spent the morning in Riverside Park. Now it was barely an hour before sunset and he was back in the downtrodden Main Street of a forgotten country town. His whiplash at being slung between these two opposing places was nearly dizzying. And now Nikki wanted to terrorize him, and what was more, he couldn't even blame her.

He sank onto one of the old swiveling stools and put his elbows on the counter, his chin in his cupped palms. He thought of New York, his apartment and his block and his life, and then he thought of Rosemary, and the stars in the impossibly dark night sky above this rural pocket of western Maryland, and the horses grazing in their pasture, the quick cutting gestures of their heads as they tore the grass free . . .

"Yes, I want to move out of the city," he said. "Anywhere Rosemary is, that's where I want to be."

Nikki slid the pie back to him. Her eyes were suspiciously wet as she said: "Then go tell her."

Chapter Forty-One

Rosemary

"Y ou're a good boy," she told Bongo, who was leaning over the pasture fence, licking her fingers clean. "You took that medicine like a pro." Rosemary glanced at Rochester, who was crowding in next to his pasture-mate with pricked ears. *"You're* naughty," she informed him in a stern tone. "You don't need any pills or potions, so stop asking."

Rochester bit Bongo on the neck and both big horses squealed and took off, cantering around the muddy clearing near the gate. Rosemary sighed and leaned down, picking up the jar of joint supplement she'd been feeding Bongo from, a medication cleverly disguised as horse cookies. He loved to take the treats from her hands, but he was deeply suspicious when she put them into his feed bin. The only problem with hand-feeding the supplement was making sure Bongo got to eat them before Rochester showed up.

"Such a brat," Rosemary sighed to herself, walking down the grassy hill between the house and the barn. The farm was looking very well on this spring day; everything was sparkling clean and ready for her first seminar on horse care. Mentally, she wasn't prepared at all; Caitlin had sprung it on her with a pealing laugh over the phone, and Rosemary was glad they hadn't been having an in-person meeting, or Caitlin would have seen how utterly horrified she was at the realization it was actually going to happen.

"It's just a couple of moms from my program and a woman I met at the fundraiser last month," Caitlin had explained. "I told them you could do it the first weekend in April. The next week is Spring Break, and they're all volunteering with me for a summer camp I'm running."

"You . . . told them . . . I could do it? That's *next weekend.*" Rosemary put a hand to her forehead. She had been sitting at the kitchen table, and the floor started to tilt beneath her. She leaned forward and rested her cheek on the tabletop, taking deep breaths she hoped Caitlin couldn't hear over the phone.

"This is what we talked about! This is what we have been working on! You wrote up a little curriculum, right?"

Rosemary had jotted down some headings, intending to fill in the rest later: *feed, hay, hooves, bedding, schedule.* "I have . . . an outline," she gasped, feeling like a fish who had jumped out of his nice, safe fishbowl.

"That's all you need. You can riff on horse care for a couple of hours, any of us could. And they'll have questions, that'll take up some time. And you can show them everything, teach them to clean stalls, show them how to weigh feed, check hay for mold, all of that. It's the Rosemary Brunner Master Class!"

"Sure," Rosemary had said helplessly. "Sounds great."

Now she sat down in the grass and tried to think of how she'd pass an entire day with these women, these four women Caitlin swore were delightful, if a little spoiled. A little prone to wearing designer jeans to their volunteer hours at the therapy sessions, and acting surprised if a manicure was wrecked while helping a child balance on horseback. Rosemary could only imagine clones of the woman in her expensive knits at the fundraiser, telling her she didn't do enough for the community.

Well, she was going to do it now. Rosemary lifted her chin, resolved. She knew about horse care, if nothing else. She knew how to rescue a horse, bring it back to health, and keep it that way through all four seasons, and she could certainly talk about it for four or five hours.

Then she'd just need to take a break from all humanity for a solid week. It was going to be fine.

White clouds were rushing through the late afternoon sky, caught in the eternally busy breezes of spring, and the countryside spilled out before her in a patchwork of shadow and sunshine. Light glinted for a moment on the rippling waters of Long Pond, and Rosemary looked over at the Kelbaughs' farmhouse. Today was her night to make dinner for her old friends; there was a stew in the crockpot. If she went into the house now, she knew, the scent would be utterly delicious. Her stomach rumbled at the very thought.

"Not yet," she told her tummy. "We'll sit here for a little bit, and then feed the horses, and then go in and taste that stew."

Rosemary looked back over her own farm, her gaze shifting almost automatically to the driveway. She watched the shadows where the tree branches met overheard, their branches interlacing over the driveway for its little wind down the hillside to the main road, and she couldn't help but sigh. The sadness crept up when she looked down there, whether she was on her front porch or in the barnyard or up here on the slope above the house. The sadness that he wasn't going to come up the driveway again, that he'd driven that old beige sedan of his father's away for the last time, and it was all because she'd told him to.

Well, she'd been right to do it. In the long run, she'd be glad. How could she have gone on with that ridiculous on-again, off-again style, always half-fighting and half in love, never sure which side would come up on top? They would end up hating each other. Better to just get over him now, and save herself the misery later.

That was the logical argument. It didn't fare well against the emotional one, which always welled up next, after she'd repeated this stern little speech to herself.

"But I miss him now," Rosemary said aloud, feeling the words like a bitter medicine on her tongue. "What if I always miss him?"

Some truths would not change just because she had sent the conflict in her life packing back to the city. Her loneliness here would not go away, no matter how many horses and chickens and do-gooder seminars she put on to while away the time. Once, a good old-fashioned spinsterhood had seemed terribly appealing. That was before she'd met Stephen. Now, her memories of him kept swamping her vision of the future.

He'd ruined so many things, she thought. How had Aileen said just last night that he would have changed her life for the better? How had she agreed so blithely that he'd been a positive change here?

"He ruined everything," Rosemary muttered darkly. She pushed herself to her feet, determined to get back to work—she could always find some work to do around the farm, that was the whole nature of farms—and then she saw, like an apparition of her own imagination, Stephen's car emerging from the trees.

"You must be joking," she said.

The car continued up the driveway, crossing the creek. A cloud rushed over, casting the farm first into shadow and then back into brilliant, shifting sunlight.

She walked down the hillside as he got out of the car, something bulky and wrapped in a plastic bag held in his hands. For an awful moment, she thought he'd brought back something he'd borrowed from her. Had she lent him a dish, sent him home with dinner one night? She couldn't think of any instance of that, though.

No, that couldn't be it. That couldn't be why he'd come back, just a day after driving back to New York. *Good Lord,* she thought, realizing how many times he'd made that trip in the past two days. He must be exhausted. He put the bag down on the top of the car and looked at her, and she saw the deep lines along his cheeks, the slack skin beneath his eyes.

"You look tired," she blurted out, and he gave her a weary grin which made her heart flutter.

"You look beautiful," he replied, stopping a few feet away from her. He put his hands on his hips. He was wearing jeans and a dark blue shirt, utterly simple but terrifically tailored, as usual. Rosemary thought of Caitlin's volunteers in designer jeans, and she had to bite back a wry smile.

"Things went wrong yesterday," he said. "I came back to see if I can get it right."

Rosemary's heart seemed to swell in her chest, nearly stopping her from speaking at all. And when she got back her breath, what on earth could she say? They looked at each other for a long moment, and he was starting to look a trifle panicked when she managed to murmur: "I'd like that."

He took a step closer to her, then stopped and turned back. He pulled down the package from the roof of the car. She eyed it curiously, and his smile broadened. "A little peace offering," he said. "To sweeten you up."

"Oh!" Rosemary's stomach reentered the chat. "Is that . . . "

He pulled back the plastic and she could see the meringue inside its clear dome. "Yup."

"You went to see Nikki first!" Rosemary shook her head at the pie, as if her friend could see her reaction. "She told you how to get on my good side."

"Was she right?"

"Of course she was." Rosemary smiled up at him. "Okay, Mister. First off, why did Barbara say you were dating Melinda?"

"We're not even unwrapping the pie?"

"I need this first."

"I didn't even know she said that until last night. And I tried to tell you last night, but you didn't respond. Barbara's not really good at reading emotions."

Rosemary had to admit this was true. "She's a little bit of a robot, right?"

Stephen nodded. "So, Melinda and I must have smiled at one another, and I guess that was enough for her to assume there was a bigger relationship there. But I think Melinda might be seeing someone up at Columbia, to be honest. I *can* assure you she's not seeing me in any capacity beyond business lunches. That ship has sailed," he added.

"You dated her?"

"Five years ago, at least. I didn't impress her, I guess. Not artsy enough."

"Oh, you're plenty artsy," Rosemary said without thinking. "A literate man is hard to find."

"I don't think that's the quote," Stephen replied, but he was laughing now. "What do you think, Rosemary?"

"Wait. But did you *kiss* Melinda?"

"I did—but wait, don't shoot! When she said she thought the school would buy the farm, I said I could kiss her. And then I did. A friendly kiss on the lips, I *swear.*"

She considered him. "That was really dumb. Why would you kiss someone in a restaurant? Don't you know that's where gossip is born?"

Stephen raked his hand through his hair. "That's what Nikki said. I can't believe I've lived my entire life ignorant of this fact."

Rosemary had already forgiven him, but she wasn't done making him wriggle a bit. Kissing women in restaurants! "Pretty strange you didn't know that."

"Rosemary, I'm an idiot. I know that now. But come on, what do you think? Pie?" He held up the dish as an offering. "And also, we can be clear about what we want from each other for once, instead of just jumping into bed and skipping the hard parts?"

"If you're *sure* that's what you want," she began teasingly, "I suppose we can just sit and talk . . . if that's really what you want . . ."

"Good God, woman, don't tempt me!" Stephen put a hand to his heart. "I want to . . . never mind what I want, I can't even say it. I'll drop dead, I swear. I love you, Rosemary. I'll do whatever it takes. Even . . . just talk." And he made an attempt at a strained smile.

Rosemary felt a rush of genuine pleasure. There was honesty in every movement he made, every word he said. She'd misjudged him, or she'd let circumstances get in the way, or . . . it didn't matter. He was here now, and she wanted to be with him.

Also, she wanted some of that lemon meringue pie. Nikki used her grandmother's recipe and that sweet-tart filling was *heavenly*. She slipped forward and watched the relief flood his face as she drew closer and pressed a soft kiss on his lips. He started to wrap an arm around her, but Rosemary was too quick for him.

"No so fast, buddy. Let's go sit on the porch and eat this pie. It's almost sunset, so we can enjoy that. But *then,* I'm afraid, you have to help me feed the horses. Oh gosh, and then we have to take dinner over to the Kelbaughs' house. I promised Aileen, since she fed me last night."

"You're saying there will be no jumping into bed, just to clarify."

"Not for a while." She smiled at him mischievously. "Can you handle the wait?"

"Wait for you?" Stephen asked, taking her hand in his. "As long as it takes, Rosemary."

Chapter Forty-Two

Stephen

H e brought Kevin down to look at the seating, arranged in neat rows in front of the farmhouse. The white wooden chairs were festooned with yellow flowers and gauzy white fabric, and a little white carpet had been rolled up the center aisle. A white trellis marked the spot where they would be standing.

"You're getting married very fast," Kevin said, "but I will acknowledge that your decorating is top-notch. It's very October."

"We've been seeing each other for six months," Stephen said mildly. "It's not too fast." He was tired of the argument, but nothing could annoy him today.

"Six months." Kevin snorted. "I've dated women I didn't even *like* longer than that."

"Lucky them," a voice said behind them.

They turned as one, and their jaws dropped in unison.

"Pick up your faces," Nikki snapped, rolling her eyes at them. "If you're that impressed, it stops being a compliment and just starts being an insult." But she smoothed the bodice of her shimmering, apple-green dress with a proprietary air, and Stephen could see the ghost of a satisfied smirk on her face.

"How does *that* work?" Stephen queried after a beat. "The whole, insult becoming compliment, thing?"

"No," Kevin agreed, shushing him, "that makes perfect sense. I'm sorry, Nikki. It's just . . . it's been awhile, hasn't it?"

She raised her eyebrows. "Has it? I just figured you were never coming back. You were last here in what, March? You missed the entire summer. We all had a wonderful time, but you missed it."

"Did that make you sad?" Kevin's voice suddenly went playful in a way Stephen had never heard, and he decided he didn't need to be a part of whatever was about to happen.

"I'm just going to go check on Rosemary," he said hastily, and hustled off before either could acknowledge him—if they even did.

Rosemary was in the barn, letting Rochester lip at her fingers. She'd consented to Nikki's entreaties that she get a wedding manicure, and her nails were a delicate shade of pink which made Stephen want to nip at them himself, but he conceded she was still Rochester's property.

For now.

"You're not supposed to see me before the ceremony," she said absently as he slipped in behind her and placed a gentle kiss on her neck. Her elegant neck, lifting out of that sweeping white gown! A shiver rattled up his spine, and he felt its twin go rushing through Rosemary. Stephen briefly eyed the hay bale resting alluringly in a nearby wheelbarrow.

"Not a chance," Rosemary announced, before he could even make the suggestion. "We are not having a pre-wedding tumble in the hay. This dress was too expensive."

"But just the words make it sound so appealing," Stephen said cajolingly. "Come on, I'll be careful with your dress. Kevin is occupying Nikki and no one else is here yet. They're all still at Long Pond. We have at least half an hour to ourselves."

Nikki's voice rang from the doorway: "Kevin is no longer occupying me."

"Damn," Stephen muttered.

Rosemary finally turned to him, her face aglow, and he felt a fresh rush of blood running to his extremities. God, she was beautiful! Tough and fragile and beautiful and perfect. His Rosemary. "Fine," he said to her, "but you have to kiss me, even if it ruins your make-up."

"You are a horrible man," she told him, but she smiled and kissed him anyway.

Chapter Forty-Three

Rosemary

Rosemary stood at the top of the little white aisle, the flower-bedecked chairs on either side filled with friends, their heads turned. She could hardly imagine a smaller wedding, and yet everyone she could ever want was there, even Melinda and Barbara, Caitlin and the new women she'd introduced to horsemanship. They were part of a team of people who seemed destined to change her life in new and amazing ways she had never conceived of, could never have imagined if Aileen hadn't talked some sense into her, if Nikki hadn't promised to defend her against all comers, if Stephen hadn't sworn she was capable of everything they said and more.

She looked at each of them in turn: Aileen and Rodney, just a few weeks from the move to Florida; Melinda and her new girlfriend Honor; Barbara and her husband Chris; Nikki and that grinning rascal Kevin. Rosemary's eyes lingered on them the longest. She had no doubt there was something blooming between those two, and she was grateful for it. Kevin would be one more person on her team. One more person she'd allow inside her walls, which were growing lower all the time, but which she'd never drop completely.

And no one would ever be so welcome as Stephen.

He was waiting for her now, beneath a trellis with a charming little crown of autumn leaves. His eyes were locked on hers, his hands were clasped decorously in front of him—the picture of a devoted groom, but she thought she saw tension in his stance. Rosemary had no doubt he was watching her to be sure she wouldn't lose her nerve and run.

She had no doubt he would chase her to the ends of the earth if she did.

There was no fear of that, but some things had to be shown in actions.

The violinist struck up a soft tune, and Rosemary stepped forward to meet Stephen.

The End

Snowfall at Catoctin Creek

Return to Catoctin Creek! Nikki Mercer inherited the Blue Plate Diner, Catoctin Creek's favorite (and only) eatery, with all of its country traditions intact. She's kept the restaurant running just as it has for generations—and just the way her customers like things. It's only on her few hours off the clock that Nikki wanders past a certain old house on Main Street and conjures up impossible dreams . . . and then goes home to cook the wild and delicious recipes that make her heart happy. She wishes she could whip up something new for paying customers, but she knows Catoctin Creek isn't ready for a change.

Kevin McRae is on the verge of collapse. Desperate for a change, positive he was never cut out for high-stakes investments, he follows his friend Stephen to Catoctin Creek, where the nights are quiet and the work pursuits feel more pure. He's certain he can rebuild his life into something satisfying away from the gridlock of the city . . . and living near the fiery Nikki, who captivated him months before, doesn't hurt. Kevin's decision to learn horseshoeing and become a farrier surprises everyone who knows him, but when he said he wanted a change, he meant it.

Romance is quick to kindle between these two dreamers, but this relationship isn't all roses. Nikki believes Catoctin Creek is too deeply rooted in the past to accept her dreams, while Kevin sees opportunity at every turn in town. She makes plans, he leaps without looking. Together, they might build something beautiful —if they can just find a shared vision of the future.

Find *Snowfall in Catoctin Creek* in paperback or ebook at your favorite online retailer, or order from your local bookstore.

Acknowledgments

Catoctin Creek has been my 2020 getaway, and I'm so thankful for it. I started this year by flying to London; by March, I was furloughed from my job and facing lockdown with my family in our (relatively) small apartment. It has been a transformative and painful year for all of us, so to write about a place which didn't look like my living room, or even the limited places out in nature I could visit, and which had no restrictions about how to live from day to day, was truly an escape.

Although most of my books are about Florida or New York, the two places I've lived most in my life, I was born in western Maryland and my family comes from very near the real Catoctin Creek. It's not a town, but a stream running in southern Frederick County, near South Mountain. I took the name and created my fictional village in northern Frederick County, where I lived for a few years as a teenager.

I borrowed the name Long Pond from Aaron Dessner's upstate New York music studio. It's true that Maryland has no natural lakes! While the Catoctin Mountains are real, by the way, Notch Gap is my own invention.

The word *Catoctin* might mean mountain or stream; whoever asked the indigenous people who lived there what they called their land didn't stop to ask. To me, the crisp consonants of *Catoctin* mean home. Although I haven't lived in Maryland for many years, those low, rolling mountains and those no-nonsense farmhouses will always have a pull on my heart. Thank you for going home with me in this book.

Thanks to my Patrons, who have stood by me in a year like no other: Kim Keller, Heather Voltz, Cindy Sperry, Rhona Lane, Princess Jenny, Emily Nolan, Lindsay Moore, Brinn Dimler, Tricia Jordan, Lori King, Mara Shatat, Megan Devine, Sarah Seavey, Cheryl Bavister, Zoe Bills, Liz Greene, Diana Aitch, Orpu, Kathy, Rachael Rosenthal, Karen KC Monaco, Kathi LaCasse, Mary, Liza Sibley, Kathi Hines, Kaylee Amons, Cyndy Searfoss, Heather Wallace, Ann H. Brown, Dana Probert, Claus Giloi, Jennifer, Di Hannel, Sarina Laurin, Risa Ryland, Silvana Ricapito, Emma Gooden, Karen Carrubba, Thoma Jolette Parker, Annika Kostrubala, Christine Komis, Peggy Dvorsky, Honey Mughal, Katy McFarland, Amelia Heath, Andrea Parker, Kathleen Angie-Buss, Alyssa, Nicole Kenney, Dawn Aguiar, Harry Burgh, Kylie Standish, Amy Flood, Jessie Chouinard, Mel Policicchio, Nicola Beisel, Linnhe McCarron, Leslie Yazurlo, and Sherron Meinert.

I appreciate all of you more than I can say. I know you're not immune to the troubles of this year, and yet you've continued to stand by me, support me, and offer feedback on my work through it all. You're all amazing. Let's keep going.

About the Author

I currently live in Central Florida, where I write fiction and freelance for a variety of publications. I mostly write about theme parks, travel, and horses! I've been writing professionally for more than a decade, and yes...I prefer writing fiction to anything else. In the past I've worked professionally in many aspects of the equestrian world, including grooming for top eventers, training off-track Thoroughbreds, galloping racehorses, working in mounted law enforcement, on breeding farms, and more!

Visit my website at nataliekreinert.com to keep up with the latest news and read occasional blog posts and book reviews. For installments of upcoming fiction and exclusive stories, visit my Patreon page and learn how you can become a subscriber!

For more:

- Facebook: facebook.com/nataliekellerreinert
- Group: facebook.com/groups/societyofweirdhorsegirls
- Bookbub: bookbub.com/profile/natalie-keller-reinert
- Twitter: twitter.com/nataliegallops

- Instagram: instagram.com/nataliekreinert
- Email: natalie@nataliekreinert.com

Made in the USA
Coppell, TX
16 May 2022

77832029R00218